BOO

Her.

Inside Island Heritage Homes (2008)

The Historical Atlas of Prince Edward Island (2009)

Building for Democracy (2010)

Building for Justice (2015)

A Century of Service of Rotary on Prince Edward Island (2017)

Historic Furniture of Prince Edward Island (2017)

On Five Dollars a Day: An Innocent Abroad in Europe, Summer 1965 (Austin Macauley, 2017)

The Spectre of Stanhope Lane (Austin Macauley, 2019)

The Mendelssohn Connection (Austin Macauley, 2021)

Forthcoming:

The 9/11 Connection

JAMES W. MACNUTT

THE ODESSA CONNECTION

Austin Macauley Publishers™
LONDON · CAMBRIDGE · NEW YORK · SHARJAH

Copyright © James W. Macnutt 2022

The right of James W. Macnutt to be identified as author of this work has been asserted in accordance with section 77 and 78 of the Copyright, Designs and Patents Act 1988.

All rights reserved. No part of this publication may be reproduced, stored in a retrieval system, or transmitted in any form or by any means, electronic, mechanical, photocopying, recording, or otherwise, without the prior permission of the publishers.

Any person who commits any unauthorized act in relation to this publication may be liable to criminal prosecution and civil claims for damages.

A CIP catalogue record for this title is available from the British Library.

This is a work of fiction. Names, characters, businesses, places, events, locales, and incidents are either the products of the author's imagination or used in a fictitious manner. Any resemblance to actual persons, living or dead, or actual events is purely coincidental.

ISBN 9781398416888 (Paperback)
ISBN 9781398416895 (ePub e-book)

www.austinmacauley.com

First Published 2022
Austin Macauley Publishers Ltd.
1 Canada Square
Canary Wharf
London
E14 5AA

DEDICATION

Families functioning cooperatively are a team unit with all the customary characteristics of a successful athletic, political or commercial group having a common purpose.

I dedicate this book to those who understand and apply the principles of the family as a team thereby creating one of the most stabilizing and supportive units in society.

Why do some families succeed during several successive generations? *The Odessa Connection*, while fictionalized history, demonstrates the answer to that question. Like any team there must be shared objectives guided by an effective leader whose position is transferred from generation to generation with predictability and acceptance.

As with the family whose story is described in the *Odessa Connection*, the strength available to a cohesive family unit having a determination to succeed in the face of external threats and challenges can achieve at many lasting levels.

This dedication is intended to serve as a reminder to learn from those who have successfully applied similar principles in their personal and family lives.

ACKNOWLEDGEMENTS

My continuing obsession with creative writing is taking me from family time I would otherwise have with my wife Barbara, two daughters Jane and Carolyn and four grandchildren Charlotte, Mark, Jack and Emma. I acknowledge their interest and support for my writing and thank them for their encouragement.

Inez Somers has been vital to the production of the nine books of mine published so far. Her extraordinary attention to detail during the typing and editing of *The Mendelssohn Connection* continues that service to me and to the publisher. The production of a book, be it fiction or non-fiction, is a team effort. No one was more vital to the team that produced this book than Inez, as she was for my earlier books.

Also on my local team is my editor Pamela Borden who as a law librarian displayed her meticulous attention to detail in each of her three edits of this book. She is also a dedicated and inspiring enthusiast for my writing, something that sustains me when doubts arise, as they do.

The Rev Dr Jack Whytock, a friend and an author in his own right, read the manuscript on a couple of occasions and encouraged me in my efforts and assisted with helpful suggestions on the text, for which I thank him.

I also wish to thank Austin Macauley and its clever in-house editor Walter Stephenson who has been a great help with creative suggestions on the text.

Prologue

AN ABUNDANCE OF disposable capital and excessive income can generate schemes that benefit others more than the owner, if in his mind he has a moral compass and a sense of public service.

The individual in this happy state came into possession of both, from an inheritance received from his father who had little knowledge of the scale or source of the assets. The latter had received a legal power of appointment under the terms of a family trust which directed him to name the beneficiaries of the assets accumulated over two hundred years of secretive and strategic investing.

Isaac Menshive – a New York orthopaedic surgeon happy in his medical career and personal independence, having survived two divorces and one near-disastrous commitment – had his self-satisfied life completely disrupted and reorganized by becoming the ultimate beneficiary of this trust, which had an estimated value of more than sixteen billion dollars in 2005.

Numerous physical attacks on him and on various of the assets located throughout Eastern and Central Europe absorbed him for the first year and a half after receiving control of the assets. He was assisted in gaining relief from the threats to himself and the inheritance by his college friend Will MacIntosh.

MacIntosh was brought into active management and administration of the financial network created out of the trust assets as a result of a tour of Central and Eastern Europe the friends had taken during the summer of 2005. During that summer the numerous trusts and companies formed by the investors were unravelled and many of the fixed and movable assets identified and documented.

During the past three years Isaac had discovered his family

roots in Russia and Germany and through his identification with those roots, largely unknown to him until the summer of 2005, he was brought back to his spiritual roots in the Jewish faith, and with it a sense of his opportunities to perform one of the principal tenets of the Jewish faith – to give charity to those in need and to work for peace.

It was now June 2008. Each year an annual review of the balance sheets of the revenues and expenses was held in that month. In each of the last three years, arrangements were made with several European governments that enabled a definitive inventory of those assets and agreements reached, as to those assets which were free from confiscation by those governments or seizure from government-connected power brokers or rapacious thieves of private property.

In the case of Russia, the rapacious thieves meant the oligarchs who had emerged from penury and obscurity into positions of power and wealth through their allegiance to Russian President Vladimir Putin, who had gained power in 2000. There had been numerous negotiations and trade-offs between Isaac's investment vehicles and the governments of Russia, Belarus, Poland, Ukraine and Germany, particularly, which resulted in interim strategic agreements with those governments. Through these the governments agreed to negotiate the potential abandonment of their interest or claim to certain of the assets in exchange for a release by Isaac to them for some of the assets. Those interim agreements included a guarantee that Isaac would be protected from interference by the oligarchs.

The four-year hiatus of conflict in Isaac's life was transformative for both Isaac and Will.

Isaac sought and received religious instruction and inspiration from Jewish theologians and historians who led him to realize the wonderful opportunities that lay open to him from the vast resources available to him – opportunities that would challenge his sense of self and purpose and could assist others of his faith and culture to new horizons.

The years 2000 to 2015, the years chronicled in this narrative, would bring extreme danger, personal and financial

PROLOGUE

growth and herculean labours to achieve a final settlement and his newly established goals.

Isaac's friend, Will, would accompany him on the journey that began in 2005. Will would prove to be pivotal in Isaac gaining such success as he would achieve.

PART 1

Smolensk

1

JUNE IN SMOLENSK, a small city in western Russia, can be a warm and engaging place to visit. Isaac had planned the 2008 annual review of his holdings in this city which he had discovered was the starting place for his family's growth to power, prosperity and position despite incredible obstacles.

Those obstacles were as frequent and potentially destructive during the Czarist era as they were in the subsequent Soviet twentieth century. An apparent interim working agreement reached discreetly with the country's president, Vladimir Putin, gave Isaac confidence that he could safely visit this city of his origins and plan for its betterment and for those few members of his faith remaining there.

Isaac was walking arm in arm with his recently married wife, Sophie Posen, in the gardens facing the Dnieper River at the back of his dacha, which had been built in the nineteenth century in the Russian Empire style. The gardens, like the dacha, were designed in a much older Italian Baroque style. Isaac's great-great-grandfather had had the house, administrative wings and farm buildings built to the style and scale of the recently rich, who wished to express their achievement of social and economic success to a standard prevalent in the late eighteenth century by others of the newly emerged upper-middle class.

The parterre, with its winding symmetrical paths and formal garden layouts, had been neglected for decades until Isaac discovered that the property formed part of his inheritance in 2005. He grew to love the place on discovering his family's connection with it and arranged to have the buildings, the gardens and the farm operation completely brought up to date.

As Isaac and Sophie walked towards the river Sophie commented: "Isaac, I love this place. It is reminiscent of similar estates in the novels of Tolstoy and Turgenev. Fortunately, serfdom is gone, but I see energetic workers around the grounds and in the fields, who are even more attached to this place and to you than serfs would have been. At least these people are free to leave."

"Yes," Isaac replied, adding mischievously, "subject to their contracts of employment." He continued in a more serious tone: "Every square foot of this property is productive now, generating a huge net profit. You are right that my staff and farm workers are pleased to be working here, and, I think, satisfied to be working for me. The place does have a serenity and sense of continuity that is very comforting. I'm glad you find it so, and I hope our son will also learn to love it. He may be only eighteen months old, but I hope we can spend enough time here to enable him to consider it one of his homes."

"My roots may be Polish, Isaac, but I feel that in many ways you and I share similar values and cultural experiences that make me feel at home here too. Like your family, my ancestors came to New York after the First World War and sacrificed a great deal to provide a future there for their family. It was a joy to me that we should visit the country house my family had near Krakow, which I discovered had been the ancient capital of Poland. I think our country house shared many features in common with this wonderful place. I am thrilled to be part of this dacha with you and Little Isaac."

They walked out onto a newly constructed wood-framed landing that extended out into the Dnieper. At the outer edge of the landing, it expanded into a large square deck almost the size of an Italian piazza. This was decorated with numerous potted trees and flowers with seating, tables and umbrellas to provide comfort and rest.

From the deck area it was possible to see a bend in the river to the north and a further bend downstream to the south.

As Sophie and Isaac sat on a double-seated sofa they were served iced tea by an attendant who had preceded them with supplies for their lunch. There was little to mar the quiet enjoyment the deck offered: few bugs, a slight breeze and a gentle warmth often found in June. Wild fowl of many colours, shapes and sounds were their companions and entertainment. There was an occasional vessel transporting goods up or down the river but not enough to be a disturbance. While prosperity had grown in this region in the past few years, the citizenry had not become addicted to consumerism so there were few pleasure craft on the river. Those that were there respected the privacy of Dr and Mrs Menshive and kept a distance from the landing – most boats were propelled by oars rather than gas-fuming outboard motors.

Their peace and solitude were soon to be broken, however, by the expected arrival of Will MacIntosh. Will was not only Isaac's best friend, he was the chief executive officer of the holding company formed three years ago to hold and manage the former trust assets – Isaac's considerable empire spanning Britain, Western, Eastern and Central Europe, and parts of North America.

Will's arrival was by a motor launch with a carefully muffled powerful motor. The thirty-five-foot vessel was as comfortable as the deck on which Isaac and Sophie were sitting. Will had picked up the vessel which was waiting for him at a dock a short distance upriver on the Dnieper where the river had a spur that led to the dacha.

The launch pulled up to the landing and as Will stood waiting for his companion to step onto the deck, greetings were extended with enthusiasm and cheer from the launch to the deck and back.

"Will, you dog, what are you doing here with my sister?" Isaac joked. "Anna, you are welcome, glad to see you. Little Isaac will be very excited. Neither Sophie nor I knew you were coming, Anna, but there's lots of room for you. We will have an extended house party – I hope you can stay for a while!"

Anna replied: "Thanks, Isaac. Yes, I would love to stay for a week if that won't be an inconvenience. I ran into Will in New York while he was preparing to come over. When he described the dacha, I couldn't resist his invitation to come too. All very last minute. I didn't call or e-mail because I knew Sophie would go to much more trouble for me than I need.

Forgive me... but I thought I was giving you less bother this way."

Sophie turned to her sister-in-law. "Anna dear, I am thrilled. We will have a chance to really get to know each other. Since the wedding Isaac and I have been flitting from pillar to post so we have not had as much time for you as we both would like," she said with genuine enthusiasm.

Isaac added, "Right. You are here, and we couldn't be more pleased. How did you get away from your current boyfriend Anthony – that control freak? *Oy*, what a character. I'm not unhappy you left him behind!"

"Hey, group!" Will broke in. "I'm here, too. I am pleased to have arrived... as scheduled, on time. Bringing Anna was a great option. I was able to arrange her flight and seating – so we could be near each other in first class during each leg of the flight," said Will.

"First class. Two seats. All the way from New York. Am I paying you too much, Mr MacIntosh?"

"You can be assured you are not paying me enough, but be assured you paid for every mile of the journey for both Anna and me. Spending your money added to the pleasure of the trip – right, Anna?"

"Isaac, I hope it was alright and that you don't mind."

"Anna. One half of this empire was left to you in Father's will. It is only mine because you assigned your interest to me. Of course I don't mind. In fact, I am happy to share as much of our ill-gotten gains as you want. I hope Will didn't bore you. He gives me endless memoranda on the businesses – and if he thinks I need upgrading on historical, artistic or political matters, I get them on those topics as well."

"Yes, chum Isaac, but do you read them?"

"Sort of, sooner or later."

Will and Anna joined Isaac and Sophie on the deck and shared in the lunch, which was laid out for three but furnished ample provisions for four.

"Isaac, you have shown me photos and iPhone videos of this place. It is much larger and grander than they revealed. The dacha is more like a palace than a country house."

"Anna, it was intended to be palatial. When our great-great-grandfather built this, he was emulating the Russian aristocracy. He was telling them he had arrived. He was rich and could afford it."

"What about the pogroms and other forms of anti-Semitism in this part of the Pale of Settlement? Wasn't it an invitation to be attacked?"

"That's right, but he situated it here in this forest twenty-five miles from Smolensk away from prying eyes. People in the neighbouring villages and in Smolensk knew the dacha was here – after all, the workers that kept the place running were all locals. One effective way the family kept peace in the valley was in treating the workers with courtesy and respect and by paying well above local wages. I gather they never had trouble recruiting new employees. In times of difficult economic conditions, the workers would be sent home at the end of the day with meat and produce from the farm. So, it appears the place was never vandalized, even during the Soviet years."

Isaac continued: "Anna, I am particularly happy you are here, because one of the main initiatives Will and I will be discussing is my proposed Jewish museum and a new synagogue for Smolensk. There is very little evidence of the Pale of Settlement in the day-to-day lives of the Jewish people in this area or of their culture and religious observance. There is a synagogue, but it is only the remains of an abandoned school. The rabbi here is disheartened and has almost given up, as have most of his congregation. This is where our family started, Anna – one of my goals is to give back something of what we have gained. I would love to have you as part of this plan," said Isaac.

To which Anna quickly replied, "Isaac, you know that I have given up my Jewish faith and converted to the Lutheran church. I did that in Berlin. In America I attend the Presbyterian Church. I am a committed Christian now, Isaac."

"You come by that honestly, Anna. You may remember our Mendelssohn connections, a double line connection. About half of Moses Mendelssohn's children gave up their Jewish faith in the mid-nineteenth century, viewing it as obsolete and irrelevant to modern life. Even cousin Felix, the composer and musician, was baptized in the Reformed Church by his father. His mother was of that faith; that appears to have led that family in the direction of Christianity."

"Isaac, I know very little of our genealogy. I would love to hear more about it. I am getting interested, particularly as I get older. This business of the trust and the adventures you and Will have gone through to discover and secure the trust assets have given me a reason to take an interest. But, Isaac, I want to emphasize and repeat, I want not one U.S. dollar of that trust. I will never have children. It really is yours to dispose of as you see fit. I would love to talk to you about the museum and the synagogue, but it is your initiative, just as it is your money."

Looking towards Sophie, Anna smiled. "Let's drop serious issues like money and stuff. Let's talk about more pleasant things. Sophie, if I am not misreading your shape, I think Little Isaac will have a playmate soon. Am I right? God, I hope so, or I have really put my foot in it."

"Anna, yes, by the end of September. All is well so far. This will be the last, however. There have been a few complications, all dealt with successfully, but my obstetrician says this must be the last. I am very happy with that advice, as is Isaac."

"Isaac, have you renewed contact with your older children? They must be in their twenties by now."

"Anna, I regret I have not had much contact with any of the three girls. Yes, one is thirty-one and the other two are in their twenties. I plan to try to reconcile with them. As usual, I have been preoccupied with the trust, as I had been earlier with my orthopedic practice. I have given them very little time. I hope you have contact with them, Anna."

Anna shrugged. "Both mothers are still bitter, angry and reject any attempt I make to contact the girls. They are all old enough to make their own decisions, but they are still heavily influenced by their mothers. I will tell you, though, Isaac, I heard from all three of them when you had the auction sale of Russian works of art at Christie's New York a couple of years ago. I think they hoped to get something out of the sale for themselves. Apparently, they know nothing of the trust. At least, none of them asked me about it. As you know, their mothers have remarried and have moved on. Yes, it would be good for me to try to build bridges with them before long."

"Isaac, Anna is correct. You must try to reconcile with the girls. I will stand by you, while you do, to the extent I could be helpful," said Sophie.

"In good time. It appears I will have little choice, with you two ganging up on me," replied Isaac.

"Anna and Sophie are simply trying to lead you to do what is right, Isaac," said Will, "In fact, the high moral standards professed by your faith require it."

"Now I have *three* of you on my case," said Isaac.

"Not on your case, Isaac, just gently reminding you of your newfound religious principles," said Will. "Enough said on this topic. It could become fractious and irritating."

* * *

Isaac arrived well before the appointed time for dinner to take a position in the dining room where he could greet his guests. As he stood there with fifteen minutes to spare until his guests were expected, he looked around, astonished. The restoration he had arranged for the dacha had been carried out with the finest materials and workmanship the world could offer, but it was the Isaac he saw in the gilded eighteenth-century mirror over the elegant sideboard that caught his attention.

"Who is that person I see in the mirror? Looks like me, although much better dressed, with a first-rate, flattering haircut. But it is a person accepting if not dictating form and style on myself and my surroundings. What a *volte-face* from my New York pre-inheritance days. A morally and ethically loose and arrogant twit, self-satisfied and dominating all those who had to deal with me. How did I get here?

"My parents were subtle in their instructions and guidance, and wise in their realization that I could succeed only if I came to an awareness of the true values of my people and my culture. By naming me an inheritor of the trust, they knew I would have to learn to support Anna in her confused voyage through life and assist her with her responsibilities with the trust. I think Mom knew Anna would reject her share, which would be the beginning of a shared generosity and interdependence. That is what appears to be happening. Dad didn't talk about Jewish culture or theology, but he knew I would be inexorably brought to them through the trust. A wise old bird, even as uncommunicative as he was. He was very proud of my success as an orthopedic surgeon, but he recognized I was emotionally a hollow shell.

"Then there's Will. It was on a whim that I invited him to join me on that mid-life escape to Europe in 2005 with our superficial agendas. It was for us both a reprieve from routine and drudgery. Neither of us knew what inner strengths and compatibility would develop. Calling on Will was the best decision I made in seeking personal support and guidance. His administrative skills have pulled the assets together effectively. He is the only person on the planet in whom I have absolute trust and with whom I can share any worry or problem. I could do with fewer Presbyterian lectures on morality, liberality and ethical behaviour; however, they have been part of my journey too.

"Sophie is a relative newcomer to my life, but through her, I have for the first time realized a perfect union of husband and wife. There are no grasping or ulterior motives. She is devoted – I don't know why, but she is, as I have grown to be to her. Our son has cemented the bond. I will be a father to Little Isaac and his sibling-to-be.

"Yes, as strange as that person is in the mirror, I do recognize myself. A model I could not have predicted five or more years ago. All of these challenges and people have brought me to the core values expressed and promoted by my faith in God as a Jew. That conversion from a scornful agnostic to embracing the faith of my ancestors has given me more solace and meaning than I could have predicted – it has given me a purpose and has proved to be one of the twelve labours that I must perform before I die."

Isaac's musings were interrupted by Sophie's arrival with Little Isaac, who twisted and squirmed with outstretched arms to his father who couldn't hold himself back from taking the child in his arms. A series of inane and incomprehensible babbling by father and son indicated they were communicating happily on some secret level. While this was going on, Sophie smiled and shook her head, pointing at Isaac. "Is this the Isaac I met three years ago? Who are you, really?"

Isaac's reply was cut short by Anna's arrival in a designer label evening gown. "Isaac, I can't believe you have actually found paternal instincts in that fried head of yours. Is it really you? What have you done to my miserable brother, Sophie? It's not that I want the old one back, but the contrast is almost too much to bear. Here! Give me my nephew. I want time with him." The time proved to be short-lived as the child's protests brought him promptly back to his mother's arms. The boy cast suspicious glares at Anna, who took it in her stride.

"Anna, give him time to get to know you. I'm glad you will be with us a week or more, so my little one can get to know you. He has a good heart. Before you leave, you will be one of his inner circle!"

"Sophie, that is one of my plans. Where is Will? He is punctual to a fault."

Isaac looked at an antique carriage clock on a chiffonier nearby which had a reading that gave Will one minute to arrive on time.

On time he arrived, also dressed in black tie to meet Isaac's sartorial standard for the evening.

"Now, Isaac," asked Anna, somewhat overwhelmed by the scale and elegance of her surroundings, "I suspect this palace is not being run by you or Sophie – I mean the cooking and cleaning – so what staff do you have?"

"When Will and I visited here for the first time three years ago, there was a majordomo in place…"

"What," interrupted Anna, "is a 'major domo'? Do you have an army? I certainly see lots of security around."

"No, no. A majordomo is the equivalent in a private home of a *maître d'* in a New York restaurant," Isaac said, before embarking on a lengthy reply. "To put it another way, he is somewhat like a butler in an English country house. He controls the workings of the inside of the house; he oversees, hires, fires and directs the household staff. While we are in residence, we have a cook, cleaners and maintenance people to clean and keep the place fully functioning at the highest level. Tonight, for example, the majordomo, Sergei, will direct the kitchen and ensure service at table is prompt, efficient and the food served hot to the menu Sophie has given them."

"Anna, the food, you will discover, is exceptional. Tonight, in honour of your family's origins here in Smolensk, you will be served a traditional Russian-Jewish meal. All household staff including Sergei are from the local Jewish community, which is thrilled we are here providing work for many of them."

Sergei arrived, having been instructed to give the family half an hour to themselves before the evening's schedule of events got underway.

During dinner, Anna asked to have a tour of the house. Isaac agreed but suggested it wait until the next day when the light of day would give her maximum views of the interior.

"And, Isaac, I don't know anything about farming, but I would love to see around the grounds and explore the farm areas."

"Anna, I will also arrange that. I will show you the house tomorrow morning after breakfast, but as Will and I have meetings in town with the mayor and some of his councillors at 11 a.m., I will leave you to the farm manager to show you the farm operation. You will not be able to see all of it – there are seven hundred acres, carefully fenced and secure. You must be accompanied by the farm manager to avoid harm. Promise me you will keep to his side and follow his directions."

"Come on Isaac, this is a farm. What harm could I do?"

"Oh, you could do harm – but it is harm to yourself I worry about. Please remember we are Jews in a predominantly Slavic and Russian Orthodox community. We are still viewed as interlopers and rich exploiters of Russia. You must not move around Smolensk or this property without a male escort. On your own, you would be a target for a number of obvious risks. Promise me."

"Alright, big brother, but you have me worried. How much at risk am I here? This place appears to be completely safe and secure."

"The dacha and the gardens are, but that is because I have security guards in several strategic locations. Usually they will be invisible to you. If they sense you are at risk to someone or something, they will intercede immediately. You will follow their directions. The same thing applies to you putting yourself deliberately in harm's way. Incidentally, and don't take this the wrong way, there are several good-looking men working around here. They are absolutely off-limits."

"Isaac, don't be so nasty. I'm not like that... well, I, too have come along a road of self-improvement. No, I won't. I can see it would affect you and Sophie more than me if I become involved with someone in your employ."

Sophie interceded before the topic could take on an aggressive tone. "Anna, the freedom in personal relations you are familiar with in New York is not known or accepted here. Yes, Isaac is correctly identifying potential problems and is wisely asking for your co-operation. Anyway, aren't you in a committed relationship back in New York?"

"No, Isaac warned me off him. And he was right to do so, I see that now. One of the reasons for my travel here to you was to get away from that man. The further away I am, the more relieved I am and the more I realize he was a pain."

Isaac turned to Will and with a gravity not seen since Will and Anna arrived, asked how Will was managing since his wife had died eighteen months ago.

"As well as can be expected. Cancer. The dreaded cancer. She had a session five years ago. It appeared to be cured, but it came back in the bones of her right hip and moved rapidly throughout. She suffered terribly. I was thankful to be there with her. Our daughters, between their squabbling, were very attentive and helpful. They're both devastated and now realize, belatedly, that their mother was their best friend. Both girls continue their education and are doing well."

Sophie had an innate instinct for expressing compassion and shifted the topic gently to Will's daughters and to what they were doing at school.

Will replied that one was training in dentistry and the other in forensic accountancy. "They both appear to have chosen fields that are compatible with their talents. I keep in touch at least once a week with both. I believe I have a good relationship with them – perhaps closer since their mother died. I must say though, Isaac, they are both intrigued by you and our adventures in 2005. I tell them only what is available in the media. Neither of them has the slightest interest in the arts, so the aspect of our story involving art, artifacts and history interests them not a bit. Perhaps it is just as well!"

Sophie offered, "Will, you have kindred spirits around this table! Tell me, speaking of kindred spirits, wasn't a girl's book *Anne of Green Gables* set in your part of Canada?"

"Yes, and the author wrapped her story around friendships, kindred spirits and the culture of the Scots Presbyterian immigrants to the province. My family was part of the community the author used as her setting – in fact, she used my great grandfather's extensive library for occasional research. She quite accurately described the period, the setting and the values of the people in her story."

"Anna, if you haven't read the book you must. I will send you a copy. It is very engaging. I have read, Will, that it is hugely popular in Japan and Poland!"

"Yes, that is true. The author, Lucy Maud Montgomery, continues to grow in popularity. Why, back in Charlottetown a musical stage version of the story has been presented during the summer season for over forty years – and it's as popular as ever."

After the final course had been served, Isaac invited Will and Anna into the adjacent sitting room for entertainment provided by local musicians. Sophie excused herself, saying her condition required early nights and extended rest. Isaac offered to accompany her, but she warmly declined, suggesting he stay behind. "I have a nurse with me who will provide the assistance I need. Isaac means well, but where nurture and nursing are required, he is best left down here."

Both Will and Anna were anxious to have an early evening as well, having travelled a great distance to get to the dacha. After half an hour of listening to the struggling amateur musicians, Isaac thanked them and ended the evening with a Jewish blessing that neither Anna nor Will understood, other than its intent.

2

"THE FARM PORTION of the estate contains 500 acres; in the unit of measurement customary here, it is 200 hectares. By Russian standards, as a property in private hands in this area, it is a large farm. It is not spread out, as many farms would be in New England, for example; it is compactly arranged around three sides of the dacha. The fourth border, of course, is the river. So, I will take you to the largest of the barns where the farm manager will show you around and answer your questions. If you like, he will take you on an all-terrain vehicle I had brought in from the States to give you a brief tour. Sorry we didn't have time for the dacha earlier this morning; something has come up that requires Will and me to be in Smolensk earlier than we had planned," explained Isaac to Anna, who demonstrated more interest than Isaac had anticipated.

"Great! I would love a tour on the ATV. I have had little experience with farms in the United States or Europe, so this will be exciting. Go, have a joyous time in Smolensk. Don't bore Will, though. He is really too nice. Don't take advantage of him, Isaac."

"Anna, there are few people on this planet more capable and willing to take care of themselves than Will MacIntosh. There are days when his instructions verge on him taking advantage of me – but I know it's always with the best of intentions and in my best interest. Behave yourself with the farm manager, Anna. He is married with children and is a devout Jew from Smolensk."

"It's not always my fault, Isaac, any more than it was yours in the past."

Isaac had an office constructed on the second floor of the former Menshikoffsky Bank building still in his ownership, despite the fall of Imperial Russia, the Soviets and the rapacious oligarchs who rose to power with Putin. From this base, Isaac planned to develop his plans for Smolensk and in other areas of Russia. It was in this office that he and Will met with the mayor and three councillors from the municipal government of Smolensk.

Will opened the meeting as the CEO of Menshive International Holdings Inc., the vehicle created to manage and develop some of the former trust assets. He had as an interpreter the resident manager, Mr Menshikovsky whom Isaac and Will met on their first visit three years ago.

Will announced that Isaac wished to make two improvements to the town, which would involve additional dedicated structures to be carried out at Isaac's expense. The two projects were interconnected and if one was not accepted the other would also be cancelled. Will emphasized that the holding company expected nothing from the city but permission to carry out the planned construction on lands owned by Isaac, and that there should be an effort by the mayor and councillors to generate support and protection for the project. He pointed out that Isaac was in a position to show his gratitude for their agreement in tangible ways that could assist the city with development plans the city might have in mind.

The mayor turned to Isaac and expressed appreciation for being included at this early state – before work began.

Isaac replied, "Thank you. Will has carefully left it to me to inform you what I have in mind. One priority is to construct a synagogue on the site where the late nineteenth-century synagogue stood until it was destroyed in the middle of the twentieth century. The new structure will be of a similar size and style. I have numerous photographs of the building that will capture the protocols and principles of a Jewish sanctuary. I plan to add to the new building a large theatre that will seat twelve to fourteen hundred people. This theatre space will be also available for civic events and theatrical performances."

The mayor and councillors retreated to the back of the room to confer. Will interrupted them, offering to give them the use of a boardroom a short distance away; the offer was quickly accepted. They remained in the boardroom for no more than fifteen minutes before returning. The mayor announced that there would be agreement in principle at the next city council meeting.

"What is the other project you had in mind, Dr Menshive? I think there was a second project – perhaps the theatre was it. If so, we are grateful for it."

"Yes, there is another major development that must link with those I have told you about," replied Isaac. "Bear with me if I appear to lecture at this point, but my motive for this next project arises because of the repetitive history of persecution of Jews in the Pale of Settlement – I know you have heard the term. Smolensk was the largest community that serviced the needs and ambitions of the Jews living or coming to live in this area of the Pale. From the middle of the nineteenth century until recent years my people have been persecuted over and over again by non-Jews in this region. It will be one of my most ardent labours to improve the standing and conditions of Jews in the city and in this region. To that end, I propose to construct what would be one of the largest museums in Russia. Russia has some of the finest museums in the world, but none on the scale I have in mind dedicated to the language, culture, origins and history of the Jewish people in Russia. It would serve the Jews of Russia, but importantly, it would become a major tourist attraction bringing scholars and Jews from all around the world to view the exhibits and interpretive devices I plan to have prepared. I need your agreement for the construction of the museum. More importantly, I need your commitment and that of other community leaders in this city and region to improve relations with the Jewish community, enabling them to emerge from obscurity and isolation. Acceptance of our Jewish community as full participants in your civic life is a necessary condition to my agreeing to construct the museum."

The mayor spoke for the group from the city council. He said that he knew Jews had been marginalized and degraded from time to time but whatever the historic reasons for that, they surely had passed. He said he would take Isaac's proposal for the museum to the civic council as well.

The mayor had hardly finished speaking when one of the councillors, a short, rather rotund, roughly dressed man, interjected, "And who will pay to keep these buildings running and compensate the staff necessary to run these places? We should have a security payment which we would hold in case the properties become a burden to us."

The mayor and one of the other councillors looked at the speaker, visibly embarrassed at this unexpected demand. "Perhaps," the mayor said, "that wouldn't be necessary if Dr Menshive is paying for them and he assures us of his continuing support.

The councillor replied with an agenda of his own. "I know our townspeople will suspect we are being used by this foreigner – particularly an American. I can remember when we were taught, not so long ago, that the Americans were our enemies. No, I think we must have money upfront to protect us."

Will answered the challenge. "We understand your worry for the future upkeep and maintenance of the buildings, but if Dr Menshive and his objectives in establishing these buildings here are honoured, he will not fail you. Please note that these buildings are intended to honour an important, historic part of your city – if the buildings are not kept to an appropriate standard it will reflect on Dr Menshive and the Jewish community here. He wouldn't allow it to happen – unless, of course, he is forced to by the citizens of Smolensk. His purpose is to build bridges, not destroy them."

The councillor was persistent. "Well, that may be, but I know there are people here who will oppose this project unless we get money in advance – money we will have the right to control."

Isaac, stood, ashen-faced and ready to leave as he assembled his concept drawings and plans. "Clearly, my generous offer is being rejected on the terms I offer – the *only* terms I offer. Let me be clear, I am not interested in helping you develop an important attraction for your city if there will be dissension and conflict in Smolensk arising because of my proposal. My motives are sincere and well-intentioned. I am not here to give money to special interest groups who would probably undermine the ultimate construction of the project. Will, it is time to leave."

As Isaac walked out of the meeting room, Will took the mayor aside with the translator and said, "Mayor, the project could still go ahead, but it is up to you and your council to take the next step. It is now dead in the water – as we say – unless the council comes back to Dr Menshive with an absolute acceptance of the terms of his proposal and a guarantee that the council and people of Smolensk will honour the terms of the gift."

The mayor and two of the councillors who had joined him assured Will that the concept was welcomed and would meet with approval.

Will replied, "That, sir, is not sufficient. Dr Menshive would require a resolution passed by the city council by not less than two-thirds of the councillors – that the exact terms of the proposal be accepted. To ensure those terms are clear Dr Menshive's property manager here, Mr Menshikovsky, will deliver the exact terms which will, if accepted by your council, constitute a binding agreement between the council for the city and Dr Menshive. The offer made by Dr Menshive today shall remain in effect for thirty days and if not accepted within that time will be automatically terminated. If it is terminated, he will look elsewhere in Russia to carry out the project. In the meantime, Dr Menshive will seek assurances and guarantees at a much higher level."

* * *

From the council meeting, Isaac and Will went to the current synagogue to meet with the resident rabbi. Rabbi Bernstein was a middle-aged successor to the rabbi whom Isaac had met three years before.

"Rabbi, I was very sorry to learn of your predecessor's death last year. I remember him well. He was very helpful to me as I was exploring my family roots here in Smolensk. He and his wife entertained me at their apartment on the outskirts of the city. I hope his widow is alright."

"Yes, sir, she is living in St Petersburg with their daughter. I write to her periodically. I will mention that you were enquiring about her. When I arrived to take up my duties here, it was before she left. She told me about your discussions with her husband. She said her husband took considerable encouragement for the future of his congregation as a result of your plans to do something for them."

Isaac informed Rabbi Bernstein of his plans for a new synagogue and community conference centre and theatre complex. The rabbi's enthusiastic response gave Isaac added incentive to persist with his plans. "But, Rabbi, I am worried about the councillor who demanded a substantial capital deposit as a precondition to considering, let alone approving, the project. I suspect the counsellor is in the pocket, as we say, of one or more local oligarchs who would take control of the funds. I must ask you, Rabbi, to make discreet inquiries about the two or three like-minded councillors. What opposition will they have, what is their agenda, and of course who are the people behind them? I won't put a penny into this community unless the project is secure, and the money will go where I decide it is to go. Please speak to your congregation to determine whether the members, both men and women, are fully in support of the project. I emphasize the women, too.

"I am here in Smolensk for another six days. I would like to hear from you before I leave. Today is Tuesday. I will attend your service on Saturday, but I do not attend for the purpose of disrupting your service. However, if asked, I could stay after the service for half an hour to answer questions."

As Isaac and Will left the synagogue, the rabbi looked ten years younger, energized and appreciative.

When they got back to their car, it was noticeably lopsided. Will said, "There is something wrong with the Merc, Isaac, or perhaps one of the wheels may be up on the curb."

"There is no curb here, mastermind. There is something wrong with the damn thing. Where is our driver?" As they looked around for him, the driver appeared coming out of what Will knew was a local watering hole that specialized in locally made vodka.

"Where have you been?" demanded an irate Isaac, "You were in charge of this vehicle. It looks somewhat lopsided. I hope there is nothing wrong with it." The driver, who was one of his outside farm staff at the dacha, not their regular driver who was ill, replied, "I'm sure there's nothing wrong, sir. I was away only a minute to go to the toilet."

Will replied with, "Like hell. Look at this tire. It is not just deflated. It has been slashed straight through – damn it! So is the front tire. Clearly, it would have taken the person who did this more than a minute or two."

Isaac followed up with, "Your employment is terminated immediately. I don't want you near any of my properties. I suspect someone lured you away with the offer of a free drink. Right? Admit it." As he spoke, he moved closer and closer to the fellow.

"Well, it was just a school friend, who wanted to share some news and a friendly chat. No harm was intended."

"Who is your friend?" asked Will.

There was a pause, a reluctance to answer was clear by his facial expression.

"Answer my question or your brother will also be fired effective today."

"He meant no harm, my friend, Dimitry."

"Dimitry who?" insisted Will.

"Dimitry Polanski."

"That name sounds familiar. Isn't his father one of the local big shots who likes to control things?"

"Yes, sir, but Dimitry wouldn't have wanted to damage your property."

"Yes, he certainly would have known what his father was up to. I want you to tell your friend what has happened to you as a result of his taking you away from protecting this car. And tell him to tell his father that I will be watching him carefully from now on."

There was a basic level taxi service that eventually found a car and driver to take Isaac, Will, and the translator back to the dacha. The Lada was diminutive for four rather full-size males. However, their return was uneventful. By the time they got back, the farm manager had already sent replacement tires and a skilled mechanic to replace the tires.

An hour before dinner that evening Anna's tour of the dacha was underway, starting in the entrance hall.

"How much information do you want, Anna – just a walk-through or an informed commentary? If the latter, you have a tag-team here who can give you what you want. Will can do the architectural history and our butler here will give the life history of the house. Which would you like?" asked Isaac, expecting Anna's limited patience and attention span to result in the shortest possible narrative.

"Oh, I'm sure Will would be a well-informed guide with his comments. This is *my* history, too. It seems far removed from New York, but I want to know all about it."

Will and Sergei agreed that Will would give an overview of mid and late-nineteenth-century Russian Imperial aristocratic life and the Tolstoy-era homes they constructed in the country. Fortunately, Anna had read both Tolstoy and Turgenev, so she had a basic understanding of Will's description. Finishing in twenty minutes, Will turned to Sergei and asked him to take the group on a tour of the house, describing the purpose and terminology applied to the rooms.

"Of course, I would be happy to do so. As I go along, I will tell you the history of the furniture and artworks as I understand them from my predecessor.

"This building is essentially U-shaped, the inside bottom of the 'U' being the principal front of the dacha; the uprights of the U are the wings that jut out into the forecourt. Like the letter U, the building is symmetrical. We are in the middle of the front, so the wing to our left is the same shape and size as the right. Mr MacIntosh referred to neoclassicism and mentioned this building is in a mid-nineteenth-century Russian Imperial neoclassicism similar to some buildings in St Petersburg of the same era. The principal rooms, sometimes referred to as the staterooms, are off to the right as one enters this hall. Secondary rooms, including Dr Menshive's office, are off to the left of the hall, as are the various rooms assigned to domestic functions needed to run both the house, grounds and the agricultural operations.

"Before you is the splendid Imperial staircase you have already explored. It is a grand introduction to the house. The balustrade including the banister and the balusters are crafted in wrought iron, each highlighted by an Italianate rococo pattern with repeated gold-leaf covered coats of arms."

Anna interjected: "Whose coats of arms? I didn't know our family had a coat of arms, Isaac!"

"Neither did I, Anna, until I reviewed our genealogical chart a couple of years ago. These are our coat of arms. You, too, are entitled to use them – although in this day and age I don't know where you would display them. The protocols surrounding their use are all passé now."

Will piped up: "Anna, you may not know that your father was, and now Isaac is, entitled to the ennobled title Baron. Isaac's technically Baron Menshikovsky."

"Don't worry, I won't use it. If I did, it would probably start another revolution. Russian émigrés fleeing the Bolshevik revolution who had titles left them behind when they moved to America, Canada or Western Europe. Only the Romanovs tended to use the titles – usually only those with close connections with the British royal family through the bloodline to Prince Philip."

"You, Isaac, a baron... no! A more unlikely aristocrat I can't imagine."

"I agree; however, remember you are of the same family and therefore of the same level of society – at least you would have been one hundred and fifty years ago. The title came to us through the Günzburg family."

"Günzburgs? Who are they?" said Will.

"Russian bankers – Jewish, of course, but with aristocratic connections. They and the Menshikovsky side of our family were somehow linked, and the title passed to us when the line of that family entitled to the title died out... Through some machinations that I don't know or care about, it came into our family."

"Do I get to wear a tiara and robes?" asked Anna

"No. Don't get inflated notions. That's why I haven't told you about the title until now. Under no circumstances are you to refer to me with the title – anywhere, and I include the USA. Here in Russia, it would set me up as a target by the many Bolsheviks still in positions of power."

"Yes, but hasn't Mr Putin recently reinterred the Royal Family in St Isaac's Cathedral in St Petersburg?"

"He did so as part of his strategy to rebuild the global status of Russia as a great power. He is using every device he can think of including recognizing Imperial history and reinstating the Russian Orthodox Church as the official state religion.

"Promise not to use the title. I am prepared to talk to you quietly and privately about it – even here in the dacha you must not use it."

"Alright. It does seem a shame. Imagine! My father, a socialist professor, was a Russian baron."

"He may not have known he was entitled to the title, so drop it."

Sergei took his captive audience through the enfilade of rooms to the right. The first to the right of the reception hall was a double parlour, both exceptionally formal. The first to be entered overlooking the courtyard was elegantly decorated in the finest Russian Empire style in its furnishings, window dressings, carpets and crystal chandeliers. The space was divided mid-point into a back parlour, also formal, but less so with its French windows that led out onto the terrace overlooking the Dnieper River.

Next to the double parlour was another space of equal size as the double parlour which was divided into three separate rooms. The front overlooking the courtyard was the ladies' withdrawing room and behind it accessible from that room and from the back parlour was a windowless picture gallery and statuary court. Many of the family portraits were mounted securely on the walls; each was reflected in the large mirrors forming part of the over mantles on the two fireplaces covered by a Russian marble known as malachite. Behind them lay an informal garden room with three French windows that led onto the terrace that ran along the full length of the back of the dacha. Next to these rooms, further to the right, was the formal dining room and behind it, overlooking the terrace, an informal family dining room. The kitchens and service areas lay beyond.

At this point, Sergei excused himself, somewhat to the relief of his audience, so that he could prepare the chef and kitchen for the evening meal.

That meal was a happy convivial exploration, as they imagined what life must have been like for an aristocratic Russian family in Smolensk in the late Imperial period. Being on their own with ample security within and outside the dacha, everyone was able to relax and enjoy themselves.

3

THE EARLY MORNING mists blanketing the surface of the Dnieper lifted as the sun rose. Will sat watching Isaac and Sophie with Little Isaac in a push-chair for infants. They each had a hand on the handle, Isaac's laid gently over Sophie's. While not a great distance from where Will was sitting, their voices were only murmurs. They were a picture of contentment, peace and love.

Sophie's arrival in Isaac's life had clearly been transformative. He had found through Sophie a sense of calm purpose and inner strength that Will had never noticed in Isaac before. Sophie, on the other hand, focused her attention and affection on Isaac while she was with him. The baby was of great importance, but it was the relationship between husband and wife that guided their lives together and was manifest on the few occasions when they were alone.

Will had finished his early morning coffee when Sergei brought him a message. It was coded, as all communications into and sent out of the dacha were – Sergei cautioned Isaac and Will on arrival that the local and national governments regularly listened in on or read messages. It was not just directed to Isaac and those in his life; it was a uniform warning to the residents of Russia. And it was one of the many methods used by the Putin government, like his predecessors, for informing the authorities on the minutiae of daily life in the country. Records were kept. Any indiscreet or unthinking remark that could be judged a threat to the established Soviet order would be used against the perpetrator. This was well known and resulted in the people appearing to be sullen and uncommunicative. They knew it was best to keep their opinions to themselves.

The coded message informed Will that Mr Ushakov, the lawyer engaged by Ivan Molotovsky, the general manager of

Isaac's extensive property holdings in Russia, would arrive at 11 a.m. by helicopter. The appointment and the method of transportation had been arranged in advance with Mr Molotovsky. The lawyer's arrival would be more private and less questioned than if he arrived by car. Isaac and Will had learned that there was a network of informers in Smolensk: these watched for and reported every arrival and departure in the city. Isaac and Will's arrival three years ago created a sensation, still recounted over a few vodkas in most watering holes in the city.

It was now 8:30 a.m. Will walked over to the landing pier where Isaac and Sophie were sitting admiring their infant creation. "Sorry to interrupt, Isaac, but our guest will arrive this morning as scheduled. I have suggested the helicopter land outside the inner gates. I will instruct the farm manager to have the gates open. There will be a lot of noise, Sophie, so you may wish to have Little Isaac inside when it arrives. No need to disturb your morning for now, but Isaac, I think we should meet at 10:30 a.m. in your office to plan for the arrival."

Both Will and Isaac arrived at the office at the appointed time. Both were somewhat rigid about meeting deadlines and being consistently punctual.

"Will, refresh my memory; why is lawyer Ushakov visiting us?"

"You will recall that before we left Moscow three years ago, I told you we needed to search the title to the numerous properties on the inventory you own here in Russia. Before we start final negotiations with regional or national authorities on what you will propose as a settlement, we must know exactly the strengths and weaknesses of our position. This certainly includes the ownership of the properties. I must admit, I am baffled why you appear to own property in Russia – I mean, why you and your family were permitted to own property in this country. However, all will be revealed. Molotovsky has assured us Ushakov has completed his search."

"Good. The inventory leaves little doubt that I own all of the properties, even giving an estimated market value for each. However, I know you lawyers like 'due diligence' and exhaust every possibility. I hope I am not wasting money on this lawyer."

"If he is knowledgeable and thorough, which I am informed by several sources – including the American and the Canadian embassies – that he is, your money will be well spent. I am sure he will also be helpful in developing our strategy when we approach regional and national authorities."

"Is he a Jew, Will? He would be less likely to have competing interests if he is of my faith and community."

"Yes, that was a condition of selection. He is an Orthodox Jew, as were your family, but is perhaps more liberal than the rigidity the Orthodox usually demonstrate. I am told he is reliable and highly ethical. He is a practising Jew and is actively engaged with the Jewish community in both Moscow and St Petersburg."

At this point the head housekeeper knocked on the office door, announcing by doing so that she had a trolley laden with a massive samovar and numerous edibles that would serve as lunch for the three of them.

"Will Molotovsky accompany Ushakov? It might be useful for him to be briefed on the legal side of things. When we met with him three years ago, I noticed he stuck rigidly to property management and did not go beyond those boundaries."

"Yes, I thought it would be helpful to have him here. He will be on the flight. If anything arises that you consider confidential and that should be kept from him, you can ask him to take a walk in the park."

The overflight of the helicopter created a heavy thumping on the roof of the dacha and a whirling vortex of sound which woke Little Isaac and sent him into competition with the helicopter. From within the dacha, he was winning.

Mr Molotovsky was brought to the office with his companion, Mr Ushakov, by Sergei who predictably announced both callers by name and then retreated.

Isaac moved forward greeting them both and he introduced Will to Ushakov, who acknowledged that he had spoken to

Will on a secure cell phone on several occasions over the last two years.

Isaac invited Molotovsky and Ushakov to join him and Will at a table set for four. The trolley was moved into place by Isaac who offered refreshments which were taken, consumed and enjoyed. Without any further waste of time, Isaac turned to Mr Ushakov and asked what his research had discovered.

"Well, Dr Menshive – I will refer to you by your American name, sir, unless you would prefer that I use your title and Russian name –"

"Under no circumstances will I be referred to other than Menshive. Yes, I am accustomed to being addressed by my professional title of Doctor and ask that we follow that practice."

"Then I will get right to it. You do not own any of the properties listed on the inventory…"

"What! Impossible. Molotovsky has been managing them for years, collecting rent and making improvements at the cost of the trust. Everyone we have met acknowledges my right to the properties. This is implausible. You must be mistaken!"

"No, I am not. But if you will hear me to the end of my research, you will better understand your position.

"First, no private person has a greater right to possession and use of the properties than you do. Let me explain the fundamental principles of property law here in Russia and in Imperial Russia, during the Communist era and now in the post-Communist period with Vladimir Putin as our new autocrat.

"The land ownership system in both Imperial Russia and during the Soviet system were similar in that all land was owned by the government, whether that government was a Czar or the Soviets. That is still the law. However, during the nineteenth and early twentieth centuries, there was flexibility. Many estates were granted by the Czar to nobles and aristocrats who owned the serfs who made the land productive. Secure possession of estates was essential to make land production reliable. The key was the serf. Serfs were owned, body and soul, by the estate owner. He had absolute power of life and limb over the serfs. Technically, however, the Czar could at will remove a noble or aristocrat from possession of an estate and transfer it to another. The serfs were tied to the land, so they were owned by whoever had possession of the estate. There were a few exceptions granted to court favourites. Exceptions started creeping in with the industrialization of Russia. To attract entrepreneurs and what you in the West call venture capital, secure title was granted in specialized situations. Several of your properties such as the banks and railways fell into that category."

"Good. Now I am regaining some comfort."

"If so, it is premature, Dr Menshive. I described the Czarist system of land distribution. After the 1917 revolution, the Communists were motivated by socialist theoreticians like Marx and Engels – both Jews, incidentally – who advocated that all land should be held by the central or the regional governments and allocated on sufferance to individuals, but on condition that possession could be recalled at any time.

"The allocation of the use of land is not like a leasehold interest in America or Canada. The rights of the possessor are much more vulnerable to arbitrary removal by the state. This was particularly the case during the Soviet era which only ended in 1998. There were favourites of the party bigwigs, there were party officials who expected and received preference, and there were the state security systems that frequently conjured false accusations of treason or illegal behaviour which would lead to confiscation of the property."

"Do I have no right at all to the properties listed on the inventory? Do I not have rights to this dacha?"

"The answer, Dr Menshive, is that you do have the exclusive right of possession until that right is terminated – ostensibly for cause."

"Can I sell the properties or leave them to my son?"

"Actually, that is where you have some security. Once the right of possession has been established, you can pass it on to your heirs – to your son, as you say. Virtually all of the Russian properties on the inventory were acquired in Czarist days, and then passed down through the trust from one generation to another.

"One of the interesting aspects of your situation is that the Günzburg and Mendelssohn properties – and there were many in the banking, railroad, and industrial sectors – were left to your great-great-great-grandfather and by him to the trust. Your ancestors were exceptionally astute. Possession was always in the name of a trustworthy non-Jewish agent. The trust to which you refer ultimately owned the assets. The trust was an administrative device helping to shelter the actual ownership. It was also an effective means of hiding the true owner from anti-Semitic attacks."

"So, if I understand any of this, I think I am entitled to continue to have exclusive possession, a sort of ownership, of these properties."

"Yes, but note the qualification on that right to possession."

"Alright, but what about the income being generated by these properties, and the market value ascribed to each on the inventory?"

"The income is that of the person in possession – you – so long as the right to possession isn't terminated. As to the apparent value listed beside each property – that is not a market value. You cannot sell these properties without the permission of the government. There is no real estate market in Russia except the black market, although one is developing. The value you see here for your dacha is not fair market value, it is the cumulative income received by the trust in Switzerland. So what has been happening is that Mr Molotovsky through his agents in various parts of Russia, Belarus and formerly Poland collected the rent. It was your money."

"I suppose there must be currency controls limiting the amount of capital in any form that can leave the country – so how did the revenue get to the Swiss bank?"

"Well, Dr Menshive, our investors were somewhat creative, devious, and perhaps illegal in how they got the money out of the country. One of the principal assets you own in Russia is a gold mine – you also have a mine that produces platinum – so what happened is that Mr Molotovsky, on a monthly basis with the monthly revenue, purchased gold or platinum from one of the mines and the mines then shipped the gold or platinum in secure containers to Berlin and deposited them in a secure bank vault there. Periodically, as the price of gold and platinum rose on the open market, your Berlin banker, who is directed and controlled by the Swiss bank trustee, ensures the proceeds of the sales are then transferred by regular interbank deposit to your master account in Switzerland. Of course, I have no idea at all what is in that account. In summary, while you do not have secure title as you would in America, you have the highest level of security in possession, transfer of possession, and exclusive right to use available to a citizen in this country. You have benefited by all revenues accruing to each property, the net amount of those revenues far exceeds the market value of the property – even if there was one.

"I should point out one quirk in the law. Development Rights. As long as the original purpose for the properties is maintained, you will be kept below the notice of the authorities. Any intended change in uses would require national or regional government approval. Your ancestors, sir, were exceptionally careful and astute not to alarm the authorities. They maintained the properties to a standard higher than other properties in the area. Most of the properties were acquired for a pittance – remember, most were bought over one hundred years ago. You could lose them all and not lose a cent on the investment, given the substantial accrual and increases in revenue."

"Fascinating. It is a brain-bender, sir, but I think I understand you. Do you have all of this locked away in that Celtic head of yours, Will?"

"Yes. I received a helpful briefing note from Mr Ushakov while I was still in Canada. Isaac, this sounds bizarre. It *is* bizarre, according to our systems of land ownership management. However, with the exception of the power to sell, you are relatively secure."

"Well, legal types – the only property in Russia I really want to have title to and absolute control over is this dacha and its seven hundred acres."

"That, Dr Menshive, is something you will have to negotiate with President Putin personally. If negotiations are conducted through third parties, one of the oligarchs will get wind of it and will acquire possessory rights. As to the seven hundred acres – this estate originally had approximately twenty thousand acres and included a strip of land two miles deep on both sides of the Dnieper running twenty-five miles south. When the serfs were liberated in the late nineteenth century, all but seven hundred acres were nationalized and distributed to the former serfs. I don't know how your investors were able to keep possession of the seven hundred acres."

Weary, confused and worried, Isaac drew the meeting to a conclusion for the day. He invited his guests to stay overnight, join him and his family for dinner and then resume discussion in the morning.

"Will, no more of this for today. I am going to get my shotgun and with the estate manager head off for some field sports. I would ask you to join me, but I know how you feel about guns," announced Isaac.

"Right. I will see you at dinner. I have several memos I want to prepare for my records. I also brought a new spy novel I would like to read. Don't shoot yourself or poor Alexi."

The pre-dinner conversation was more reserved, with Will and Isaac distracted in their own worlds, neither offering very much to the conversation. It was left to Sophie and Anna to entertain Mr Molotovsky and Mr Ushakov. They eagerly inquired about shopping in Smolensk – what was good, bad and indifferent? Where should they shop? Did any carry designer goods? The replies mostly from Mr Molotovsky were negative, but he recommended they tour the Kremlin – believed to be the largest in Russia – even though it offered none of the splendour of the Kremlin in Moscow. However, he said, there were stalls nearby selling local crafts that might appeal to them. The reaction to this advice established that there would be little shopping in stalls for them.

"I remember from my music history courses that the celebrated early Russian musician and composer, Glinka, was born and lived here for several years. Is there a museum or historic house to visit?" The negative answer is what was expected. "The house is there, but somewhat reduced. You can walk by. The neighbourhood has fallen into a state of disrepair. Be sure to have security with you if you go anywhere in the city outside the historic centre. Even if you stay in the centre you should have security." Mr Molotovsky was defeated in his efforts to engage the women in further conversation and the room fell into silence.

Sergei had suspected that the conversation would lag at dinner, so he had arranged for two balalaika players to perform during dinner. It proved to be the salvation to a rather miserable gathering.

Before separating for the night, it was agreed that Isaac and Will would take Sophie and Anna into town with them the next day. Mr Molotovsky agreed that he would go into town with Alexi in a farm vehicle that required mechanical attention. Mr Ushakov was left at the dacha to enjoy a day of quiet relaxation and possible recreation with a fishing rod.

4

FORTUNATELY, ALEXI HAD stockpiled spare parts and tires for the Merc. He explained that the nearest professional mechanic qualified to work on a Mercedes Benz was in Moscow and supplies for the car were only available there as well. After the tire slashing incident in Smolensk the day before, the car had been towed back to the dacha by one of the farm vehicles. It depressed Sergei to see friends and relatives of his lining the street in Smolensk with happy smirks on their faces as the car was being towed.

The drive into the city brought them on time for Isaac and Will's meeting with the mayor and councillors. A change in plan was put in place when Anna suggested that she and Sophie take Little Isaac into town. They could take him for a walk in his push-cart while they explored the city. Isaac expressed reservations about the walk-about but was too distracted to pursue his point.

Two security guards were left with Anna and Sophie. They were directed to accompany them everywhere and not let them out of their sight.

Isaac and Will walked to the city council offices for their meeting with one security guard. It had been arranged that the meeting would be with the mayor and his principal administrator only. When Isaac and Will walked into the meeting room, they were faced by the same crowd with whom they met a couple of days before. The meeting had been called by the mayor. Isaac's deadline gave them until Sunday, their planned day of departure for Moscow.

The mayor started the meeting by thanking Isaac and Will for coming so soon after the initial meeting. Isaac nodded, waiting for the purpose to be explained.

"Dr Menshive, the council met in special session and wishes to have additional information and give its preliminary thoughts on your proposal. First, as you heard from one of our councillors, there seems to be agreement that you should pay a deposit to be held by the council as security for completion of the project and as a pool of money to meet our expenses as the project is discussed, plans developed, and construction is undertaken."

"How much?"

"Well, sir, we know you are opposed to the deposit, so we thought a modest sum would be more likely to be acceptable to you. The council has decided that as a condition of considering the proposal further, we would need a cash deposit of two million U.S. dollars."

"Who would control that money – make decisions as to its depletion by charges against the deposit?"

"Oh, you can trust the council to respect your deposit and to take withdrawals from it only as necessary."

"You haven't answered my question."

The mayor looked anxious which turned into embarrassment as he said, "Well, we have struck a committee of persons in whom council has confidence to do so."

"And who are they?"

"I can't reveal private information about how the council works. Be assured they are honourable men in whom you can put your trust."

"Their names, please."

"As I have said, I can't give you that information."

Isaac rose, and said, "This meeting is terminated. I agree to none of your requirements. You have until Sunday, today being Wednesday, to accept my proposal as presented to you."

Without waiting for a reply, Isaac and Will left the room. As they did so, Isaac turned to Will and the security guard, who both had the latest mobile phones in hand with the capacity to take excellent digital photographs, "Did you get any photographs of those in the room who were hangers-on?"

"Yes, I took several," said Will, whose assurance was also given by the guard. "Now, Frank, I want you to forward these to the bank in Zurich. Mr Molotovsky, do you know the identity of those in attendance?"

"Some, but not all. I will go over the photographs with our local banker; he should know them."

"I suspect I know that that kid Polanski's father was one of them. I know him to be linked to one of the prominent oligarchs. Let's get our background information together before we go further. Incidentally, I am in no rush to start this project if there is local resistance to it."

Isaac had barely finished his sentence when Anna came running across the street to Isaac waving her arms frantically, calling for Isaac to stop.

"Isaac, Sophie and the baby have been kidnapped! Yes, both of them. We kept together with the bodyguards, but when Sophie had to go to the toilet, she insisted on going alone and then she changed her mind and said she would take Little Isaac with her. When the bodyguard asked to go with her, she refused. She was in the room where the facilities are for more than fifteen minutes. When we went in, she was gone. My God! What can we do? I'm devastated. I was watching her, I promise I was."

Isaac turned purple with anger, clenched his fists and exclaimed, "This meeting was a setup. They got us into town hoping we would bring Sophie and Little Isaac."

"Isaac, I will have Ushakov contact the Russian security police in Moscow and ask for immediate help. I will then contact our friends at the American Embassy to help. This will be an embarrassment to Putin in his attempt to seek re-election. They can't afford to have this stand-off last. He is personally aware of the generous plans you have for the people of Russia. Isaac, you have to contact the American Embassy in Moscow. In the meantime, we go international with this. CNN, BBC, NBC; whoever we can engage to cover the story. We'll make our calls out on our cell phones now, and then get back to the dacha as our base. Frank, you will remain here and, with your backup, you will check for clues and do your best to find Sophie and the boy. Remember, Sophie is seven months pregnant."

Isaac completed his call to the embassy. His shaking and

scarcely controlled voice was barely able to get his message across.

Before they entered the Merc for the drive back to the dacha, several emergency vehicles converged at their car, firearms held in flailing arms demonstrating more panic than skill in an emergency. Mr Molotovsky explained what had happened, described Sophie and the child and her condition. Frank was designated to be their contact person with Isaac.

Mr Molotovsky explained who was present at the meeting and told them about the tire-slashing incident and its possible connection to Polanski. The local constabulary promised Molotovsky they would follow up and would gain the release of Mrs Menshive and the child very soon.

Back at the dacha, Mr Ushakov joined Will and Isaac in the office. He immediately called the local rabbi, instructing him to get the Jewish community activated in the search, and he called Rabbi Levin in Moscow from whom he received assurance that Levin would discuss the situation personally with President Putin and with the Patriarch of the Russian Orthodox Church. Levin expressed the same worry that Isaac and Ushakov had: that the situation had the potential of creating a full-blown uprising by Russian Jews in the middle of Putin's election campaign.

Within an hour BBC and CNN were carrying the story, more exaggerated than the reality, but even that level of publicity was helpful.

Two hours later Frank returned, with no news. He said he had retraced the steps Anna had described and examined the washroom area and adjoining room. He said there was no sign of violence, but that meant only that Sophie was forced into the kidnappers' custody, quickly and without physical violence. It was possible that she was taken at gun or knifepoint.

Isaac started shaking uncontrollably. Fortunately, one of the nursemaids Sophie had taken with her on their trip to Russia, a woman named Anastasia, was a trained registered nurse. She had a sedative that calmed Isaac as soon as it was injected into his shoulder.

The cell phones and landlines were alive with incoming calls all night with updates on what efforts were being made to find Sophie and the child. Isaac gave interviews to CNN and the BBC World News. A bleaker picture of security for Jews in Russia couldn't have been created by the Western media. Although Isaac tried to indicate there was apparent cooperation with Russian internal security – but he knew he was in a state in which lying and disinformation were the norm.

Will took several calls from Sophie's family and from both Rabbi Levin and Rabbi Bernstein, who were controlled but almost on the verge of panic. Bernstein had a genuine concern for Sophie and Little Isaac, but he was equally worried for his congregation about the growing anti-Semitism in Russia. Already there were demonstrations in Smolensk, Moscow, St Petersburg and Novgorod by both the Jewish and non-Jewish communities, each one verbally attacking the other.

At midnight, Will went to bed. He knew the next few days would be considerably worse than today. Isaac was given a sedative strong enough to put him to sleep.

Isaac's clinic in New York called at 3 a.m. and informed Will that it was sending a team of doctors for Sophie, the child and Isaac. They were to leave by midday on a private jet that would land at an airstrip near Smolensk by noon that day. Vehicles had been rented by the clinic, via telephone, in Moscow which would be at the airstrip when the jet arrived.

Sophie's parents were invited to join the team on the private jet. They gratefully accepted the invitation.

What really disrupted the life of the citizens of Smolensk, however, was the army of private security: both Russian security forces and American Embassy officers hired to cover the scene in Smolensk. The message was clear: find this woman and her child and return them to their family in good condition immediately or your town will be completely taken over. Putin was effectively powerless to resist being involved, given the international interest in the story.

5

AT SEVEN THE next morning Will had already conferred with the security detail he trusted and the Russian police on the case. Will said, "I expect a ransom note from the kidnapper demanding money or something of value. What it may be, we will only know when it arrives. Is there any sign of one?"

"No, Mr MacIntosh, no sign yet."

"Has anyone looked out at the gate or at the top of the road leading to the dacha for a note or a message?"

"No – I did look at the front of this building. There was nothing there."

"There wouldn't be. The intensive media and police coverage would intimidate the kidnappers from coming near the property. Continue to have a close look at the double gates leading into the dacha and at the top of the road. Also, Isaac fired his driver for inattention to the Merc which resulted in the tires being slashed a day or two ago. Check his area of work on the grounds around the dacha. He should be questioned in Smolensk if he can be found. Take the farm manager with you, and a translator. Have you checked out the pier and deck area on the river? That was a favourite spot for Isaac and Sophie. Someone could have reached the pier by boat and left a message there."

"Right. I'm on it. I'll get the security detail divided into sectors and put them to work."

Before Frank left the breakfast room, Sergei came in and said quietly, "Sir, the mayor and a delegation from the city have arrived and wish to meet with Dr Menshive. I did not think it wise to bother him at this time."

"Thank you, Sergei, you are correct. *I* will meet with them. The meeting will be in the farm manager's office once he has had time to straighten it up and assemble enough chairs.

Coffee and tea will be offered. No food will be necessary. Thank you."

Will immediately called both Mr Molotovsky and Mr Ushakov who were staying at the dacha and asked them to join him in Isaac's office immediately.

When Will explained that the mayor and his group were insistent on a meeting, he turned to Mr Ushakov and asked: "Any ideas of why they want to meet with Isaac? Incidentally, I am not telling Isaac about the meeting. I will handle it."

"My sources," said Mr Molotovsky cutting in, "have been in contact with me several times during the night on my cell phone. From what I can gather when it wasn't cutting out, the city is in a state of chaos – everything is shut down and the relations between the Jewish population, as small as it is, and the others are past boiling point. I suspect the delegation from the city wants Dr Menshive to intervene to try to cool the situation."

"What do you advise, Mr Ushakov?"

"Let events flow as they may. This may be the test these people need to learn to get along and accept the Jewish population as equal citizens."

"Thank you. Let's meet with them and find out what they want." Frank joined them, along with two of the more robust farmworkers in the farm manager's office.

After introductions had been made, little civility was extended by Will or those on his side of the room.

Will remained standing as the mayor rose to speak. A few predictable platitudes and regrets were offered and ignored by Will and his group.

"We have come from the city to meet with Dr Menshive."

"He is not available. You meet with me and my colleagues or you leave now."

The delegation gathered and whispered among themselves. The mayor continued.

"Will you promise to give our message to him?"

"Only if I consider it helpful to our search for his wife and child abducted in your city yesterday – strangely while

Dr Menshive and I were distracted by being with you at a meeting you styled as urgent. Say what it is you wish to say."

"The city is in chaos. Commerce has come to a stop. All public services have been curtailed by uprisings in the streets. We cannot tolerate this any further. You or Dr Menshive must intervene."

"That, neither Dr Menshive nor I will do. I warn you that the situation as you see it now is going to get a very great deal worse. Your national government has a large security force arriving any minute – its purpose is to find the lady and her child. Civic order will be secondary. You and your group have chosen the wrong victims. Let me tell you, if any harm comes to Mrs Menshive or the child you and your group will pay an exceptional personal and civic price. You want this problem to go away, Mayor? It will when Mrs Menshive and her child are returned safely – and we find those responsible. President Putin has assured us that the full weight of Russian law will fall on them. I know you are aware of his personal authority in this country. Do you have anything else you wish to say to us on this side of the room?"

"Yes, we will try to find them and those who are responsible."

"You know damn well who is responsible," replied Will. "I suspect one of them is in this room now. The farm manager and our security personnel will see you up to the main highway. Communicate with me only when you have something helpful to tell me. Otherwise, enjoy the mess, as you describe it, that you and some or all of your group have created."

By mid-afternoon, a large group of locals had formed a militia and assembled at the first set of gates into the dacha. They brought with them enough firearms, knives and scythes to intimidate the local constabulary and the citizens of Smolensk. Calls were received by Frank and interpreted by Ushakov that demanded immediate withdrawal of the security forces brought in by Isaac's supporters.

A stand-off resulted that neither side was prepared to break.

Will realized that with the increasing volatility of the situation he would have to include Isaac in the planning.

When Will arrived at Isaac's private quarters in the dacha, he found Isaac in the sitting room adjacent to the master bedroom bent over a computer, working on something.

"We have a situation underway near the dacha that requires your involvement. Your security people have a recommendation for dealing with it, but it requires your attention and agreement. The risk to the dacha, to you and probably to Sophie and Little Isaac grows by the minute."

"I have been watching the crowd growing up the lane. I have an excellent vantage point from the windows in this part of the building. I think I have a sense of what is happening, but tell me what you know and what our people recommend."

"Well, Isaac, first there is no news on Sophie or Little Isaac; second, we have assembled a substantial security force, part of which is in Smolensk looking for Sophie and Little Isaac and the other part here at the dacha ready to defend the property and us. In all, we have about eighty heavily armed, skilled private security guards on the ground. They assure me they are a match for anything the locals can bring against you. There is probably little increase in the risk to Sophie or Little Isaac because of the threat our security guards are giving the locals."

"Alright, that is some comfort. What about Putin and his reaction to this uprising? Has he indicated what he is prepared to do?" asked Isaac.

"No, although through our communication channels set up yesterday, he says he will not take sides with the locals and will do his best to negotiate Sophie's safe return with Little Isaac – I wouldn't trust anything Putin would say one way or the other. He will do what he considers to be in his personal best interests without any consideration for you, Sophie or Little Isaac, but given the international interest in this mess I think he will try to remain neutral. My guess is that he will leave it to the locals to deal with the situation, no doubt with covert advice from his security forces."

"Has anyone come up with a theory of where Sophie and

Little Isaac are, and what the objectives of the kidnappers are?"

"No, but it was a very high-risk step on their part. They will have an objective, but it may be as simple as to intimidate the local Jewish population and perhaps to force you to put your money into projects they want. Don't make any decisions until we know what they decide to do," explained Will.

Before Isaac had time to reply Frank burst into the room without a knock warning or invitation.

"Dr Menshive, it has been reported that Mrs Menshive and Little Isaac were seen last night in Smolensk, around 1 a.m. They were with a group of five or six people, genders unclear, who were wearing masks. According to the report, Mrs Menshive looked unhurt… but both she and Little Isaac were clearly terrified. It looked like they were being moved from one location to another when they were seen," announced Frank.

"Who is our source? Can that person be useful in contacting the kidnappers?" asked Will.

"The information came from the local constabulary who would not disclose the source. However, the constabulary know or suspect they know who the kidnappers are."

"Alright, Frank. Thank you. Please remain while Isaac and I decide what to do now." Will turned to Isaac saying, "Isaac, this is a positive development. It appears we may be able to communicate, though I suggest we do not as it would show panic and weakness on our part which the kidnappers will use to their advantage. Let's wait for another twenty-four hours or so before attempting contact. The delay will also give our security team a chance to gain some control over the situation and give us at least some tactical advantage, which we do not have now."

There was a pause before Isaac could reply to Will. He was profoundly emotional, shaking uncontrollably, with tears streaming down his face.

"Will, you know I have abandoned my duties as a husband and father without a thought in the past. I am learning now how that must have felt to my exes and to my children. This situation is teaching me a lesson I will never forget, and that is to do my duty to those relying on me. *Oy*, if I could only take back my past – if I could, I suppose I would not be experiencing 'pay back' as I think I am getting now."

"Isaac, that is not helpful in dealing with the immediate. Do you agree with my suggestion or not?"

"Yes, of course. I am in no shape to decide anything on my own. What about offering the mayor and his henchmen a million U.S. dollars to secure Sophie's and Little Isaac's return?"

"They can't accept it, Isaac, as you should know. Acceptance would be acknowledging they are responsible for the kidnapping and the military-style assembly of locals at your gate. Definitely not. I suggest, however, that the reverse message should be sent back, namely that if anything happens to either Sophie or Little Isaac you will leave Smolensk without investing a ruble for anything. That should be sent right away."

"Agreed. I can't wait to get the hell out of this place and this miserable country," was Isaac's reply.

A couple of hours after Will's message was sent, a message was received from an unidentified spokesman for the city council, stating that Isaac could take his money and stuff it.

"How do we read this message, Will? I want your opinion as well, Frank."

"Isaac, it is a bluff. That they answered as they did surprises me, not because of what they had to say, but that they answered at all. After all, by sending the message they have admitted to being complicit. I suggest we instruct our security people to intensify their investigation of the mayor, each councillor and each person who has a vested interest in getting the support of the city council. It must be someone who has a major project or request requiring the help of the council. We need to know the background and interest of all of them. A little subtle greasing of the palms may help in obtaining that information. Do you agree, Isaac?" proposed Will, seeking a decision from his friend, who at the moment was unlikely to be able to come up with a plan of his own.

"Yes. I am settled on that. If money will bring Sophie's and Little Isaac's release, whatever money as is needed will be made available."

Before Isaac, Will and Frank separated for the night, a couple of visitors were announced by Ushakov.

"Who is here at this hour and what do they want?" asked Isaac.

"Sir, the one who acts as spokesman for the two describes himself as an agent of Rabbi Bernstein and someone who appears to be from the American Embassy."

"Thank you, Ushakov. Show them into Isaac's library. We will be there in fifteen minutes. We need that time to prepare Isaac for the meeting. Also, prepare two bedrooms for them. They will stay the night," Will instructed. Isaac simply nodded his assent.

* * *

The library was in the east wing of the dacha. It was a large room with windows overlooking the river and a terrace, access to which was provided by a double set of French doors, both securely locked in advance of the meeting. Isaac changed his mind and decided to join Will at the meeting. After the heavy drapes were drawn across the doors, Will instructed Ushakov to request the visitors to join them.

"Gentlemen, Isaac welcomes you, but I will act as his spokesman. As you can see, he is emotionally distraught by this situation. He will remain with us as long as he feels strong enough. Please give us your message."

"Dr Menshive, Mr MacIntosh, we are here on behalf of Rabbi Bernstein and your country's ambassador to this country. Neither knows where your wife and child are yet, but we are instructed to inform you, you will have the unqualified support of both our principals in bringing your ordeal to a satisfactory and safe conclusion."

"Right! And just how do you propose to do that?" asked Will.

"That is not clear to us at the moment, but we have

authority to tell you that there may be a process that could lead to that result. Contacts have been made to President Putin to engage a mediator who could act discreetly as a go-between to see whether an agreement can be reached," answered Rabbi Bernstein's spokesman.

"There is nothing to oppose in that idea," said Will, but he added, "Why do you think Putin is to be trusted, and why do you think the locals, if they are behind the kidnapping, would listen to a mediator?" asked Will.

"The message the ambassador has received from the Kremlin is that the government of Russia is embarrassed by this situation. Particularly in light of President Putin's current presidential election campaign in which he has been preaching national unity and 'Russianness' embracing all Russians. I have also been informed by the ambassador that Putin wishes to have a final agreement with you soon dealing with all your assets located here in Russia – and some assets you hold in other countries which he thinks should be brought here."

"Oh! Could it be that Putin is behind this kidnapping as a device to force me to make generous concessions in his favour that would benefit his campaign?" asked Isaac.

"That, sir, is the opinion of Rabbi Bernstein and the Ambassador."

Will interjected: "You will inform Rabbi Bernstein that how this plays out will have a lasting impact on Jewish-government relations in the future. Your community will have to establish that you cannot be manipulated or coerced into a particular course of action through physical intimidation."

"Yes, Mr MacIntosh, Rabbi Bernstein is cognizant of that problem. He thinks, however, that with his involvement a solution may be framed in a way to protect the Jewish communities in Russia."

"Well, I think he is incredibly naïve if he thinks so. However, Dr Menshive will agree to your proposal. We have nothing else as a strategy. Let's see where this will take us. However, there are conditions. One, we require proof that both Mrs Menshive and Little Isaac are in good health. Two, Mrs Menshive's nurse must be allowed to join her with whatever drugs or supplies she considers necessary for Mrs Menshive and for Little Isaac. Three, the talks start tomorrow at 2 p.m. here at the dacha. I am aware of the distance between Moscow and this dacha. A helicopter which Dr Menshive can arrange will bring the participants to us. Four, Dr Menshive will not leave this dacha or Smolensk until his family has been safely returned to him. Five, we agree that no press release related to the mediation will be issued for forty-eight hours, other than indicating the situation is fraught and unsettled. And six, ten members of Dr Menshive's security detail of his choosing will be at the dacha, some inside, some outside; all of whom will be fully armed. The delegation may have five security, army, or police officers here at the dacha – outside only – but they shall be subject to my instructions. None of these conditions is negotiable."

The two representatives asked to have a private meeting and a secure place where they could each obtain instructions.

* * *

An hour and a half later the meeting resumed. A decision was received, agreeing to Will's conditions.

6

ONE OF THE ironies Will and Isaac encountered in Russia was that architecture and the decorative arts appeared to be heavily influenced by either France or Italy, even though France was the country's principal enemy in the Napoleonic era. During that period in European history, France dominated virtually all of Europe. In the same way, the attraction to the Napoleonic ethos in politics, law and military process was to be the nemesis of Russia in 1812 and would pose a threat to Russia in various ways throughout the nineteenth century – it was a moth to the flame attraction.

Will was considering this dichotomy and sharing his thoughts with Isaac while they sat in the library waiting for the delegation to arrive by helicopter. Will, the pedant, and somewhat informed on the applied arts, tried to distract and relax Isaac by engaging him in a discussion on the elegance of the library in which they sat and the quality of the furniture, fittings and works of art.

Isaac customarily would have been interested in such a discussion, but he struggled to clear his mind from the reality of the peril in which his wife and son found themselves. When Will drew his attention to the oil paintings hung with skill, each piece positioned to complement the whole ensemble, he became focused and engaged. Will pointed out that all of the paintings in the library were the work of the most celebrated Russian painters of the nineteenth and early twentieth centuries.

The discussion brought both back to the auction sale of some of Isaac's Russian paintings in New York three years before, which appeared to flush out those pursuing him and attacking his assets. The sale established a period of peace that lasted the last three years.

"Isaac, what do you think the calibre of these paintings is as compared to the works you sold in New York?"

With some animation, Isaac replied that there were at least four separate periods or schools of artistic styles represented in the auction and the top five Russian artists were included. "In my opinion, what I see in this room exceeds the quality of what was sold in New York. Very little art from this period, created here in Russia, was exposed to the West. The Russian artworks known in the West were primarily the works of Russians living in Paris whose works established the known standard of Russian art. I will take it as one of my missions, Will, to promote the best of the Russian artists in the West. They deserve to be known and celebrated. Have you noticed that of the ten artifacts represented in this room, seven were crafted by Jews? – Although they obscured their Jewish origins, like Trotsky, who hid his origins as he advanced in politics during the early Communist era. I think Putin and his government are determined to expose and promote Russian art in the West, if for no other reason than to advance the reputation of Russia as a centre of exceptionally sophisticated creativity, which it was."

It was a cold blustery day for the time of the year, so Sergei had laid a fire which created a calming, pleasant atmosphere. The atmosphere, Sergei knew, would be conducive to the effective planning and discussions that would take place when the delegation arrived that afternoon.

"The two fireplaces are particularly attractive, Isaac. Both surrounds and mantels are crafted from malachite, that distinctively Russian material similar to Italian marble, but uniquely identified with Czarist Russia. The deeply rich green with its distinctive graining gives it animation and interest. While similar to the French Directoire style, this room is Russian and could only be Russian. I hope the members of the two delegations will be impressed and will be more open to useful discussions as we have planned."

Their discussion was interrupted by Sergei announcing the arrival of the trio of musicians who would provide some relaxing background before the weight of the discussions got underway. Sergei suggested the balalaika player start playing traditional Russian folk songs as the delegation arrived, and then during the early 'get to know the representatives' phase of the meeting, a conventional string ensemble would play classical pieces written by Glinka, Tchaikovsky and even Stravinsky.

Isaac agreed with Sergei's proposed arrangements and directed him to position the musicians on the balcony extending across the north wall of the library, access to which was provided by a wrought iron semi-circular stairway containing numerous Jewish religious symbols and traditional neoclassical decorative elements.

By the time the central library table was laid for lunch, Isaac was visually more relaxed and focused on the agenda that would ensue that afternoon.

During their simple lunch comprised of borscht and heavy Russian bread served with exquisite Russian tea poured from an eighteenth-century samovar, Will reminded Isaac of the agenda.

"First, of course, Sophie and Little Isaac's release is a priority for the discussions. We will have to assess the degree of candour and honesty in both the Putin reps and those of Rabbi Bernstein's delegation. I am glad the rabbi will be joining us. That will add substantially to the significance of the meeting and any plans that may emerge during the discussions. He will also add to the solemnity of the occasion. I will leave it to him to raise the subject of Sophie and Little Isaac's release. I know he made some contacts already and will emphasize that the discussion relative to the assets will go nowhere if Sophie and Little Isaac are not promptly released. It may seem strange to them that we would host a meeting of this kind with these elegant settings while we are searching for your wife and son, but I am sure that at least part of the reason they were abducted has to do with the assets. If we can move forward with successful proposals for allocation of the assets, I am sure it will help pave the way for their release. I hope so, anyway."

Will continued: "Second, further plans for allocating those

works of art you own in Russia's major museums and agreements for your continued use of the real estate of which you are the publicly identified owner or possessor – given that in this country all land is technically owned by the central government: a system and method of creating ownership-like security and stability for your possession of the real estate is essential to Putin's government in encouraging economic development in Russia.

"Third, we must try to finalize the working agreements in place allocating the art, antiquities and archaeology that will be transferred to the central government and that part of the collection that will be securely yours. No assets will be transferred until the final agreements have been reached. I have an idea for both solutions, Isaac, but I won't bother with it now.

"Fourth, the Jewish museum you plan to construct here in Russia and the endowment you are prepared to settle on the museum for its future administration and development. As I see it, Isaac, we can't get to number four, even though it is important to you, until we have successfully dealt with the first three. I have prepared an agenda which Sergei has printed for me. It will be there for just you and me at the beginning of the meeting, but if we are satisfied that the discussions will be useful, then we can distribute the agenda to those present. Incidentally, I have asked Sergei to be present as our recording secretary. If the delegates agree, I propose to record the discussions. The library is already planted with recording devices. As a formality, I will inform the delegation of the recordings. We will discontinue the recordings only if there is a heated objection that we cannot settle."

"Will, remind me, how many do we have coming from the Putin government and how many with Rabbi Bernstein?"

"Each has an allocated number, the same number – five in total, three men and two women. I have insisted on the women given Sophie's vulnerable situation. I hope a female point of view will be helpful in getting her and Little Isaac released."

* * *

Promptly at 2:30 p.m., both delegations were ushered into the library where they took up the seats assigned to them. Tea was served from the samovar and aquavit was made available to those who wanted something more fortifying. No one took the aquavit, which pleased Will who knew that liquor of any type or strength could lead to a reduction in civility.

Isaac stood extending greetings and then, excusing himself from acting as chair, turned the proceedings to Will as prearranged.

Will introduced each member of the two delegations, explaining in detail the background and stature of each in their professions or occupations and thus demonstrating the exceptional talent and high offices held by each delegate. The delegates were given an opportunity to reply to Will's instructions. They each extended sympathy to Isaac and pledged to assist in the recovery of Sophie and Little Isaac.

When the formalities were completed, and the agenda agreed to, Will circulated the agenda.

Sophie's abduction was discussed at length, no one having anything to add to the information already obtained. No one had any theories as to who was responsible or what their motives were, but one of the Putin delegates assured Isaac that the government of Russia would do all in its power to secure their release.

Will then gave his theory of the abduction and the role and obligation he expected each delegate to assume. He assumed the motives for the abduction were the assets, money or influence for some purpose. The motives, he believed, were a form of blackmail, even though nothing had yet been received as a claim or threat.

Will went on to say that government personnel, at some level, might intend to use the kidnapping as pressure on Isaac related to the division and use of the assets. Money could also be an objective from government interests – perhaps not even known in the Kremlin. He went on to say that he was equally worried about the Jewish community as a possible source of the pressure on Isaac.

There was a gasp from the delegates on both sides of the

table. Will explained that the trust assets, all of which were now Isaac's personal property, were acquired over a period of almost two hundred years. It could be that there was someone out there who believed they had an interest in some of the assets, including money. Also, he said, it could be that there were factions within the Jewish community here in Russia or elsewhere who wanted to force Isaac into making some, as yet unknown, decisions with the assets.

The discussion continued for four hours. Nothing constructive was achieved because Will refused to move to agenda items two, three, or four until Sophie and Little Isaac were safely returned to their home at the dacha. Before the meeting broke up for dinner, Will emphasized that each delegate had an obligation through their contacts to gain as much information as possible and to return to the meeting the next afternoon at 2 p.m. with what they learned. The government delegates were clearly irritated that there was no discussion on the assets and decisions between Isaac and the government of Russia. The Jewish delegates were offended on behalf of their community that there would not be any involvement by the Jewish community in Russia or elsewhere in the asset negotiations. Isaac, dutifully following Will's advance instructions, simply nodded assent when Will finished his comments.

As the delegates rose from the table, the musicians stood, gathered their instruments and started down from the mezzanine, awkwardly climbing down the circular stairway. There was suddenly a loud metallic crash as a case fell from the hands of one of the musicians. As it hit the floor it burst open to reveal a submachine gun.

The delegates expressed surprise and outrage, to which Will said simply but with finality, "We had extra security for your protection. Clearly, it was not here to pose a threat to you." No one demurred, but all left knowing Isaac was determined to have his wife and son safely returned.

7

EARLY THE NEXT morning Will arranged to meet separately with Isaac's security team; Isaac was left to rest as best he could.

Frank, speaking for the security team at the dacha and in Smolensk, stated that inquiries were made but nothing was learned. Will asked him who was making the inquiries on Isaac's behalf. Frank informed him it was a New York security guard and two Germans – to which Will replied that they only got what they could have predicted: nothing. Locals would not expose themselves to censure among their community by talking about the activities of members of the Jewish community to foreigners.

Will instructed the guards to discontinue wearing fatigues and the heavy firepower evident around their waist. They were to wear simple clothing as similar as possible to what locals were wearing; they were not to try to communicate with the locals – Rabbi Bernstein would appoint Russian Jews to conduct the inquiries. The security guards would be there to provide protection for the Jewish interrogators. "Keep it simple and as informal as you can... as little intimidation as possible."

The delegates brought with Rabbi Bernstein arrived next. Having already spoken to the rabbi and obtaining his agreement to the plan, Will informed three of the Jewish delegates that they would conduct the inquiries accompanied by the security guards. Each protested such a role. When Will explained the rabbi's position and the consequences of their not fully cooperating, each pledged to do so.

Next, Will drew Frank aside and reminded him of the New York sale and the disruption that had occurred during the Christie's sale. In particular, he mentioned the three Russian oligarchs who were the principal bidders and the behaviour of Anthony Cann, Anna's former lover and the convicted killer of the Menshive family's New York lawyer, was now known. He instructed Frank to have the New York security detail divide the potential suspects among them and to make inquiries. Particularly, Will wanted to know what telephone, computer, internet, and other forms of contact any of them may have had with persons in Russia in the last month.

"Mr MacIntosh, why would we bother with Cann? He is now in a top security prison somewhere in the Midwest."

"That means nothing, Frank. Even the most secure prison in the United States is a leaky ship when it comes to delivering messages to and from inmates. Assume he has an office in a public library with an open-door policy. Assume he has as much access to contacts here in Russia as he had before incarceration – he probably has more now."

When he finished with Frank, Will met with the rabbi's principal assistant who continued to demonstrate the same level of resentment and anger as he had after the meeting yesterday. Will dealt with that promptly. The assistant persisted:

"I am expressing an opinion and giving you directions expressed to me by Rabbi Bernstein. He and all members of the Jewish community in Russia are more vulnerable and at greater risk arising from the abduction of Isaac's family than our community has experienced in decades. If you wish to challenge my instructions, speak to Rabbi Bernstein and see how you get along. For myself, I can see several ways in which Jews, local and foreign, might want to manipulate what Isaac is intending to do."

Will was left alone, having been given guarantees that there would be total cooperation and he would actively participate in the inquiries accompanied by the security guards.

He next met with the Moscow delegates representing the Putin government. Will asked whether they had instructions from Putin or a senior person in his office. He was given a surprising answer: "Yes, sir. We have clear instructions in writing directing us to engage in finding Mrs Menshive and her son. The president understands the dynamic of your predicament. If Mrs Menshive and her son are not returned to Dr Menshive unharmed, there is little chance of a discreet negotiation with you about all these assets in Russia."

Will replied that they understood fully and that there would be no wavering from that position by Dr Menshive or by Will as Isaac's team leader. A plan was formulated by the Russian delegates, to which Will agreed, that would engage Russian security experts in the investigation. Their work would get underway within hours. Will asked them to check telephone messages from the United States and within the Jewish and Russian community in Smolensk. Evidently, access to that information was more readily available in Russia than in the United States. There seemed to be little concern about privacy or citizens' rights in Russia. "That may be to our advantage," thought Will.

During the early afternoon, while Will and Isaac were discussing Will's meetings earlier that day, Frank abruptly entered the library without knocking. He came straight to the point: "I think we may have a lead. Mr MacIntosh, you were right – our inquiries worried the locals. The Russian people you delegated to the task calmed them and appeared to bring them onside. One of the city councillors who would not identify himself (but we know who he is) has informed us Mrs Menshive and the child are still in Smolensk and are being taken care of. They even have a Russian midwife to assist her."

Before Frank could utter another word, Isaac exploded: "Don't you let that bloody woman near my wife! Get that message through to where she is being kept. We have a highly qualified nurse with us who we'll send to be with Sophie and Little Isaac. There won't be any peasant hocus pocus on my wife or son."

Frank assured Isaac he would do his best but asked whether the nurse would agree to go to the hiding place.

"She will – she'll damn well go. Don't worry about that. Take her with you when you leave." Isaac paused. "I interrupted you; what else have you heard?"

"Only that there are factions in the Jewish community, one

of which, out of fear, is collaborating with the city councillors who are in control. The other faction is loyal to Rabbi Bernstein but is not privy to the location where Mrs Menshive and the little boy are being kept or the motives for the abduction."

Will intervened to compliment Frank on getting helpful information and to insist that he was to get back to the investigation immediately.

Frank had left the library only a few minutes before Sergei arrived, running at full throttle, an event never before witnessed by either Isaac or Will.

"Dr Menshive, there is a telephone call for you on the secure telephone you gave me. It is from Chicago in the United States. It is something about a Mr Cann. I think you should…"

Before Sergei could finish, Isaac and Will doubled Sergei's speed and made their way to the secure telephone.

"Dr Menshive is here; I also have Mr MacIntosh here with me on speakerphone. Who is calling?"

"Sir, I am Gus Trombley, the acting lead among your security detail in the States. We have gained access through a special court-issued warrant to search Mr Cann's phone records for the last six months. He would not be aware that we have gained that access. He is in a high-security prison in Missouri, outside St Louis. He has made several telephone calls to persons in Moscow and in a place called Smolensk. The calls were recorded because he is a federal prisoner. During those calls, he talked about Dr Menshive and his considerable wealth in Russia. He was trying to enlist members of the Russian Mafia, the 'Bratva', to take Dr Menshive and his family into secure custody and to force Dr Menshive to gain their release by paying Mr Cann an unbelievable amount of money."

"Do you have the names and contact information for the persons Cann had contacted?"

"Yes, we have telephone numbers but no names. Cann was using a combination of letters and numbers to identify the people he was contacting. I think it was this subterfuge that alerted the prison and the FBI that the calls should be recorded. We will provide this information and anything new we get to your people. Should we inform the Russian authorities?"

"No, absolutely not," said Isaac. "Will MacIntosh, my agent and spokesman in all matters relating to me, is in charge of making all the decisions you will need. Take instructions from no one else. If I contact you personally, I will provide proof of my identity at that time."

Will added: "We won't take any more of your time. Report back to me this evening at 7 p.m. Moscow time."

8

THE ANXIETY ISAAC was feeling was not abated by the promising reports from the security detail delivered to him yesterday. He knew Sophie so well that he knew she would be worried about him and his ability to cope with the chaos that the situation had created for the family. His first priority for the day was to get the nurse, Anastasia, delivered safely to Sophie.

Anastasia was not surprised at being asked to leave the relative security of the dacha and to go to a place that might put her personally at considerable risk. "Dr Menshive, I am not worried about the risk to my safety in going to the kidnappers. I am terrified knowing that madam and our precious Little Isaac are alone and each needing me. If there is any way of getting me to them, please do it. I can take care of myself and them if I can get to them."

* * *

Will's conference with Frank and the two security guards disclosed that one of them had heard from a local in Smolensk that Sophie and Little Isaac could be found in a particular part of Smolensk. It was agreed that a mediator who could be trusted by both sides was necessary. The best option they could think of was obtaining a representative of the local Jewish community and one from the Russian Orthodox Church. Neither would be suspected of hostile motives adverse to the objectives of the kidnappers.

Frank left the dacha by 7:30 that morning with Will to visit Rabbi Bernstein at his apartment. Arrangements had been made by Mr Molotovsky with the senior cleric in the Russian Orthodox Church in Moscow for him to select a couple of trustworthy members of the congregation in Moscow to join

Rabbi Bernstein. They would be joined by two representatives of the Russian Orthodox Church who wished to show solidarity with the Jewish community. While the team was being arranged, Frank and his men continued their inquiries to find a representative of the kidnappers with whom the clerics could talk.

While Frank was working in Smolensk, Isaac and Will, with their supporters flown in from Moscow, continued their attempts to obtain information from their sources.

At 10 a.m., a Putin government secret security officer asked to meet privately with Isaac and Will.

The group assembled in the dacha library, which had become the control centre for their search efforts. The security officer, after identifying himself as Igor and providing proof of his credentials, informed Isaac that he had information that could assist in the search.

Through information sources he did not and declared he would not disclose, he had discovered that Anthony Cann was the precipitating cause of the hostile activities in Smolensk.

"He didn't direct someone to do it… he set the wheels in motion that gave others the motivation to achieve their ends by abducting Mrs Menshive and the boy," said Igor.

"Who did Cann contact and what was his interest?" asked Will.

"We traced the calls made to citizens located in the Smolensk region from the United States over the past four weeks. There were a few. We were able to identify the calls from Cann both because of the frequency of the calls and the place from and to which the calls were made. As I am sure you know, Dr Menshive, Cann is incarcerated in a high-security prison in the United States. We had cooperation, I should say, from the CIA in the United States who are well connected on this matter. Cann's telephone calls were recorded, and I have a transcript of those messages being sent to me as we speak. He called a local member of the city council here in Smolensk. His contact was an agent of a dangerous person you in the West refer to as an oligarch. His name is Poliakov. What he was telling this fellow was that you and your family were here at the dacha and that you are very rich and that you have a lot of money that is his. He was asking Poliakov for help in putting pressure on you, Dr Menshive, to get money for himself and to send the rest back to Cann. Cann even gave him a secret account in the Cayman Islands to which the funds were to be sent."

"Did he mention kidnapping as a device for getting the money?" asked Isaac.

"No, his calls were directed to attracting the interest of Dimitry Polanski. Details of what he claimed – in particular, how much money he wanted – were not specified. The calls could have been understood as neutral and friendly if Cann's role was not known from his earlier involvement with you and your family, Dr Menshive."

"Well then, who did abduct my wife and son and what is their motive?" asked Isaac, white-faced and agitated.

"That is not clear. I think we can assume Polanski, aided by Poliakov, are part of the conspiracy. Whether they were part of the abduction, I don't know, but it is likely they both are. I can tell you my team and I will call on Polanski within the hour. We will get from him whatever he knows. We have methods. We have successful methods that seldom fail," said Igor with a smirk. Clearly, he was going to enjoy the next few hours.

* * *

Frank was briefed on the interview with Igor and he then suggested, "I think we need to gag Cann in terms of telephone access to anyone outside that prison. I will have the prison officials freeze outgoing calls to Russia and a couple of my men in the States will interrogate Cann with the assistance of prison officials this afternoon. He will be left deeply regretting his attack on your family. Remember, we will have complete cooperation from the prison officials – he has broken just about every rule of which inmates are subject and if the abduction can be linked to him, he can write off the next two decades of his life in the outside world."

"How does this bring us any closer to recovering Sophie and Little Isaac?" asked Will.

"It appears that Mrs Menshive and the child were held here in Smolensk at least until the last day or two. You have an effective team making inquiries in the city. I think it is probable they will report this afternoon with information that could prove helpful," said Frank.

* * *

After lunch, a member of the team of clerics was ushered into the library. The spokesperson for the team got directly to the point: "We have discovered that Mrs Menshive and your son are being held in a 'safe house' here in Smolensk. The abductors have been contacted by an intermediary who has obtained their consent to the nurse being sent to your wife right away. Incidentally, the message I am getting from the cleric spokesman is that the abductors did not expect the scale and skill of the investigating team. They expected it would be fast and easy to get the money they wanted. They know that if anything happens to Mrs Menshive or the little boy their lives will not be worth living."

The nurse Anastasia was dispatched with the cleric who brought the news. She was eager to get to her patient and Little Isaac. In light of the comments made by the cleric, neither Isaac nor Will considered Anastasia at risk in going to Mrs Menshive.

The clerics joined by the GRU (Soviet Military Intelligence) security officer met with Isaac and Will at five that afternoon. One of the Russian Orthodox priests was the first to talk. "I can report that Mrs Menshive and the boy are well and now have the nurse with them. We are informed that the abductors never intended harm to come to them – events grew out of control when outside interests became involved. It appears that Cann contacted Polanski, who in turn assembled a small group of three or four locals including his son. Led by his son, a female cousin, and a local policeman, Mrs Menshive and the boy were encouraged to join them for tea at the city council chambers, where they were told you, Dr Menshive, and your sister would be attending a welcoming reception. When they got to City Hall, they were blindfolded and taken by a police car to the place where they are being held in captivity. It appears that the involvement of the city officials is much greater than we originally thought. We now know that there was to be a demand for more than money. The demand was that the plans for a Jewish museum and new synagogue would be dropped by Dr Menshive and that the money for these buildings would be diverted to a new city hall with new facilities that would suit them. They assumed it would be easy to intimidate Dr Menshive and his friend the Canadian lawyer. A problem arose for them greater than was posed by Dr Menshive.

"The Bratva in Moscow is now in control of their side of the situation. They had an informer in the city council who no doubt for a price told them of the abduction. They have taken over, excluding the original group on the city council. Mrs Menshive and the boy are still in this region but have been moved from where they were."

Will intervened, asking the Russian Orthodox priest who appeared to be in control of the investigation, "Can the GRU and Putin-appointed security people be trusted if the Bratva is involved?"

"That is difficult to know at the moment. The president's office has its tabs on the known Bratva groups. I will contact the President's office and have it trace the group involved. Dr Menshive, you ask, 'Can President Putin's office be trusted in this?' I think so. It is as interested in getting this problem resolved as you are. Putin wants a final answer on the distribution of the art, real estate and antiquities. Also, he doesn't want any more adverse news in the West about the way the Russians treat the Jews. Remember there is a national election soon. I think you will have the authorities on your side," was the priest's reply.

* * *

At six that evening, while Isaac and Will were mapping the probable locations of the abductors in the region, a telephone call came in. Will took the call. The caller identified himself as a person interested in helping to free Mrs Menshive and he stated that he would incur major expenses in getting her release. If Dr Menshive could arrange to have $150,000 in American dollars delivered to a particular drop-off, the caller would assist in gaining Mrs Menshive's release. Before Will could reply, the caller hung up.

Will had placed the phone on hands-free mode to enable Isaac, Frank and the GRU agent, Igor, to hear the call.

Igor instructed Isaac not to comply with the demand. He informed Isaac that all calls to and from the dacha were being recorded and monitored. Normally, Isaac would have exploded on hearing that his privacy was so compromised. However, he wisely recognized the benefit he would have from the records of the calls. Perhaps tracing the call could lead to the place where Sophie and Little Isaac were being held.

Less than ten minutes after the first attempt at extorting money from him, Isaac received another call, this time from Moscow. This call was not of the same amateurish type. It was made by a woman with little English and a heavy Russian accent who put her demand quickly and concisely. "Your little boy will be hurt if we do not receive 1.5 million U.S. dollars by noon tomorrow. The money is to be left at a safe place I will identify before noon tomorrow. If you fail to have that money for us, I will chop off one finger per hour, starting at 1 p.m. tomorrow and one every hour thereafter. He has only ten fingers. Don't delay. We won't." With that, she hung up.

Isaac lost all self-control, screaming and crying uncontrollably. Will, Frank, the rabbi and the Russian Orthodox cleric tried to comfort him. Will remembered that the nurse had a bottle of pills she occasionally used to dispense to Isaac if he became agitated. The pills were found and administered to the patient. Will took Isaac to his bedroom, put him on his bed and covered him. By the time the blanket was firmly in place, Isaac was asleep. Will instructed the majordomo to sit outside Isaac's door to watch him in case he had an adverse reaction to the drug.

By the time Will returned to the library, Igor had contacted President Putin's office which was able to consult with the president who promised immediate intervention by his security forces.

* * *

At 11 a.m. a message was received from Putin's office. The Bratva group responsible had been identified by checking telephone calls, and an undertaking given by a known senior member of the group involved that all demands and claims would be dropped.

Will and those surrounding him in the library were engaged in trying to develop a plan for finding and returning Sophie and Little Isaac.

It proved to be futile. As they were putting the finishing details to their plan of action, lights flashed into the interior of the library when several vehicles entered the compound in front of the dacha. Suddenly, Will's cell phone rang; he found it buried under maps and numerous plans they had developed over several hours that evening. When he took the call, the vehicles had stopped outside the front of the dacha. One car had pulled up into the porte-cochère at the front door. It was raining heavily, but the shelter of the porte-cochère provided protection for a heavily wrapped person who was being assisted in getting out of the vehicle. It was not apparent who it was. Will feared it was someone from the Bratva bearing hidden firearms.

The front door rattled with forcible banging that announced the arrival of this visitor.

The majordomo was with Isaac, who was woken by the noise and came to the library immediately. A woman from the kitchen area arrived to answer the door. Will was afraid it could be an invasion, so he dismissed her and stated he would answer the door.

In fact, it was Will assisted by Frank, the GRU agent and the clerics, who stood at the door as Will opened it.

Will was greeted with squeals of delight that emerged from the greatcoat covering the person Will saw leaving the vehicle. Little Isaac threw himself into Will's arms and was joyfully hugged and caressed by him. The greatcoat, muffler, fur hat and face-covering were hastily removed, revealing Sophie, who was weeping with tears of relief and joy.

Isaac was greatly relieved by their return and a reunion ensued, demonstrating even greater joy on his part than the returned captives had expressed.

* * *

Weather in western Russia in late summer can be highly changeable, as both Napoleon and Hitler found to their dismay. The sun rose in a cloudless, pristine sky, showcasing the Dnieper River visible from the principal rooms at the back of the dacha.

Absolute silence prevailed both outside and inside the dacha. All farming and maintenance work were suspended, which was unusual for a midweek day usually busy with each part of the farm operation preparing for harvest, and the maintenance crew preparing the house and grounds for winter, which often arrived even in early September.

It wasn't the sun and warmth with its invitation for rest and relaxation for the family that caused the shutdown. It was the instructions of Will MacIntosh which created the stillness. Before Will retired for the night after the arrival of Sophie and Little Isaac, he gave firm orders that Isaac and Sophie were to be left alone the next day until they chose to join the rest of the household.

Isaac and Sophie were able to achieve solitude because of the layout of the dacha. Like many early nineteenth-century country houses in Russia, it was designed on eighteenth-century neoclassical principles. The main house was the centre of a shallow, U-shaped semicircle. On each side of the main house, ancillary offices and spaces for domestic activities were located. The farm operation was conducted from offices on the right-hand side of the semicircle and the maintenance and business operations were conducted from the left.

From each side of the main house as a connector or hyphen to and from the offices, there was a projecting wing styled as a 'pavilion'. Isaac and his family occupied the two-story pavilion to the left of the principal front. The library, study and office used by Isaac were in a similar structure on the right.

The passageways to and from the private family quarters were designed to be securely closed. This was not only to provide privacy for the family; it was primarily to enable isolation and security for the family in the event of an uprising or attack. During the nineteenth and early twentieth centuries, these happened with regularity in the form of pogroms where Jews would be attacked and terrorized, often with the loss of life.

The dacha was designed to provide maximum security, which enabled maximum privacy.

Isaac, Sophie and Little Isaac were safely ensconced in their quarters after Sophie's arrival. They were provided protection by their security guards who remained as invisible as the situation allowed.

9

AFTER BREAKFAST THE following day, Will assembled Frank, the majordomo Sergei and Anastasia, the nurse who had been sent to care for Sophie.

"Nurse," Will asked, "what is Sophie's condition? Does she require medical care, or will a few days' rest be sufficient to help her get over her terrible ordeal?"

"Mrs Menshive is over seven months along in her pregnancy. She had a few difficulties in the early days, but she recovered well for most of her term until this abduction. I have been attending to her for forty-eight hours now. I am concerned for her emotional and physical state. She was unfailingly cheerful for Little Isaac, not letting him sense there was any danger in what was going on around them. I have observed, however, that she has begun 'spotting' again." The nurse looked around the room at the men listening to her, in case they needed more explanation of the term 'spotting'. They did not, or at least chose not to ask for one. "It may mean nothing, or it could be the sign of problems with the pregnancy. She could deliver any time now, but the baby would be premature and would require specialized care she could not receive here."

"Then Mrs Menshive must be moved immediately to the nearest medical facility with first-rate obstetrical expertise. How can she be most safely moved, nurse?" asked Will, with his customary taking control of a situation that required decisive action.

"Aircraft of any kind would not be suitable because of the reduction in air pressure which could induce labour or sickness. I think the only way of getting her to a medical facility would be by a car or SUV," replied the nurse.

"Alright, when Mrs Menshive indicates she is ready to leave her quarters, I will discuss this plan with her and her husband.

Sergei, please make arrangements for food to be prepared with non-alcoholic drinks. Nurse Anastasia will give you advice on what should be prepared. Isaac will require something much more substantial. We don't want him to become agitated because he doesn't have a good supply of food and beverages – but no alcohol of any kind. We don't know what we will face on the road. I want him alert and in control of himself at all times until we get to the facility. As to the facility, leave it with me to make the arrangements. They will be announced only after I confer with Dr Menshive."

* * *

Isaac met with Will in the library by ten that morning. He looked as if he had the first good night's sleep in many days.

"Well, thank God that is over! We can take a few days and relax. Sophie needs time to get over the ordeal. I will arrange for the housekeeper to prepare meals and the nurse can take them up to her."

"That is a plan, Isaac. However, I would like you to consider some thoughts I have had over the last few hours," suggested Will.

"Now, Will. I don't need complications. I want to stay here quietly. I want time off. Certainly, Sophie needs time to rest."

"I agree. It can't be just now though, Isaac. The nurse tells me that Sophie is having an issue with her pregnancy. Remember the warning she received after her miscarriage that she was not to have more children; this pregnancy has always been high-risk. She must be taken to appropriate medical care to monitor her health and that of the baby. I have arranged to have them moved there to arrive at one o'clock this afternoon. Frank will accompany you and Sophie in the car behind the lead vehicle, which will have security personnel. Also, there will be a security detail behind you. You are being taken to the specialized international medical facility we used four years ago after your car was attacked in Moscow. I have checked with the facility. You continue to have diplomatic standing which was arranged for you when you used the facility the last time. As your wife, Sophie is also entitled to the use of the facility. I have called Dr Rayskill, Sophie's New York obstetrician. He agrees that Sophie must be taken to the Moscow facility immediately. Neither he nor I would trust either a private or government-operated medical facility in Moscow. The international medical care facility will be best. He is leaving New York by private jet any time now on a direct flight to Moscow. All appropriate arrangements have been made through the U.S. Embassy in Moscow and the State Department in Washington."

"*Oy*, Will! Well, I guess you are right, particularly if Dr Rayskill agrees. Sophie has absolute confidence in him, so I guess that is best. I will discuss this with Sophie. She will have the last word…" was Isaac's decision, although he knew the decision had already been made.

* * *

Sophie, Little Isaac and Isaac were packed and ready to be picked up as scheduled at the appointed time. Sophie had readily agreed with Will that she should be under the care and ministrations of Dr Rayskill. She turned to Will, surprised and said, "Why are you not prepared to leave with us, Will? Where is Anna? Neither you nor Anna are being left here. Both Isaac and I want you with us in Moscow. Isaac, we should have told Will we needed him."

"I assumed you would be coming, Will. Sophie is correct. I need you with us in Moscow. And you must bring Anna and take care of her, too. I know there is another Merc in the barn that can be used. You have half an hour to prepare – those are my orders! I get to give some occasionally, Will. It feels good to give them now and then, you know."

"Can Anna get ready in half an hour? She tends to be somewhat slow-moving before 5 p.m., Isaac!"

"Go to her and tell her that she must be ready. I doubt she unpacked after getting here. She will accept your instructions, Will. She won't follow mine, but for some reason she will listen to you."

***

The motorcade left at 2 p.m. that afternoon. Will, with Anna, was in the car behind Isaac and Sophie. Neither Isaac nor Sophie were advised that the first vehicle with Frank driving and the last vehicle with Frank's '2-I-C' (second in command) were fully armed in case of an attack similar to one Isaac and Will had experienced when they last took this route to Moscow four years before. Additional security was provided on this occasion by a GRU-operated helicopter with continuous radar and internet location positioning technology.

As the motorcade moved through Smolensk, a crowd had formed adjacent to the war memorial in the central square across from the Kremlin. The mayor and Rabbi Bernstein moved forward, waving and asking the motorcade to stop. Each of the four vehicles in the motorcade was interconnected with a telephone. Will called Frank asking if Frank considered the crowd to be a threat or whether the motorcade should stop. It was Frank's opinion that there was enough firepower in the motorcade and above it to take out everyone in the crowd in minutes. He expressed the opinion it should be safe, but perhaps Will should get out first to find out what they wanted.

Will got out of his vehicle and met Frank in front of the mayor and the rabbi.

"Mr MacIntosh, we would like to address Dr Menshive. We will not hold you up more than a minute or two."

Will walked over to Isaac's vehicle which by this time was surrounded by four security guards; each with weapons poised for action should it be required.

As the mayor and the rabbi moved forward with hands extended in a friendly gesture, there was a commotion at the back of the crowd.

The shouting was punctuated by a couple of gunshots. Quickly, the crowd turned as one on those creating the threat and promptly wrestled the two instigators of the disturbance into strangle-holds. The firearms were removed and silence prevailed until the mayor and rabbi walked forward and said to Isaac: "We apologize for this threat to you and your family, as we do for the abduction of Mrs Menshive and your son. We wanted to say that the community has met in an open public meeting. It is the unanimous opinion of this city that you are welcome here, and that the citizens of Smolensk will do all in their power to protect you. Almost as important, we have addressed the anti-Semitism that has been flaring up. The citizens of Smolensk promise to treat and accept the Jewish population as equals and as a valued part of our city. We promise to support and protect them. Also, we would welcome your planned museum devoted to Jewish life in Russia and your proposed synagogue. We had hoped to deliver this message without interruption. You can see how our citizens reacted when the terrorists threatened you – they were also threatening us, as well as Dr Menshive and his family. God speed. We will welcome your return."

* * *

The drive from Smolensk to Moscow on a relatively straight flat road in reasonably good condition should have been uneventful. It wasn't.

Sophie started moaning and demonstrating discomfort about two hours out of Smolensk. She was attended to by nurse Anastasia in the very cramped back seat of the car. As Sophie's problems intensified, Little Isaac became increasingly fearful, crying and violently thrashing out against his father, as his father tried to comfort him. Isaac instructed the driver to pull over after signalling by telephone to the other three vehicles that there would be a pull-over stop.

The stop was a short distance from a large farmhouse to which Sophie was then taken. Nurse Anastasia was given access to a bedroom on the ground floor where she took Sophie and in private, examined her. The examination lasted no longer than twenty minutes. She provided some assistance that involved bandages or wrappings. As they were leaving the house an older woman gave Sophie and the nurse some strong tea which calmed Sophie somewhat, and before they left the house the woman took Anastasia aside and said to Anastasia that she was the local midwife and recognized the symptoms of an early birth – offering to allow Sophie to remain until after the birth.

Isaac had virtually no knowledge of obstetrics and deferred to nurse Anastasia when she told him that Sophie was in medical distress which could result in a high-risk premature delivery. Isaac's reply was prompt and decisive. Sophie had had difficulties with Little Isaac's birth that resulted in a Caesarian section. Sophie required specialized medical care immediately. The decision was made to move on as fast as possible to Moscow.

Nurse Anastasia explained to Isaac that Sophie was discharging blood and fluids that could be precursors to a vaginal delivery. She stated as emphatically as Isaac had expressed his opinion, that Sophie would require prenatal care that would involve towels and what medications would be required; all of which involved both space and a calm atmosphere, which she recognized could not happen in the car with Isaac fussing in the seat with them.

Isaac was moved to the first car with Frank, and Little Isaac to the car with Will and Anna, with whom Little Isaac had developed a strong bond and affection.

Will notified the police, who were tasked with patrolling the highway through the American Embassy of the emergency, and was given clearance for such speed as would be necessary.

From time to time the motorcade stopped to enable Sophie to have comfort stops. With nurse Anastasia's expert attention Sophie seemed more relaxed and demonstrated fewer of the threatening symptoms. During one of the stops, Will asked the nurse whether the trauma of the abduction could have brought on the symptoms Sophie was displaying. The answer was "Yes. And a trauma as intense as what Mrs Menshive has gone through could also affect the baby, both before birth and in its childhood." She emphasized that the trip to Moscow had to be conducted as quietly and calmly as possible, which meant that Isaac should continue to be isolated from his wife.

Isaac was genuinely supportive and affectionate with his wife, but his anxiety and persistent fussing were causing her distress. "There is no place for a husband near his wife at a time like this," was the nurse's opinion. As this was expressed to Will and Anna they agreed and said they would do what they could to calm and distract Isaac.

PART 2

Moscow – St Petersburg

10

ARRIVAL IN MOSCOW six hours later proved to be without incident and the admission to the medical facility went smoothly.

Dr Rayskill had arrived at the facility only a few minutes before Sophie was admitted. A physical examination was undertaken immediately. He remained with Sophie for what seemed to Isaac to be an eternity. Finally, in the early morning of the next day, Dr Rayskill called for Isaac, Will and Anna to meet with him in a conference room a short distance from Sophie's room.

"Isaac, I have examined Sophie continuously over the last several hours. I did not meet with you sooner as she needed my personal attention. The profound shock and anxiety she experienced from the abduction was, I think, the cause of her medical distress. I needed to calm her, which took considerable effort. I avoided drugs that could have affected the baby. I can tell you she is now relaxed, and the signs of early labour have passed. There is no doubt, however, that she must remain here until the baby is born. She can have no worries or problems that can be avoided. Nurse Anastasia has Sophie's confidence, so I recommend she be the immediate caregiver. Additional round-the-clock special duty nurses must be engaged to tend to her, to assist Anastasia and to take over from her when she requires respite."

"Dr Rayskill – Ben, if I may – thank you for all you have done. I think you have saved Sophie and the baby. Can you stay here in Moscow for the next few weeks until the baby is born? You know that money for your fees and occasional travel to return to the States is not a problem."

"Isaac, I have been Sophie's obstetrician during both of her pregnancies. No one knows her medical situation as well as I do. The big task at the moment is dealing with the impact of the abduction on her health. Yes, I will remain as her principal physician, but I will have to return to my clinic occasionally. We can work out the details as we go along. As to the impact of the abduction on the baby, the duration of the abduction was short, and Sophie was reasonably well taken care of, so I don't think there is much risk or lasting harm to the baby. But we must keep Sophie as calm and happy as possible."

"Well, Ben, I recognize in your comments that there is a path for me to follow going forward. I will keep my impatience and mercurial temperament under control. My friend Will, here, and my sister Anna will make sure I do."

"Isaac," Will added, "we can use the next few weeks to work on the project that brought us here. It will be a sufficient distraction to keep you away from bothering Sophie. Anna will be a great help in keeping Sophie company. They have become great friends. Thank heaven she joined us on this trip."

* * *

Isaac returned from a visit with Sophie with Little Isaac in hand and he turned his son over to Anna, who received him with joy and took him off for ice cream and chocolate sauce.

"Isaac," said Will, "now that the personal care arrangements have been completed, I want to get down to our plans for the allocation of assets as we discussed generally on our previous meetings with Putin's government. If we can formulate a reliable plan that is acceptable to Putin's government, it may be, should be, a template for dealing with the other national governments where assets are held.

"A gentle reminder, however. We must follow up with Anthony Cann and his Bratva accomplices here in Russia, including Dimitri Polanski and the oligarch Poliakov, who have their covetous eyes on you and your assets."

"Let's get at it now, Will. I need a distraction and something to occupy my mind."

They left the medical facility and met at the lavish suite made available to Isaac and his family in a nearby hotel where their discussions continued for several hours, aided by substantial quantities of coffee.

A plan was devised and documented on a computer which resulted in a ten-page printout.

The fundamentals had been clear for the last three years but could not be implemented until the full details of the inventory were completed and an appraisal of each asset established. The appraisal was two-fold: a monetary value and an assessment of its cultural importance to each of the national governments where the assets were held. There was also an opinion expressed by a panel of experts on the competition for each asset by other national governments. An agreement could be reached with one government only to have implementation blocked by hostility from another government. Dealing with one government necessitated dealing with others with an interest in the object. Will pointed out that the best example of this was the Trust's collection of Scythian gold objects:

"Isaac, the Russian authorities will expect you to give them the extraordinary treasury you hold of Scythian gold located in Russia – but the governments of Bulgaria and Ukraine will strenuously oppose giving them all to Russia. After all, the Scythian works in gold were primarily crafted along the northern and western shores of the Black Sea. So, in terms of modern geographical boundaries, Ukraine and Bulgaria would have an equal, if not superior claim – but the Russians will be adamant that the gold stay here, even though it was your family who assembled the collection and brought it here.

"To start, I propose we convene a meeting with the senior government representative responsible for each category of assets. For example, I suggest we start with the National Museum of Art and Antiquities Director Kutuzov, in Moscow. You remember, we met him as we were fleeing the fire that we started in Borodino four years ago. We cornered him in his apartment parking lot, not knowing who he was and had him drive us into central Moscow, which probably saved our lives. We will need to know from him what his mandate is in the collection and preservation of ancient art and archaeological treasures. From there we will gradually identify each director or specialist with whom we must deal. It is only after dealing with the specialists that we can determine what competing interests there will be. So, the art, archaeological, and architectural assets must be the start. We have flexibility and trade-offs in the form of the real estate and ultimately money, of course."

"That is the plan, Will – I accept it, but what should be my ultimate objective in dividing assets now apparently worth at least forty-four billion dollars, probably more? I need very little of it, but I am not going to give it all away."

"Isaac, by a rough estimation I think you should try to retain half of the goods by value – some goods like the Western art and the real estate being more useful and capable of reinvestment and assembling in a manageable form. To obtain any agreement with the rapacious governments of Russia and its neighbours you must appear to be generous, if not foolhardy, in your choices of what to release, and other requirements attendant on the gifts."

"In terms of priorities, Will, first a Jewish museum in Smolensk with an associated new synagogue and peace institute for better relations among ethnic groups here in Russia and its neighbours; second, a major museum identifying Jewish craftspersons and their creations. I want it located in a city which will confer on it a world-class standing that will attract visitors from all over the world. I haven't decided which city, but it must be a cultural capital of Western art, stable politically and secure in terms of risk against terrorism and theft; third, a wing added to my orthopedic clinic specializing in pediatrics – a world-class, preeminent facility; and fourth, I want a new college to be added to one of the most senior universities in the world such as Oxford, Cambridge or Harvard, in which a rounded, non-denominational liberal education is provided in an atmosphere sympathetic to a spiritual life. That's it for now."

"Alright, that is an excellent set of objectives. As we explore those, others will emerge that are necessarily symbiotic to and supportive of the ones you identify," was Will's enthusiastic reply. "Let us start with Kutuzov. He knows us and will be pleased to be engaged in the early planning stages."

* * *

The division of the assets held by Isaac, which was accumulated over one hundred and sixty years by Isaac's ancestors, would not be easy to accomplish. Virtually every object or building on the inventory would have several competing claims or alleged interests. Both Will and Isaac realized that an effective plan for the assets required a detailed identification of those who had competitive interests; what those interests were and what weight would be applied to those interests.

"Alright, Isaac, who are our demons? – The demons we are going to fight in preparing and implementing a successful scheme that will encompass all of our trust-related assets. Oh! I meant to ask you whether you will include any of your personal collections of art and antiquities."

"No, what I had before the trust came to me, I will retain together with pieces I will acquire specifically as additions to those collections. I am separating those from the trust assets because I have decided that my personal collections will be kept in my family to be divided among my children and of course Sophie. I hope to engage them all in a family trust to benefit each equally. It may be a way of re-engaging with my older children and enabling them to become part of the family I have with Sophie. As you know, Will, that collection will include my father's substantial collection of neoclassical statuary and a few other things he collected."

"And what about your sister, Isaac? You have benefited from her generosity. You and your family are her only relatives. You must include her in this family building plan of yours. I know she is well-endowed financially but her inclusion in a family trust seems appropriate, don't you think?"

"I had overlooked Anna. As you know, Will, we were not very friendly as adolescents and young adults but that has changed very much for the better since the trust came on the scene. It has brought us together. I have accepted a duty to care for and protect her. I recognize she looks to me now for that. Yes, I will include her in the plans you, Will, will prepare as an outline for this family trust."

"I wish I had kept my mouth shut. As I was talking, I recognized my likely involvement. I will prepare a draft family trust. I was involved in preparing several in my private practice. Actually, I will look forward to preparing a proposal for you to consider but it will take time given that our priority must be the old trust assets.

"Back to the demons as we struggle with your labours, Isaac. I would start with Cann, then continue with the Russian oligarch Poliakov. Minor as he may be, he is obviously eying you as a target for enlarging his current holdings and status here in Russia. Then we must discover the identity of those other oligarchs who are threatening you for your assets here in Russia and in Eastern and Central Europe. They pose a certain risk because we do not yet know their particular identity even though we know they are there. The auction held in New York three years ago may give us some help. We also have an idea of who wants some of your property holdings over here.

"Apart from the oligarchs who pose particular threats, we then have the Bratva – perhaps the Italian Mafia; although we have seen no evidence so far, when they discover your substantial real estate holdings in western Europe and in North America they will happily leave the Eastern and Central European assets to the Bratva over here and will concentrate on those assets within what they consider to be their area of interest.

"We must also recognize that even within the Jewish community there will be competing interests. Cann aside, there will be factions wishing to establish their own agenda as far as the plans for the museums and the synagogues are concerned. Any initiatives involving education and peace, for example, will generate special interest groups already in those fields who could be highly adversarial.

"The single most difficult adversary will be the national governments. Putin appears to be onside at the moment and we can thank him for assisting in freeing Sophie and Little Isaac, but he had self-interest at the root of his cooperation. He wants a lot of your assets held here in Russia. But when it comes to competing claims by various governments such as Ukraine, Poland, Bulgaria, Romania and Germany for the historical material, your wishes will have little influence. We will be left to out-maneuver them – perhaps outwit them." Such was Will's analysis. Isaac agreed, but he added that he was worried that involving his own children in the family trust might lead to aggressive attempts at involvement by them in the distribution of the former trust assets.

"My children in America really don't know me, and I don't know them. So they, too, are unknown entities in this puzzle. I worry that they will consider themselves entitled either to the assets or an equal say in the historical assets assembled by the trust. Also, I worry they may become targets.

"There is no doubt we have demons ready to pounce. Demons who must be identified, controlled and engaged according to our plans, Will. This will be a huge task I certainly didn't ask for or want, but I am stuck with it."

11

THE CLEVER, AUDACIOUS and effective investments made by Isaac's ancestors and their successors at the Swiss bank were a complex and interconnected roster of assets. To Isaac, Will and the experts retained to assist them in arranging the distribution of the assets in a manner that would deflect as much opposition and attack as possible, the task was proving to be more difficult than they had anticipated. The difficulty was quickly compounded after arriving in Moscow: difficulties that left the Smolensk experiences seeming minor by comparison.

Molotovsky, the manager of the real estate and other assets generating an income in Russia, laid before Isaac and Will a comprehensive list of the real estate holdings in Russia. Fifteen pages closely printed itemized over three hundred properties. Isaac and Will knew those located in Smolensk well and had had a cursory examination of some located in Moscow years ago.

The list produced by Molotovsky for Isaac this time was twice the length of the list provided earlier. The additional properties were located as a result of detailed searches on bank records conducted by a lawyer practising in Moscow, Peter Dolgoruky, who was an expert in international law as well as in the principles and laws that applied to ownership or long-term possession of land and buildings by non-residents. The research conducted in Russia under his supervision was augmented by bank officials in Zurich, particularly in tracking leasehold interests.

At a meeting held shortly after Isaac and Will arrived in Moscow, the Molotovsky list with multiple copies lay before Isaac, Will, Dolgoruky and Molotovsky. Will invited Dolgoruky to brief them on the nature of the ownership in terms of possession of each property. He had carefully broken the list into four categories, each weighted in terms of security of ownership; the fourth category being the weakest containing those properties most vulnerable to government confiscation. Dolgoruky started with the fourth category.

"For the purposes of this meeting, Baron Menshikovsky, I start with the weakest group because I think we can deal with the threats that will arise to your continued occupation and use of each. Those individuals who are most likely to benefit and challenge you can be identified. It is a good place to start as it will give you an indication of what you face with the other categories as well, even if perhaps less risk to you…"

"Mr Dolgoruky, I am an American. We do not recognize titles in America or when Americans travel overseas. I understand the courtesy intended by using my Russian title and I thank you for it. My friend and agent, Will MacIntosh, here, has given me a brief profile of your family. As a member of the pre-revolution aristocracy, your family lost several titles, a great deal of land and sources of revenue. I would prefer to have our conversation based on the American familiarity of first names. Would that be acceptable to you?"

"Yes, that would be acceptable, but I should advise you when we, descendants of former aristocrats meet in private, we like to resume our identification by our more formal titles… those to which we would be entitled if 1917 had not occurred in the form in which it did. I meant no disrespect. In fact, I thought I was simply recognizing you as one of us – as someone, therefore, you could trust."

Isaac replied, obviously mollified and slightly embarrassed: "I appreciate the courtesy and generosity with which you addressed me, but first names it must be. Please remember I have no experience of any kind with the protocol appropriate to socializing with any aristocrat, let alone a Russian one."

Will felt it was time to wrap up this awkward dialogue. "Isaac, I think you would find it interesting and potentially helpful to explore this aspect of your inheritance with Peter. As I told you earlier, the Dolgoruky family is one of the premier families of Russia today and not just because of its pre-revolutionary standing. His connections are truly extraordinary. You will need to learn more than the law and family connections from him to survive successfully in this Hydra's den."

* * *

The fourth category contained properties none of which Isaac, Will or Molotovsky were familiar with. Peter explained that possession of each property was held through a series of trusts and holding companies, the ultimate owner appearing to be domiciled in Russia. However, he commented that "…it appears, Isaac, that the Russian ownership is in turn held by a legal entity domiciled elsewhere – perhaps in Switzerland. I don't know."

"What do you mean, Peter, 'domiciled' in Russia? No doubt Will understands you, but I don't."

"The term," Peter answered, "is one applicable in those countries in which the English common law became established; at least in part, and that includes the United States. The principles underlying the term have become an accepted rule of international law; so, it applies here in Russia, too. Simply put, it means the place in which the courts of a country have jurisdiction and the laws to be applied in those courts. It is highly important in this third category because many of the properties have weaker title than in the first category. So, it is the law of Russia and the day to day practices or common usages in Russia, or a particular part of Russia that apply for those properties located in Russia and the same for each country in which real property is located." "Typical lawyer's answer, Peter," said an exasperated Isaac, "I understood less than half of your answer. What is 'real property'?" "Simply put, land and buildings on it, just as it would be in the countries in which English law is the basis of the law of property."

The properties on the category four list were almost all in Smolensk, Moscow, Novgorod or St Petersburg. They were almost all the locations where industrial or commercial activities have been or continue to be carried out. Dolgoruky explained that an industrialist or merchant banker, like Isaac's family, would often simply acquire what appeared to be the outstanding claims for creating an interest in a property. The properties when acquired were worth very little, so if possession was lost, the investor lost little. It was the commercial activity carried on there that had value – the property, if lost, would be abandoned and the factory or commercial activity abandoned or relocated. What makes the properties on this list interesting, Isaac, is that with the passage of time the location of many of these properties is no longer marginal; they are in the centre of urban sprawl, often in the middle of twenty-first-century real estate development."

"Right, okay. So, let's just sell our interests; whatever they may be, strong or weak, to the nearest oligarch," was Isaac's prompt solution.

"Not so easily carried out, Isaac. Virtually every property on this list will have several highly competitive and ruthless oligarchs with an interest in acquiring them. They remain in your possession simply because the oligarchs haven't yet discovered who has control and possession. When it becomes a burden, as it will, when it becomes known that you have the controlling interests, you will become the target of each of the competing oligarchs. I think you already are. Remember, many of the richest oligarchs have friends in the highest offices in the land. I believe it to be true that President Putin receives a substantial percentage, as a commission, on every purchase he assists an oligarch in achieving. It is an ugly marketplace out there, and one you will have little power to control."

"Can we simply stop paying taxes or use some other process that could result in the public sale of the properties?" asked Will. "Isaac does not need any of the properties on this list or the money they could realize in a sale. Getting rid of them would be in his best interest," stated Will.

"Not so easy. Government would come after him for millions in fabricated claims for taxes, municipal utility charges or community-share expenses. No, that will not work. A formula must be found that will give Isaac a clear exit from these properties with or without money being paid for them," was Peter's advice which was readily accepted.

"Peter, I had no idea that being rich could have so many

problems. Before I came involuntarily into ownership or whatever, of these properties I was rich, modestly rich, by American standards. It was, however, legal, clean and straightforward. I guess I can't just renounce it all and walk away?"

"No, your competitors, the oligarchs, will pursue you ruthlessly to force you into their particular camp which will bring you into competition with others equally ruthless. You are likely to be nothing more than a pawn in the property wars underway among many of the oligarchs." Peter's opinion was expressed with polite but vigorous self-assurance.

As the conversation turned to the other three categories, it became clear that the problems with category four properties applied with similar risks to Isaac but on a diminishing scale.

"When, Peter, will it be advisable to start a process of divestment?"

"Only when you have a comprehensive plan that applies to all of them."

Will offered the following suggestion: "Peter, it seems to me there is one constant in any solution for divestment and that is government. Government will favour the oligarchs; however, unless we have a queen on the chessboard to checkmate or capture the king – President Putin. I believe we have such a player. The assets acquired by the trustees were carefully weighted and balanced. Offsetting the real estate are substantial government loans which if made public as owed by Jewish interests would be a huge embarrassment to government. However, it is perhaps the historical and cultural artifacts that are the most important levers in this machine. The historical and cultural artifacts have both nationalistic importance here in Russia and elsewhere in Europe, particularly which when divested will generate fierce competition among countries believing they are entitled to ownership. The artifacts also have a monetary interest on the open market – Christie's auction sales come to mind. Putin cannot interfere with that marketplace. His oligarchs are among the most engaged and competitive in that arena. If Putin jeopardizes that marketplace, he will be putting the oligarchs who are his principal source of personal wealth and power in a financial position that could destroy them. That, they wouldn't accept. That is how I see it. I think we start at the top with each national government; starting as close to the top as we can in Russia dealing comprehensively with each category of asset but with a comprehensive solution. I am a simple country lawyer, Peter, but I suggest that is the strategy we need to follow."

Peter asked to have an hour alone to consider Will's recommendation. He took Molotovsky and the current comprehensive list of assets and left for a secure meeting room nearby that had been screened carefully for listening or recording devices.

Dolgoruky and Molotovsky returned not in an hour but in fifteen minutes. Peter started the discussion: "Isaac, I see why you have placed so much trust and confidence in your Canadian friend. I agree that his strategy is the one to follow. I recommend you follow it."

"Peter, Will and I have discussed this on several occasions," replied Isaac. "I, too, think it is the correct route to take. Now, we need your help to carry it out. Who do you know that can bring us into contact with Putin in negotiating a settlement? You should know that we have had meetings with Mr Kutuzov and his equivalents in several fields in which I have connections in public institutions here in Russia. Putin's office will be aware of me and in a very general way of my negotiations with Russian cultural institutions. In fact, my wife was recently abducted in Smolensk; I suspect either directly or indirectly through the work of one or more oligarchs – or it could be the Bratva although the line is blurred between the two. I believe the time has come to go to the top and slay the nine-headed Hydra, as Will refers to these oligarchs."

A meeting was scheduled for two days hence to receive a recommendation from Dolgoruky as to the mechanics for putting the strategy in place.

* * *

Assurances of Sophie's health and the cessation of her labour comforted Isaac and with Sophie's admonitions that he was in the way with his endless questions and need for reassurances of how well she was, he was firmly instructed to find something else to do with his time.

His hurt and disappointment lasted for only a few hours. A message was received by e-mail from Molotovsky that a branch of the real estate management office in St Petersburg he was using had found something that would prove to be interesting. Caution arising from fear of their telephone calls, e-mails and faxes being monitored had resulted in clear rules of communication being agreed among the team supporting Isaac. He was left to wonder what the something interesting might be.

Will called Molotovsky and he was informed the information they found was probably very important and should be examined in St Petersburg as quickly as possible. Molotovsky was asked to go to St Petersburg immediately and to meet Isaac and Will at the central railway station in Moscow early the next morning.

Sophie failed to hide her extreme pleasure in being informed Isaac had to go to St Petersburg for a day or two. "I'm sure," she said, "You will need to be there at least a week. Don't rush back. It's important you be thorough in this investigation. Just let me know where we can reach you. Remember I have another four weeks to go. Anna and Anastasia are here with me continuously. Dr Rayskill is available on call when needed. I will feel guilty resting here in Moscow having all my needs met in this safe and secure environment when you are out there fighting your battle. I will try to hold up Isaac, worrying about you."

The not-so-subtle message was not lost on Isaac, who accepted that he was in the way in the nursing facility in Moscow and that he might as well move on to the resumption of his quest.

12

ISAAC AND WILL, accompanied by Frank, an auxiliary security guard and Peter Dolgoruky arrived at the station at the scheduled time early the next morning. They took precautions to avoid being recognized. The tickets were bought in Dolgoruky's name and their arrival at the station in Moscow was just minutes before the departure of the train. Their compartment, while small, enabled them to keep out of visual range of anyone watching for them.

Molotovsky had arranged with the station manager, after a suitable monetary inducement, to allow Isaac's car to pick him up at the VIP lounge where they shed their long coats, fur hats with earmuffs and scarves which had effectively hidden their identity. The luggage was limited to carry-on cases carefully chosen to be as common and uninteresting as possible. Each of the travellers arrived carrying his own case, as a group of senior businessmen would. While travelling in plain sight, they kept inconspicuous their arrival and departure from the station.

Isaac had not visited St Petersburg before, but he had been briefed on the properties located in the city itemized on the inventory. Molotovsky announced that they were going to the central business district located on the Neva River. The district bordered the Neva on the north and west and the Fontanka River to the south and east.

Will, ever the keen tour guide, had visited St Petersburg twenty years before and so started a dissertation on the history of the city and in particular the characteristics of the district in which their destination was located. Isaac as usual became restless and about to object, but not before Will was able to inform him that the building they were going to was an eighteenth-century palace on the Fontanka River, one of the most beautiful urban areas in the world. He was cut short just as he was warming up on his favoured subject of the architecture and aesthetics of the district in which the palace was located.

Dolgoruky, trying to keep the peace and to be helpful, stated that he knew the Fontanka very well. It was the equivalent of the Grand Canal in Venice, but more lavish and almost as consistent in its building styles: although primarily eighteenth century, every bit as beautiful. He offered to arrange for a boat tour of the city's rivers and canals later if they had the time. He added an inducement he suspected would appeal to Isaac: "My family still has possession of part of a palace on the Fontanka, close to the building we are going to. We have a private motorized launch which I can arrange to use as a discreet tour. Yes, I heard your whisper, Mr MacIntosh; I will give you a running commentary as we go along."

The cars used to get Isaac and his group from the central rail station stopped some distance from their destination. They were taken by water taxi which took them along the Fontanka until they reached the palace. Not a word was spoken as each traveller was awed by the beauty and scale of the ornate buildings observed on the Neva, and when they turned onto the Fontanka most of the buildings had a similar scale and complementary architectural façade. For a mid-October day, it was unusually warm, and the sun gleamed off the gold-leaf encrusted neoclassical ornamentation decorating many of the buildings.

When the taxi stopped, Molotovsky spoke; only he spoke, as his accent was a nondescript local vernacular of Russian that would not attract interest from the boatman, or anyone in other vessels plying the river nearby.

A watergate in the palace opened immediately on their arrival. Those inside had been alerted to their arrival and had been instructed not to allow the travellers to remain outside for more than a minute or two.

The watergate led to stairs that gave access to the palace. The main entrance was comprised of paired doors, huge in size, designed to enable eighteenth-century horse and carriages to enter and to gain access to a central courtyard which provided a private and unseen access into the palace.

In the courtyard, Isaac could hold his reaction to his surroundings inside no longer. "Reuben Molotovsky! Are you sure I have some interest in this incredible structure? I mean, it is a palace, larger and grander even than the dacha in Smolensk. *Oy*! How could Jews have acquired this property and kept it until now? Frankly, I am embarrassed even to go inside."

In reply, Molotovsky said simply, "You, Dr Menshive, not only have sole possession of this palace, but you also have as much ownership as Russian law allows a private citizen and you certainly own all it contains. I will explain how and why when we get inside."

* * *

Each of the travellers insisted on having an hour to freshen up and to be given the use of the suite set aside for them while staying in the city.

Will, predictably, completed his 'freshening up' in record time and bolted with considerable enthusiasm to explore the palace before the meeting started. He was amazed at the number of staff who appeared to be service workers around the building. Each greeted him with a forced smile – Russians, he had learned, have an aversion to smiling. He was recognized as a guest, which led him to conclude that photo IDs of the guests had been circulated in advance of their arrival. That was both comforting and unsettling. He worried whether the identification had been sent and circulated in a secure fashion. He must remember, he thought, to question Molotovsky about this when they meet. His tour was at breakneck speed, more an orientation than a museum-like tour, which he knew would be provided later.

The meeting was held in the former library which had remained amazingly intact. The elongated central table easily sat twenty-two, more than enough for Isaac and his guests.

Isaac moved to a chair on one side of the table, not on an end as would be traditional for the chairman of a meeting in New York. He was overwhelmed by his surroundings and endeavoured to be as withdrawn as possible.

"Dr Menshive, sir, in Russia you are correctly seated on the side of the table where traditionally the Chair would take his position, but may I suggest you take the chair opposite you – the large carved and upholstered chair. That is where the master of this house would sit and take control of the gathering. I mention this because we will certainly be meeting with high-ranking politicians, bureaucrats and collectors in the next few days. They will be watching you closely for your sense of confidence and control."

"Will, you will chair any meetings we have here in St Petersburg. I am just a bones doctor from New York without much training in protocol or social graces. I can control a meeting of opinionated and difficult medical people in America, but I am a fish out of water here. Will, you must," was Isaac's plea for help.

Dolgoruky spoke up, answering for Will. "I understand your reticence and sense of unease in this place. They were deliberately designed as places to intimidate and establish both a presence and a superiority over others. That is what we must ask you to demonstrate, Dr Menshive. Will can certainly chair our meeting today, but I must ask you to do so at any meetings held here with your guests from the city; some may also come from Moscow. The way our society works today is very little different from the way it did when this palace was built during the reign of Catherine the Great. The master of the house must project confidence and sophistication. Failing that, you will be treated as inferior and controllable. You will be taken advantage of. It is essential here to project mastery when dealing with others. I was brought up in that environment and in the legal world of lawyers, judges and clients. I continue to function in that environment. If you will permit me, I can give you some training that will assist you. Mr MacIntosh, I know you are more accustomed to these standards, but I invite you to join us because some local social peculiarities should be known to avoid unwitting offence."

Both Isaac and Will quietly, if not timidly, agreed.

***

Will assumed the finely hand-carved chair of state and drew towards him an agenda that Molotovsky and Dolgoruky had prepared.

"The first item is somewhat obvious: why are we here – what, Mr Molotovsky, have you discovered that you consider requires our presence here?"

"First, I wanted Isaac to see this building, the Alexander Palace. It is just one of several strategically, historically and monetarily important buildings on your list of assets. The list is more comprehensive than the one the Swiss bank provided you with. In fact, the new list which you will find attached to the agenda was found as part of what I consider to be one of your most significant group of assets."

"Where was the list found and what else was found?" asked Will.

"I will review each building as to its use, age, importance, location and value either at this meeting or perhaps tomorrow. I think you will be more interested in what else I have discovered," was Molotovsky's answer. "Now, the really intriguing discovery we have made. In preparation for a visit that I knew Dr Menshive would make to visit his assets here, I had the staff go through every square inch of this palace looking for and documenting its contents. Two of the maintenance men while searching the basements found a closed and sealed door which they pried open. It was what we call a 'strong room'. Every bank and substantial business had one. Count Dolgoruky informed me every significant palace also had one, so I gave specific directions to search for one. As I said, it was found. It contained five safes, each with a combination lock and other security devices. I have not had those opened. I knew I should wait until Dr Menshive was personally present to do that. I have a locksmith, Jewish, who can be trusted. He will be here tomorrow to open them. What we can deal with now are the items lying on the shelves. I have arranged for staff to bring in a representative sample on trays. I will call on the staff to bring them in now."

Isaac turned to Will and with what he considered to be an inaudible voice said sneeringly, "More Russian art, I suppose."

Before Will could reply with his usual admonition, the trays arrived. There were several: each solid silver polished to their highest level of perfection, each borne by a staff person dressed in the full livery of a nineteenth-century footman. Fortunately, Isaac was distracted by what the trays contained before he could comment on the costumes.

There was a highly audible gasp from each person around the table. The trays were slowly and dramatically emptied, giving time for each piece to be revealed and studied.

Over four hundred separate pieces were decorously arranged on the table in front of those attending the meeting. A more incongruous assemblage of artifacts Isaac and Will couldn't have imagined.

Since these pieces had been crafted, the Romanovs had lost their throne, the nobility dispossessed by the Soviets and several cultural purges instigated by Stalin and his successors had taken place, communism had imploded, a brief trial with democracy had failed and Russia under Putin had returned to an autocracy not unlike a Czarist monarchy.

The pieces displayed were all Fabergé-crafted: coronets, crowns, rings, hair pieces, bracelets and decorative items for the home, containing some of the largest, most brilliantly cut precious stones anyone in the room had seen before. The early morning rays of the sun pouring into the room from the east through the French doors overlooking the Fontanka were caught on every facet and highly polished gold and platinum surface.

The room remained silent for over half an hour as each guest viewed and tried to understand the origins and the 'why' of this phenomenal collection.

Will broke the silence by turning to Dolgoruky and gently asking "Sir, this horde is more of your background than mine or Isaac's. What are we seeing? And are they authentic?"

The reply was almost too quiet to be heard. "This collection equals the collection of jewellery in the Armory Museum in Moscow. I haven't seen such a display in private hands anywhere within or outside Russia in terms of Russian craftsmanship. My grandmother Princess Dolgoruky was a specialist in Russian jewellery. She instructed me, my brother and sisters in the various forms of eighteenth- and nineteenth-century Russian jewellery and where and when each piece would be worn. We were instructed in the various craftsmen and the characteristics of each in their work. What I am viewing is of the highest quality, most of which is of the Fabergé manufacturer. I am absolutely breathless." The count paused, then let out a cry. "God in heaven! That piece in the middle of the group in front of Dr Menshive... no, sir, you must be Baron Menshikovsky, in this room now. I insist on it. I see a fabulous diadem I haven't seen except in photographs taken of my great-great-grandmother in full court dress. That was part of my family's collection lost during the turmoil and thievery following the 1917 Revolution. That piece was reputed among the nobility to be the very finest of its kind – Fabergé, of course."

Count Dolgoruky's comments were terminated by his tears and emotional struggle as he faced an object that had been a central item of identity for his noble family. Everyone around the table sat mute out of respect, waiting for the count to regain his composure. Finally, he said, "I don't know how this palace or this collection of jewellery came to be identified with your family, Baron Menshikovsky, but I suspect the answer to that question will give you the insight and answer to virtually all your questions about the assembling of all of your trust-related assets. I suggest we call on a decorative arts specialist I know – who can be trusted to be discreet – to inform us more fully on each of these pieces. I will try to have him join us this afternoon after lunch."

Isaac quietly asked Dolgoruky the question each person around the table had on his mind: "Were these pieces legally obtained? Could they be here in storage for others to claim later? How could they have been collected by Jewish bankers? What mess do I now find myself in? This may be just the start; we have the sealed safes in the basement to be opened. What do they contain?"

Dolgoruky replied, "We don't yet know the answers to those good questions, but we must find out. Nothing of this collection should be made public or disposed of in any way until we understand the answers to your questions."

Isaac quickly and firmly agreed. Before the meeting adjourned that afternoon, Will brought out his new cell phone with a built-in camera and with Isaac and Dolgoruky's consent he photographed the table, its contents and those in attendance from several different angles. This, he said, would serve as a record of what had been presented that morning and those present to verify the items on view. The images taken were immediately forwarded to the Swiss bank and to Isaac's lawyer in New York with strict instructions that the images were confidential and not to be disclosed to anyone.

* * *

The mystery of the origins of the trove of jewellery was intensified when Isaac was informed the collection was priceless and without parallel in any private collection in the world. It reminded him that no reliable information about the astonishing range and diversity of the assets assembled by the trust had yet been achieved. He worried that there had to be illegality or at least unethical practice that had led to the assembling of such treasures. His instinct from the beginning of his receiving the trust was to abandon or renounce it. This was the solution he took into the afternoon meeting.

He shared his anxiety with Will, his confidant in all matters relating to the trust. Will was able to give him little comfort other than to say that the specialist expert in the decorative arts and jewellery would join them as scheduled that afternoon. That might give an answer to Isaac's dilemma. They were both reassured that Dr Vorontsov who would be attending was himself a descendant of an ancient noble family. He was recognized by the Armory Museum in Moscow and the Museum of Decorative Arts in St Petersburg as the foremost expert in this field of research. Isaac insisted during his discussion with Will over a light lunch of borscht and a sandwich that full disclosure of whatever facts Dr Vorontsov required would be provided. "I cannot have anything to do with such priceless objects without absolute assurances that they are legitimately mine."

* * *

The meeting was reconvened as planned at 2 p.m. Isaac took the chair and remained there, but he quickly transferred leadership to Will who would be assisted by Dolgoruky; the last person arrived shortly after the meeting was convened.

The first surprise was Dr Vorontsov's immediate approach to Dolgoruky, giving him a bear hug and, "Greetings, Cousin Peter. I suspected you would be here. I am glad for it." He was seated next to Dolgoruky. Proceedings paused while polite inquiries about families were completed.

It was only when Vorontsov's attention was removed from his cousin that he focused on the treasures assembled on the table.

"My God! Is it possible? I have never seen such a collection in Russia or elsewhere other than perhaps in the Armory Museum in the Kremlin. This is indeed an exceptional grouping of treasures."

Will, having been instructed to probe the expertise of Dr Vorontsov, asked: "Can you tell us, Doctor, how this trove could have been assembled by Jewish bankers in light of their vulnerability to confiscation by public and private interests?"

"I can think of only one way. If I am correct, Dr Menshive legitimately owns everything you see before you. First, you must understand that I can identify pieces that date back to the Napoleonic period, and pieces crafted through the nineteenth century up to the Art Nouveau period, just before the 1917 Revolution. Second, you must understand the nature of warfare. Napoleon invariably threatened war before actually invading a country. In his warning, then confirmed in his declaration of war, he threatened that on successfully invading and conquering a country he would seize as prizes of war all such art, cultural and historical artifacts as he chose. His motive was to enrich the collections in the Louvre to make Paris the world centre of culture and artistic influence. Many of the oldest pieces I see here were acquired in this manner by Napoleon, but then lost by him as his Grande Armée retreated in disarray and disgrace from Moscow. Those wagon loads of treasures seized in what are now Western Russia, Poland, the Czech Republic and Germany (formerly parts of Prussia and Lithuania which included much of Poland) were seized by Czar Alexander I and stored in St Petersburg. The jewellery was distributed among the nobility for services rendered to the Imperial family. Well, then how did they get out of those hands? I will answer.

"After the 1917 Revolution, the Bolsheviks were desperate for money. The country had been virtually bankrupted by the 1905 Russia-Japanese War and the Great War of 1914, which ended for Russia in 1917. The Bolsheviks realized that a fast and easy source of cash was to confiscate precious jewellery in the hands of the nobility and the Imperial family and sell it. They did just that with swift efficiency. The purchasers were both local and international. The money was so desperately needed that they sought local purchasers. Well, about the only people with the cash needed to acquire such treasures were the bankers. The bankers were almost exclusively Jewish. You, Dr Menshive, come from three extremely successful banking families, the Mendelssohns, Menshikovskys and the Günzburgs – from the latter I know you received your ennoblement as Count Menshikovsky. There may be proofs of purchase, but I am willing to stake my professional opinion on the date and method of acquisition as post-revolutionary Russia in 1917 or 1918 – purchased with cash readily available to your families, sir."

"Why would they have wanted such artifacts? No one in my family, except perhaps the Günzburgs, would have used them," replied Isaac. "I am wrong. The Günzburgs may have used them during the Imperial period when they endorsed and paid to support the Imperial government in St Petersburg. But of course, that era had disappeared, if as you say these treasures were acquired in 1917 or 1918."

"May I refer to you today," asked Vorontsov, "in the presence of this fabulous reminder of Imperial Russia, as Count Menshikovsky? I would like to. It would dignify our proceedings. I think cousin Dolgoruky, himself a Czarist count and I as a prince of Imperial Russia, would feel more at ease with that atmosphere in this wonderful palace and in a library that dates to the reign of Czarina Catherine II."

"Yes, of course," was Isaac's embarrassed reply, "but I am not now nor shall ever be comfortable with the title. However, if you both would like that connection with your history, I allow you to use it."

Vorontsov continued: "To your question, sir, as to why your family would have acquired these jewels when they would have little use for them? The answer is given by reminding you of the horrific slaughter of Czar Nicholas and his family at Ekaterinburg. You may have read that when the family was being shot in the basement of their place of confinement, numerous shots were required to kill the Czarina and the daughters of the Czar and his Czarina. The Czar and Tsarevich were killed instantly, but not the women. The reason was that they had sewn diamonds, hundreds of them, into their corsets. The bullets were deflected by the diamonds until the shooters aimed for more vulnerable areas of the precious bodies. They had the diamonds not to protect them in case of an attack, but as highly valuable commodities they could sell when they got to the West to generate substantial capital to live on. Just as the Royal family saw uses other than personal adornment and noble attire, your ancestors knew that these wonderful works of art and craftsmanship could be broken up, and the diamonds used to generate capital if they had to flee the country.

"It appears these fabulous pieces of jewellery have been kept in secret storage here in this palace since the early twentieth century."

Will, thinking of the inventory and valuation of the jewellery, asked whether the items had a value only for the precious stones embedded in them or whether, as works of art apparently almost unique, they would have a premium price on the open market. A reasonable question a hard-headed descendant of practical Scots thought appropriate.

Both Vorontsov and Dolgoruky blanched, Vorontsov stating with vehemence that they were valued beyond mere monetary worth. They were an essential part of Russian history that must be kept, conserved and displayed.

"Alright, they were stored in this building. How do we know they were not hidden by others, expecting to collect them in the future – even if I own this building? I do not understand why I have this building or my inventory. I discovered only yesterday that it appears to be mine," was Isaac's worried contribution to the discussion.

"I will answer that question," Dolgoruky said. "You own this building. Like the jewellery, it was purchased like any of your other St Petersburg real estate after the revolution from members of the nobility. This, sir, was one of the premier palaces in St Petersburg dating back, as we noted earlier, to the reign of Czarina Catherine the Great. I can give you much more history another time. After the Revolution, the nobility were targets for exploitation and confiscation by the ruling Bolsheviks and their supporters. Cash. Your family, sir, had cash and were willing to assist the nobility to escape by purchasing this building and its contents. Yes, the nobles who sold their properties may have resented that they were selling to rich bankers, but they were desperate to generate enough capital to leave the country and to start a new life in the West.

"However, as far as this building is concerned, the noble family who sold it knew only that it was being sold to a bank, the Günzburg Bank; yes, a Jewish bank, but the person with whom they negotiated and to whom they sold was thoroughly Russian, a leading member of the Duma and the Russian Orthodox Church. What the sellers did not know, and I can assure you would not have cared, is that the purchaser was a trustee acting for a London-based trust, which in turn was owned by a highly secretive international company, owned, sir, by your trust!"

"*Oy*! What webs were created to deceive? Should I consider this building mine?"

Both Dolgoruky and Vorontsov replied in unison, "Yes, of course. The method of purchase was a device used by the rich, not just aristocrats, throughout Europe, the United Kingdom and America. You alone have the rights to this building."

"Well, how did it remain as an asset of the trust? We certainly would have lost it if it were known it was owned by Jews."

"Your family, sir, were amazingly astute businessmen… clearly. The fortune you have received from the trust is a testament to that. To answer your question, as far as civic officials and national politicians are concerned, this building is now owned by a Gentile bank in Zurich.

"This palace has been leased to the City of St Petersburg for public events and for the entertaining of visiting dignitaries for years. Some of the revenues produced from the rentals have been remitted to Mr Molotovsky, your manager, who was acting then as agent for the bank. The largest part has been paid over to the City of St Petersburg. There was no need to change the ownership. It was generating a substantial income for the city as it was. There was no suspicion of anyone other than the bank owning it. We are here today because no events were scheduled for the palace, so we were able to rent it from the city as a sublease."

"Incredible! I am impressed by the skill my ancestors employed in acquiring their assets. Can I then accept that the contents of the house, including these treasures and whatever is in the safes in the basement, are truly mine?"

"Yes," replied Dolgoruky, "there is no doubt, but I recommend that the Swiss bank continue to appear to be the owner."

"I certainly agree with that. I will retain and use the dacha in Smolensk, but I would have no use or comfort in taking possession of this palace. It might be nice to have a part of it for occasional use. However, its contents are another matter. I will have to do something with these. They cannot be kept here. Now that they have been discovered, they will be a target for oligarchs or Putin's personal interest."

Tea, Russian tea, was served late in the afternoon. While each guest along with Isaac and Will enjoyed the superb tea and comestibles, with gloved hands they examined each of the more than four hundred pieces laid out in front of them.

13

LAND OWNERSHIP IN Russia had been a preoccupation of Will's for at least three years – since his involvement with Isaac in identifying the assets held by the trust, which included an extensive portfolio of property in Russia. He had sought and received the opinion of legal scholars recognized as knowledgeable in the laws and practices of property ownership, and transfer of ownership by will, gift and sale.

The results of his inquiries added to what had been disclosed by Dolgoruky. The additional information provided to him was in the form of comprehensive legal opinions which proved to be confusing and unsatisfactory from a land titles point of view as understood by a Canadian lawyer. The experts engaged by the Swiss bank in Zurich, however, came to as definitive a position as any he had received; all property in Russia after 1918 had been confiscated and held and distributed by government on an 'as needed' basis until the 1920s, when there was a short period in which the Communist government allowed a form of conventional ownership. That lasted, apparently, less than ten years, when the laws reverted to absolute ownership and control by government. Will was informed that as far as the laws of the country were applicable that remained the case. Yes, it was well known that since Putin's assumption of power a large number of his cronies and international investors had acquired something very like absolute title, such as is the law in the United Kingdom, Canada and the United States. In fact, those acquiring such properties had the 'rights or privileges' that went with them. They could be sold for valuable consideration. The properties were subsequently sold over and over again by the oligarchs at prices reflective of fair market value, as if the properties were in Canary Wharf in London or in the Manhattan district of New York City.

What, then, did Isaac have? How did the trust maintain possession, exclusive possession and use?

Each of these questions, Will knew as a lawyer, had to be definitively understood as Isaac considered how he should arrange the sale, distribution or retention of the properties. He had Dolgoruky's opinion, but that might not be reliable or acceptable to a non-Russian purchaser.

This issue came forcefully to mind yesterday as Will sat in the library of the Alexander Palace on the Fontanka River in St Petersburg, one of the most architecturally, culturally and historically significant buildings in Russia.

Over a private breakfast with Count Dolgoruky, these questions and observations were put to the Moscow lawyer, hoping his experience with property transactions in Moscow and St Petersburg would enable him to give Will a definitive answer. He shared the opinions he had received from the Swiss bank.

"Everyone has assured Isaac that he is the owner of this inventory of land and buildings in Russia and that he is free to treat them as commodities on the open market much as he could in London or New York. I don't see how that could be. Please help me with an answer – an answer I can use as we consider what Isaac can and should do with the Russian properties. Let me be clear, he is not prepared to simply continue the status quo – he wishes to divest most of the property held in Russia. I need to know what laws or procedures apply that can enable us to do that."

Dolgoruky poured himself a hot cup of tea from a Russian samovar which itself was of museum quality. "Your question I was expecting. I know you need the answer to enable you to move forward. My assurance yesterday was not enough for you as a Western lawyer. Dr Menshive has told me privately what your general plans for divestment are. I have considered the issue carefully and have taken the liberty to discuss the matter with the Ministry of Justice and a senior judge of our Supreme Court, the court which would oversee and hear any challenge that would arise as to the sale of Dr Menshive's interest in any of the properties. He has the sole interest which is saleable."

Before Dolgoruky could continue, Will interjected, "Surely that is flummery — as I understand it, Isaac can be dispossessed of each of his apparent properties simply by confiscation by Putin's government without remedy."

"I will consider and answer your challenge as I explain the way property holdings and transfers actually work in Russia. This samovar is full, the tea excellent and the biscuits worth eating. My explanation may take an hour or more, so please tell me if this is not a good time. Nothing, I mean nothing, in Russia since the Revolution was, or is, what is on the statute books or government policy papers. What happens is usually arbitrary, but predictable with the correct connections.

"A quick history of the early twentieth century of the ownership of land here in Russia continued until the 1920s, and as it relates to Isaac's other assets, is necessary to understand how the properties listed on the inventory remained in possession of the trust.

"During the First World War, the Russian economy during the Romanov Monarchy was a shambles and the country had lost hundreds of thousands of its citizens to the ravages of war and famine. There was very little productivity. Tax revenue was almost non-existent. A tax on wealth would have helped, but the aristocracy were exempt from taxation. There was tax on land but it amounted to little in relation to the needs of the Imperial government.

"Obviously, money was needed to finance ongoing government operations and, of course, the war. The war alone was costing the Imperial government well in excess of what revenue it had coming in or could finance.

"Dr Menshive, your ancestor Baron Günzburg financed the government of Czar Alexander the First as it struggled to pay for the Napoleonic Wars. Your ancestors, the Mendelssohns, did the same for Prussia and many of the German states that were in a loose confederation. It was the Günzburg, Mendelssohn banks and several smaller banks such as the Menshikovsky bank in Smolensk, Moscow, Odessa and St Petersburg which advanced the cash to finance both government and the war. This is documented, and the proof is readily available. Virtually none of that money was repaid. In exchange, however, for the cash being advanced by the lenders they were given exceptional privileges not available generally in the marketplace. They were given the right to accrue land and historical, cultural and artistic assets as they wished. Not just government was dependent on those banks for money; my family borrowed from the Günzburg Bank, for example, about double the worth of the assets owned by my family. We were, simply put, insolvent by the end of the Romanov era. I know that virtually everything my family owned was delivered, often in wagons, to the bank. When I viewed that spectacular treasure trove on the library table, I recognized a number of pieces as you now know that came from my family – to pay in part the debts they owed the banks.

"Let me assure you, everything on that table is owned either by the Swiss trust or by Dr Menshive himself. I would be the first to attest to the validity of his claim – a claim superior to that of any other claimant. Part of the funding agreements between the Imperial government and your ancestors was a guarantee that such security as was given by government and private individuals would take precedence over any laws that would be embraced in the future, to the contrary; yes, I know how limited that assurance could be. However, the guarantees were honoured in the months before the Revolution by the Imperial government. Everyone knew we Russians were going to have a change of government, just when and what form it would take were not clear until 1917.

"Most of the aristocracy recognized that their favoured life in Russia was ending and they chose to leave. Even though the security held by the banks was well in excess of the value of assets held by the borrowers, the banks were generous in advancing cash in exchange for deeds.

"All of the properties on the Russian part of the inventory were conveyed legally during the Imperial period – all were conveyed for what you in Britain and Canada call 'fair market value'. Let me tell you, we were thankful for the generosity of the banks in financing our departure."

Will interjected: "That is all very well, but in 1918 the Bolshevik government nationalized all property in the country, outlawed leases and long-term tenancies. I know there was a brief respite in the twenties when some form of capitalist experiment was tried, but that didn't last long."

"You are well informed, Mr MacIntosh," Dolgoruky replied. "That brings us then to the Communist era, which as you have noted began in 1917, but became fully operational, after a fashion, by 1920.

"From the commencement of the 'Communist' system of economic management the revenues never reached anywhere near what was needed to run the Soviet government. The Communist model was about the least efficient and effective form of economic management operating in the twentieth century.

"Just as the Imperial government before it, the Communist government was perpetually short of money – massively short. They followed exactly the practices of the Imperial government, and using the Imperial government's documentation as useful precedents, they borrowed from – not the banks, they had been confiscated – but from the former owners of the banks who were – mostly – living in the West. Why did your family, the Mendelssohns, Menshikovskys and others lend the money? Because they were given assurances, none of which were actually kept, that the vast inventory of assets held in Russia would be left alone. The only reason the assets were not seized by the government was because government politicians knew they would have to go back over and over again for loans, as they did right up to the Gorbachev period.

"At no time during the Communist era did your relatives guess the trustees of your family trust held the vast scale and value of the assets held in Russia. They were exceptionally well held in trusts, companies and joint ventures that were impossible to trace. In fact, sir, I believe one of the principal trusts is domiciled in Canada – on a small island near the Atlantic Ocean, called Prince Edward Island. Why, I don't know, but it was a key structure in the ownership scheme that hid your families' Jewish background or that all of the assets on the inventory were actually owned by the same family.

"How the Mendelssohns and Günzburgs and Menshikovskys shared the assets, I don't know, but it appears all of their assets are now held in the Swiss trust, which in turn is owned and controlled by a Canadian trust. This I have just discovered. It is unimaginable. I believe Dr Menshive is the current trustee and the only person having any right or interest in the trust."

"That is correct, Count," said Will. "Isaac shared the termination and assignment of the trust with his sister, but she renounced her interest leaving Isaac with the only interest in the assets. A new trust, successor to the historic trust, has recently been created and operates, maintains and will develop the assets. What rights does Isaac have that enable him to divest or transfer any of his Russian assets? Does he actually have anything in Russia that has a value and that is saleable?"

"The answer is yes. Starting with President Gorbachev, assurances and plans for a form of free enterprise system of trading, in commodities and land, for example, were being developed. But long before any legal structure was formalized the Russian economy was restructured to encourage and actually accept an open marketplace within the confines of a centralized and controlled economy.

"You may have read, Mr MacIntosh, that President Putin has announced that in the next two or three years a form of free enterprise will be structured with ownership guarantees.

"So, in response to your question, the answer is that now Dr Menshive has undisputed ownership and control of all his assets but, and I must emphasize this, some of his assets such as historically or archaeologically significant objects will not be permitted to leave this country. That is not unlike the protections afforded similar objects in the United Kingdom or America, and I suppose you have similar restrictions in Canada.

"Simply put, Mr MacIntosh, the trust was hidden in plain

sight, never revealing who was behind the controlling interests. The players and investors were exceptionally astute in planning and executing the purposes of the trust. There was no benefit to the national government in challenging the trust's possession and control because the central government was making more money through the trust's management and revenues, shared with the state through heavy taxation, than it could have done on its own."

"Thank you, Count, for your helpful explanation. Please provide me with what we call a legal opinion, with suggestions as to how we could divide and distribute the Russian land and buildings as assets. As an example, the only property Isaac wishes to retain is the dacha in Smolensk, although I think he and his wife would enjoy a condominium or equivalent here in the Palace in St Petersburg. I suspect any arrangement decided will require the consent of the Putin government, which may involve forgiveness of payment of some of the debt owed to the trust by the Russian government."

To which Count Dolgoruky replied, "Allow me to comment that the only reason the trust and Dr Menshive have the exceptionally strong bargaining position they have here is because of the skilful acquisition and management of the assets – including not attempting to divest them during the Communist period."

* * *

The meeting that had adjourned reconvened the next day early in the afternoon, time being allowed for Will's separate meeting with Dolgoruky that morning. A visibly relieved Will took the chair and when asked by Isaac what he learned from the discussion he said simply: "More of what we have discussed over the past three years but with a substantial level of comfort as to your right to sell land and buildings. We will discuss how it affects our plans later – but nothing I will tell you will affect our overall strategy."

The meeting was then directed at its primary objective both for the meeting and for the visit to St Petersburg – what lay in the strong room with its safes and the recently discovered sealed room that led from the strong room.

"Mr Molotovsky, what do you suggest we tackle first – the documentation and objects on the shelves in the strong room, opening the safes and examining the contents, or unsealing the adjacent room?"

"I recommend that we examine what is now available on the shelves. It will take some time as each document must be recorded and a file opened. With Dr Menshive's consent and some helpful suggestions from both Count Dolgoruky and Prince Vorontsov, I have taken my two sons who will clerk for us and will follow the form of recording that we have been recommended to apply. I think this should take about an hour and a half. I can say that, as I have had a preliminary examination of the open contents of the room. My sons are there now, already working on it."

Prince Vorontsov, an expert conservator and museum administrator in his own right, said with firmness: "I have instructed the young men to record where the items are found, photograph before recording the space and putting each item back exactly where found. We need every bit of information we can obtain. Often it is a minor, or seemingly minor, bit of information that can give meaning and an effective interpretation."

Molotovsky meekly replied that he had given the same instructions, and before they started the room it was methodically photographed on a grid plan and each sector of the grid numbered so the records would predictably link to each sector, to enable accurate records as each piece was examined and characterized.

Unfortunately, the strong room was not insubstantial in size, as Will had expected. It was about twenty-five feet square. There was no natural light, but Molotovsky had brought in extension cords and set up lighting that brought every square inch into clear visibility. In the centre of the room, a table with sufficient chairs for everyone including Molotovsky's sons had been arranged.

Will spoke first when they took their seats. "I suggest we

invite Prince Vorontsov to lead us in our investigation to ensure an orderly process. Will you accept that role for us, Prince?"

"Of course. This is very much part of the professional role I perform at the Museum of Decorative Arts, a little further up the Fontanka River on this side. I invite you all to visit it in a couple of days when we are finished here so that you can put what you have discovered so far, and will be viewing, into the Russian historical context. I have my staff arranging a private exhibition for our use only that should be helpful."

Murmurs of grateful consent were heard around the table to Vorontsov's obvious satisfaction.

* * *

One and a half hours later, as predicted by Molotovsky, the prince announced that a summation and interpretation of the objects on open shelving could be made. He said that lesser jewellery in terms of quality and size to those viewed yesterday were found there, but said, "You will have observed numerous small pieces by Fabergé including a few of the firm's famous Easter eggs made on order by the Imperial Family. It is not surprising that they would be here. The Bolsheviks saved what jewellery they could retrieve from the Imperial residences. The Imperial family occasionally gave Fabergé works as gifts to family and those who had provided a service to the family. Some were ordered and delivered by the British Royal Family as gifts within the family. Fabergé works are highly sought in the west, and at Christie's or Sotheby's sales would sell for exceptionally high prices. I have quickly estimated the value of what is on the shelves in the range of eighty to ninety million dollars. Let me be clear that these are Dr Menshive's. The government of Russia would not interfere in their removal from the country or sale. I can say, however, that a national museum would wish to make an offer to purchase a significant number of these artifacts or exchange claims for other assets for the Fabergé objects. I will arrange for a 'proposal to purchase' to be prepared by the ministry and delivered to Mr MacIntosh.

"Please note that of the most celebrated jewellers who operated in Russia, we have excellent examples here of each. I will list those to whom I refer. Jeremie Panzia, a Swiss-born jeweller whose most accomplished work was achieved here in St Petersburg. It was he who fashioned the celebrated dual hemisphere crown made for Czarina Catharine the Great in 1762. There is little left of his work in this country, but I have found twelve pieces in this collection. Truly remarkable. The Bolins family of jewellers, whose original craftsman was the Swede Bolins, and Andrey Remplon, a native of Saxony. Remplon made a substantial amount of regnal and personal jewellery for Paul I and Alexander I; some with his son-in-law Bolins. I should note as an indication of how important that firm's work was that your Queen Elizabeth II, Mr MacIntosh, has a spectacular diadem made by this firm. The firm of Ignaty Sazikov which survived from the late eighteenth century to the late nineteenth century produced wonderful pieces, some of which were included in the Russian display at the 1851 Great Exhibition held in London. Sazikov was referred to with praise as 'Russia's Benvenuto Cellini'. Very high praise indeed. The examples I have found here would justify such high praise. Then there was Ivan Khlebnikov whose workshop was in operation by 1871 from where he provided the highest quality jewellery to most of the monarchs in Europe in the late nineteenth century. Each monarch was in competition to augment his or her jewellery collection as oligarchs are now. Two other jewellers whose work I have found here are Pavel Ovchinnikov and a firm known as Keibel, who serviced the pre-revolutionary period producing the contemporary style which was highly popular with the *Beau Monde* and newly rich. The collection in this room alone is outstanding and has the best range of jewellery crafted in Russia from the eighteenth century to the end of the Imperial period. The Revolution brought all manufactory of this type to an instant end. I have taken time to give you this overview as you must understand the significance, let alone the value, of what you have here, Dr Menshive, – my apologies, again in this setting, with objects of this kind, I must refer to you, sir, as Baron Menshikovsky."

There was nothing to add, so after a moment or two of reflection, Will requested the Molotovsky sons to open the four safes. While these had not yet been opened, the double combinations on each lock had been discovered. Molotovsky himself went to a safe and said: "I believe this safe is the oldest of the group. I propose to open it first." To which Vorontsov agreed, saying he was familiar with each of the firms that made the safes and could identify their date of manufacture. "As we have no other guide as to the sequence in which to open the safes, I suggest," he said, "that we proceed with the date of their making. The contents may reflect that date".

Molotovsky opened the safe and found it full of legal and sales transactional documents. Both the Prince and Count Dolgoruky went through them quickly and stated one after the other that the contents included deeds to most if not all of the Russian properties in the trust. Dolgoruky looked at Isaac and announced, "This is the confirmation of your ownership I was looking for; most of our deed registry documents in the public records offices were destroyed during the Revolution or during the Stalinist era when Stalin tried to obliterate the historical records in his attempt to rededicate and create a new social and economic order. These records are exactly what we need to support your claim, Baron Menshikovsky. I have seen the deed to the Smolensk dacha you would like to keep and the one to the Alexander Palace. The record is what is needed."

"As you go through the documentation, is there any record of who was the guiding hand in structuring and making the investments?" asked Isaac.

"Yes, in the early years it was Baron Günzburg, his heirs and successors. As you know, his son died leaving only a daughter who married a Menshikovsky, hence the connection between the banking families and flow of assets from Günzburg to Menshikovsky. I expect to find evidence of who his successors were up to the time of the Revolution in the next safes."

The other three safes were opened and predictably they produced similar documentation establishing a coherent chronological order of the acquisitions and the managers and investors. When the contents of the last safe had been examined carefully, Dolgoruky turned to Isaac to say, "I now understand how the trust came to your line in the family. As you recall, your mother was a second cousin of your father, both having a common ancestor on both the Mendelssohn and Günzburg sides. Your father was not the predictable heir to the trusteeship. His first cousin, also a Menshikovsky, was the manager and investor who at that time dealt with the Swiss bank, actually living safely in Zurich. However, after the Revolution, when he worried the trust's assets were at risk and did not understand the lawlessness that characterized the Revolution, he travelled to Moscow and then to St Petersburg to discover what he could do to protect the assets. He was dealing with Mr Molotovsky's grandfather at the time. While in St Petersburg he inadvertently while walking to his hotel got caught up in a mob scene and was one of several dozen protesters who were killed. This history is recorded in detail by Mr Molotovsky in journals found in safe number 4. It is also recorded, Baron Menshikovsky, that the family tree was examined and because of your parent's dual connection to the two families, your father and mother each a descendant of the Günzburgs and the Menshikovskys were jointly named as the trustees."

"I had no idea that they were designated as trustees," said Isaac, somewhat bewildered. "I don't think they were engaged in the management of the trust or in plans for investments."

"No," said Count Dolgoruky. "I don't think they were in any way involved, other than being told that in their wills they would have to designate one or more beneficiaries. There is nothing in these records to indicate that they were informed of the scale, location or value of the assets. Their role was limited to naming successor trustees with a notation that the time had come to assign the capital and assets to a beneficiary.

"You see, that was possible because before leaving for Moscow in early 1918 your cousin assigned interim trusteeship to the bank. It was under that authority that the bank operated between 1918 and your father's death as the successor of your mother and himself.

"No doubt the bank will have other documentation, but from what I see here the chronology and sequence of trustees are clear. Incidentally, your cousin, actually your mother and father's cousin, was a young man of thirty-five, unmarried, without children, although the records indicate he was engaged to another cousin, a third cousin on the Günzburg side.

"The path of trusteeship and designation of you and your sister is now clearly established in these records as it probably is in the bank's records. It is clear that the bank accepts you as the true heir."

As Will and Isaac walked around the room after the close of the meeting, they each identified many other artifacts not mentioned during the meeting including historic maps and marble portrait busts of exceptional quality.

"Isaac, as we leave this room all is revealed establishing your absolute right to all of the trust assets. We have to meet tomorrow morning to unseal that room on the far wall. Heaven only knows what is in there – leave it until tomorrow. We both have more than enough to ponder from the events today. In the meantime, back to our rooms above us in the palace, to prepare for a special dinner Prince Vorontsov has arranged for us at the Museum of Decorative Arts. It is just a short distance away, let's walk to it."

Isaac nodded assent, fully preoccupied with his own thoughts.

14

UNSEALING THE ROOM which had been hidden for almost one hundred years and which was observed during examination of the strong room and its contents took little time. Molotovsky and sons came prepared with the equipment necessary to do the job. Complying with Will's instructions, the younger son who had photographed and recorded the contents of the strong room by video and photography arrived with devices necessary for those purposes as well.

Isaac was overwhelmed by what he had found in the last two days at the Alexander Palace. His surprise was to be no less so as the adjacent room was unsealed. Will observed that the discovery of the several layers of treasures so far was similar to Lord Carnarvon and his crew discovering room after room sealed with hidden artifacts stored as part of Pharaoh Tutankhamun's tomb in the Valley of the Kings opposite Luxor on the River Nile in Egypt.

The door was opened, revealing absolute darkness. Artificial lighting was required and was promptly brought in with the help of several extension cords. As the lights were brought to shine on the interior, it became clear that the strong room was only an entrance to the much larger chamber beyond.

As the room became illuminated the odour of the long-sealed room spread unpleasantly into the strong room. The witnesses, becoming accustomed to the artificial light, looked eagerly to identify the contents, and Isaac let out an expletive that expressed the reactions silently felt by everyone in the strong room.

Amid the contents of the room, all of which were covered in sheets, there were five chairs mounted on a dais in the middle of the room. The chairs were occupied by desiccated, mummy-like human bodies, each still wearing blindfolds and restraining ropes around their wrists and ankles. The odour to which Isaac responded was familiar to him at his hospital when, as a student, he was required to accompany a pathologist to examine human remains which had been left to decay for an extended period of time.

Dolgoruky spoke first: "This is obviously a crime scene. We must notify the appropriate police authorities before moving anything in this room."

A debate ensued amongst those present, Will taking a contrarian view that calling the police would remove the secrecy and confidentiality necessary to protect Isaac from prying eyes. Unwarranted attention would lead to the contents of both the strong room and this room becoming known to interest groups who would threaten confiscation of Isaac's ownership or planned use of their contents.

Count Vorontsov agreed with Will that secrecy was essential.

Isaac listened to various opinions expressed, many conflicting, even from the same person. Finally, he quietly said to Dolgoruky and Vorontsov that the solution to the mysterious deaths had to be found here in St Petersburg and that he would agree to nothing that would put him in an adversarial position with Russian law or Putin's policies.

Finally, Vorontsov offered a solution. "I have been engaged in numerous archaeological digs that involved the discovery and management of ancient human remains. From what I observe from the way these men are dressed and the state of decomposition and mummification, it is my opinion that these remains have been here for many decades – I would guess they have been here since about the time of the Great War. You will notice that they are wearing clothing typical of the Bolshevik peasant recruits that were formed before the Bolsheviks had achieved supremacy. They remained the principal authority for law and order until the new government was able to establish a more orderly and trained police force. If I am correct, while this is a crime scene, there would be no one alive now to be accountable for the murders.

"I recommend that you permit me to contact my friend and fellow museum director, Kutuzov. I think he would agree with me that this is more an archaeological site than a crime scene. If we take that approach, the bodies would be considered artifacts and would be removed and examined as if they were ancient mummies. That would leave the site intact."

Isaac agreed immediately.

Will added to Isaac's reply that Dr Kutuzov was known to Isaac from their visit to Moscow four years before.

Vorontsov added his comments that whatever arrangement Isaac would wish to make with respect to any of the contents of the palace would necessarily involve Dr Kutuzov and his agreement. The sooner Dr Kutuzov was contacted the better, was Dolgoruky's emphatic advice. He directed Molotovsky not to go further into the room, as he was about to remove a dust sheet nearby, as were his sons. "This room must be treated as an archaeological site and left to experts to examine and document."

It was agreed that one condition would be imposed on Dr Kutuzov. It was that Molotovsky and sons would accompany Kutuzov and his officials as they conducted their examination of the room and its contents. "There will be no interference with or recording of the bodies and their removal," said Dolgoruky. "This must be handled with sensitivity and deferring to the policies and practices of the archaeologists. With a professional approach to the archeological services, we should find them sympathetic to our requests."

It was left to Vorontsov, as one of the most senior museum administrators in the country, to contact Kutuzov who in turn would have to discreetly engage the support of the archeological services.

Isaac had been informed that the process of arranging the next step in examining the treasures held in the Alexander Palace would take a few days. In the meantime, it was agreed that the premises must be made secure. Vorontsov agreed to contact the St Petersburg official responsible for subleasing the site, giving her only enough explanation to justify sealing and securing the building.

* * *

The rest of the day was taken by Isaac and Will exploring the city driving and walking by some of the more significant buildings on the list. They were only faintly aware of their surroundings and spectacular vistas before them. Their thoughts were perhaps focused on the strong rooms at the Alexander Palace.

As they sat in the lobby bar of the hotel next to the Alexander Palace musing about the recent developments in the basement of the palace, Isaac observed that his situation daily grew weirder and more inexplicable. What were the Bolshevik guards or police doing in strong room number two? Will replied that none of what they encountered in the palace in the last day or two made sense. He suggested that an explanation could only be found by obtaining the services and explanation of an historian specializing in the 1917 Russian Revolution and post-revolution history of Russia. Isaac agreed and directed Will to discuss the idea with Dolgoruky and Vorontsov and get their advice on who would be a trustworthy person. They both recognized that the historical connection was also part of giving a proper understanding of the artifacts and the most suitable method of disposing of them considering both Russian interests and his own.

When they returned to their suites at the palace, Isaac was informed that Anna had been trying to reach him for several hours. While both Isaac and Will had cell phones with them during the day, their location in the stone and concrete bunker that was the basement of the palace blocked the signal.

* * *

Isaac left Will immediately, found a location in the palace where he could receive a good mobile phone signal and called Anna, making contact within minutes.

"Isaac, Sophie's problems with her pregnancy have returned. Anastasia and Dr Rayskill are both with her and have completed several tests. They are with Sophie. I was asked not to be there. It must be serious. I think you should return to Moscow as quickly as possible. I haven't asked Sophie... I am telling you what I think you should do."

Isaac readily agreed with his sister's advice. Arrangements were made through Molotovsky to have a private jet hired to take Isaac and Will to Moscow. Within three and half hours of Isaac's conversation with Anna, they were landing in Moscow. Molotovsky accompanied them and made the advance travel arrangements, leaving his sons to monitor security arrangements at the palace.

Isaac's Merc and his principal security guard Frank, with two support staff, took them from the airport to the international medical clinic where Sophie was being treated.

Within minutes of his arrival at the clinic, Isaac was with Sophie and Dr Rayskill. Dr Rayskill gave Isaac a briefing on Sophie's condition, explaining that the symptoms that she had on the way to Moscow had returned in a more serious form. He did not offer a prognosis and Isaac had the presence of mind not to ask for one. He was gently holding Sophie's hand as Dr Rayskill spoke.

Sophie listened intently and when Dr Rayskill paused for breath, she turned to Isaac and said quietly and with little breath that she could feel the baby and that she was feeling much better, to which Isaac replied with a kiss on both cheeks as he rose to leave. While Sophie was distracted by Anastasia taking her blood pressure, Isaac signalled to Dr Rayskill that he would like to meet with him outside the room.

Twenty minutes later Dr Rayskill joined Isaac in a conference room further along the corridor on which Sophie's room was located.

"Ben, I have Will here with me because he may be needed to deal with my sister Anna or to make particular arrangements. So, please tell me what is going on."

"Sophie has internal and external bleeding in and from the uterus. This is very serious. I am afraid of infection. You are well aware of the consequences of an infection in a situation like this. I think the baby is still alright, but I am worried about Sophie's health. She is weakening rapidly. She is six weeks from her due date. It would be safe to remove the baby by Caesarean section, but I worry about whether Sophie is strong enough to endure the surgery."

"Should she be flown to Berlin or London?" asked Isaac.

"No, the changes in air pressure could not be endured... nor could any air turbulence. What we need must be brought to us. I have ordered what I anticipate I will need from my clinic in New York. With the supplies, I have one of my best juniors coming. She has assisted me in some of my most difficult cases. She is particularly effective in diagnosing and treating infection and bleeding. I called for them early this morning. It is now 7 p.m. here in Moscow. I expect them here at the clinic any time now."

"Alright. Now, the most difficult issue we must face. Mother or baby? Is that an issue here, Ben?"

"It could be."

"The mother is the priority, Ben. If possible, save them both, but if a choice has to be made, Sophie must be spared."

"Isaac, I did not raise this issue with Sophie, but she raised it with me this morning while she was quite strong and certainly clear in her analysis and decision. She made her wishes known to me and insisted Anastasia be present to hear them, that if a choice must be made and it is either her or the baby, it must be the baby who survives. She made me swear that I would comply with her wishes."

"We must operate on the assumption that her wishes were expressed before she understood the gravity of her condition. Her instructions may have been different if she knew the real risk she faced. Ben, I will make the decision when I know on the balance of the medical facts who is more likely to survive. I can only hope – and yes, pray – that I am not left with that decision to make."

A nurse arrived and called Dr Rayskill to attend to Sophie. Isaac and Will sat in a state of shock, fearing the worst.

"Isaac, may I discuss this with Anna? I think she should be kept fully informed. She needs to be prepared to be strong for Sophie and to assist Sophie no matter what happens. Anna is the closest female relative available to Sophie. I know Sophie will be comfortable with Anna."

"Yes, Will," said Isaac, "but I am going to leave it to you to talk to Anna. I must do something now I have until recently scoffed at and frankly ridiculed; I am going to pray. And by God, I am going to pray with a commitment and conviction I did not know I had."

"Shall I request Rabbi Levin for you?"

"Yes. Frank has the number."

15

SOPHIE'S CONDITION STABILIZED during the night, giving some comfort to her and reassurance for Isaac that all would be well. He knew from the birth of his first three children that pregnancies and birthing were not as simple and uncomplicated as the over-population of the world would suggest.

He met with Sophie early that morning, leaving it to her to select what she would choose to talk about. Isaac had been warned by Dr Rayskill that the ultimate decision he and Isaac discussed yesterday should not be raised unless Sophie herself chose to raise it. During their time together there was no talk of illness or threat to the baby. Sophie was exceptionally animated and ebullient, uncharacteristically so. This worried Isaac. He had observed similar behaviour in patients, usually pre-surgery, who while in denial as to their medical situation, appeared to have an adrenalin rush almost to the point of hysteria. There was nothing negative in her conversation, nor was it forced in any way; it was simply a voluble stream of babble from an anxious mother-to-be.

By noon Sophie had tired of Isaac's company and decided she would like to rest that afternoon. "Isaac," she said, "the time has come for you to move on to your projects. It was a great comfort to have you with me, but your endless chatter has tired me. You need something to occupy your time. As I remember, you were in St Petersburg a couple of days ago; nice of you to come back to see me, but as you can see, it wasn't necessary. Anna is taking excellent care of me. In fact, we have become very good friends which makes me happy. I want my children to know their immediate family and to have them as an active part of their lives. Anna will be as great an aunt to the baby as she is now to Little Isaac. I'm almost jealous, though, that Little Isaac isn't missing me much because Anna is occupying his time so well. Now, enough of your chatter, go… I will be interested to hear all about your discoveries later. I shall be incarcerated here in this bed for the next couple of days at least so there is nothing for you to do here. Just call me occasionally on your cell phone – wonderful gadget, I must learn to use one."

Ben met Isaac outside Sophie's room and replied to Isaac's concern about Sophie's uncharacteristic behaviour. "This is common among patients who appear to have avoided a medical disaster. It is a combination of relief, happiness and suppressed anxiety coming out as excessive euphoria but she is deliberately not dealing with the continuing medical crisis she is having."

"Is she really any better? Is the baby out of danger?" asked Isaac with more concern than Sophie had expressed.

"The vital signs for mother and baby are much better today than yesterday. That is positive, but I have to caution you that we have not identified the cause of the crisis yesterday – we know the symptoms, but not the cause. Sophie has told you to carry on with whatever it was that took you to St Petersburg. If you haven't finished with that work, I suggest you return and get back to it. Call me two or three times a day; that will be enough for now. Remember, at this stage in her pregnancy, particularly given the trauma she faced in Smolensk and the medical problems since leaving there, she is in her own world of fighting for survival for herself and her baby. She simply needs to know you are emotionally with her at all times and available to come to her here at the clinic if necessary. I will keep you updated on events here. Incidentally, I have taken a two-month leave of absence from my clinic in New York. I will be on full-time attendance on Sophie for that period of time. Go and do what you must in St Petersburg. I would like to visit it sometime."

* * *

Molotovsky had followed Will's instructions to have the rented private jet on long-term lease and ready to take Isaac and his family where and when required. The jet was ready for Isaac, Will, Molotovsky and Frank when they got to the Moscow airport used for government officials and those who receive VIP access to the facilities there. This included Isaac as a result of arrangements made by Vorontsov with the cooperation of Kutuzov.

On arrival in St Petersburg, Isaac and his party were taken to the Museum of Decorative and Applied Arts, where they met with Vorontsov and Dolgoruky and others invited by them to meet with Isaac.

The others included the historian who had been engaged earlier to provide genealogical and historical information for Isaac's family and generally the Jewish community in Russia. Dr Kutuzov and his deputy director Dr Antonov were welcome additions to the meeting, as they enthusiastically demonstrated for Isaac and Will customary Russian bear hugs which almost dislocated their spines.

Dr Vorontsov took control of the meeting, welcoming each guest to his facility, the Museum of Decorative and Applied Arts. He gave a brief history of the facility which proved to be useful background to Isaac's research.

"This facility was created from a private collection of paintings, sculptures, drawings and expressions of Russian applied arts. The collector was a leading member of the Russian Jewish community in the nineteenth century.

"I refer to Ludwig van Stieglitz, who was the founder of Stieglitz and Company which became one of the most important Russian banks by the middle of the nineteenth century. His fortune was assembled beginning with the Napoleonic invasion of Russia when he acquired and financed a substantial part of the military material required by Czar Alexander I, who came to rely on Stieglitz as one of his most trusted advisers. The relationship reached its high point when Czar Alexander appointed Stieglitz as court banker and subsequently ennobled him as Baron Stieglitz, one of the very few Jews to be ennobled in Russia. In 1878 Baron Stieglitz founded our facility's predecessor, the School of Technical Design. It proved to be instrumental in the fostering and recognition of the distinctive Russian excellence in the decorative arts; for example, in the West that excellence is expressed in the late nineteenth-century work of the Fabergé factories. Then, between 1885 and 1895, the baron constructed this exceptional architectural monument to the arts and donated from his collection the core of what was to become an institution or museum of world-class significance. The museum was built by Baron Stieglitz with his own money and the transfer of his collection was a gift to the nation. Baron Menshikovsky, you will see considerable similarities to your family history here in Russia.

"I should add that the Stieglitz Bank went into voluntary liquidation in 1863 and formed the nucleus of the newly created State Bank of the Russian Empire. Baron Stieglitz's son Alexander, who incidentally succeeded his father in the title, became the head of the State Bank in 1860."

Turning to the historian, Will asked what had been a primary question discussed frequently by Isaac and Will. "Why did the Günzburg and Menshikovsky banks survive the formation of the state bank?"

The answer from Dolgoruky surprised Isaac. "Simply because the two banks you refer to operated as private banks serving very rich, influential and financially needy clients, including the Imperial Government. I should add that the formation of the State Bank had been discussed for several years before it happened. Your ancestors responded in a typically brilliant fashion: they had identified themselves as branches of the international Mendelssohn Bank with its headquarters in Berlin. This, it turns out, was something of a sham, as the Günzburg and Menshikovsky banks each maintained a separate legal status. Now, the most effective aspect of your family's response to the creation of the State Bank.

"Both banks, through a series of secret holding companies and trusts, were actually incorporated in Switzerland and were recognized in Russia as foreign banks. During this period, for example, several English and French banks operated in Russia quite freely. They were permitted to operate as independent banks because it was in the best interests of the Russian government to have most of its loans made to it by foreign banks which at that time could be held as secret transactions; thereby disguising the level of the Imperial Government's debt. This was particularly important during the disastrous Russo-Japanese War of 1905 which left the government virtually insolvent. That situation became eventually worse of course with the Great War."

At this point Vorontsov took over: "Your family hid in open view, but no one knew or cared about the actual ownership and control of your banks. You should know, Baron, that not one artifact in this museum is not yours. I know there are some of your artifacts in other Russian institutions, but having examined the inventory carefully, I can tell you that the loans were highly strategic – made to satisfy the Imperial and Soviet governments that your holdings were maintained in a form that was in the best interests of the government of the day – and just enough – to make the government beholden to your family."

"Why," asked Will, "weren't the numerous and highly important artifacts nationalized?"

Dolgoruky answered: "The ownership was spread over numerous apparent owners. No one in Moscow or St Petersburg had a composite, comprehensive list of the Baron's family's assets. The bits they would have identified, by my estimation, included at least 250 separate apparent owners, all of whom were foreign companies or trusts and all of which were ultimately controlled by your family. The governments of the day could not afford to alienate those foreign investors such as your family who skillfully continued to finance the government in a way that could be kept hidden from scrutiny."

Vorontsov added: "The amazing artifacts we observed at the Alexander Palace and those you have viewed since arriving in Russia were mostly purchased during the turmoil and desperate need for money by the nobility and both the Imperial and the Bolshevik governments during the Revolutionary and post-Revolutionary period. Why didn't Lenin or Stalin shut you down? First, they had no idea of the scale of debt held by your family and, more importantly, the credibility of their governments rested on efficient fiscal management. At no time could either of them admit or disclose the true level of debt their governments carried. They had to propagandize the Communist system of government as the most efficient and effective, and one that as a socialist form of government most effectively provided for the needs of the people."

Molotovsky then spoke up to comment, "The artifacts were almost all acquired during the historical period you referred to, Dr Vorontsov. But where did the cash come from? By answering that question I disclose the single most brilliant aspect of the functioning of the trust created by your family's banks – all revenues received from properties and investments in Russia, including loan payments made by both the Imperial and the Soviet governments, were paid over to the Swiss banks, going first through the Warsaw branches of the banks and then to a central clearing house in Berlin, from which the money was transferred to the Berlin branch of the Swiss bank. All neat and tidy and, at that time, untraceable. As an example of why it was untraceable, there was a trust that ultimately owned both banks. That trust, Mr MacIntosh, was domiciled in Charlottetown, Prince Edward Island. Not a penny of the bank's money or any of its assets were transferred there. It was a paper trail. One of the documents we found in the fourth safe was a detailed ledger showing the paper trail through Prince Edward Island. I am not sure why that place was chosen but I am certain Mr MacIntosh could tell us.

"It was with the money in the Swiss bank in Berlin that the purchase of virtually all of the artifacts was made. The money necessary for the purchases was forwarded through various channels to companies in Russia owned by the Günzburg, Menshikovsky or Mendelssohn families. Fascinating, yes, but that is not what is most important at the moment. We must get back to the contents of the Alexander Palace."

Vorontsov circulated three memoranda to each of those attending the meeting. It was agreed that the meeting would be adjourned for the day to give each person a chance to read them. The meeting would resume the next day promptly at 9 a.m., Will announced.

16

BOTH ISAAC AND Will were exhausted physically and emotionally by the events to which they had been subjected since their arrival in Smolensk. It had been only six weeks since they had entered the grounds of the dacha outside Smolensk. They had learned a great deal about the origins of the trust to which Isaac became the ultimate beneficiary. They had also become targets for those who envied and avariciously coveted Isaac's inheritance. His initial response had been to reject the burden the trust had created for him. He wished to renounce the gift the assignment made by his father had created. That, he thought, might end the troubles and problems the inheritance created. The problems far exceeded even what he imagined when he started the journey to investigate what he had fallen heir to. What affected him personally also endangered his pregnant wife and their son. He was also becoming increasingly worried about exposing his friend, confidant, and trusted ally Will MacIntosh to harm.

Isaac identified with descriptions given by swimmers who almost had drowned in rough seas. His life flashed by repeatedly before him. As he had these flashbacks he tried to identify where he must have gone wrong in his efforts to control the endless barrage of attacks against him and those close to him. His most pressing worry was for his wife who should be in a secure natal unit in London or New York. He had the connections to put her in the best facilities with the most accomplished specialists, yet he consistently found himself powerless.

Will recognized the signs of distress and anxiety Isaac demonstrated. He tried his best to shelter his friend but the forces against Isaac and those associated with him were overwhelming and beyond any experiences Will had in the past which could assist him and Isaac.

They were standing in front of the Museum of Decorative and Applied Arts on the bank of the Fontanka River, close to where it joined the Neva River. As they viewed the museum Will suggested they take a walking tour along the banks of the Neva to view the Strogonov Palace and the Kazan Cathedral among other celebrated architectural wonders of St Petersburg.

Isaac's reply to this suggestion was less appreciative and accepting than Will had hoped. Isaac made it clear with some considerable vocal force that he was not in the mood for a lecture on any topic, let alone on architecture. Somewhat mollified, Will suggested as an alternative that they simply take a walk along the Neva to the Winter Palace and back to the museum along the Fontanka River assuring Isaac that the sole topic of conversation would be the weather. Isaac agreed to this proposal.

The walk, a quiet, non-challenging stroll was what they both needed. As they were about to set off, Frank and one of the auxiliary security guards joined them and they agreed to accompany them.

The early morning sun, even on a cold November day, caught and highlighted the magnificence of the neoclassicism of the buildings, the bridges and the street and riverscapes. November usually brings winter to St Petersburg with bitter cold and blowing snow. On this morning, however, they were fortunate to have some warmth available from the still air.

From time to time Isaac casually examined a map Will had given him but he demonstrated no interest in questioning the connections between the maps and what he was viewing. Will offered no interruptions, noticing that Isaac was showing signs of being somewhat more relaxed and apparently happy.

As the foursome passed in front of the Stroganov Palace, Will couldn't resist the comment that the Alexander Palace and the Strogonov were remarkably similar.

Isaac was about to reply, his mouth open and poised for a negative reaction, when a series of rapid-fire shots whisked past them. Frank immediately tackled Isaac and the auxiliary guard felled Will. Both guards were armed and took their handguns out, but the shooters were unimpressed. After all, they were firing from Kalashnikov guns, against which the handguns offered little protection.

The auxiliary, with one leg over Will and the other leg giving him support for his arm firing the hand gun, took a couple of bullets to his free arm but stood his protective stance over Will. Frank redoubled his efforts to protect Isaac, lying him face down and trying to serve as the target.

The bullets kept coming for what seemed to be an eternity. They then stopped as suddenly as they had started. The reason became apparent when a police patrol of more than fifteen sharpshooters arrived and started returning fire. Two of the policemen came to Isaac and Will and in English explained that they had been commissioned to offer security protection to them.

Isaac was too much in shock to offer thanks which were extended by Will. The reason for Isaac's silence and his state of shock became clear when large red patches spread across his chest through his winter clothing.

An ambulance and additional police protection arrived momentarily. They provided shelter as Isaac and the auxiliary were transported by ambulance to a hospital nearby. While the foursome was on their way to the hospital, Will called Dolgoruky on his cell phone and briefed him on the attack. Dolgoruky said he would take control of the rescue and would secure medical attention.

Isaac and the auxiliary were transferred to an ambulance and were taken with Will and Frank to a hospital which they were assured was safe and secure.

When they arrived at the hospital, located a short distance from the museum, both Vorontsov and Dolgoruky were there to meet them. Isaac was in critical condition from a substantial loss of blood. The wounds sustained by the auxiliary were superficial.

Will remembered that Isaac was to call Sophie at least three times a day to comfort her. Isaac was obviously in no condition to speak to her. Will took Isaac's mobile phone and he put a call through to Sophie. As quietly and as calmly as he could muster, Will told Sophie that Isaac had had a minor slip and fall during a walk that morning that required a brace to be applied to his right leg – "Otherwise he's okay, Sophie. He will be furious with himself, but you know with his extra weight he is awkward and prone to trip, usually over himself."

Will was relieved when Sophie accepted the lie and she simply laughed at Will's comment. She asked Will to pass on her message to Isaac that she was well and she expected to get out for a walk later that afternoon. Before ringing off, Will asked her to have Dr Rayskill call him as soon as possible as an issue had risen relating to his passport. She accepted this story as well and she assured Will she would pass on the message.

Will had no time to regret the series of lies he was telling Sophie before the phone rang, with Ben Rayskill on the other end. Will informed him of the actual details of the incident. To Ben's obvious concern for Isaac, Will could only reply that Isaac was receiving blood transfusions and that his condition remained critical. He quickly informed Ben of the lies he had told Sophie to try to protect her. Ben agreed it was the correct thing to do and that Will should leave it to him to inform her of Isaac's injuries. He strongly recommended that Isaac be moved to the international clinic in Moscow where Sophie was receiving treatment. He would deal with the American Ambassador, requesting the transfer. He assured Will that Sophie would not be permitted to leave the clinic and he would alert the security guards on duty to redouble their protective measures.

When Will arrived at the emergency department at the clinic, he was informed that the transfusions seemed to be improving Isaac's condition: he remained in a critical condition and in an induced coma but his vital signs were improving.

Dolgoruky was a great help to Will in dealing with the hospital and police authorities. A room was found for him to spend the night at the clinic in case he was needed. As he stood outside the room assigned to him, Will asked Dolgoruky whether the meeting could reconvene the next day if Isaac was up to it. A ruse, another lie, Will thought, could be fabricated to explain Isaac's absence. Will explained that it was becoming abundantly clear to him that Isaac, Sophie, Anna and he should return to New York as soon as possible, so the time he had in St Petersburg should be used as productively as possible. Dolgoruky agreed and he assured Will that arrangements would be made for the next day at 9 a.m. depending on Isaac being well enough to attend. He would be met by an armoured vehicle driven by a reliable security guard. Frank, he was told, would be with him. Isaac was surrounded now by enough guards to repel even a Napoleon.

After he took possession of the hospital room assigned to him, Will called Anna. She must be told the truth; not only was she Isaac's sister, she had become Sophie's closest companion and confidante. She might be called on by Dr Rayskill to help if he had to tell Sophie the truth – particularly if it was bad news.

"Anna, a difficult situation has arisen here in St Petersburg," stated Will. "I have to ask you to listen quietly and not repeat what I am telling you as Isaac has again been physically attacked. This afternoon, during a simple walk along the Neva River in St Petersburg, we were ambushed by a group of attackers armed with machine guns. I was only grazed on my arm. That was nothing. Our auxiliary was hit twice. He is being treated. It was a serious attack… yes, Isaac was hit… I didn't tell you straight away as I wanted to warn you how serious the situation was. Yes, he was hit. Yes, he is alive but in critical condition. They have put him in an induced coma. He is receiving competent medical attention in a secure hospital.

"I am sharing this with you because you should know, of course, but I have lied to Sophie, telling her Isaac sprained an ankle and he was unable to call her. She will be asking where he is tomorrow morning. We must get our stories straight. Dr Rayskill knows the truth; he will help you deal with Sophie. You are completely safe where you are, but you must not, I repeat, must not leave the clinic for any reason unless I, and only I, tell you it is okay and I tell you where you are safe to go. Do you agree to accept my advice?"

There was an extended pause in the conversation while

Anna tried to regain her composure. Her weeping and strangled breathing caused an unaccustomed bout of tears from Will. He suddenly realized that he had been repressing the emotional trauma the journeys with Isaac had brought them both. He also realized that his emotions were also intensified because of the emotional attachment he and Anna were developing for each other.

When Anna regained sufficient composure to speak, she assured Will that she would follow his advice and she thanked him for his unstinting help to her, Isaac and Sophie. Before hanging up, Anna said quietly: "Will, I share your feelings. I hope we have the chance to fully be together. I have always loved you since you visited Isaac at home, when you were both attending Dalhousie University. I now know that the paths I took were stupid and wrong. Dad always told me so. But perhaps we will have time now."

17

WILL, ISAAC, FRANK and the auxiliary bodyguard were transferred to the clinic in Moscow the following morning. Almost at once Will, only just settled in his new hospital room, met with the GRU Chief Investigating Officer Nicholas Golovine. Golovine's stated purpose was to investigate the shootings in St Petersburg which he termed an "assassination attempt." His knowledge, not only of the incident itself but also of Isaac's reasons for being in Russia and the attempts on his life and assets over the past four years, was remarkable. It was as if he had been present at each event and knew the details and their outcome.

After making appropriate inquiries about Isaac's condition as well as Sophie's, Golovine was about to move forward with his interview when Will informed him how his friends Isaac and Frank were that morning. Golovine was far better informed at that moment than was Will. Inspector Golovine rose to his full five foot five inches and through foggy glasses he informed Will that Dr Menshive remained on the critical list but was expected to survive. Isaac's wife, he said, remained unaware of Isaac's shooting and treatment at the clinic; however, she appeared to be in good spirits and was looking forward, she said to the inspector, to seeing Isaac when he returned from St Petersburg.

Will was apprehensive of the GRU's involvement in Isaac's affairs. Golovine assured Will that the Russian national police and security services were well aware of Isaac's reasons for being in the country and that they were under instructions to assist in his protection and security. He assured Will that there was no hostile or threatening interest by Russian authorities in Isaac's investigation of his holdings in Russia; in fact, he said, it was recognized that it was in the best interests of Putin's (the 'National') government to protect Isaac and those travelling with him. It was known that Isaac wished to make substantial transfers of his holdings to the people of Russia.

Restraint on Will's part prevented him from pointing out that those same police and security forces had failed Isaac in St Petersburg and in Smolensk on his tour of the country. He managed a wry thanks and encouraged Golovine to continue his investigation with the security services, but he had little confidence that anything useful would come of the GRU's promised role.

Golovine informed Will that preliminary investigations suggested that one or more of the Russian hooligans known, he said, "In the West as 'oligarchs'," were behind the shootings. When Will twitched with a muscle spasm and pain from the wound he received during the shootings, Golovine excused himself for failing to inquire about Will's condition after the shooting.

Will replied that it was a glancing shot or two to his right leg and it had been well treated at the clinic. He was well enough, he assured Golovine, to continue the investigation Isaac and he had conducted on this trip to Russia. Golovine smiled dismissively and carried on with the results of the GRU investigation: "Yes, Russian hooligans. We think we can identify one or two who may have been involved but it is too early in our investigation to reveal who we think they may be. We don't want to identify people who may not be the villains. I am sure you understand."

Will agreed politely and he assured Golovine that he would have the cooperation of Isaac's team and his security unit identifying Frank as the contact person for the GRU investigation.

The interview concluded as it began, as a pro forma routine visit that would be recorded in the public records of the GRU in the most flattering terms to the GRU. Will was left knowing that the investigation and identification of the shooters would be left to Frank and his team.

As Golovine left Will's hospital room, Frank entered. He informed Will that Isaac and Sophie had exceptionally tight security which was being provided by Frank and his team and which was now augmented by a security team consisting of two senior investigators from both the German and Israeli security forces. To the extent that Isaac and Sophie's safety could be protected, Will was satisfied that all that could be done was being done.

Will informed Frank that he was returning that morning to St Petersburg to continue the exploration of the Alexander Palace and to investigate the assets there and the shootings. He arranged for Frank to remain with Isaac and Sophie, with the caveat that he was also to provide security for Anna and Little Isaac. Frank gave Will the assurances he was looking for and he committed to providing Will with his own security detail which would be comprised of Gus Trombley, head of the American security team who had been engaged four years before to lead the North American security unit and who had been flown in last night from New York. He would be joined by one of the security detail who had been with Isaac since they arrived in Smolensk.

The well-oiled hinges on Will's hospital room door then admitted two familiar faces: Pavel Ushakov, who had been the long-term legal adviser to the Swiss bank in its administration of the Menshikovsky trust assets, and Sergei, the majordomo employed at the dacha in Smolensk. A somewhat unusual combination at this time, perhaps, thought Will; however, he knew Ushakov had effective connections with the appropriate Russian authorities in keeping the trust assets safely in Isaac's possession. Will was so trusted by Isaac that Isaac had put him on the board of directors of Isaac's new holding company Menshive International Holdings Inc., technically owned by the Canadian trust to obscure the actual ownership by Isaac. It was in that name that the current management of all of Isaac's assets received from the Swiss trust was conducted.

Sergei, the majordomo, was called to be part of the current operational team as his loyalty had been tested and proven during the episodes earlier in Smolensk. Sergei had also established an excellent sense of Russian attitudes, behaviours and opinions on a wide range of topics of importance to Isaac and Will. He would serve as a confidant and sounding-board for Will while the latter remained in Russia. Will trusted the advice he had received so far from Dolgoruky and Vorontsov but he had deep-seated lingering worries about both of them.

Those worries coloured his interaction with both Dolgoruky and Vorontsov. Underlying those worries was the unanswered question: how had two members of the Imperial nobility managed to survive Bolshevism, Stalin, Khrushchev and Putin? What they were, what they represented, were the antithesis of what Lenin and his successors espoused both privately and in the policies followed by their governments. Will kept asking himself, "Have they been compromised? Are they truly on Isaac's side? Could they be the tools of those who oppose Isaac?"

There was no immediate answer to these questions, but until he had satisfactory answers he would continue to deal with them with caution but apparent candour. He hoped that Sergei and Ushakov would assist him in reading them correctly. The more dealings he had with Russians, and by now he had had many encounters with Russians of all walks of life, the less he trusted his assessment of the character and motives of those he met. Not only did Russians avoid smiling, they avoided any interaction that one could interpret as friendship and reliability. "Just as they avoid humour, which invokes a personal connection with another person, that profound reserve seems to lead to a fundamental falsehood in their interaction with others – particularly non-Russians."

Frank and his security detail, together with Ushakov and Sergei, would remain with Will for the balance of his stay in Russia. As Will moved from pillar to post in his tasks, each of those individuals formed a tightly knit team and operated as a unit advising Will and dutifully following his instructions.

So it was when Molotovsky entered the hospital room. At this point, it was standing room only. Will asked him whether there was any further information on the shootings. He was informed there was not and gave his opinion that there had to be an insider leak of information on Isaac's movements in St Petersburg. That was the only way, he surmised, that the shooters could have been ready for action as Isaac walked along the Neva River embankment only moments after deciding to go for the walk.

Frank agreed with Molotovsky, and he added that technology could be a source of information. The only way an insider could have communicated so quickly was by cell phone. He suggested that everyone present before the walk had begun give their mobile devices to Frank to check their records for the particular time. Will asked him to include both Dolgoruky and Vorontsov.

Sergei and Ushakov rejected this idea immediately.

"Why not? After all, they must establish their bona fides, too!" said Will.

"No, sir," said Ushakov, "they would both find the request demeaning, rude and hostile to their dignity. Russians live on dignity, particularly those of the former Imperial nobility. We have many survivors of that class in modern Russia. They hide their backgrounds as best they can but the authorities know who they are. They are scarcely tolerated and when they come into contact with politicians, the police or other authorities they are suspect and dismissed as unreliable in terms of the standards of modern Russia." Sergei agreed and he added that even something as reasonable as Will's request might appear to be, the request for their mobile phones or other equipment capable of rapid electronic connections could turn them against Isaac.

"Mr MacIntosh, you need Mr Vorontsov and Mr Dolgoruky on your side. Treat them with caution, but don't alienate them," was Sergei's advice.

Will responded: "Well, if they are so suspect in the eyes of the current government, why are they permitted to hold such high offices?"

"Simply because," offered Molotovsky, "they represent cultural superiority and an elevated level of courtesy and dignity that ordinary Russians could not present – particularly to foreigners. Their roles are not only involved in dealing with other Russians in esoteric fields like culture, museums and management of national treasures, they also have to deal with foreign governments or their equivalents in similar cultural institutions in London, Paris and New York, for example. They present a face of Russia only they and their type can offer. We need them, but don't really accept them as part of modern Russia."

Will listened carefully and understood that he now had the answers he had looked for, but he asked one more question, "Can they be trusted? You saw Vorontsov's covetous reaction to seeing some of his family's jewellery on display at the Alexander Palace."

"We won't know whether they can be trusted until we can fully test them and observe their behaviour and the actions they take supporting you as we move forward with the investigation."

Turning to Molotovsky, Will requested him to arrange a resumption of the meeting with Dolgoruky and Vorontsov that afternoon. "Please ask them to join us at the Alexander Palace. We know it has been checked for surveillance equipment. It will be the most secure location available to us for our meeting in St Petersburg. Before we leave for the airport I need to have half an hour to meet with Mrs Menshive and her sister-in-law."

The hospital room visit with Sophie reassured Will that she was being well cared for and she appeared to be in good health — certainly she said she was. She asked where Isaac was, to which Will, with a little white lie (he said to himself) told her that he was still in St Petersburg receiving treatments from a physiotherapist for his strained ankle. He continued the tale by adding that Isaac was unable to call because the mobile phone service in the building where he was receiving his treatments blocked mobile service. Sophie was content to accept Will's story. Anna, who was in the room with Will and Sophie, said she had received a text message from Isaac sent from a different location by one of the security guards with him. The message included directions to Anna to pass on affectionate greetings on his behalf to Sophie.

From Sophie's room, Will walked to the end of the corridor on which her room was situated to the room occupied by Isaac. Two physicians, including Isaac's New York family doctor, were present with him. The family doctor, Dr Philip MacGregor, had been flown in overnight at Will's request. His birthplace of Glasgow, Scotland was evident in every syllable, vowel and consonant he spoke. Dr MacGregor informed Will that he had no reason to believe that Isaac would not fully recover, although the two bullets to his chest were close to the sites of the bullets he had taken four years before in Russia. Will was assured that he would not be needed in Moscow for a day or two and that MacGregor would keep him informed of any developments in Isaac's condition.

Greatly relieved, Will joined his group and headed to the airport, where on schedule the private jet took off for St Petersburg.

* * *

On the flight to St Petersburg Will had the first distraction-free opportunity to consider his situation. He had become the personal caregiver and decision-maker for both Sophie and Isaac under agreements signed in New York before leaving for Smolensk a few weeks ago. It didn't occur to Will, Isaac or Sophie that Will would now also become their legal guardian, for both their persons as well as their assets. His responsibilities were further compounded by becoming the legal guardian for Little Isaac as well. The cumulative effect of which was that he was the sole decision-maker for the whole family, including the investigations Isaac had been undertaking in the last few weeks; he was now accountable to both Isaac and Sophie for any decisions he made.

Decisions that had been made with, or on behalf of, Isaac during the past four years had been made by Will in consultation with Isaac after an issue was thoroughly discussed with him and a mutual decision was made on the next course of action. That had changed dramatically. He was on his own.

What would be Isaac's physical and mental condition after this last shooting? What decisions would he have to make for Sophie? The answer to these questions would be his even if reached only after consulting their medical providers. His vulnerability to legal accountability in a court of law was weighing heavily on his mind.

Will kept a thorough ongoing journal recording the events of each day, the issues that arose, and the process of reaching decisions. All decisions would have to be made on the day on which the events occurred. Will's legal training came to the fore to assist him in his planning. In Canada and England, documents were admissible as proof of the evidence of the events, if the documents were recorded by that person on the day on which the events occurred and decisions made. The journal had been started and would have to be continued. Where would he find time to do this clerical work on top of all his other responsibilities?

Should he have someone accompany him every day to make the primary record, to which he would add his own observations at the end of the day confirming or altering what the primary recorder had prepared?

The question, then, was obvious; the answer, not obvious. Who could he engage to be the primary recorder who would be impartial, have both Isaac's and Sophie's best interests at heart and who could be reliable to give him the time necessary to carry out the tasks involved? That person or someone else would have to record all decisions made with respect to Little Isaac as well.

Could he identify anyone among the team in Russia or near at hand in Europe who could be engaged for one or both purposes? That person would have to be in Russia with him. The only person who could fit the requirements was Isaac's sister Anna.

Anna brought with her considerable baggage, however. It was through Anna that Anthony Cann had discovered the Swiss trust administered by her parents and an indication of the nature, location and extent of the assets. She might be a witness in future legal issues, probably of a criminal nature in New York related to Cann. It was possible that Cann may have been involved through surrogates not only in the Smolensk incidents but also in the shootings in St Petersburg. Also, Will was aware that Anna had quickly rejected any responsibility for the trust or the assets by transferring her interest in them quickly as one could to Isaac.

Would Anna be a sensible choice? Even if she said yes, would she prove to be more trouble than a solution?

The two-hour flight to St Petersburg involved more emotional turmoil for Will than the exceptionally turbulent flight.

By the time he was greeted by Dolgoruky and Ushakov he had made his decision, but one he had to discuss in the abstract with the two lawyers seeking their advice and guidance.

On the drive into St Petersburg, Will explained to Molotovsky that he needed a period of rest at the Alexander Palace before convening the meeting that afternoon. The meeting would have to be postponed by thirty or forty minutes, but the issues facing him were more important and had to be resolved. In fact, he knew he could only hold the meeting when he had made his final decision.

During his 'rest period', he met with Ushakov and Dolgoruky. This was a confidential arrangement and had not been disclosed to anyone else but them. Will agreed with Molotovsky that advance insider information had been necessary as to Isaac's intended route along the Neva River embankment.

He did not know who he could trust. He decided that the least likely to betray him and Isaac would be the two lawyers. He felt he had tested them both during earlier meetings and he would now have to rely on his assessment of their characters.

The planned half-hour meeting lasted a full two hours as a result of the intensive discussions the three lawyers had as they considered all the factors related to maintaining the journal.

Anna Menshive would be requested to serve as Will's recording secretary and advisor on all personal issues relating to her brother, sister-in-law and nephew. The lawyers would serve as primary recorders for all other events. Will requested Ushakov to brief Anna on the seriousness and legal implications with respect to the services she was being asked to provide.

That role had to be performed by someone like Anna who was independent without a vested interest in the assets. Will and Anna had been much more than acquaintances many years before when Will would visit Isaac in New York during semester breaks at the university they attended in Halifax, Nova Scotia. Their relationship had recently been renewed but Will realized he now had to distance himself from that connection as well so that Anna would appear to be an objective arms-length recorder of events. It was left that Ushakov would serve that role of informing Anna of the additional role she was to take.

* * *

Will convened the meeting just before two o'clock after the conviviality of a shared lunch had eased the tension in the room. Everyone present was aware of what had occurred on the Neva embankment and that an insider must have been responsible for the tip-off.

The first order of business was for Will to announce that until Isaac's health enabled him to resume control of his person and his assets, Will would do so holding the unrestricted legal right to make such decisions and to issue such directives as might be required – that, he said, extended to entering into written agreements. He assured his guests that he and Isaac had discussed all of the issues over an extended period of time and he was therefore well aware of what decisions Isaac would likely make. Will concluded his remarks by assuring those present that he did not stand to personally benefit in any way from any decisions he would make. He would be acting as guardian and trustee for Isaac. He was legally prohibited by New York law from personally benefiting from his role. He managed to get a polite laugh from the guests by informing them that any misbehaviour on his part would result in an extended stay in a New York upstate penitentiary that had fewer benefits than the Alexander Palace.

The balance of the day, which extended into the early evening, involved the creation of several separate groups that would consider each classification of asset Isaac held in Russia. It was fortunate that the only cash on deposit in Russia available to Isaac had less than $5,000 U.S. dollars in it. "Cash is not on the agenda and will not be, except to the extent that a transfer of an asset or group of assets will result in an exchange of title documents for cash. If so, let me be clear," Will said, "that money would be paid in U.S. dollars and would be transferred immediately by a U.S. bank having a branch in Russia to an account in New York."

Numerous preliminary discussions and meetings had been held over the past four years relating to each group of assets. It was known to each representative of the Putin government what was on the inventory for the group of assets to which each was the representative.

Will reminded the guests that there had been full and open disclosure of all assets located in Russia that were known at that time. He stated that it was now time for each group representing a category of assets to meet and to prepare a proposal for distribution of the assets.

"Dr Menshive has made it abundantly clear," said Will, starting the meeting, "that he is prepared to release his interest in many of the assets in exchange for a reliable benefit to him. He does not need or expect an equalization by value, but does expect fairness and goodwill.

"Note, you are not working in your own vacuum here, however. Many of the assets located in Russia will be of interest to other governments which will require your government's resolution of predictable conflicts relating to them. As an example, I refer to the fabulous collection of Scythian gold artifacts that will be claimed by Russia, Ukraine, Bulgaria, Turkey and perhaps Greece. Dr Menshive will not interfere in what bilateral agreements are made, but he expects goodwill, good faith and generosity to prevail. Similar issues may arise with respect to the decorative arts as well as the former property of the nobility sold during or after the Revolution to generate capital to enable them to finance their escape from

Russia. I repeat, all competing claims are to be resolved by you, the principal representatives of the institutions having responsibility for Russian national interests in the various categories of assets. Dr Menshive expects to simply sign off, take what is to remain his and leave quietly without any further involvement with the authorities in this country or any other that may be involved.

"I am available to each of you should you wish to consult with me on behalf of Dr Menshive in undertaking the process."

After extensive discussions, mostly of a procedural nature, the meeting adjourned. Will joined Dolgoruky, Vorontsov and Kutuzov at a private dinner arranged for them at the Museum of Decorative and Applied Arts further up the Fontanka River from the Alexander Palace where the meetings had been.

Before Will joined his hosts in the museum's private dining room he called Anna for a report on the patients. She gave him a detailed account that gave him comfort that the family members were being well cared for and that Anna was capable of intelligent and focused conversation. It was at that point that Will made his final decision to ask Anna to serve as his personal assistant and recording secretary relating to Sophie and Little Isaac. He realized earlier that these formal terms were necessary in establishing their new relationship to ensure the arms-length objectivity necessary for the relationship to work effectively. Before Will could hang up, he was required to listen for over half an hour to Anna describing the wonders and perfections of her nephew, 'Little Isaac'. She was certain that never had humanity created such a phenomenon.

The dinner was served with the protocols and standards of service Will had read about describing formal dinners in Imperial Russia. He enjoyed the elegance and dignity of the event. He also contrasted it with the barbarity, crassness and violence of the Putin government. The more he observed of Russia in the twenty-first century, the more he realized there were in fact several types of Russians, becoming aware of the disparities and contrasts in their social standards.

During the dinner, both Dolgoruky and Vorontsov floated

an idea that they had discussed with Kutuzov who could not remain longer than for pre-dinner drinks. They suggested the possibility of the creation of two museums formed out of the principal artifacts in the collection. One would be in Moscow and named after the Menshikovsky family which would have a focus on Russian Jewish craftsmanship, accomplishments in the arts and in collecting. The other, they suggested, would be an international foundation that would establish a similar museum focused on European Jewry. They suggested that an appropriate location could be found for it in Central Europe where it could attract the growing members of cultural tourists.

Will's response was cautiously positive, but he expressed skepticism that Russia and other countries in that region would be able to agree on a location.

Dr Vorontsov offered the suggestion that Isaac would have to be called on to make that final decision and that his decision would be a precondition to all other settlements. Will agreed to the concept but he emphasized that for the foreseeable future he had the sole authority to make decisions. He privately continued his reservation that an agreement on location could be made.

"Mr MacIntosh, the international museum would serve as a reminder to all nations in Europe and the Americas as to the formative role Jews had in the cultural achievements of modern Europe."

18

AN EARLY MORNING call to Anna the next day alerted Will to a change in the situation at the clinic in Moscow. She reported that Isaac had emerged from the coma into which he had been induced to enable his body to recover from the several blood transfusions, shock and the trauma of the bullet wounds. "Enough time," she said, "to enable Isaac to gradually adjust to the shooting and his serious injuries, particularly since this was a repeat performance."

Will inquired whether Isaac was sufficiently alert to talk and to express himself coherently. Anna replied that he was certainly vocal but there was a notable change in his personality, or perhaps, his way of dealing with the stresses he had encountered since arriving in Russia. "Will, you will find him very changed. I hope it is temporary. He is a bundle of nerves and unable to talk sense. You are the only person who will be able to assess the severity and meaning of what I and the medical types treating him are observing. He has been asking for you and when I informed him you were with that group in St Petersburg he could not contain his rage at being 'left out', as he expressed it. I think you should come back as soon as possible."

* * *

Back in Moscow, Will met with Anna before joining Isaac in his room at the clinic. He explained the role he would like Anna to perform as his personal assistant recorder and adviser representing Isaac's family. Will knew that even if Isaac wished to resume control, he was not fit to do so. Isaac had deferred to Will consistently in the past to make decisions for him and to carry out the actions necessary to implement them. Will was confident he could make the decisions Isaac would have made if he were well. After what seemed to Will to be an unnecessarily lengthy debate on whether Anna should accept the responsibilities Will wished to impose on her, she reluctantly agreed, concluding her comments with: "This, Will, alters our relationship a lot. I hope you know that. I guess you know that and decided it didn't matter. Okay, I will do as you ask." Will was uncertain as to her meaning but had the answer he was looking for, so he decided not to pursue it any further.

Will left Anna in a pensive mood and he walked towards Isaac's room. He could hear Isaac's voice but it did not appear to come from his end of the corridor. As he walked further towards his room Will realized that Isaac's voice was echoing through the corridor from a location behind him. Turning, he saw several nurses and security people converging on the room Sophie had occupied when Will was last here.

He arrived at the site of the commotion at the same time as Anna. They found Isaac on the floor in severe pain, literally screaming for pain relief. He was promptly placed on a stretcher and taken to his room. As the noise Isaac was creating diminished, Will heard Sophie crying out for Isaac to come to her, asking, "What's wrong, Isaac? Why are you carrying on like that? Tell me. I can't take this new pressure."

Anna turned to Will as he was about to follow Isaac and said, "No, Sophie needs our attention first. The medics will inject Isaac with something to calm him. We must tell Sophie what has happened to Isaac and try to reassure her everything will be alright."

Anna, taking the lead in entering Sophie's room, gasped when she saw Sophie and ran to her side taking her hand and murmuring what were intended to be comforting thoughts. But Sophie had become delirious and was screaming for Isaac; she repeatedly clutched her abdomen.

Will called for Anastasia as the clinic staff seemed paralyzed with indecision as to what to do. Anastasia arrived quickly and took Anna's blood pressure, and while reading the gauge examined Sophie's eyes and hands. Her diagnosis was not what anyone wanted to hear. "Her blood pressure has spiked into a range that could result in a stroke, unconsciousness or convulsions. Any of which could be seriously harmful to the baby, with her uncontrolled thrashing about on the bed and clutching at herself. I think she may be suffering from an infection again. We were able to keep it under control by keeping her temperature down and maintaining her in a calm state. I will have Dr Rayskill join us immediately."

Nothing further could be done to carry out Anna's intention to inform Sophie about Isaac's condition and the reasons for it. Taking uncharacteristic control, Anna turned to Will and ordered him out of Sophie's room, directing him to go to Isaac. Will obeyed, aware of the change in the balance of power that Anna had created; however, he was wise enough to recognize that in this situation wisdom required compliance.

Isaac was in bed, inert and apparently quite calm when Will arrived in his room. A moment or two observing Isaac gave Will a clearer understanding of what was happening. Isaac was in a straightjacket that tied him effectively into inactivity. His mouth was full of a device that prevented him from speaking or biting into the sides of his mouth or his tongue. A drip feed into Isaac's arm informed Will that Isaac was being heavily sedated.

Will walked over to Isaac and took his hand, and as with Anna and Sophie, gave him what he thought might be comforting words. They generated no response from Isaac.

Having done his best with Isaac, Will returned to Sophie's room to find her in a somewhat similar state to Isaac, but without the straightjacket. The drip into her right arm was probably the same supply as was being forced into Isaac.

"Anna," Will ventured to say, "let's step out and have a talk with Sophie's and Isaac's lead physicians. We have to know what to do – what instructions to give them and where... and I mean *where*. Should they be moved to another hospital with more extensive facilities than here in Moscow, or to London or New York? In either city they would both receive the best medical care available on the planet."

The lead physicians assembled and met with Anna and Will about half an hour later in a conference room far enough away from the sick rooms not to be heard by either occupant.

Sophie's condition appeared to be more threatening, so Will asked Dr Rayskill for a status report on her health and that of the baby.

"I am worried, very worried," said Dr Rayskill, "about the health of both mother and baby. Apart from the infections and the baby's current position in utero having shifted to a breech position, Sophie is displaying the symptoms of post-traumatic stress disorder. If I am correct, it will be exceptionally risky, no matter what treatment plan we adopt and follow."

"Do you need instructions on the treatment you advise, Ben?" replied Will. "As you know, I have the legal authority to make those decisions while Isaac is incompetent and therefore unable to make the decisions. Good God! I certainly don't want to have to make such a decision, but with Anna's help and advice the decisions will be made. However, can we wait for a few hours, perhaps a day or two, hoping Isaac will resume his senses and make the decision himself?"

Isaac's physician Dr MacGregor interjected, stating: "Dr Menshive's current condition is as much mental as physical. His physical condition is gradually improving. I believe he will fully recover after one or two more rounds of surgery to repair the internal wounds created by the paths of the bullets. It is the mental side of that equation that gives me the greatest worry. I have been observing Dr Menshive on the psychological side, as has Dr Rayskill with Sophie. We have been assisted by a trauma expert here in Moscow highly recommended by specialists in Berlin and Geneva. They tell us that, like Mrs Menshive, Dr Menshive is displaying early signs of post-traumatic stress disorder. You will need to talk to Professor Doctor Alexander Valentin. He will be joining us by 3 o'clock this afternoon. No decisions are needed before then assuming you approve the treatments you have observed this morning."

Will took Anna aside and asked her opinion about those treatments. She replied that she had no training in medicine and felt she had to take their advice. Will replied that he agreed. He added that they should ask Dr MacGregor to be with them to continue to advise them on future decisions on the medical side.

After the consultation with the medical team that morning, Will suggested that he and Anna meet to discuss the position they were now in personally, particularly in light of Will's request that she act as his recording secretary as events moved forward solely in relation to the physical and mental health of the patients. Will gave her some comfort in informing her that Will's meetings and negotiations related to the division and distribution of the assets would be recorded by Ushakov, the Moscow lawyer who had been advising the Swiss bank on the management of the assets for several years, and by the trust's Moscow lawyer, Ushakov.

"Will, you know my views on those hateful assets – give them away. Just get rid of them. Isaac doesn't need them. He was independently wealthy before getting this pile of problems. As to me, I renounced them and have never regretted it. Dad left me comfortable and Isaac has given me more money than I could ever spend. The movable objects and real estate are of no interest to me. All I want is a cozy cottage in the Hamptons. I have all the money I need for one person. Therefore, I leave all decisions relating to money, the trust and those damnable assets to you. And I mean that. If you want my advice, ask away, but I will follow your advice. I don't want to sound unhelpful but there is my honest opinion – and it won't change."

"Anna, I know well that your mind once made up is unalterable. As I remember I was a victim of that once before," replied Will, with a wan smile.

"Yes. I didn't say, though, that I don't sometimes deeply regret some of those decisions. However, we are where we are and now have other problems which require our attention."

"One last point in terms of consultations: I know you have become a card-carrying Lutheran, but you would know when Isaac and Sophie should have counselling from a rabbi. I expect you to tell me when arrangements should be made for either Sophie or Isaac – particularly if an extreme situation should arise."

"Yes, I can advise you on that point. I don't consider myself to be Jewish now, although my mother certainly brought me up knowing the theology, standards and practices of Judaism. I am well aware of Isaac's resumption of the Jewish faith – as highly improbable as that was – and I know, too, that Sophie is a practising member of Liberal Judaism."

When they returned to the corridor containing the temporary quarters for their friends and family, Will went to Isaac and Anna to Sophie.

Isaac was still under physical restraint but he was no longer struggling against it. His eyes were open and when he saw Will, he spoke: "I guess I made a fool of myself a little earlier, Will. Philip MacGregor told me. He said it was important that I not deny my transfer of authority concerning my person and agency for these damn negotiations. He was right – is right. Nothing I have said was meant to revoke or change my transference of guardianship of my person and the general power of attorney in you. I have made it clear to Philip and Ben that regardless of what I may say or do while in delirium, nothing should change the powers conferred on you. Forgive me, though, for putting you in this hellish situation and for being subjected to my awful behaviour. You know you are more than a brother could be to me, Will. Continue to bear with me, please."

"Of course I will. I made that commitment to you long ago and I will continue that commitment. I want you to know that I will use the decision-making authority only when I think you're not able to confer and able to assist me in making decisions."

"Thank you. However, I am – I mean – we are now in a new world that I occupy. I have been informed by Philip and Ben that I probably have post-traumatic stress disorder. I will be meeting this afternoon with Dr Alexander Valentin, a specialist psychiatrist in PTSD. I can recognize some of the symptoms myself. I think I have had a mild form of it since our last visit here in Russia four years ago. My adventure on the Neva embankment a few days ago has intensified those symptoms. I really worry about that because those symptoms include profound depression and a tendency towards violence to the people closest to me, the sufferer. You will have to be vigilant about any attempt to strike out at you, as you must watch to protect Sophie. She is particularly vulnerable, because one of the symptoms of PTSD is assaulting loved ones who are themselves in a weakened state. *Oy,* what a mess I find myself in. I hope my rabbi friends can help me, too."

At this point, Isaac slipped into a deep sleep. As Will looked at his friend, he realized that not once had Isaac asked about Sophie or their baby she was carrying. He decided that might be Isaac's way of sheltering himself from this intensely emotional side of his life.

The day closed with Isaac and Sophie heavily medicated alone in their hospital rooms, with neither asking to see the other.

That evening was taken with Will instructing Anna how she must diarize the events of the day. At the conclusion of the session, she understood and accepted the importance of the records she and Ushakov would be keeping.

19

CONCERN FOR BOTH Sophie and Isaac's health intensified overnight. A meeting was convened early in the morning at which all attending physicians were in attendance, including Dr Valentin who by now had examined both patients. At the conclusion of their *in-camera* session, Anna and Will were invited to join them for a briefing.

Will asked Dr Rayskill to chair the meeting but requested that the meeting be concluded in two hours, as he had a later meeting scheduled with Putin government officials.

Starting with Dr Valentin, Dr Rayskill informed the meeting of the results of his examination of Sophie. He stated that in his opinion the medical crisis she was experiencing on the way from Smolensk to Moscow was in part induced by the terror, separation and intimidation she experienced during her captivity in Smolensk. Separation in Moscow from Isaac further aggravated her condition. What brought her crisis to the highest level was her discovery from an indiscreet nurse of Isaac's having been shot and being in the clinic with her, but unable to see her given the severity of his condition and the medically induced coma in which he was initially placed. Her response was typical of a PTSD patient: she withdrew into herself, repressing the increasing threats she felt toward herself and to her baby. Valentin diagnosed Sophie as being in a severe state of PTSD which required expert clinical treatment and personal care.

As to Isaac, Valentin said simply that his PTSD was even more severe than Sophie's, arising from the numerous traumas he had faced over the past four years, including his intense worry about Sophie and his failure, as he saw it, to protect her and their child. Long-term clinical care, counselling and drug therapy would be necessary to see any improvement in his condition.

Dr Rayskill reported on Sophie's obstetric issues. He stated that Sophie's extreme fluctuations in blood pressure and anxiety, aggravated by the infection she had sustained in the uterine area, gave the pregnancy a very high risk of failure, particularly as the baby was now in breech.

Will asked the question that was on everyone's mind: "Where should the patients receive their treatment and specialized care?"

Dr Rayskill spoke for the medical team, stating that London was the best location for the quality of professional and institutional services needed by both patients.

"Why not New York?" asked Anna.

"New York would offer comparable expertise and facilities but it is an extra two hours from Moscow," Dr Rayskill said. "Moving Sophie, in particular, to London would be high-risk, but less so than leaving her in Moscow. The four-hour flight to London on a private jet with appropriate air pressure and temperature control would be manageable. I have already contacted colleagues with whom I have conducted several internationally acclaimed research studies on PTSD in pregnancy from which we have co-authored papers that have received praise and recognition. This is best dealt with in London. Remember the IRA bombings and the extremist Muslim attacks there. The impact of these events has frequently been felt by pregnant women, particularly if they were present when the terrorist attacks took place. You may remember the bombing of a double-decker bus on Russell Square in London a few years ago. Many were killed. Of the few who survived, there was one seven-month-pregnant woman who required treatment for her pregnancy which was, as a result of the bombing, at high risk of failure. The expertise available in London was able to help the baby and the mother survive their ordeals. Yes, London is my advice. If you need someone from New York, that person can be brought in."

It was agreed that the sooner the patients were removed the more likely there would be a satisfactory outcome. Will interrupted the medical commentaries with the observation that wherever Sophie and Isaac were going, Little Isaac,

Anna and he must accompany them. If the flight to London would involve obvious stress and overt anxiety by either of the patients it would be detected by Little Isaac, so he stated with considerable vigour, that Little Isaac, Anna and he should be on a separate flight.

Before Will allowed the meeting to terminate, he informed their guests that he and Anna must meet to discuss the medical recommendations. They needed, he said, a private opportunity to discuss all they had heard. The discussion between Will and Anna lasted no more than half an hour. There was no debate or challenge from either of them as to the recommendations they had received. They spent their time considering where in London they should establish a temporary home and what arrangements should be made for Little Isaac.

It appeared that the hospital to which both Sophie and Isaac would be taken was near Harley Street in Marylebone, just north of Oxford Street. Will checked the inventory of real estate owned by Isaac in London and found an apartment in nearby Fitzrovia that by very good luck was vacant. Will told Anna he would try to find a small bachelor pad nearby. The reaction he received startled him with its intensity. Anna, with an expletive or two similar to those her brother was accustomed to using, made it clear that Will would be staying with her, Little Isaac and a full-time nanny who would be engaged. "You, Will, have been a parent, I haven't been. I will need your practical experience in dealing with Little Isaac. I'm sure we will find you room under the service stairs for a pull-out bed and sleeping bag."

As Will examined the description of the apartment, he realized there would be enough room to accommodate the Canadian diplomatic contingent in London, which was not small. Whatever alterations were required could be made under his supervision by the UK manager of Isaac's properties and other assets located there.

PART 3

London

20

EDWARD THORNHILL, THE manager of Isaac's properties in the United Kingdom, met with Will and Anna at the apartment two days later. The description Will had of the apartment's location and quality was incomplete. Mr Thornhill informed them it was located on Fitzroy Square in one of the numerous surviving buildings designed by Robert Adam in the late eighteenth century. The apartment itself was comprised of two floors containing the original decorative elements. The plaster work had been refreshed, conserved and gilded to its original state. The reception rooms were the principal rooms in two lateral apartments opened to form one unit. In all, the apartment comprised over 4,000 square feet. It turned out there would be ample room for Will on the second floor of the apartment, in a suite that consisted of a large double bedroom, a modern bathroom with all the mod cons and a sitting room. Anna would occupy the lower floor which contained a double parlour, formal dining room, kitchen and library. The cook, maid and nanny were to be housed on the lower ground floor which would include a well-insulated playroom for Little Isaac.

The apartment required little refurbishment. Remarkably, it was fully furnished in late Georgian furniture with some original oil paintings by artists Will recognized.

The major advantage of the apartment was its location which was no more than a ten-minute walk for Will's long legs to reach the clinic where Sophie and Isaac were receiving treatment.

Will's meeting with Mr Thornhill gave him the opportunity to discuss security arrangements for Isaac and Sophie and for the residents of the apartment. Frank was scheduled to join Will as soon as he could extricate himself from the continuing Moscow-based GRU investigation of the shooting. Arrangements were made for rooms on the lower ground floor for Frank and two other security guards.

Will realized that a move from Russia to the United Kingdom was tantamount to a royal progress by the first Queen Elizabeth. Unfortunately, unlike Queen Elizabeth, Isaac would be picking up all costs associated with the move. Will knew that the expenses would only slightly dent Isaac's cash reserves – which brought to mind that he should have the Swiss bank send a couple of the trust managers to London to establish bank accounts, methods of financial reporting, and exchanging invoices for all expenses that were being incurred.

Will himself was unworried about his own cash requirements. Isaac had established an exceptionally generous salary and expense account for him, with payments being made into a secure personal account held by the Swiss bank and accessible by Will at a prominent national bank in major cities in Europe and North America, including a nearby bank in London. As it turned out, Will had little need for cash. Virtually all his expenses and needs were provided for by Isaac through arrangements made with the bank. However, he thought, while in London this would be an excellent time to review the current systems to ensure they were working well for himself and for Isaac's whole family.

Will, over many earlier visits to London, had walked through Fitzrovia across Portland Place into Marylebone. He knew London well and he felt at home there. After his meeting with Mr Thornhill and having discovered that Thornhill was a descendant of the celebrated painter Sir James Thornhill, painter of the 'painted hall ceiling' located in the Old Royal Naval College in Greenwich, he walked with a calm confidence of security he had not felt since leaving North America to join Isaac over a month ago. No one outside the immediate circle of his and Isaac's contacts would know where he was in London even if they had discovered he was in London. As he walked north along Portland Place before crossing over to Marylebone, he passed the Royal Institute of British Architects reminding himself that he had to visit its remarkable library as he had often done on earlier visits to the city.

It was with considerable apprehension that he entered Isaac's room at the clinic, fearing that Isaac's physical and mental health would have deteriorated since he had last seen him earlier that morning on the flight from Moscow.

Isaac was aware but subdued and uncommunicative. When Will asked him how he was feeling, Isaac simply turned his head away without answer. When Will asked whether Isaac had any instructions for him, Isaac shook his head in a barely perceptible manner. When Will asked whether Isaac wanted him to continue his work with Isaac's full authority and to make whatever decisions were required, there was only a simple tilt of Isaac's head to demonstrate his agreement.

Will had never observed Isaac in such a depressed state. Will had hoped that a change of venue to London would improve Isaac's disposition; he was keenly disappointed. He knew Isaac liked London as much as he did and that he found the challenge of the antiquities and art salesrooms to be irresistible. Will asked him if he looked forward to a visit to Christie's or Sotheby's, expecting some enthusiasm. There was no reaction at all. This, more than the shooting and medical diagnosis in Moscow, alarmed Will profoundly. His friend was in a different place, and not a happy one. Will asked his last questions, knowing he had to test this ground as well: "Have you visited Sophie? How have you found her?"

There was no verbal response from Isaac but his tears welled and flowed and his chest heaved rhythmically until he closed his eyes and ceased to connect with Will.

Next, Will visited Sophie who, he observed, was in a similar state to Isaac. Ben Rayskill came along the corridor as Will left her room. Will asked for a medical status report. Ben advised him that both mother and baby remained at high risk. No decision was required yet. Sophie needed all the rest she could get, but there was little rest, he reported. Her agitation was deep and continuing. When Will asked whether it would help Sophie if Isaac were brought to him, perhaps in a wheelchair, Ben replied that it would not; it would simply remind Sophie of the severity of Isaac's condition, and this would alarm her even more.

Feeling dejected and worried about what his next steps would be, Will walked down to Christopher Place near Selfridge's store where he entered a restaurant that had always provided him with a particularly fine meal on his earlier visits to London. There he was able to find a table in the same location where he always ate. The server recognized him from the year before and was cheerful and welcoming. Will tried to rise to the occasion but simply felt flat and defeated by life in general.

That evening Will and Anna had a simple take-out Italian dinner which he picked up on the way back to the apartment. Anna was able to provide some comfort by informing him that a nanny and cook had been hired, though not before Frank had checked them out and interviewed them. Much of Anna and Will's time together was spent in mute solitude, even in each other's presence.

21

A STROLL THROUGH Regent's Park north of Fitzrovia on a warm mid-November morning refreshed and revitalized Will. London was almost a second home to him; he had visited it almost forty times over the same number of years. His interest in history, architecture and the Westminster system of government led him back to the city every fall for ten to fourteen days per visit. It was a place of comfort, ever energizing and stimulating, even as the traffic and congestion of people and vehicles made traversing each district chosen for exploration challenging and irritating. The sublime visual delights of the street-scapes made the negative recede before all of the benefits of London. The cultural amenities, such as the incredible displays in museums and galleries, appealed to him as they contained the highest levels of creative accomplishments in his own cultural heritage.

It was therefore in a state of conscious happiness arising from the landscaping of the park that Will again took stock of his situation with Isaac and his role towards his friend's family. Any thought of returning to his quiet and secure life in Charlottetown, the capital of his home province in Canada, was ruled out by his obligation to his old friend.

Will realized, too, that over the past week his commitments to Sophie, Little Isaac and the unborn baby were now intensified. He also had to contend with Isaac's sister Anna, whose role in his life was now ambiguous. Before Isaac's shooting, it appeared to be moving in one direction, but afterwards, with Will and Anna's need to act as a team in providing personal and child care and legal services as guardians and trustees, a more professional and business-like relationship was required.

The steamy moisture of the rising morning mist, while warm, was coolly refreshing at the same time. The weather forecast, as so often in London, was for rain later in the day.

Will took this advantage to get out and walk to get exercise and to plan the next few days. He assumed that Isaac and Sophie would be safe where they were in the clinic. They would require little of his bedside attention. Anna had assured him she would take on that duty.

As he considered the location and nature of the assets on the Swiss bank inventory, Will recalled there were extensive assets in London as well. The assets included the elegant period-furnished apartment in the building designed by Robert Adam on Fitzroy Square. The list of properties included real estate in the Pimlico, Kensington and Notting Hill districts of London – technically parts of the City of Westminster, which to a visitor is adjacent to and virtually indistinguishable from 'London'.

The assets held by Isaac in the Greater London area included some art and creations in the decorative arts. They were not as numerous as in Russia or other areas of Central and Eastern Europe but they had a substantial value, being in the hottest and most expensive real estate market in Europe. Will decided that having discretion as to his daily agenda for the next few days he would visit each listing. "At least in London," he thought, "I am able to openly and safely explore the assets held here. I will not have to worry about security issues, but to be on the safe side I will take Frank or one of the other security guards with me."

Still in Regent Park, Will saw the Queen Mother's famous rose gardens coming into view. At home in Canada, there would be nothing to see or sense in a rose garden at this time of year, but this was London. This brought to mind the peculiarities of micro climates which reflected Will's stream-of-consciousness mental processes. His home town was located at latitude 46.51 degrees north, whereas London is significantly further north at 51.51 degrees; indeed, about 4 degrees further north than Saint John's, Newfoundland. The point being, he reminded himself, that the geographical position of a place on earth was no absolute predictor of its weather pattern. It did make visiting a rose garden in November more interesting and enjoyable, however.

Bending to examine what was described as a 'Queen Elizabeth' rose and inhaling the sweet scent, Will was transported back in time to his own gardening efforts, which included an attempt to grow roses. He even attempted competitive rose growing. This involved showing them at the annual rose show, where his failure proved to be absolute. However, his well-known penchant to organize everything with which he was associated prompted members of the local Rose Society to elect him to the chairmanship of the society and in that capacity to organize the annual shows two years running.

"How on earth did I find time to get involved in and chair so many organizations? My professional life occupied all daylight hours, it seemed, and what spare time there was from that was devoted to family." As his thoughts were back in Charlottetown, he remembered his law practice and his pleasure in that role. In this fleeting frame of mind, he was consciously brought back to Isaac's trust, which then brought him to the allegations of a connection between the Swiss bank, the trust and the organizational structures on which the assets were held. "Right. I must visit the law firm here in London that has been retained to manage the British and North American trust assets." The firm was located in the Lincoln's Inn area of Holborn north of the Strand, near the Royal Courts of Justice.

A walk from Regent's Park down Portland Place to Regent's Street through dense crowds of tourists led him down past Piccadilly Circus to Carlton House Terrace overlooking St James Park, another of the several royal parks in London. It was a short walk through Admiralty Arch into the Strand and from there to Lincoln's Inn Fields where he found the address of the law firm identified on the Swiss bank inventory. He didn't have an appointment but he could use this occasion to inquire whether he could make one.

The suited receptionist, her hair, somewhat blonde with a grayish cast, in a bun, presented Will with a glance that was manifestly an assessment of whether he met the standard of clientele she was familiar with. Will was up to the scrutiny and in a somewhat subdued but demanding stentorian tone presented her with a letter of introduction given to him by the bank. When she appeared to have completed her examination of the letter, she typed something into her desktop computer and then surfaced with a frozen-faced announcement: "I will contact Mr Roger Smythe to see if he is available to see you."

Will sat while she replied to the person on the other end of her computer. This was interrupted by a telephone call which she took while she continued to type. Her answers demonstrated a challenging line of inquiry. Eventually, Will was asked a series of questions; his answers passed muster. As a result, his new companion informed him that 'Lisa from Mr Smythe's office' would come for him shortly. This surprised Will. No appointment was necessary – he had expected only to be able to arrange an appointment today.

It was twenty minutes before a clone of the receptionist arrived in the entrance hall and announced, butler-like, "Mr Smythe will see you now. He is however very busy and may have little time for you." Without waiting for a response this figure turned her back on Will, expecting him to follow, which he did.

Will's own legal practice was operated from a Victorian neo-Georgian building he had rebuilt in the interior to accommodate his practice and that of the other lawyers in the practice. It was a simple but elegant space with a particularly attractive staircase that he had designed and had installed. The walls were covered with antiquarian first edition engravings. As he was being led through the narrow corridors of this office, he could not help but contrast what he was viewing with the standards of law offices he was familiar with in Canada, where forceful presentation of competence, intelligence and taste were on display in law offices in Canada to assure clients that they had chosen their lawyer well. On the other hand, this firm, which had a history extending back over one hundred and fifty years, was dull and unassertive other than to declare, "We couldn't give a damn about our surroundings; our firm is sufficient to impress you by reputation alone."

"There lies a major difference between the Old World and the New," thought Will.

Finally, he was shown through a door into a chamber of considerable size occupied by a short, round man with more gleaming skin than hair on his cranium. Will struggled to stand; once he managed it, he extended his right hand as a greeting. He attempted a smile at the same time, although it came out as a wince.

Mr Smythe asked Will a few questions of a qualifying nature; when Will produced his passport, the English lawyer rather ostentatiously held it up to compare it with what he had on file from the bank. Smythe appeared to be satisfied that Will was who he represented himself to be.

Will explained in general terms what his specific role was with the Menshive inheritance and his immediate position as sole decision-maker, briefly explaining that health issues had prevented Isaac from being with him.

Smythe, with a note of boredom in his voice, asked Will how his firm could be of assistance. Will responded that he had understood that Smythe's firm had assisted the Swiss bank in structuring the ownership of the assets. At Will's request, Smythe agreed to provide Will with an organizational chart of the various corporations, trusts and sole proprietorships involved which had never been successfully challenged.

A management structure was in place for administration of the assets and fully operational. The structure, Mr Smythe proudly informed Will, was created by his firm. When asked when this had happened, Smythe answered that the original management structure was created about the time of the Russo-Japanese War of 1905. As the geographical extent of the assets grew, so did the complexities of the corporations and trusts created to hold and manage the assets.

"The original organizational structure, Mr MacIntosh," explained Mr Smythe, "was a trust created for the Swiss bank by my firm which was domiciled here in London. You see it on the chart down at the bottom.

"In 1905, following the Russo-Japanese War which was a disaster for Imperial Russia, it became clear that the loss of that war would lead, in 1914, to what we know historically as the First World War. This war was also a disaster for Imperial Russia.

"The repeated military losses and losses of lives in the millions resulted in the outbreak of the 1917 Russian Revolution. With its new Communist government in place, assets in Russia had to be better protected, so a new corporation was formed here in London, technically owned by the trust but stripped of all its assets which were transferred to the new corporation.

"That company purchased several properties in the London area to demonstrate that its domicile and principal place of business was London. That corporation then formed a second corporation, again controlled by a board of directors appointed by the Swiss trust. There was no public record of directorship at that time so it was impossible to connect the two companies with the Swiss-based trust. The London corporation was in turn owned by a foreign trust.

"As the success of the Russian Revolution and its politicians espousing communism became clear to the London corporation, many of the extensive assets formerly held directly by the Swiss trust were transferred to the principal corporation. The board of directors was restructured to be appointees of a new trust which was to be the principal organizational element. That trust was the foreign trust I referred to. It was established in a Canadian province called Prince Edward Island with which I understand you are familiar, Mr MacIntosh. The lawyer who formed the trust was a respected member of the bar there with extensive family and business connections, a Charles Longworth, QC. Are you familiar with him, Mr MacIntosh?"

"Yes, he was a double first cousin of my great grandparents. I am somewhat familiar with his law practice which did involve a number of English-based trusts. I think I know why Prince Edward Island was selected as the domicile for the trusts."

"Indeed," replied Smythe. "Your province was selected because it was about the most advantageous jurisdiction in which to settle a trust. There was virtually no public register or scrutiny of such trusts in that jurisdiction. The English common law governing the creation of trusts applies there – and still does, I gather. So, the real pyramid of corporations and trusts used by the Swiss bank for the acquisition and holding of assets on both sides of the Atlantic Ocean were all ultimately owned by the 'Isle St Jean Trust'. Why that name was selected perhaps you can inform me, Mr MacIntosh."

"My guess would be that as it is not a name currently connected with the province, it was selected cleverly to throw off the scent of anyone trying to locate the place of domicile of the trust. Isle St Jean was the name given to what we know now as Prince Edward Island by the French when they occupied it as part of their North American colonies. When the British defeated the French in the mid-eighteenth century they used the English translation of the French to 'The Island of Saint John.' The island was renamed in the 1790s as Prince Edward Island. The name change was the result of too many St Johns in that region which led to constant confusion. So I guess that those who named the trust hoped that confusion would divert interest away from Prince Edward Island."

"Very clever. I have been the attorney primarily charged with responsibility for the Isle St Jean Trust. I am delighted to discover the origin of the name. I can tell you that no one has connected the trust with your home province. However, as a trust established there it has legal standing in the United Kingdom. From London, we have created a network of corporations that own assets located in specific countries. Now, as to Russia, we created a double-blind. We have a separate company that does nothing but own a trust created by the Swiss bank. That trust owns or has the sole private rights to the assets located in Russia. No one can link the assets to Dr Menshive without having that chart and the names of the trustees and directors. As you know, Dr Menshive and his illustrious family are Jewish. That fact had to be hidden. If the connection between the assets and Jewish interests had been known in Russia and other areas of Eastern and Central Europe, they would have been confiscated in the name of nationalism. The ownership structure is one of utmost secrecy and effectiveness."

Will listened spell-bound to the profound connection between the trusts, assets and trustees and his home province. That connection was made more immediate by the fact that the lawyer who had skillfully created the trust, Charles Longworth, was his distant relative.

As Will walked back to Fitzroy Square through Covent Garden and Bloomsbury after a libation or two at a Georgian-era pub, he had a sudden awareness of why Isaac had chosen him from Isaac's many friends and colleagues – "It must be the Prince Edward Island connection and therefore my knowledge of the law of trusts in that province – and my connection with the creator of the trust and where to this day the originals of those documents lie in Charlottetown." He and Isaac had been friends, but this connection made Will's selection as his companion invaluable, perhaps inevitable. It had proven to be successful for both Isaac and Will. "What an interesting circle this creates," he said *sotto voce* to himself.

22

WHILE WILL WAS enveloped in a garden of roses and engaged in considering the connections between Isaac's several trusts and his own Prince Edward Island, Isaac remained in isolation at the medical clinic in Marylebone, his wife a few doors away also in isolation.

Isaac's condition had improved to the degree that he could be released from the restraints of the straightjacket. The several gunshot wounds were being treated successfully, but it was his mental health that was proving the most worrying aspect of his recovery. During the past four years, after receiving the assignment of the trust assets from his parents, he had been subjected to no less than four physical attacks, three of which were life-threatening. His prior life as a highly regarded orthopedic surgeon and hospital administrator had led him to accept his superior skills in dealing with emergencies and catastrophic issues – but only as they related to others. His pre-trust life had been free of any challenges to his person or to his authority.

The shooting on the Neva Embankment in St Petersburg was only the latest intrusion on his sense of security and superiority. The earlier physical attacks, while initially amusing and not without a James Bond-style *frisson*, gave him a reason to develop and act in disguise the role of other characters as methods of hiding from those who would harm him. The fun stopped in Smolensk when his pregnant wife and toddler son were kidnapped and held hostage. He was shaken to the core and for the first time in his life he felt powerless – and for the first time in his life, too, he felt a love for another human that surpassed his love of self. His love for his wife and son exceeded any emotion he had ever experienced before.

In spite of the liberation of his wife and son, he continued to feel as vulnerable as they were and he had become powerless to assume command or control of subsequent events. He had relied on his friend Will for four years and he had been deeply grateful for Will's companionship and competence in planning the next steps in their task to discover the truth about the origin and ownership of the assets. His decline into depending on others began in Smolensk. What remained of his self-confidence was shattered on the Neva Embankment.

Isaac's coma had been a medically induced state, a state into which he returned from time to time, seemingly to enable his body to heal. It did not stop the brain cells and synapses from functioning. While he lay in the coma his mind was racing at a feverish pace, repeatedly revisiting all of the events of the past four years. In doing so, he continually aggravated the emotional trauma his body was endeavouring to cope with. His attending physicians knew he was psychologically in distress but were reluctant to give him anything other than medium-strength dosages of an anti-anxiety medication, for fear that they were not identifying the location of the injury in the brain. They also worried that anything stronger would not be monitored effectively, given the profound crisis Isaac's physical body was suffering. In the battle of dealing with the physical injuries and the psychological injuries, the physical had to have priority. The psychological would have to wait until Isaac's physical recovery enabled him to interact with psychologists or perhaps psychiatrists to assist him in dealing with the mental trauma.

By midday, Isaac had gradually emerged from the coma but he remained isolated in his own head-space, not engaging with his medical help or with Anna who was with him at his bedside as often as she felt it was possible to be away from Little Isaac.

Little Isaac did not notice the change in his routine for the first two or three days after Isaac's return to London following the shooting. His mother's absence he understood because she was sick and he was being taken to see her periodically by Anna. And he was able to see his father several times a day although there was no verbal communication. He and Anna had established a trusting and deeply affectionate relationship, but the absence of both parents in his life was creating separation anxieties that Anna was doing her best to deal with. She wished that Will was around more because he and Little Isaac had become great friends and companions playing with the Lego set and racing toy cars by remote control.

Anna was torn between her duties to Isaac, Sophie, Little Isaac and the new role she had accepted with Will, becoming in effect his personal assistant. She, too, was becoming emotionally drained and prone to tears and to stress relief of a more liquid form.

When Isaac had become aware of his surroundings, Anna endeavoured to engage him in conversation. She assumed his refusal to talk or engage with her was because of his worry for Sophie and the unborn baby. She tried to talk to Isaac about Sophie but the moment her name was mentioned Isaac, without a word, turned his head away from Anna, refusing to listen. She tried telling Isaac amusing stories of Little Isaac's activities but these did not interest him either. Anna thought that these emotionally sensitive areas were too much for him, so she tried to talk to Isaac about Will and what he was doing on Isaac's behalf in London. That did result in a reaction, but not one she expected. Without saying a word Isaac grimaced as if he had had a tooth pulled without anesthetic. That topic, she thought, wouldn't work either.

After discussing her plight with the attending physicians, they advised her to simply sit by his beside, perhaps occasionally talking about happier times, for example their childhood. Their message was clear: it would be Isaac who would decide when he would leave the safety of his closed world and engage with those around him. When Anna asked the physicians whether Little Isaac might help his father if she brought him more frequently to Isaac, she was instructed not to bring him. It could be deeply distressing for the child and cause him to act out while with Isaac. No, she was told, wait until Isaac asks to see the boy, but talk about him to Isaac so that Isaac will know the child is alright.

After a couple of hours with Isaac and his medical team, Anna walked down the hall to Sophie's room. She walked in to find a team of medics furiously working on her. Anna stood there for over half an hour, not interfering but with an increasing foreboding of impending disaster.

Finally, the immediate crisis seemed to be under control, which liberated Dr Rayskill. When he saw Anna, noticing her state of shock, he invited her to a conference room next door, closed the door, and gave her an explanation of what she had observed.

"Sophie continues to have a high fever from the infection she incurred earlier. We thought we had it under control, but it flared up again early this morning. You know the baby is in a breech position. With her limited strength, she cannot deliver the baby naturally. That leaves a Caesarian section. We cannot proceed with a Caesarian while she has a high fever. When you came into the room a short while ago, Sophie was in distress and having a convulsion which had to be treated immediately. Sorry, I cannot stay with you now. I must get back to my patient. I suggest that Mr MacIntosh should be contacted and requested to be here as soon as possible. He holds the power of attorney and guardianship of the person for both Isaac and Sophie. I may need his instructions."

Anna reached into her shoulder bag and took out her gleaming new cell phone. She took the steps to turn it on but nothing happened. She tried it several more times without success which resulted in tearful frustration. A young female doctor saw her and knew she was part of Isaac and Sophie's family and came up to her, giving Anna words of comfort.

Anna with a sharpness amounting to rudeness, said, "It is not Isaac or Sophie – it's this wretched thing," holding out the cell phone. "Dr Rayskill has instructed me to get in contact with someone we need here right away but I can't get this to work."

The young doctor heard her own mother in that voice when similarly trying to use these 'damn things'. The doctor took Anna's cell phone and led her out to the front steps of the clinic.

"You can't call out, from in there," the young doctor explained. "The mobile phone signal will not penetrate these ancient walls. But we should be able to get a signal here, Ms Menshive. I will need your password to get into your phone."

"What password? I have no idea what word that would be!"

"Actually, it's a four-number code you type in here," said the doctor pointing to the numbered keypad on the phone.

Anna did not know the number required and she was prepared to throw the phone on the concrete step, when in mid-flight her right arm was gently stopped by the doctor, who with a quiet laugh said simply, "So like my mother's reaction to new technology."

The doctor took out her own cell phone and asked Anna for the number she was calling. The cell phone rang several times without answer. They waited another fifteen minutes and tried again. No answer. The doctor excused herself and said she had to get back to her patients. Anna was left frustrated, angry and bewildered. What should she do next to comply with Dr Rayskill's directions? She realized there was nothing more she could do. She didn't know Will had been smelling the roses in Regent's Park and had moved on to having a pleasant conversation with a lawyer in Lincoln's Inn Fields about one of Will's distant cousins.

* * *

Anna's day continued to be a rotation from one hospital room to the other. Neither patient asked for the other. She knew it was not a sign of indifference or anger, but rather a simple self-absorption with the medical crisis each was facing.

She had hoped for help from Will and in the absence of his appearance at the hospital or at least a telephone call, she was becoming increasingly irritated at what she considered to be Will's lack of cooperation.

At the end of a long day, she returned to the apartment in Fitzrovia where she was met by a cheerful, if not buoyant Will, who was prepared to share his adventures of the day with her. He was taken aback by her frozen demeanour and lack of greeting. It turned out that Will was as skillful in the use of cell phones as Anna. It had not been turned on, hence the lack of reception. After mutually commiserating on the impositions imposed by the ever-increasing technical challenges of the new devices, they settled into a peaceful conversation, each telling the other of the happenings of the day.

Will was very concerned about Isaac and his detachment, which he knew was uncharacteristic. Indifference to Sophie and Little Isaac, he recognized, was a symptom of a deep underlying psychological trauma that Isaac was dealing with: this required professional attention. Sophie's lack of interaction with Anna, he was sure, was based on her health and in particular the infection which was elevating her temperature.

Both Will and Anna recognized that their immediate attention had to be given to Little Isaac. They agreed that they would each structure the next few days to have a specified time with Little Isaac, Isaac and Sophie. Anna understood that Will had continuing duties related to the asset investigations and the management of the assets, particularly those located in London – most of which had not been explored. They also agreed that together they would seek the assistance of some bright person under age thirty-five who could instruct them on the use of the mobile phones cluttering their existence. The most likely place, Will decided, to find such a genius would be at one of the specialty shops selling the devices nearby on Oxford Street.

Anna had no time or interest in hearing about what Will considered the remarkable discoveries he had made during the day. This, Will knew and accepted, was consistent with the renunciation of her half interest in the trust assets four years earlier. The mobile phone was only marginally more interesting.

23

A CALL TO the apartment on Fitzroy Square from the clinic alerted Will and Anna that there was a serious medical crisis at the clinic which required them both to be there as soon as possible. They were fortunate to have had the flexibility in their schedules to be able to comply. Anna had been successful in hiring a nanny from an agency recommended to them by the clinic. While it was only 5 o'clock in the morning they went up to the nursery and first had a brief visit with Little Isaac, assuring him they would be back soon and would take him on a promised walk to see the birds on the ponds in St James Park.

Ms Ellis, the nanny, took control and reassured Little Isaac that Will and Aunt Anna would be back soon after he had had his breakfast. That was the plan; it would be thwarted by events not of their own doing or control.

* * *

At the clinic, Anna went immediately to Sophie and Will to Isaac.

Isaac was in a highly emotional state – thrashing around, swearing and shouting that he couldn't "take the abuse anymore". What that abuse was, Will was determined to find out. After conferring with Isaac's lead physician who had been with him all night and with the duty nurses, he discovered that Isaac's rantings were directed at him. Will was flabbergasted! He had devoted the better part of four years to Isaac, his inheritance, and he had supported Isaac during the numerous physical attacks to which Isaac had been subjected. Until three days ago Will was a boon companion and the one good and reliable person outside the family on whom Isaac could rely.

Dr Walter MacKenzie was Isaac's attending physician who had been arranged for him by Isaac's clinic in New York. Dr MacKenzie was a man of middle years, who was skilled and accredited in several specialties, having served with the British Army in Northern Ireland early in his career. He would put all his skills, experience and insights into practice with Isaac.

Dr MacKenzie entered Isaac's room shortly after Will had arrived and observed the shock, hurt and look of helplessness on Will's face. He took Will gently by the arm and took him to the conference room next to Isaac's room, but before leaving he prescribed strong sedatives that Isaac was to be given intravenously for more immediate results.

"Mr MacIntosh, I observed your reaction to your friend's behaviour and rantings a moment ago. I will give you my diagnosis and describe the treatments Dr Menshive requires and I will give you my prognosis for him.

"Dr Menshive is suffering from several recent physical traumas brought on by the shootings in Russia. Those wounds were exceptionally close to wounds Dr Menshive received a few years ago, also in Russia. The fresh injuries reopened the scars from the earlier wounds, compounding his overall injuries. Our clinic has some of the best trauma surgeons in the UK. We were successful in staunching the blood loss, replaced the loss with three transfusions and continue to monitor him watching for possible infection. There is none yet, but I think there will be… Indeed, I think I see early signs of one. Our most immediate physical problem with Dr Menshive is that two of the bullets from the recent shootings remain lodged in his chest. When we opened him up we did not detect them because the site of the injury was a pulverized soup. Our immediate task was to stop the bleeding and pull things together as best we could. I ordered an X-ray and an MRI yesterday afternoon. Both should be available to me shortly.

"Now, the most serious aspect of Dr Menshive's condition, in my opinion, is his mental state. He is displaying most of the classic symptoms of post-traumatic stress disorder. I have observed the same symptoms in terrorist attacks in Belfast when I practiced there twenty years ago. In Dr Menshive's case, not unlike patients in Ulster, where there had been more than one traumatic event, such as being severely wounded in a paramilitary-style shooting, the psychological impact is often more damaging but more unpredictable as to its outcome. In Dr Menshive's case, I know there were earlier attempts on his life and most recently while in St Petersburg and a place in central Moscow; his pregnant wife and son were kidnapped and held for days, earlier in Smolensk. It is my assessment that the post-traumatic stress disorder has been building for months, if not years.

"Why is he railing on about you, Mr MacIntosh, in such a hostile and mean fashion? Simply because right now, in his subconscious, you are the one person in whom he has had absolute trust and faith and on you he has subconsciously projected responsibility for safeguarding his wife, son and unborn child. The mind in such a feverish state is not logical, nor is it reasonable. You are not in any way responsible for what he is now blaming you for. You must ignore his ravings and understand that underlying that behaviour is a troubled mind seeking solutions to get him out of his current predicament and that of his family. There is nothing, Mr MacIntosh, you can do except remain the true and loyal friend which you are; carry on being his friend and supporter. You should know that, from my experience, when Dr Menshive has had an opportunity to heal he will have forgotten everything he has said in his agitated state of madness."

Will listened intently and he took considerable comfort in what Dr MacKenzie had told him. He was not greatly reassured next, however, when he heard from Dr MacKenzie that the prognosis for recovery was long-term and he could not guess what the chances of recovery of the psychological issues would be. When Will told him that he held a power of attorney and a guardianship agreement that kicked in when a qualified surgeon certified that the patient was incompetent, Dr MacKenzie asked for the document and he called for a nurse to make several copies to be returned immediately with his professional seal. The guardianship papers were signed and sealed promptly. Will was given five original copies; Dr MacKenzie kept two for himself and one copy he would leave on the clinic records. Will explained that he had similar guardianship papers for Sophie. Dr MacKenzie took those as well, then left the room and went to find Dr Rayskill.

During the half-hour that Will was left alone in the conference room, he considered his situation. Not only was he one hundred percent responsible for the assets, the ongoing investigations and the upcoming negotiations for an allocation, division and calculation of compensation for assets transferred; he again reminded himself he now was responsible for Isaac's physical care and psychological treatment. Which brought him to Sophie.

Before he could dwell on Sophie, Dr MacKenzie returned to the conference room with Dr Rayskill who held a bundle of papers in his hands.

"Mr MacIntosh, I have certified that Mrs Menshive is incompetent and that you should have – I will say, we at the clinic *need* you to have – guardianship. We need someone with authority to make decisions for Mrs Menshive. I regret to worry you that we are now at a point in our care of Mrs Menshive that we need some decisions respecting her care. I will go further to give you a sense of the urgency that without hard decisions being made now, Mrs Menshive's condition will rapidly decline, becoming life-threatening. You have the sole responsibility and duty to act as Mrs Menshive's guardian as is clearly set out in these documents. I understand they were prepared in New York by Dr Menshive's legal counsel," to which Will simply nodded assent.

"What is Sophie's current condition and that of the baby?" Will asked with temerity, fearful of the answer now that he knew that she was at the very least mentally incompetent.

"She is in a state of delirium from the infection which is now systemic. That is compounded by the baby being in a breech position. Also, I think the umbilical cord is wrapped around the baby's neck. The medical condition of both mother and baby could not be much worse. I recommend that you inform her parents or siblings that they should come to her as soon as possible. As for the baby, it could be viable if born now. Natural childbirth, as you know already, is out. I have informed you that a Caesarian section would be extremely risky because of the infection, but we may now have no choice. You know the umbilical cord protects the baby from most sicknesses the mother may incur, but if there is a systemic infection or if the umbilical cord is compromised, as I think it is, the infection can enter the baby's system and cause it grievous harm. In summary, Mr MacIntosh, it is the unanimous recommendation of the team working with Mrs Menshive that a Caesarian section be performed without delay."

Will requested Dr Rayskill to bring Anna to the conference room and to remain with Dr MacKenzie and Will, as Will asked for Anna's opinion.

The discussion with Anna was brief. She had observed her sister-in-law's condition, heard the discussions among the medical team, and she had come to expect this recommendation. Will was surprised and comforted when Anna came over to him and gave him a hug that lasted longer than necessary and told him she agreed that surgery should be performed immediately. In the presence of both doctors, she took her hands and gently put them on the sides of his face and thanked him for his loyalty and services to her family. "I will stand behind you and support you, Will, no matter what the outcome. I know from Sophie's medical team that they do not know what the outcome shall be. In fact, one or both may die. The only hope, I know, lies in immediate surgery. Perhaps one or the other may survive." She took Will's hand in hers and both could not resist silent tears. The doctors went back to work, leaving Will and Anna to wait and cope as best as they could.

No sooner had the doctors left than there was an irritating, persistent and penetrating buzzing sound. Will looked at Anna, she looked at Will, and they looked around the room for a speaker, finding none. Finally, Will said, "Could it be my cell phone ringing?"

The call was from Mr Smythe who stated that he had been

contacted by Isaac's New York law office and by Mr Ushakov calling from Moscow. The call from New York was in answer to Will's own call, asking to have a senior partner and the managing partner handling Isaac's assets in the Swiss bank confirm that they were on their way to London.

As a frugal Scots Canadian, Will directed Frank to make reservations at a four-star hotel on Russell Square, a short walking distance from Fitzroy Square. It was arranged that Will would meet them in Mr Smythe's office which would become the centre of Will's management of the assets for the foreseeable future.

The diversion offered by the telephone call was a welcome break for both Will and Anna. It brought them back to the real world outside the medical one in which they were trapped.

A nurse arrived shortly after the telephone call was completed. She informed Will and Anna that the surgery was underway at that moment. There should be a report back to them shortly.

Before they could react to the nurse's information the prevailing quiet on the ward was shattered by a piercing announcement of a code that Anna informed Will meant someone was in a life-threatening state. There was a flurry of activity on the floor with nurses in particular running to the adjacent ward where Will and Anna knew the surgery was being conducted.

Isaac had not been forgotten. The sedatives and anti-depressive drugs had taken effect leaving him in a semi-comatose state. "At least Isaac doesn't need any of our attention at the moment," was Anna's comment, justifying her own exclusive focus on Sophie.

A few minutes later Dr MacKenzie and Dr Rayskill entered the conference room both bathed in sweat, covered in blood, and uncharacteristically dishevelled. Immediately Dr Rayskill turned to Will and said, "We may be able to save Mrs Menshive but not the baby. We could try our luck and see if both might be able to survive. It is our collective opinion that Sophie's survival is more likely, but I must warn you it is only a possibility. I think the baby is already stillborn and beyond recovery. What are your instructions, Mr MacIntosh?"

Never had Will faced such a dilemma. Even when his wife was in her final stages of cancer, each step, including the decisions necessary for the termination of the life support systems, was obvious. Will looked at Anna and said that he and Isaac had discussed this possibility during happier times at the dacha. Isaac had given his firm opinion that if a choice was required, Sophie's survival must be the priority. Will also said that Sophie had given Isaac the opposite instruction.

Will looked at Dr Rayskill in particular and he said that if there were a possibility of saving Sophie, that was to be the priority. Both doctors left immediately and knew what they had to do.

* * *

While Will and Anna waited at the clinic for the results of the Caesarian section, they visited Isaac in his room.

They were with Isaac when Dr MacKenzie entered the room and he greeted them with a sombre demeanour and in a quiet voice informed them of Isaac's condition, telling them that Isaac had occasionally emerged from his stupor and he had tried to speak before falling back into his quiet solitude of oblivion. Will strode over to Isaac's bed, sat next to Isaac's right arm and put his hand there as he tried to attract Isaac's attention. There was no response until Will, in a forceful tone insisted Isaac wake up and speak to him. "Isaac, I know you can come out of that fog – I need you to talk to me. Sophie is in a bad way. I must prepare you for what might come, and you must become alert to help Sophie."

There was movement of Isaac's limbs and rolling eyes behind shut lids, but there was no awakened engagement with Will and Anna.

Even though Will's attention was required, Dr MacKenzie cautioned Will that he should not be too forceful with Isaac, to which Will answered, "I know this man well. He can and must move beyond his own demons and get ready to deal with Sophie and her predicament."

Will then took Isaac's right hand in his and gave it a tightly compressed squeeze which resulted in Isaac opening his eyes as he shouted, "Stop, you bastard! You hurt me." To which Will said simply: "Good. Now we talk. Don't release or you will get another jolt."

Dr MacKenzie was on his feet, moving towards Will and about to stop him when Will stood, put his hand up in the universal 'stop' position and pointed to the chair from which MacKenzie sprang.

Anna stared in wonder and panic at what she was observing. She worried about Isaac's condition and whether Will was being too forceful. She saw Will staring intently into Isaac's eyes at close range and Isaac looking back, clearly paying attention.

While Will had Isaac's attention he explained Sophie's condition and that of the baby to him. He didn't hold back the probable outcome of the surgery being conducted as they spoke. "Isaac, you will be upset and perhaps angry just now about what is happening here and in the operating theatre, but you must ready yourself to help me make decisions and you must gain sufficient control of yourself to talk to Sophie. If the baby is lost, she will need your support and understanding. Remember, none of this is your fault… but she may say it is your fault for bringing her to Russia instead of leaving her in New York. You must remain calm and take whatever she throws at you. Over time she will understand. But you must be alert and help her."

Silence. It was several minutes before Isaac spoke his first words in many days. "I heard you, Will. I think I understand. I know you have made decisions already for Sophie and me. That's okay. You had to. Sorry," he said in a strangled voice, breaking into tears and sobbing uncontrollably.

"Forget me, Isaac," said Will, "I did what was necessary. Now get control of yourself so we can be ready to deal with Sophie's emotional and medical needs."

"Alright, you Celtic bully, I'll try."

"No. There's no trying. You *will* rise to the occasion." Isaac's reference to Will as a 'Celtic bully' gave Will immense satisfaction as it indicated that something of the old Isaac had survived the horrific ordeals he had faced and he could summon their accustomed style of speaking.

Dr MacKenzie watched with Anna on the other side of the bed as this scene played out. Anna continued crying but managed to bring it under control as Isaac turned to face her. To her he said, "Thanks, Anna. I really need your support. Thanks. Who would have thought...?" She smiled and understood.

Dr MacKenzie looked at Will and said: "I did not think that possible. Your performance was truly remarkable." To which Will replied, "That could have had good results only between friends who deeply trust and respect each other. Subconsciously he knew I wasn't out to hurt him and he knew he had to rally as directed. So let's find out what is happening in the OR". MacKenzie ran ahead of Will, who was pushing Isaac in a wheelchair while Anna held his hand.

Before Isaac and his group reached the operating room, MacKenzie brought Dr Rayskill from the OR. Rayskill spoke first: "Isaac, my friend and colleague. I do not have good news, I'm sorry to say. The Caesarian has been concluded. The baby lived for only a few minutes. It was strangled in utero by the umbilical cord. If she had survived, she would have been physically and mentally impaired. Even so, I know this is a great loss for both you and Sophie. As to Sophie, Isaac, she is very sick. She has a systemic fever – an infection that has been increasing for many days now. She has slipped into a coma which may enable her to develop her healing. We have started her on an aggressive plan of antibiotics and sedatives. I think she will emerge from this physically improved but probably deeply depressed and in a weakened physical condition that could last for some time. I am more worried, though, by what I observed a couple of days ago. I think her post-traumatic stress disorder has deepened, removing her from consciousness."

In answer to Will's question about treatment for PTSD,

Dr Rayskill reminded Will they were very lucky to have available to them one of the world's leading experts in that field, namely, Dr MacKenzie.

Dr MacKenzie replied to Dr Rayskill that he would be pleased to continue to provide treatment for Sophie if Isaac wished to retain his services. Will replied quickly, "Yes, Dr MacKenzie, I engage your services on behalf of both Dr and Mrs Menshive. I do so under the guardianship agreement you know both husband and wife have conferred on me. I turn now to Isaac to confirm that I continue to have that authority." Isaac nodded his head in assent and then fell asleep.

It was agreed that Sophie would remain in the clinic until her physical health returned to a level where she could be transported to Dr MacKenzie's treatment facility, which had a much less institutional feel than the clinic. Isaac was to go to that facility in a couple of days, a delay required only in case Sophie needed him by her bedside. Arrangements were made for Anna and Will to take bedside sessions with Sophie and to make daily visits with Isaac.

Anna and Will discussed the ongoing asset investigations in which Isaac and Will were engaged; Anna expressed no interest in being any more involved in that process than she had been, in fact saying she wished the whole 'kit and caboodle' could be burned and buried.

* * *

Will kept his promise made to visit Little Isaac that evening. When Will entered the nursery with arms open and a big smile for Little Isaac, the child responded happily and with enthusiasm. Before Will could suggest Legos and Dinky toys, he was led to a large table in the corner of the nursery which was set up for building a town with many roads, hills and valleys where the large collection of toy cars and trucks could be employed with imagination and fun.

Little Isaac displayed an eagerness to build with the Legos and he began the happy task as he directed Will as to what he was to do as Little Isaac's assistant. Will was amused at the role he was assigned and Little Isaac took assumed command naturally, expecting Will to fall in line.

After they had been playing at the table piling the Legos into building-like structures, Little Isaac came around the table to Will and, almost pushing his face into Will's, asked him where his mamma was. Will decided that a direct honest answer would be best.

"Your mother has been very sick, Little Isaac, and so was the baby she was carrying. The baby became so sick it needed peace – it couldn't struggle any longer and died. Your mother misses you very much and would like you to be with her. Right now she needs a lot of sleep and medicines which means she has to be very quiet. We have the very best doctors for her who are helping her right now. Your aunt Anna and I will be taking you to see her in a day or two. Right now she needs you to stay here in this apartment with Nanny Ellis, Anna and me. We all care for you and will play with you. Tomorrow I will take you up to Regent's Park where we will visit the zoo. It has lots of monkeys and even a giraffe." Little Isaac's eyes shone with happiness.

Will was not surprised that Little Isaac had not asked about his father. Isaac had been away much of the child's life. Will decided that Isaac's role as father would have to be much improved and involved as soon as he was well enough.

24

ANNA HAD BEEN diligent in creating and keeping her journal as requested, and every day or two she would review it with Will to discuss whether corrections were required. None were. She surprised herself at how much she enjoyed her scribe-like role, keeping a detailed record of the events and decisions made by each of their fellow passengers on their ship from hell.

The journal, as Will and Anna reviewed it after the events surrounding the illnesses and loss of the baby, proved to them the essential merits of the record. The journal assisted them to identify the path forward for each of the several tasks that lay ahead for both of them.

The most obvious on that morning over coffee was the reminder that they had been so absorbed by Will and Sophie's crisis that Little Isaac had been neglected. His need for love, support and continuing contact with those he knew and trusted, was proven the evening before while Will spent over an hour and a half playing with Little Isaac.

"We must work him into our daily schedules," Anna suggested. "I know very little about raising children but from what I have seen of Sophie and Isaac's interaction with Little Isaac before this horror happened, we, I mean you and me, Will, must fill that void until Sophie and Isaac are back to full health and able to resume their roles as parents."

"Right, I agree, but let me give you what appears to be a timeline on how long our new roles with Little Isaac's care are likely to continue from my conversations with Dr Rayskill and Dr MacKenzie in particular. A diagnosis of post-traumatic stress disorder has been made for both of them as you know. Some of the root causes are similar for each of them, but there are profound causes that go well beyond the last few weeks. Dr MacKenzie has cautioned me to expect the recovery of both patients to be long and unpredictable; it is likely to be characterized, once they are over their physical ailments, by depression, by periodic hostility to those close to them, including each other – and that can include physical violence. This means, he tells me, that we must watch them carefully and protect each from the other both physically and verbally. This extends to Little Isaac, too. The hostility there may be more verbal than physical but it can be as damaging, with long-term effects on him. Little Isaac has Mrs Ellis to provide for his physical needs, but she has shown few signs of open and robust nurturing and demonstrable love customary in Jewish families in an American setting.

"Anna, you know you and I are now his surrogate parents. You may not have had children and decided you did not want children but you are now, as we say in law, *in loco parentis*. As acting parents, and I include myself, we have to organize our lives to meet his needs. Having said that, I have a huge task to complete in terms of Isaac's inheritance. Not only will I be discovering and then organizing the assets, but I will be preserving them for Little Isaac. Long-term planning was an issue that Isaac and I discussed in the past, but in general terms. Greater detail is now required."

"Do Sophie and Isaac have wills and other legal documents in place needed at a time like this?"

"Yes. I prepared wills for them which have been duly signed and the originals delivered to the New York law office. They were sent a few weeks ago. As for my role as manager of his assets with authority to investigate and deal with them, that authority was conferred on me jointly with Isaac four years ago in Switzerland. That authority made it clear that my authority survived any incapacity Isaac or Sophie might have. My authority extends beyond assets to their persons under guardianship agreements. I have guardianship of their persons in the event of a mental incapacity such as we now face with them both. Incidentally, that authority means that I have a duty to do what is needed, and that now includes something I have to talk to you about."

"Oh God! What can that be?"

"The baby. As Jews, I know Isaac and Sophie would expect end-of-life and funeral procedures customary to their beliefs. I know who to contact to find out whom I should deal with here in London, but I don't know what family traditions they have that might be expected. Sophie's parents are arriving tomorrow. They will help, but we can't let them take over. With Isaac's recent reengagement with his religion, I need to know which sector or belief-system in Judaism he adopted – and I know there are several; some are non-specific as to the usual theological divisions prevalent in Judaism, as are many American Jews."

"In our family, Will, like almost everything else related to family traditions and European culture, there was no practice or beliefs discussed or practiced. For example, my mother's funeral, as well as my father's, was at a local funeral home – it was a Jewish funeral home, and some Jewish rituals were involved but very little. You see, they had suffered so much vicariously during the Nazi years and from the Bolsheviks that they simply forgot, or chose to forget, anything connecting them with their religion or the customs of the places their parents came from in Europe."

"Alright, that means it is up to us to create a ceremony that seems to us to meet the spiritual needs and historic cultural expressions of your family. We will put a plan together and will then discuss it with Mr and Mrs Posen. Of course, I will try to discuss our plans with Isaac as you and I will do with Sophie. I am leaving you out of discussions with Isaac only because you have each gone on separate paths with regard to religion and culture so I don't want any reason or opportunity for discord between you two. You have grown together very well over the past few weeks and have come to respect and actually like each other. I am not going to jeopardize that." To which Anna had no reply.

* * *

Will called Rabbi Levin in Moscow and he explained the dilemma he and Anna were in with respect to the death of the baby and in light of Isaac and Sophie's medical and psychological conditions. The rabbi gave Will several helpful suggestions; the most important of which was the name of the foremost rabbi in the branch of Judaism in London he thought most compatible with Isaac's emergent beliefs. He had not discussed religion with Sophie but believed she would accept Isaac's wishes in regard to plans for the religious elements of a funeral. He congratulated Will on an important decision Will had made.

"In our faith, Mr MacIntosh, life is sacred. A baby having survived full term but stillbirth is considered to be a member of our faith and is entitled to the full rites of the church at a time like this. Thank you for being respectful and understanding. One more thing: you know that Dr Menshive met with me several times to discuss our faith and his conversion to it. We became friends as well as confidants. I would ask your permission to come to London to attend the funeral and to meet and try to counsel and comfort both Isaac and Sophie. Would that be acceptable?" Will and Anna, in unison, affirmed that his visit would be welcomed and they insisted that he conduct the service, if possible, in both Russian and English. He was pleased to be asked. Before ringing off, Rabbi Levin offered to contact Rabbi Cohen, the rabbi he had recommended, adding, "I know Rabbi Cohen well, having worked with him on various aspects of Jewish history in Russia and Jewish genealogy. It will be a privilege to meet him again. I know he will take an interest in and will be active in supporting Dr and Mrs Menshive on their journey of grieving and healing."

* * *

Will and Anna visited the clinic as soon after the phone call to Rabbi Levin as they could. They had to safeguard the baby's remains before she was ceremoniously cremated which was the custom, Will had discovered.

They arrived just in time at the clinic meeting with the director. The clinic's director had attempted to discuss with

Isaac and Sophie what they wished to do with the remains but he had not been able to engage them in a conversation of any kind. The baby was in the mortuary in the basement of the clinic, prepared for cremation. When Will proved his authority to deal with the baby on behalf of her parents, his directions were accepted and promptly followed. The baby was returned to the refrigerated holding unit.

Will went to Isaac and Anna to Sophie as quickly as they could. Will tried over the period of an hour and a half to reach into Isaac's unconsciousness to engage him in discussion related to the baby. At first, having no response of any kind dealing with the baby as gently and compassionately as he could, but failing, towards the end of his time with Isaac Will tried a more direct, if not brutal, manner to bring him into consciousness. He explained his baby daughter was dead and arrangements had to be made for her burial. Isaac's directions were required, Will explained. The more direct and forceful Will became, somehow the more withdrawn Isaac became, although at no time did he demonstrate any consciousness.

Anna met with Sophie and she had a similar response from her. Will joined Anna with Sophie after leaving Isaac and he witnessed a similar reaction or lack of reaction from Sophie, other than observing Sophie's eyes were full of tears which poured from behind closed eyes.

Will and Anna understood that they were now left with the responsibility of organizing the funeral and arranging for Isaac's and Sophie's involvement in the service, even in their current states, to make plans for them to be taken to the synagogue for the funeral.

Before Will left the clinic, while he was waiting for Anna to compose herself after the hospital room visits with her brother and sister-in-law, Will received a call on his mobile phone. It was a remarkable achievement for him to have identified the ring, its source and how to activate the call. It was from Rabbi Cohen. The rabbi's highly cultivated Oxbridge accent gave Will an immediate sense of the man's authority and an inherent comfort from the competent authority he exuded.

Rabbi Cohen asked few questions. He recommended an

eighteenth-century synagogue in the City of London, Bevis Marks Synagogue on Heneage Lane. This was London's oldest synagogue, a short distance from St Paul's Cathedral. Will was pleased on behalf of Isaac that the sanctuary was one containing ancient dignity and tradition. He looked forward to viewing it and observing the funeral service. Arrangements were made for the rabbi to meet with Will later that afternoon.

* * *

Over tea that afternoon at Fortnum & Mason on Piccadilly Street, Will and Anna sat pensively, both trying to devise a plan to resolve the immediate issues related to the death of the baby and the health of the baby's parents. Each issue required their attention and it seemed each denied priority over the others, changing from one minute to the next relating to the funeral and disposal of the baby's remains.

The elegance and calm of the Fortnum & Mason restaurant were enhanced by the attentive and nicely attired servers. It was a different world from any they had occupied in the last few months. When conversation ceased Will and Anna sat in silence, happily enjoying the tea, sandwiches and sweets. As they were leaving to meet with Rabbi Cohen at the Fitzroy Square flat, Anna turned to Will and said quietly, "For me, this place offers the calm refuge some people find in a church. This will be my 'go-to' place when I need to be alone to regroup my emotions."

In reply, Will suggested, "Yes, there are two other places I have visited often to which I will take you with a similar atmosphere. I suggest, however, that as you have recently converted to Christianity, you might find solace in attending a church service. If you would like I will take you to a service at St Martin-in-the-Fields on Trafalgar Square, technically the Royal Family's chapel in London, on Sunday morning." Anna's only reply was a broad smile displaying her happiness with the suggestion.

* * *

Nanny Ellis had Little Isaac dressed and groomed to a standard suitable for an audience with the Queen. Anna had him sitting on her lap as she explained that his 'momma and poppa' were getting better but still needed a lot of sleep so they should not be disturbed. He understood and accepted that reason for not being able to see his parents. While Sophie was confined in the early months of her pregnancy and frequently after they left Smolensk, Sophie had required quiet time to rest. Little Isaac accepted Anna's explanation as a simple confirmation of the pattern he had become accustomed to with his mother. As to his father, he was usually away anyway, so any explanation sufficed.

Will and Sophie decided it would help Rabbi Cohen to meet Isaac and Sophie's child as arrangements were made for the funeral. He would be able to pass on his observations to Rabbi Levin. It had been agreed that Rabbi Levin would deliver the meditation on death and participate with Rabbi Cohen in the religious ceremonies. Each would need a sense of the family in order to give meaning to the funeral meditation.

Rabbi Cohen proved to be much younger and more vibrant than either Anna or Will had expected. He was a tall, fit and robust man with a mellifluous voice that would need no amplification in the synagogue. After an hour of the rabbi meeting Little Isaac, Will and Anna said goodbye but it was Little Isaac who stole the show, bringing more tears to Anna, and in this instance to Will, when he said, "Rabbi, I know all about God. I am happy Baby will be with Him and that you will help get her to God." The rabbi turned as quickly as he could without frightening Little Isaac. Will saw tears in the rabbi's eyes as he was shown out of the apartment.

25

ANNA JOINED WILL as he travelled by the Central Line on the London Underground to St Paul's Station, from where they walked to Bevis Marks Synagogue. They met Rabbi Cohen there as scheduled at 10 a.m.

The building was difficult to find. It was tucked away down a well-hidden lane near Liverpool Station. As Will stood in front of the structure, he recalled an earlier visit during a specialized architectural walking tour of the ancient places of worship in the Square Mile. He launched into one of his stream-of-consciousness rambles on architectural history. He pointed out that the synagogue was built in 1701 and contained transitional architectural features, some of which were late Baroque and the majority early Georgian neoclassical, with evidence of Jewish symbols as decorative elements.

He suddenly jolted back into the present and he turned to Anna, apologizing for his pedantry. He explained that his travels through over seventy countries were to study, interpret and memorize the features of prominent buildings so that he could compare and contrast with others he encountered during his travels. He expected Anna to demonstrate the impatience and boredom usually expressed by Isaac, along with a threat of a competing medical lecture on 'total hips'.

Anna turned away from looking at the front elevation, as Will referred to it, and she said to Will, "Why did you stop? I am interested. Remember, I took a fine arts course at Columbia University in New York. I know Isaac has interest only in knees, hips and lesser joints. I have no interest in them as I suspect you don't. Share your knowledge of the history and architecture of our surroundings. I will be attentive, but beware I will have questions and may appear to challenge you – but that is only my method of learning."

Will stared at her for a few moments, somewhat stunned into silence, since his wife and very few of his colleagues and friends were prepared to listen to his monologues.

"Alright… We are here in this secure little courtyard carefully tucked away out of sight. I have visited this city over forty times with expert guides who took me here and there and toured me through numerous buildings, so I am full of details many could find trivial. Thank you for being prepared to listen to me; I think it will be helpful to you when we discuss the funeral. There are traditions in the conservative Jewish tradition practiced here that you might find offensive."

"Come on, Will, my family was not devout but I attended our local synagogue in Upper Manhattan on several occasions. My mother told me about the status of women in the old traditions. I expect that is what you are talking about." A nod from Will confirmed her guess, although it wasn't much of a guess. "I will be very happy to see my little niece given an old-fashioned Jewish funeral. I know that is what both Isaac and Sophie would have liked if they could have made the arrangements themselves."

They walked through one of the double doors that led into the sanctuary. Anna immediately described each sector and point of importance to Will.

"I remember what I was told, but I am not part of that tradition and spiritual belief system now. I have more Mendelssohn genes than Menshikovsky or Günzburg genes, I think. Like my distant aunts who had converted to Christianity, I too find my conversion to Lutherism, not specifically what is known as Lutheranism, very relevant to me and more satisfying."

Will was impressed with this woman who had always struck him as a 'flake', as Isaac called her. She was always a great sport and had been fun to be with when they briefly dated while Will visited Isaac in New York during holidays from Dalhousie University. She had been a rebel then, associated with undesirables like Anthony Cann, but she seemed to have outgrown that phase.

Anna smirked as she watched Will: his reaction was obviously amusing to her.

They walked to the front of the synagogue from its elevated position halfway between the seats and railings on the principal floor and the balcony above. Will pointed to the railed enclosure formed by a balustrade in the centre of the main level reserved for men and said that he related to the layout of this ancient synagogue since it was similar to the late-eighteenth-century Presbyterian churches built in the New England States and older British settled sections of the Maritime Provinces of Canada. Within that enclosure, the elders of the Kirk would sit – all males in formal attire, silent, dignified and authoritarian.

"Very much like the Jewish elders in this church, I think," said Anna.

Rabbi Cohen joined them as he led Rabbi Levin into the sanctuary. Both theologians on entering conducted a ceremony difficult to understand to Will but clearly one of submission and obsequiousness to their God. After Rabbi Cohen gave his colleague a brief history of the structure and the functional elements of the sanctuary, they joined Will and Anna.

Anna was the first to speak: "Gentleman, while I was born Jewish, I have long abandoned that faith in favour of Christianity which espouses equality of the sexes – so I must ask your forgiveness if I am in a part of this sanctuary to which women are prevented from being in."

Rabbi Cohen replied, "Ms Menshive, I thank you for your courtesy in recognizing that in the conservative Jewish tradition women are confined to a lesser, some would say, inferior role. I don't agree with that interpretation, but many modern women do have that opinion. Now to reply to your comment about parts of this sanctuary to which you are not entitled to be in, let me assure you that the funeral is a private ceremony. All who attend will be accorded the same privileges, access and welcome. That of course includes Mr MacIntosh. No, our planning for the service that will be conducted here will not in any way relegate anyone attending to an inferior place or role. In fact, Ms Menshive, I am asking you to read the Prayer for the Dead, a prayer that has been part of Jewish funerals for many centuries. And I would like Mr MacIntosh to read from the Pentateuch, one of the first five books of the Old Testament. Rabbi Levin and I will select the readings before you leave this morning. I will ask, however, that you not join us here in the area that in a Protestant Church would be referred to as 'the chancel'. Rabbi Levin and I will occupy this space, although certain of our elders will have ceremonial tasks that are performed here."

Anna's assent was immediate and she said simply, "Thank you, Rabbi, for accommodating me in the form, timing and ceremonies of the funeral for my family to enable us to have a traditional Jewish funeral here tomorrow."

Will felt a momentary guilt as he realized he was looking forward to the funeral service with its many exotic features — exotic to him, he reminded himself.

After the schedule of events for the service was discussed, approved and rehearsed, Rabbi Cohen invited Rabbi Levin, Anna and Will to his office next door to the synagogue. While next door, it had its entrance from the same courtyard as the synagogue. It was a modest, nondescript structure on the square — deliberately intended, Will surmised, not to be in conflict with or compete with the impressive front of the synagogue.

When the group was comfortably seated in the rabbi's office, Rabbi Levin turned to Anna and asked whether there would be any objection to the 'Menshikovskys', father and two sons, attending the service. Anna looked blank. Before she could ask who they were, Will explained their very distant connection to her family and more significantly their role in managing the land and buildings now owned by Isaac in Russia. Anna said she would be happy to meet them and thank them for attending. She couldn't resist, however, in asking how they would have known of the baby's death in time to make travel arrangements and to actually get to London. No one had an answer, but Will said he was glad they would be in London at that time as he planned a meeting at the lawyer's office in Lincoln's Inn Fields in a couple of days, to which he would invite the senior Menshikovsky. It did bother him, too, how that information had travelled to them so quickly.

When the conference with the rabbi ended, Will approached Rabbi Cohen and he asked how Isaac and Anna could be brought to the funeral and where they would be placed. The rabbi explained that Will should leave that to him. All the arrangements had been made including transportation to and from the clinic, their method of entry into and placement during the service. Will was thankful that at least in that matter he had no decisions to make. And as a follow-up, he asked what had been arranged for the baby to be brought in and where the internment would be. He was informed that the conservative Jewish traditions at Bevis Marks prescribed the protocols for every aspect of the funeral for a baby. The internment of the ashes, he said, would follow the service in a consecrated burial plot used by the congregation for which express authorization had been given by the proper authorities.

As Will and Anna returned to the apartment, Will suggested to Anna that Isaac would want a suitable gift to be given to the synagogue and to each of the rabbis for their cooperation and conduct of the service. Anna agreed and without thinking asked whether there would be money available to Will to make a donation and discreet fees paid to the rabbis. Will assured her there was and that he had full management of the funds necessary for the purpose. That brought him back to the relative isolation Anna had chosen to have in relation to the trust assets left to her and to Isaac and to what had been discovered since she had assigned her interest to Isaac. Will promised himself that a priority later in the week would be to have a conversation with Anna, giving her a briefing on the current status of the assets now in Isaac's possession that came from the trust.

Thinking of the former trust assets brought Will's consciousness to Isaac's personal assets, namely those he had before the inheritance. He and Isaac seldom discussed those assets and when they were referred to, it was only in passing.

Will realized he now had an obligation under the power of attorney to look into and protect those assets as well.

Fortunately, the meeting scheduled with Mr Smythe would include two specialists from the Swiss bank. This, too, was another topic he would have to discuss with Anna.

The early evening hours were spent with Little Isaac, who greeted Will more like a buddy than a parental figure. He showed Anna affection but Anna had not learned how to return it in a way that Little Isaac would recognize. There was affection but little interaction.

While Will and Little Isaac were busy building their castle, houses and barns, Anna went to her sitting room and sat down to prepare her day's entries in her journal.

* * *

Earlier in the day, Will decided he needed the peace, solitude and relaxation a concert would provide. He discovered in the Evening Standard newspaper that a concert was scheduled at St Martin-in-the-Fields Church at 7:30 p.m. that evening. Little Isaac was worn out by 6:00 p.m. that evening, so Will left him in the care of Nanny Ellis. He had offered to take Anna but she declined without giving a reason. Will was somewhat relieved, but only because he felt drained by the many people he had been dealing with in close quarters. A time-out was needed.

He took the Northern Line from Tottenham Court Road Station to Embankment Station and from there he had a leisurely walk to the church. As was his habit from numerous previous visits to the church for concerts, he went to the basement area where an excellent buffet dinner was served virtually every evening – certainly every evening that there was a concert.

After his light meal, enhanced with a dessert laced with quantities of old-fashioned, delicious custard, Will went up to the sanctuary where he rented a cushion for his thinning backside that increasingly objected to hard wooden seats. A comfortable pew was now a necessity in his life.

During the concert, he revelled in viewing the late Baroque architecture created by Aberdonian James Gibbs in the early eighteenth century. The space in volume, decoration and simplicity never failed to provide him with peace and a sense of happiness.

In truth, he heard little of the music. It was simply a distraction that enabled him to concentrate on the real issues requiring his attention. He was able to attend to those issues without distraction and he only occasionally listened to the music.

26

ANNA AND WILL arrived at the synagogue ten minutes before the scheduled time of the funeral. They were met inside the entrance by Sophie's parents Levi and Helen Posen who were standing on either side of the wheelchair in which a slumped and inanimate Sophie had been seated. To assist in Sophie's security a large strap encircled her body and the chair, affixing her to the chair. Adjacent to and a hand's reach away from Sophie's chair was a duplicate with Isaac similarly secured.

Efforts were made by several people to engage Sophie and Isaac with even simple condolences, but such utterances were lost in the breeze flowing into the sanctuary from the open doors admitting mourners.

Will had advised Mr and Mrs Posen the night before that they should expect a very small attendance – no more than eight or ten mourners. In fact, the service was delayed for twenty minutes as an increasing number of people arrived to join the family and to extend their sympathies. By the time Rabbi Cohen was able to commence the service, there were over one hundred people present. Neither Sophie nor Isaac acknowledged the presence of so many who had come to show their support. The indifference shown to the congregation was reflected in their behaviour with each other.

Anna whispered to Dr MacKenzie who stood behind the family, asking why Sophie and Isaac did not recognize or communicate in any way with each other. His reply answered the question in a way that confirmed his diagnosis for each of the patients. "It is a classic symptom of post-traumatic stress disorder; they would withdraw into themselves from a state of emotional numbness. They cannot leave their solitude to recognize or take part in what is happening around them. It is important that they be here. It may assist them in returning to the world around them."

Mrs Posen, in a state of emotional breakdown, heavily medicated and almost comatose, heard what was said and she said simply, "Is that why my dear Sophie won't talk to me? I need her to talk to me." Her husband gave her a prolonged hug which appeared to give her some comfort.

The service proceeded according to the order of service Rabbi Cohen had outlined during their meeting the day before. The Jewish Prayer for the Dead was read with considerable passion and conviction by Rabbi Levin in both Russian and Hebrew. *El Malei Rachamim* had been recited at the funeral of the baby girl's ancestors for many hundreds of years, giving her existence a spiritual life it had not possessed in this world. The casket was placed on a table in front of the congregation behind the mourners and below the rabbi. Its diminutive size was such that few in the sanctuary noticed it until at the close of the service a young rabbi assigned to the task by Rabbi Cohen came forward to carry it out of the sanctuary. As he picked it up there was a collective sigh and tears were spontaneously displayed on the faces of all present. Even though a casket of a size to accommodate a two-year-old was chosen to lessen the shock of a size appropriate for a newborn, the scene of a hulking young man gently carrying the diminutive box was a summation of the life and loss in the pathetic scene observed by those present.

After the service, a reception was held at Rabbi Cohen's office and meeting rooms visited by Will and Anna the day before. The reception room was filled with flowers and tables laid with small sandwiches and hors d'oeuvres. Three teenaged girls circulated salvers carrying glasses of sherry.

The family was ushered into the reception room first, with Sophie and Isaac brought in by clinic caregivers pushing their wheelchairs. Mr Posen came over to Anna and asked whether she would object to Sophie being taken to a room next to the reception room where only family could be with her. Anna agreed and instructed the attendants with Isaac to take him as well. Dr MacKenzie accompanied Sophie and Isaac. Will and

Anna stayed with them long enough to observe Dr MacKenzie gently but urgently talking to Sophie and Isaac, trying without success to engage them.

Those in the large crowd in attendance were identified as they went through the reception line comprised of Mr and Mrs Posen, Anna and Will. Anna and the Posens insisted that a reluctant Will be in the line-up, as he now represented both body and worldly goods. Also, he was the only one of those in the reception line with sufficient composure to assist the others.

As people went through the line at least one-third were family members of Isaac and Sophie. The Posen family had flown over from the United States in large numbers and they proved to be a considerable comfort to Levi and Helen. The Menshives were represented by two second or third cousins who had been contacted by Isaac's first wife. They were also represented by all three of Isaac's daughters. Anna uttered a gentle gasp of recognition and welcome as they approached her in the line. The receiving line was held up for some time while arrangements were made for them to meet the next day at the flat for a reunion. Will requested them to call on their father in the next room and asked them to identify themselves first to Dr MacKenzie who would handle the introductions. Introductions were particularly necessary for Sophie as she had never met them.

The Russian branch of the family was represented, as expected, by the Menshikovskys, father and sons. Sergei, the majordomo at the dacha in Smolensk, requested to be present and arrangements had been made by Menshikovsky senior with Will's consent.

The remaining visitors were a mixture of people Will had met in London on Isaac's business such as lawyer Smythe and his young associate, and there was a large component of members of the Ben Marks Synagogue, many of whom had Russian or Central European origins. Will was particularly interested in three older men who came up as a group and introduced themselves as distant cousins of Isaac's through the Mendelssohn connection. As members of the congregation at Bevis Marks they had heard of the death and on making inquiries of Rabbi Levin they had discovered the connection with Isaac and the deceased infant.

With Anna's consent, Will arranged to meet with them two days hence. This meeting, he reasoned, could provide further information on the Mendelssohn family linkages with the Menshikovskys and the trust assets.

The love and encouragement extended to Anna and the Posens was remarkable and gave them some solace, to which Anna's comment was revealing for many displaced and transported families: "It takes a crisis like death, particularly the death of a child, to bring people together who have been lost to each other, in our case for generations."

At the conclusion of the public reception Anna, Will and the Posens joined Sophie and Isaac in the next room. They were happily surprised to see that several ladies of the congregation were doing their best to attend to Sophie and Isaac. As Will entered the room he observed one very short, rotund woman with a smile that could melt an iceberg bending over Isaac, patting him on the cheek and talking to, or more accurately talking *at* him. Suddenly, Isaac turned to her, focused on her and smiled and he expressed his thanks. She continued to talk to him for several minutes. He continued to listen and to watch her intently.

Another member of the congregation, a young woman about Sophie's age was giving similar attention to Sophie. Mrs Posen was the first to observe that Sophie started to cry, the first indication she was actually concentrating and listening to the woman, who continued talking. As she spoke to Sophie, the woman became highly agitated and became intensely tearful as she explained to Sophie that she, too, had lost a baby shortly after her birth. Sophie actually raised her hand and patted the woman's arm.

After the private visitation had been underway for almost an hour, Dr MacKenzie advised the Posens, then Anna, that the patients should return to the clinic. He expressed his surprise that Sophie and Isaac had responded so well to the stimuli of the funeral and reception. He cautioned Will and

Anna that the road to recovery from PTSD was long and uncertain but, he said, it appeared it had begun. Progress could be made only with the patient reverting to an early stage in the condition. He repeated his opinion that both Sophie and Isaac had profound PTSD and that the families should not expect a rapid recovery.

* * *

The Posens joined Anna and Will at the apartment for an early dinner. "This will be more like what they call here, Helen, 'high tea'."

During their time together Levi asked Will whether money was needed to pay expenses, to which Will, with surprise, informed him that there was sufficient money to meet all expenses, including continuing support for Little Isaac who had greeted and visited with his grandparents for over an hour when they arrived. Will realized that neither Isaac nor Sophie had revealed what they were doing in Europe. It was time for Will to brief them on Isaac's purpose for being in Europe and on his personal role as attorney, agent and guardian for both Isaac and Sophie.

When Will finished his monologue, brought to a conclusion by Anna who noticed Mrs Posen nodding off, he concluded by saying there was sufficient money available for both Isaac and Sophie to provide whatever medical and psychological treatment and counselling they might require for whatever period of time was necessary.

Mrs Posen expressed disappointment that her daughter would have appointed Will as her guardian. "In the States that is always a close family member unless there is a family split, but as far as we knew that wasn't the case."

Will replied that there was no indication of dissension in the family. The decision was based on the nature of the investigation Isaac, Sophie and Will were undertaking relating to the inheritance. There was risk to them all, Will said, so it was important that someone was with them with a knowledge of the background to step forward to make decisions quickly if required. Mr Posen said simply, "Very sensible. Thank you for your care and support for Sophie and Little Isaac. I understand that you, Mr MacIntosh, will remain guardian for Little Isaac as long as he requires a guardian – with your loving help, Anna."

Anna agreed that was the case. Will added that the role he was now playing was both investigatory and administrative, which directly involved protecting Little Isaac's interests; hence the need for Will to be the guardian. Both Mr and Mrs Posen agreed.

Anna reassured them that they would have access to Little Isaac when and how they wished, to which lawyer Will replied, "To the extent it does not interfere with his parents' treatment and my continuing role as guardian."

Will was relieved that neither Mr nor Mrs Posen asked about the nature or value of Isaac's assets and income. Refusal to disclose that information might have been viewed as distrusting and exclusionary.

Mrs Posen asked when Sophie and Little Isaac would be returning to the States.

Will replied that they would be staying in London for the foreseeable future. Dr MacKenzie, he explained, was a foremost authority and treatment specialist in PTSD. They were both better off here at his clinic for their ongoing care. It was essential that Little Isaac be near at hand to assist with his parents' recovery. Sophie would remain with her husband. Both were receiving the best medical care the world could provide.

Anna turned to Will and asked, "Will, is there a flat on the inventory list in London which could be available to Mr and Mrs Posen where they could stay when they wish to come to visit in London?" In fact, she knew there was a vacant flat on the ground floor in the building they were in. Will's answer surprised her. "Yes, there is," and to Mr and Mrs Posen he said, "It is fairly close by on another square called Russell Square, in a district called Bloomsbury. About a fifteen-minute walk from here. I will have it made up for your use when you need it, assuming you would like to have it when Sophie is in London after her recovery. I should say, though, that the nature of our investigation will require frequent travel, so I will need to know in advance when you will need it. Having said that, it will be set up for your sole use and you can leave what you like there for your next visit."

This response gave both mother and father satisfaction that they could visit Sophie and their grandson when they chose. It might be frequent because they had only one other child, a son who persisted in his unmarried state – without offspring.

"Before you leave, Will, you have referred to our future accommodation as a flat and your accommodation as an apartment. Isn't a flat and an apartment the same thing here in England?"

"Well, Helen, in this situation a flat is a rental unit such as you would have in New York. When I use the term 'apartment', in London real estate language it is a 'maisonette', or a house-like large part of a building used as accommodations. The distinction is even more significant because the whole building is owned by the occupier or his family. I hope that clarified the use I made of both terms. 'Apartment' would be used by few Londoners... but I think it explains more accurately what this is."

"Thank you. Does Isaac own a lot of real estate in London?" asked Mrs Posen.

Will replied briefly but in a way that did not invite further inquiries. "Yes. A lot."

27

WILL AWOKE THE morning after the funeral having shared with other family members the intensely emotional loss felt by Isaac and Sophie. He was drained and lifeless. It was a struggle to get ready to meet Anna at breakfast, knowing she would be in even worse shape: this would require his efforts to lift her spirits somewhat, assuming he could.

Before leaving his bedroom he paused for a moment of self-reflection: "I need to take stock of where I am, why I am here and how long I can remain at this."

As he sat stiff-legged on a Windsor chair – never very comfortable at the best of times, particularly one two hundred years old, as was this treasure – he had flashbacks to the stages of his involvement with Isaac over the past four years.

He recalled the beginning of this journey with Isaac: out of the clear blue as he was working with his usual drive and concentration at his law office in Charlottetown, Prince Edward Island, comfortable and confident in his well-ordered life, he received a telephone call from an old friend. His receptionist announced that Dr Isaac Menshive was on the line. He was surprised and intrigued, as he hadn't heard from Isaac for a few years. They had been great friends and companions at Dalhousie University in Halifax, Nova Scotia while in their undergraduate years. Isaac went into medicine at Dalhousie, Will into law. With their diverging career paths, they gradually lost much of the familiarity of their former friendship. From time to time on visits to New York Will had lunch with Isaac and he tried to keep up with Isaac's professional achievements and his varied and inconsistent family life. Isaac on two or three occasions took a new wife or companion to Prince Edward Island where he would visit with Will and his family.

The call was unexpected, not only because their friendship appeared to have naturally run its course, but also because

Isaac was frequently in the news with some major orthopedic innovation with which he was connected.

Will had taken the call bracing himself for bad news. Isaac's voice was as forceful and loud as it had been at university; stronger than Will had remembered during their occasional meetings since those idyllic days.

Isaac announced that he was taking a leave of absence from his practice and his senior ownership and management position with one of New York's most prestigious orthopedic clinics. Without a pause, he informed Will that Will would be accompanying him during the sabbatical which Isaac planned. It would take them to Europe that summer for about four months. Before Will could catch his breath to interject, Isaac informed him that his father had recently passed away and in his will had given trust assets to him and to his sister Anna.

"You are essential to the success of this venture in Europe, Will. The assets are located in Eastern Europe controlled by a Swiss bank with lawyers at every turn and style – bloody vultures. I must have you with me. You can take time off from your practice. You have others in your office who can fill in for you. It's just legal work, after all. Incidentally, don't worry about money. All expenses are mine. It appears there is a lot of money involved. I will live like a lord and so will you."

Just as Isaac was taking a deep breath to resume his instructions, Will managed a question or two. "Why me, and what is the purpose of exploring the assets? The Swiss bank will have them meticulously documented."

"You?" said Isaac. "Because I trust you. I remember that you studied Russian and expressed some knowledge of the history and culture of Russia and the former Comecon countries. Not many Americans of my acquaintance have that background and those few I wouldn't trust. You I trust. Now, I plan to leave in six weeks. We will meet up in Berlin. I will have your first-class tickets from Toronto to Berlin on Lufthansa Airlines sent to you the first of the week…"

Will recalled saying: "Hold it, I can't do that! I have family and professional responsibilities. Even on this little sand spit I live on there are legal issues requiring my attention – and many of its residents find my services helpful. I can't just leave like that, even if I wanted to."

Will's memories skipped over the arguments, discussions and reflections that ended three days later, when he had agreed to join Isaac on his madcap adventure. An adventure was all it appeared to be. He was in mid-career, successful by local modest standards and somewhat bored. An adventure was what he needed to revitalize himself. A week before, he recalled, he didn't know he needed revitalization, but the intensity of his happy response to Isaac's proposal convinced him he did indeed need it.

"Why didn't I stop and get off this frenetic pace of life I was leading long ago?" The truth was that his law practice had brought him excitement, challenges, many successes and a sense of real achievement. "However, a form of sabbatical with respite from my day-to-day life and routines would be a welcome diversion," he supposed.

"I am now prepared to engage in Isaac's travel plans even with all my work and responsibilities here in Charlottetown. The truth is that I can't abandon it now. Every element of creativity, inventiveness and professional ability I have will be engaged in Isaac's investigation as well as involvement with every aspect of Isaac's life. A return to my pedestrian law practice and daily routine is unthinkable. This may indeed be an interesting adventure."

As Will was reconfirming his commitment to Isaac and his family, he reminded himself that along with Isaac's underlying mental health issues, Isaac was both suffering from a post-traumatic stress disorder and also was attempting to heal from several gunshot wounds received recently aggravating those he received a few years ago. Will was now the guardian of Isaac's person and legal attorney of his assets, having full authority to manage all aspects of the vast network of multi-dimensioned asset holdings which required continuing and immediate attention – his.

"Can I abandon Isaac, Sophie, Little Isaac and the new trust management at a time like this? I am where I am and will have to continue to be."

***

No less dispirited and feeling overwhelmed by his responsibilities, Will joined Anna for breakfast. After they exchanged a few brief words of greeting and commiseration, Little Isaac joined them. There is nothing like the enthusiasm, affection and blind trust of a child to engage a person's better feelings. Certainly a few minutes with the child was enough to recharge Will's batteries, particularly when he remembered that at law he was now *in loco parentis* to this child. He was legally responsible in a parent-like manner for this child's welfare and happiness – he had Anna to assist him now, but as she was a recent addition to Little Isaac's day-to-day life, she had none of the legal responsibilities imposed on him. She had become an integral part of Isaac's family since her arrival in Smolensk a few weeks before. Will was thankful for her presence and for her help with Little Isaac during Isaac and Sophie's recent medical and personal traumas.

"Anna, I want you to know that I could not have managed all of the challenges of the last few weeks without your help and loyalty to Isaac and Sophie. You know that while Isaac and Sophie are struggling to cope with their own physical and mental problems, we are left to carry on their lives in all aspects of their fractured worlds. I hope you will continue with me to be of service to them. This goes well beyond family duty – this is effectively living their lives for them for the next few months. I hope it will only be a few months, but it might well be longer."

"Will, thank you for your implied offer to release me from the here and now and likely future. I am *in*. It's not just a family thing. I have never felt more fulfilled and needed. I have Little Isaac as my immediate family. I had no idea being a mother could be so emotionally important to me. I think I was meant to be involved. I am gradually learning to be a mother. Will, I feel a spiritual calling to being here. Yes, you couldn't get rid of me if you tried!"

"There's no possibility of that. Your role with Little Isaac, Isaac and Sophie is going to get greater in the next few days or weeks, while I have to continue our investigations and negotiations over the assets…"

Before he could finish his lawyerly rhetoric, Little Isaac came to him, standing chest against Will's right leg, imploring Will to come to his bedroom to continue building a Lego castle. Off they went, both happy with each other's company. One of Little Isaac's attractions to Will was that he was not a little girl. Will had had children of his own. Only two girls had survived birth, so through his experience with Little Isaac, he re-engaged with his own childhood and a whole new parental experience.

Will's route after leaving the flat was to walk again through Fitzrovia over Tottenham Court Road and from there he made his way to the clinic where Isaac and Sophie continued to be patients.

As had been scheduled with Dr MacKenzie after the funeral yesterday, he met with MacKenzie and Rayskill, this time in the clinic boardroom. After the predictable expressions of grief were expressed, surprisingly intense on Dr Rayskill's part, Will thought, Will asked each to provide a prognosis for each patient and their recommendation for the future care and location for the care.

Dr Rayskill spoke first: "Will, Sophie continues to suffer uterine infections that require continuous nursing care. She also suffers a post-traumatic stress disorder as you know. It is not abating as far as I can see at this point. The former must be treated here, I suspect for a couple of weeks. Then I suggest a transfer to a clinic specialized in treating PTSD patients. Eventually, she will be sufficiently well enough to return to her home. When that will be is outside of my area of expertise. I leave that to Dr MacKenzie to deal with. I recommend that Isaac and Sophie be brought together as often as possible. They may ignore each other for days or even weeks, but the healing process will bring them together eventually. Also, Little Isaac should be brought over to Sophie every day, but for a few minutes until she starts to react and engage with him. We don't want him traumatized by his mother and father's conditions, particularly their apparent indifference."

Dr MacKenzie agreed and said that Isaac too should remain at the clinic for about a week, primarily to have immediate access to Sophie. His care should then be transferred to the PTSD clinic in Chelsea where MacKenzie was the senior specialist. It was also the clinic to which Sophie would eventually be taken.

Will requested MacKenzie to make the necessary arrangement at his clinic and then added, "Dr MacKenzie, I find confusing the English protocol of referring to some physicians as 'Mr or Ms' and others as 'Doctor'. I am going to be American in my approach. You will all be 'Doctor'. It will be easier and I won't be struggling to keep you all sorted. Please advise your people at the clinic. I hope I haven't insulted you by repeatedly referring to you as 'Dr MacKenzie', even though I think you are properly referred to as 'Mr MacKenzie'. Too confusing."

That comment managed to evoke a smile from both doctors and it helped to ease the tensions and formality in the room, which was Will's intent with this *non sequitur*.

Will then visited Isaac and he found him asleep. The nurse was tucking Isaac in and attempting to make him comfortable. After being asked, she informed Will that since he returned to the clinic after the funeral he had dropped into a dormant state, not comatose but certainly in another place mentally and not responsive to any stimuli. Will gave the nurse his cell phone number and told her to call him if Isaac resumed awareness and was willing to talk. The nurse had been recommended as a special duty nurse by Dr MacKenzie to provide extra care for both Isaac and Sophie. She was thirtyish, blonde, buxom and tallish with legs that would attract Isaac when he resumed his old habits. She was also familiar with mobile phones and she assured Will that she was proficient in their use, having one herself. She also assured Will she could be contacted any time by the clinic, Isaac, Sophie or Will. The potential immediacy of this device, still largely foreign to him, was to be a comfort to Will, knowing considerable distance would not prevent him from being both a guardian and an attorney for his friends.

* * *

After a light sandwich lunch near Trafalgar Square, Will arrived as planned at Roger Smythe's law office to discuss the continuing investigation and management of the assets. Smyth had with him two representatives of the Swiss bank, one a lawyer and the other the senior asset manager. He also had a face present whom Will had not seen before. Smythe introduced the lawyer as Penelope Wright. Her titian hair was pulled in curls to the side of her face, framing it and defining its symmetry; her spontaneous smile attracted Will immediately and ensured her acceptance as part of the team.

"Now, Smythe," said Will, "I have to ask whether one of the many peculiar protocols in the English world apply to Penelope. It is a strange custom for men of similar status to refer to each other by their surnames, even if they have knowledge of each other personally for decades. Do I refer to Penelope as 'Wright' or something else?"

This resulted in a strangled gurgle of mirth from Smythe, but it was Penelope who answered. "Mr MacIntosh, I ask you to call me by my first name since I suspect we will be working closely together for the foreseeable future."

"With pleasure, Penelope. It will be easier to remember which style of address I should use if I use the first person form. It can be very confusing, as I have discovered, in addressing doctors and specialists. You are masters of complicating your social protocols here – particularly for North Americans!"

"And for Europeans, Will," was a comment from one of the Swiss bankers. The familiar 'Will' was established by agreement between Will and the Swiss bank officials over the past four years. The Swiss, in particular, were more comfortable with rigid formalities, but Will had not the patience or the inclination to allow the formal to interfere with his direct personalized form of address. He knew well that he would need to give direct unequivocal instructions to each of these people and that they were most effectively given through use of the first name.

'Roger', as Smythe had now become, handed Will an envelope that had just arrived from St Petersburg. Will opened it and announced: "It is a report from two of our Russian team, Dr Dolgoruky and his colleague Dr Vorontsov, on their investigation carried on since we left Russia. I would like to take this extensive report to a private room to read and consider it. It will have a bearing on what we decide are our next steps, which is the purpose of this meeting. It couldn't be better timed for its arrival."

* * *

Will returned after an interval of half an hour. His startled and confused appearance had the team baffled until he explained. Investigations at the Alexander Palace had revealed an unknown source of much of the internal investment planning that had been transmitted to the Swiss bank investors. It had long been obvious to Will that the investments made in Russia and elsewhere in Eastern Europe required someone in the decision-making process, or some persons, located in Russia and elsewhere in the region who were observing, understanding and formulating investment strategies and opportunities. According to information obtained from the sealed chamber in the Alexander Palace, that person – or a group of persons performing that role – was located in Odessa, a Ukrainian city on the Black Sea.

Will had informed the Swiss bank and Smythe earlier of the astonishing treasures found in the Alexander Palace and the sealed chamber yet to be opened.

"It turns out that the sealed chamber contained treasures unlike anything found so far. The treasures were extensive investments and purchases of artifacts made by individuals who had inside knowledge of economic conditions in Eastern Europe and had access to the statistical and political information that enabled skillful investment decisions. These decisions were transmitted from southern Ukraine to St Petersburg and from there to Zurich," Will said, "by coded messages from one or more persons in Odessa."

"Why would a Ukrainian city be chosen for that purpose?" asked Smythe.

"That takes me back to two events that enable me to answer your question. Ukraine was culturally distinct for centuries but had become part of the Russian Empire created by numerous Czars and in particular, one Czarina. Peter the Great expanded the boundaries of Russia, creating his window to Europe by building St Petersburg and accessing Europe from there by sea and by land through what is now Poland and Lithuania. Czarina Catherine the Great provided an equally valuable economic link to Europe and the world beyond by wars that resulted in what is now the southern half of Ukraine being captured by Russia from Turkey. This provided her with control of the north shore of the Black Sea; with that acquisition, she instructed her former lover Potemkin to create a seaport along that coast. As with all of her biddings he complied. Odessa was the result. It was to become one of the most important seaports in Russia. Yes, Russia. Ukraine then was nothing more than a region of Russia. That brings me to the second point which is the control of the Jews in Russia. They were tolerated and were used when convenient to the Czar. In order to achieve the economic benefits Catherine's new port of Odessa offered, it was necessary that the port be developed by skilled business people with established links to the Mediterranean and northern European regions. The Jewish communities in Russia were recognized as the single most accomplished investors and business managers in the country, added to which the Jewish communities had many family and economic connections with their confrères in Europe and in America. It was primarily the Jews who developed Odessa, the Black Sea shipping and trading routes and gave the city much of its culture and economic success."

The assembled listeners were becoming restless at the history lesson. By now Will had learned to observe the signs. He stopped and said, "There is one more important connection to the trust assets and their acquisition. You know about the Menshikovsky family connections with the Günzburgs and the Mendelssohns. It was the Günzburgs, a banking and entrepreneurial family par excellence who were among the Jews who established the family in Odessa. Junior male members of the family served in Odessa as agents of the primary interests located in St Petersburg. It was this group who were part of the entrepreneurial development of southern Russia. Their knowledge and skills were put to work by the Günzburgs and later the Menshikovsky families in making clever entrepreneurial decisions, most of which turned out to be successful at a macro level.

"The researchers acting for Isaac have discovered in the sealed room detailed ledgers and business records that itemize the acquisition of a substantial number of the assets currently held for Isaac by his new trust. It is the opinion of both Dr Dolgoruky and Dr Vorontsov that a visit to Odessa is essential to follow up with this lead. They have informed me that during the post-1917 Revolution period Odessa became a backwater for everything other than espionage. They think more records, probably more significant ones, still exist in Odessa.

"They were able to find an address for the headquarters for the Günzburg Bank in Odessa. Dr Vorontsov informs me it is near the newly refurbished Bristol Hotel in an area of the city that is largely as it was in the nineteenth century. Both he and Dolgoruky are familiar with the address and they believe the building is still standing. Our business manager in Moscow has searched our inventory of real estate holdings there and has found a record of the bank building continuing to be held through the trust. In light of that, it is my opinion that I should visit Odessa and explore the address we now have."

The proposal advanced by Will was discussed in detail by the team. Everyone knew that if Will had decided it was a good idea he alone had the authority to make that decision, but what was discussed was the strategy of doing so, particularly in light of the fact that the city was now effectively in the control of the Russian mafia. Which in turn was manipulated by some of the country's more ruthless oligarchs.

By the end of the afternoon, it was agreed that Will should have a 'cover' for the visit. That of a tourist was the most plausible. In turn, it was suggested that Will not travel alone – suspicions of his motives would be lessened if he was accompanied by a young woman who could appear to be his romantic partner.

For reasons they did not yet understand, Odessa would prove to be a place where that profile worked well.

PART 4

Odessa

28

COMFORTABLY SEATED IN First Class on an Air Austria flight from Vienna to Odessa, Will and Penelope took the opportunity to take the measure of each other. Will in particular knew that absolute trust in this young woman was essential if he had any chance of succeeding in his mission to Odessa.

Penelope came highly recommended to Will as an informed expert in Russian and Ukrainian law and current political events in the region. She was a thirty-two-year-old graduate of the University of London Law School with post-graduate studies in Russian and Ukrainian law. Her interest in the subject came naturally to her. Her mother was born, raised and educated in Kiev, the capital of Ukraine, during the period of the Ukrainian Soviet Republic, part of the group of states known in the West under the collective name of the Union of Soviet Socialist Republics, or USSR, but very much a satellite of the USSR's main player, Russia.

Smythe, Penelope's senior partner at the London law firm, advised Will before they embarked on the investigation in Ukraine that Will should become familiar with Penelope's background, so he could appreciate the full range of attributes and attitudes she brought to the purpose of the visit.

Penelope's answer to an inquiry from Will about her connection to Ukraine added to what he already knew, that her mother moved from her home in Odessa to the capital Kiev, where she had taught history and economics at a university there. While a sessional lecturer and very junior on the academic staff she applied for and received a sabbatical to study at the London School of Economics. It was while she was studying there that she met Penelope's father who was a junior lawyer at a firm in Lincoln's Inn Fields, a short distance from the London School of Economics.

Penelope's mother was fluent in both Russian and Ukrainian and she had an academic but working knowledge of English. When she and Penelope's father married, her mother took her husband's surname and as her English developed she lost virtually all of the Slavic verbal overtones in her spoken English. Her accent, which was passed on to her two children, was an academically perfect English, spoken with a slight exotic accent few recognized to be of a Slavic origin.

Will asked her to give him more details about her family's political and spiritual beliefs. He knew many western professional women would find the question intrusive and offensive, but the information was essential in Ukraine, particularly in Odessa where prejudices and underlying attitudes were deeply established and they might influence strategic decision-making. And they would influence how locals would observe and react to Penelope.

Penelope demonstrated an openness and candour which Will found encouraging. He was satisfied by her answers that she understood the importance of his questions and his project on behalf of Isaac.

"My mother was the formative influence on me as I grew up in London. My name is thoroughly British but my attitudes are divided between British norms and those of Ukraine. I am well aware of biases and strong opinions that I have received from my mother as a result of her upbringing. My father knew my mother's influence on me and was careful to temper those influences, giving me a British perspective. I can say that his role has been successful in enabling me to see my prejudices and to take a reasoned and objective approach to issues related to the history of Ukraine and Russia."

Will knew the next question as one that would be considered inappropriate and offensive in a professional work environment which their roles were on this trip to Ukraine. "What are your spiritual or religious views, Penelope? I know the history of Odessa quite well, having visited the city on my own five years ago."

"Mr MacIntosh, you are correct. Attitudes based on political, historical, ethnic and religious values underline and are formative in the opinions and actions of people in western Ukraine, particularly in Odessa. My mother was born Jewish and was raised secretly – as secretly as was possible – as a Jew. After the war, those Jews not exterminated during the war made every effort to escape to the West. My mother was able to get out through her academic sabbatical. It was a rare opportunity and available to her only because she appeared to espouse the Communist theories and values. It was a ruse, and they were abandoned on her flight to London. If anything, she became more pro-British and pro-Western than most citizens in the West. So, yes, I was born and raised Jewish but I frequently attended Anglican Church services with my father and his parents. Five years ago, I formally converted to Christianity and joined the Anglican Church – what you in America would know as the liberal end of the Anglican theologies – not the *Oxford Movement*, far right."

Penelope went on to explain that she continued to have deep roots in Ukraine. Her mother had three sisters and two brothers. Two of the sisters left and made a home for themselves in the United States, as did one of her brothers. One sister and one brother remained in Eastern Europe. Penelope's aunt and her family remained in Ukraine, living in Kiev, while her uncle had become enmeshed in the Russian Soviet governance of Ukraine. With Ukrainian independence in August 1991, he moved to St Petersburg and continued as a bureaucrat in the Russian government.

"Does his role with Putin involve Ukraine in any way?"

"I don't know. Frankly, sir, he rejected my mother and her family many years ago – even before independence. He also severed ties with his siblings in the United States."

"What about your aunt in Kiev?"

"I don't know. We have corresponded but only at a familial level. There is never any reference to politics, religion or other topics that could be controversial."

Will explained that his reasons for the questions were grounded on the risk Penelope might bring to Will's investigations related to Isaac's assets in western Ukraine. He had to know what boundaries were required for Penelope in terms of her role with him during the visit. Penelope assured Will that she thoroughly understood that Dr Menshive, and by extension Will, were her principals in a solicitor-client relationship and that she owed them a high professional standard of confidentiality, privacy and loyalty.

As the aircraft was landing at Odessa International Airport, Will fell silent to prepare for landing – always a time of anxiety for him – and to ruminate on his conversation with Penelope.

* * *

As Will and Penelope passed through customs and emigration, an official, after taking Will's passport and Penelope's, turned to Will and asked whether Will and his daughter would be staying long in Ukraine. The difference in surnames did not suggest a different relationship. Surnames and identities, he was to discover, were highly flexible, even on official documents such as passports issued in Eastern Europe, where these could be acquired on the black market with ease. The reference to the age difference did serve as a reminder to Will that he was well into middle-age rather than the young-seeming, mid-career professional that he sometimes thought himself to be.

Penelope demonstrated her usefulness as they left the terminal, immediately stepping forward with confidence and authoritatively hailing a taxi for them. Will was taken aback by her somewhat aggressive demeanour. He had observed only a compliant, soft-spoken, rather deferential young woman. "She has depth, this young woman. I hope she won't be too threatening to the locals, however!"

Penelope asked where the taxi should take them. Two words were the reply, a place Will knew from his last visit to the city would be readily understood: "Bristol Hotel." The taxi driver replied with a simple "Da". Penelope turned to Will and said, "Sir, the Bristol was the most elegant and sophisticated hotel before the wars, but I am told it has fallen into decay and ruin."

"Thanks for the caution, Penelope. However, the hotel was remodelled, modernized and brought back to five-star quality about five years ago. It is now the best in the city and one of the finest hotels in Europe. You will enjoy it, I'm sure."

"Please don't misunderstand, I am not worried about its standards for myself; I know you would expect an international level of quality. I was afraid you might have been influenced by an out-of-date guidebook. Also… I should point out that it had a reputation as a place that attracted Mafioso, political activists and espionage."

"Penelope, again I thank you for your helpful comments. I am well aware of the history of the Bristol and its current status in terms of its clientele. Yes, by reputation it has attracted a crowd similar to its past. In fact, the hotel, by reputation, was refurnished by an oligarch working with local Russian *mafiosi*. This is one of the reasons I have selected the Bristol. We shall discuss my reasons later."

The six kilometres from the airport to the city passed in silence while both passengers observed the landscape and, in Will's case, the buildings both old and new, trying to read them for the origins of their architectural features – his form of relaxation.

* * *

After checking in and taking their respective accommodations Will and Penelope met in the living room of Will's suite. Penelope's shock at the lavish elegance of this set of rooms could not be disguised as she took the seat pointed out for her by Will, who was amused by her reaction. "Actually, Penelope, your reaction to this hotel and to my rooms is a great place to start my briefing and schedule for the next week," said Will.

To which an embarrassed reply from Penelope emerged before Will could carry on with his plans. "I'm sorry, it was rude of me to react as I did. I did not mean to imply that you were wasting your client's money – what I am seeing is so much more lavish and extravagant than anything my mother described – I was not prepared for this. In fact, there are few hotels in London so overstated."

"I am mindful of my client's financial situation, Penelope, but I am also well aware of image. In this place, appearances lead to respect, which in turn leads to a smoother exercise of authority and compliance with requests. That is not just within the hotel. My inquiries will quickly identify me, and by extension you, as someone of interest, if not suspicion. I must appear to have the authority that my inquiries will suggest I should have. We will talk further about our demeanour and methods of dealing with people here as we conduct our investigations. And by the way, my client and I have worked together well for over four years. I am aware of what expenses he is prepared to accept. I also know he would expect me to conduct myself as I propose to do, while here in Ukraine. He and I have dealt with bureaucrats, oligarchs and politicians here in the former USSR. To be effective a certain personal presentation in public on our part will be essential to achieve the results Dr Menshive and I require.

"You have been referring to me as 'Sir' and 'Mr MacIntosh'. Please continue the tone of submission and deference. In London that would be expected given our ages and relative seniority at bar, but here there is an added dimension to the relationship. I mean of course, that as a junior, particularly as a young female junior, you cannot appear to be equal to or in a position to give orders. At a personal level, Penelope, it would not bother me at all if you did. I am used to thoroughly liberated women – having been married to one and raised two more. I simply refer to this location and time which requires a certain style of communication. Any indication to those with whom we will be dealing that I am weak or subject to the dictates of a woman would reduce my effectiveness here to nothing. Simply put, 'When in Rome do as the Romans do' – substituting Odessa for Rome.

"Normally I would invite you to speak to me using my Christian name. I must ask you to continue with, 'Mr MacIntosh', but use my surname as sparingly as you can. Confidentiality, where possible, should be our mantra.

"Even though it is early evening here in Odessa, you must be tired and ready to have time to yourself after travelling for several hours today. We will meet tomorrow morning at 8 a.m. here in my suite. This room will be our headquarters and business office while we are here. This room is working space we will need – it is not necessary to satisfy my ego."

With that Will saw Penelope to the door. Shortly after she left, after making a few adjustments to his appearance, he left the building through the service entrance.

* * *

A warm evening greeted Will as he left a side entrance to the hotel. He was scheduled to meet with two of his security guards at the Potemkin Steps, a pleasant walk away from the hotel. It was mid-September, the sun still strong enough creating clear visibility, but its angle slowly dropping giving heightening colour and contrast to the city.

As he reached the park bordering the Black Sea and the boulevard across its upper reaches, he reminded himself that the semi-tropical plantings in the parks and squares were in marked contrast with those of his home on Prince Edward Island. The contrast was even greater when he recalled his research on the relative latitude of Charlottetown and Odessa. Remarkably, they were both 46° north, in line with a circumferential circle that included Lyon in France, Lausanne in Switzerland and Bolzano in Italy. The cold North Atlantic left his home province with a less congenial climate but one with similar daylight hours which gave him a sense of being in a somewhat familiar place.

He walked by several buildings he would be visiting the next day, each of which he had visited on his last trip to the city. On this occasion his visit had specific objectives on which he was going to brief his security detail, and as needed Penelope too.

The Potemkin Steps were only indirectly named after Catherine the Great's lover and, under her direction, the founder and initial developer of the city in the image she conceived for it. The steps were actually named for a Russian battleship that bore his name and that was engaged in a post-revolutionary naval skirmish staged by insurrectionists opposed to the Czar. The relevant revolution was one of several waged against the absolutist Czarist government, in this instance in the 1840s. There had been a mutiny on the battleship Potemkin. Then, in the post-1918 Communist era, the event was celebrated annually as an early revolutionary movement against the autocracy. The steps were named the Potemkin Steps to commemorate the battleship and its early role in the sequence of revolutionary activities in Russia.

Will stood at the top of the steps looking out to the sea; to the south, in the invisible but real distance, was Turkey. As he watched, he engaged in his surroundings and thought of the role the city had played in the Second World War and during the Cold War as the scene of incessant subterfuge, espionage and massacres, particularly massacres of the Jewish residents.

A quiet voice behind him alerted him to the arrival of his security team. Both men were dressed casually, indistinguishable from American tourists exploring the city during a day excursion from a cruise ship, of which there were many since the relative stability Ukraine experienced following its independence in 1999. The disguise adopted by the security guards would be their primary attire during the Odessa mission. Will was similarly dressed. As boisterous Americans, they hid in plain sight and were of no interest but of some irritation to the residents of Odessa.

Will led them up the hill from the steps to a statue in the centre of the street where it expanded into a small park. The statue was of Czarina Catherine the Great, whose vision and purpose for this city was in furtherance of her attempt to emulate Peter the Great and his expansion of Russia northwards, creating a window to the West by building the original features of St Petersburg. Odessa was Catherine's expansion of Russian Territory through Turkish-held territory along the north coast of the Black Sea and built at the western edge of that territory on the site of an ancient Greek port and later Turkish fishing village.

The statue of Catherine was a statement of her role in the founding and development of Odessa, and from her elevated position on the hill looking south to the Black Sea, she could see the Potemkin Steps, continuing her overview of the memorial to Potemkin.

Will took the two guards to a café with an outdoor sitting area overlooking the statue and he suggested they all have an early dinner. While they were enjoying the Ukrainian cuisine on offer at the café, Will explained his objectives and the role the security detail was to perform. After emphasizing the physical risk he had from both the oligarchs and the Russian mafia who would either be acting in their own interests or on behalf of one or more oligarchs, he reminded them of his role as the voice representing Isaac's interests and that at least while they were in Ukraine his opinions and directions were final and absolute.

"You are familiar with my usual interaction with Dr Menshive. Even though he relied on my advice and expected me to decide what was required, I engaged him at all times to explain the reasons for my decisions. That is not possible at this time. There will be no opportunity for consultations with Dr Menshive. I am on my own – with his full legal authority – but I require your constant observations of my movements and protection by whatever means are available to you. Perhaps you will tell me what you have in hand as surveillance devices and firepower."

Frank, his senior security officer, explained that neither the sophisticated surveillance devices they required nor the firepower they were accustomed to having could be brought into the country. Knowing this in advance, Frank had purchased what he required in Istanbul through a non-questioning cooperative dealer who accommodated everyone for a price. The purchases were shipped as boxes of books – scientific titles, which would be of interest to no one – and delivered to a port on the Crimean Peninsula, and through the help of a paid agent, they were transported by rail from Yalta to Odessa, arriving yesterday as arranged, for Frank's assistant to pick up. His assistant was a Ukrainian sympathetic to his country's independence from Russia, and was as trustworthy as could be arranged.

Frank informed Will that he had a detailed operational plan designed to protect both Will and Penelope. One part of this involved a guard each for Will and Penelope who would 'tail' them twenty-four-seven. There was a new aspect of security put in place during the Odessa mission: electronic listening and communications devices.

"Great. Frank, Penelope comes to me as a result of the recommendation of a lawyer in London. He appears to be honourable and trustworthy, but I do not know that for sure. Ms Wright should be known to you as Dr Adamchuk – incidentally, the name of the architect who designed the Potemkin Steps. She has an Odessa background and is a product of the Jewish community in this country; her relatives here have diametrically opposing political loyalties. She is probably alright, but we cannot assume she is. I doubt the lawyer who arranged for her to join me checked into her security background. She will be helpful as a translator and as an expert in both Ukrainian and Russian law. Beyond that, we must be careful to the extent we use her and inform her of what our plans are only in generalities. This is not being unduly suspicious. You, Frank, well know the attacks that have been made on us – one of which has left Dr Menshive in his current disabled condition."

There were two other members on Frank's team. Both were engaged as researchers. Both were young and keen graduate students directed to follow specific leads on the assets and on family business connections linking Isaac and an extensive inventory of real estate. The discoveries at the Alexander Palace in St Petersburg cited business records said to be located in Odessa which had to be discovered, retrieved and removed to safety. "Frank, please inform each student that you hire that you are on an academic exercise conducting historical research and a better understanding of international business connections with firms in Odessa and possibly Kiev. I require a report in English from each of them twice a week. You alone will meet with them. They will not meet me or

Dr Adamchuk. We will monitor their research and their activities outside their research to make sure they are not selling or sharing their research. Emphasize that their work is for an academic in England who wishes absolute confidentiality fearing competitive academics getting the information first."

Frank concluded the meeting as the sun was setting, its afterglow giving the sea an intense darkness that gave one explanation for its name; a more congenial explanation than its real meaning, that it was black because the sea was effectively dead to life, being without oxygen except in small areas.

The dual walkway through the park was filled with walkers, mostly locals Will thought, judging by the style, simplicity and shabbiness of the clothing. The joy of those walking the pathways showed their indifference to the opinion of any who would criticize their appearance.

When Will returned to his rooms at the Bristol hoping for an early bedtime, his cell phone had a message for him to call a number he recognized as Anna's.

Will returned the call. Anna answered promptly, and quickly apologized saying: "Isaac has taken a turn for the worse. He was resting comfortably, we thought, until this afternoon. Someone or something has made him agitated and anxious. He is angry and thrashing about. His doctor is medicating him but afraid to overdo it. I think you need to know this in case his condition is the result of someone talking to him and upsetting him."

"Your call is important. I want twenty-four-seven in-room security for both patients. I will arrange that here. You must inform the doctors and the chief administrator at their current place of residence. Please keep me informed. A new number for this device may be required. It is a short-term rental so I will call you tomorrow at this time. Before I ring off, how is the other patient? I wish I were there to attend to them. Does it appear the doctors there are in control and know what they are doing?"

There was a long pause before Anna understood Will was implying he was the attending physician. "Yes, doctor, they have your instructions. As head nurse, I am watching them carefully and can say they check your chart frequently and appear to follow your instructions. The other patient is no better than she was a week ago – but no worse."

* * *

Will delayed his bedtime by a couple of hours to review his objectives and schedule. Now that he was in Odessa he was able to put the logistics into better focus. The city was compact and his walk that evening enabled him to gauge the timing of his activities with greater precision.

To prepare for the next day he had picked up a copy of a locally produced guide to the city entitled *A Travel Guide: Odessa and its Environs*, published only two years before his visit. Reading a timeline of historical events, he was startled to read that a Count Vorontsov had been the Governor-General of Novorossiya between 1823 and 1846. Novorossiya (literally 'New Russia'), Will recalled, was the name of the region and administrative district of Russia of which Odessa was the capital. The name had been applied by Czarina Catherine as part of her annexation of this region into Imperial Russia.

Will read that during his years as Governor-General in Odessa, Count Vorontsov was active in the life of the city, donating, among other things, his extensive library to the new university he established in the city. He was instrumental in the construction of several important civic buildings. As a reward for further Czarist development of the city, he was ennobled as Prince Vorontsov.

Continuing his reading of the history of the city Will came to a reference to Vorontsov's successor, A. G. Strogonov.

Both these names had currency with Will, having met a Vorontsov whom he knew styled himself as Prince – or perhaps it was Dolgoruky. The Strogonov reference was more remote but still interesting, since the Alexander Palace was designed by the same architect as had designed the Strogonov Palace in St Petersburg and was constructed about the same time as the Strogonov Palace. Intriguing, but maybe not relevant to his investigation; however, he knew the Günzburgs had business interests in Odessa during the period of the Vorontsov and Strogonov administrations. "Maybe," he said to himself, "it is nothing, but given Vorontsov's involvement with us on the Menshive investigation, and we know the trust assets at the Alexander Palace had some of the Vorontsov jewels included in Isaac's collection...". The suspicion of an ulterior motive for Vorontsov's involvement could not be discounted until proven to be irrelevant.

With a head swirling with competing scenarios Will attempted to overcome jet lag and the day's events with some sleep.

29

THE PURPOSE OF the visit to Odessa was uppermost on Will's mind as he planned the next few days. He had limited time available to him away from his duties in London. He realized he had to maximize the time he did have. The Odessa connection to Isaac arose recently during the exploration of the Alexander Palace in St Petersburg, during which documents discovered in the safe room adjacent to the treasury referred to Odessa as the location of some early business dealings of the Günzburg and Menshikovsky families that appeared to link to the creator of the original trust.

The documents found in the Alexander Palace had been translated and reviewed in detail by Will and by Smythe's legal team in London. Penelope's exceptional facility in both Russian and Ukrainian made her invaluable in understanding the documents, particularly with her specialized study in the nineteenth- and twentieth-century laws of both Russia and Ukraine. The documents found were ledgers and journals containing numerous business transactions, but they appeared to be copies and were incomplete, failing to disclose the individual or business for whom they were originally created. It was clear, however, what the nature of the business was: private banking for an individual and later as records of a privately owned bank lending money to select individuals and businesses. The dates of virtually all of the transactions were omitted on the records found in St Petersburg.

Isaac and Will hoped that investigations in Odessa would find additional records and would fill in the most important details of the copies in St Petersburg. The research in Odessa, he hoped, would provide the motivation for the creation of the Russian trust and its subsequent reconfigurations that led to the creation of the core trust domiciled in the Canadian province of Prince Edward Island.

Where would he look for the missing documents? It was unclear what the name of the individual or the business was, so conjecture based on the knowledge gained so far would be his sole guide.

* * *

Will had an early, very early, breakfast in the elegant dining room at the Bristol Hotel, so recently refurbished that he could smell the new paint, carpeting and furniture. His concentration was frequently interrupted by identifying some new detail he hadn't noticed before. The overall style was neoclassical but with a mixture of period styles which identified the date of design and construction as 1899. Forcing himself to concentrate on his limited Russian, he made several notes on a compact journal he carried for the purpose. His notes were divided into columns, each having an identifier of subject matter heading each column.

The column identifiers included: individual business transactions dates; the nature of the transaction; the purpose of the transaction; value; and the other party or parties in the transaction. Will had recently been introduced to computer spreadsheets as a format for recording and manipulating the information each column contained. His handwritten notes would be transmitted to London where they would be entered into a computer.

Each column remained blank. His initial efforts were to systematize the information he obtained so that he and his team, including Penelope, could efficiently pursue and evaluate their inquiries.

Penelope joined him before eight that morning, later than Will's usual time for starting his work day, but she had needed extra time to sleep off her jet lag.

* * *

After discussing the draft spread sheet with Penelope and adding several helpful suggestions she offered, they got down to analyze where those categories were likely to lead them in finding the information they required.

Will and Penelope agreed quickly that the legal documents might still be held by a law office in the city. One of the researchers was to be assigned the task of researching the legal firms dating from about 1820. Banks existing at that time in Odessa were also to be researched and assigned to the same researcher, hoping relevant information would be in public records.

The surnames known to Will associated with the trust were also to be thoroughly researched as to their businesses, politics, family connections and records contained in local newspapers. The list of names given to Penelope, as Will spoke in an ad hoc and spontaneous manner, included Menshikovsky (and variants on that name such as Menshikoffsky), Mendelssohn, Günzburg, Vorontsov, Dolgoruky, Cann, and Trotsky.

The last name shocked Penelope. "Why Trotsky? What possible connection would Dr Menshive's family have to Trotsky?" To which Will replied that Trotsky's grandmother was Jewish, possibly also his father, although his parents appeared to be largely unreligious as many intellectuals were in late nineteenth-century Russia. He said that it appeared Trotsky's grandmother had a sister who married a Cann who in turn had a daughter connected by marriage to the Menshikovskys. "Good grief, sir. That is remote."

"Family connections," replied Will, "particularly those remote to money or status, are often reinvented as immediate family to gain advantages through the connection. That appears to have happened with the Cann/Trotsky family – claiming a close familial connection with the Menshikovskys that did not exist.

"The most likely names of banks were the Menshikovskys, Mendelssohns and the Günzburgs. However, it is probable that the family names would have been subverted by names suggesting the nature of the banking business, for example, the Ukraine Railway Development Bank, the Ukrainian Agricultural Bank or the Industrial Development Bank of Ukraine. These are suggestions. I have no idea whether such banks actually existed. The family names may or may not have been included. What we do know is that Odessa was established as the capital of the Ukrainian *oblast* or county of Russia in 1798. It was systematically planned and developed as a city and as an economy. It was an open free port city with a highly favourable climate for commercial and industrial development, more so than any other part of the southern Russian Empire and as such, it attracted investors and highly creative entrepreneurs from all over Europe, not only Russia. I think we can assume that each of the families we identified was aggressively engaged in business by the 1820s or 1830s. If we cannot find banks or businesses publically linked by name with our families of interest, public corporate registers were maintained in the city which would identify the directors and officers of companies formed in or elsewhere operating in the city."

"What do you hope to find, Mr MacIntosh?"

"The origins of the investments that ultimately were rolled into the Swiss trust and the reason why they were segregated and domiciled elsewhere. Why hidden? What were they afraid of? What was their objective? From this research we may find records of the investments being made and, importantly to Dr Menshive, their ultimate purpose. In making his final arrangements for a distribution of the assets held in Eastern Europe, Isaac needs to have that knowledge to assist him in making decisions that comply with and honour those purposes."

"Well, Mr MacIntosh, I suggest we start with the Jewish connection," suggested Penelope. "There are four prominent Jewish organizations, some religious, in this city. I remember my mother talking about them. I spent part of my evening yesterday reading online helpful tourist literature and I found the names and locations of the four. I suggest we concentrate on two. I am thinking of the 'Hillel Jewish Culture Centre' and the 'Beit Grand Jewish Culture Centre'. The latter is associated with the main synagogue in Odessa. I suggest we start there. I suspect it will have extensive records of all Jews who have lived here, particularly all prominent families as each of Dr Menshive's families were."

Penelope left before 10 a.m. to make contacts and to set up appointments. She was especially anxious to arrange an appointment with the Chief Rabbi in Odessa for background on Jews in the city. Both Will and Isaac knew that there were periods of horrific violence in which Jews had been victims. Will and Penelope had discussed the likelihood that the secrecy and absolute control provided by the trust arose because of one or more of such events.

They agreed to meet again at 2 p.m. in Will's suite where there would be as much confidentiality and privacy as could be obtained. Will knew that in coming to Odessa he was visiting one of the most active espionage centres in Europe during the twentieth century and even into the twenty-first. Competing interests were always represented in Odessa. In 2008 it was not so much political as it was financial and economic interests competing ruthlessly for advantage in a city and district that offered some of the best economic opportunities in Eastern Europe.

* * *

During the four hours of solitude available to him, Will again became an archetypical American tourist in appearance, including cameras (two) and a rucksack with stuff spilling out from its innumerable pockets including a water bottle and a sunscreen tube on display. His sun hat was pulled down as far as he could make it without suggesting he was deliberately disguising himself. 'Hide in plain sight' was his mantra, he kept reminding himself.

From the Bristol he passed the former part-time residence of the celebrated nineteenth-century poet Alexander Pushkin, whose grand residence had been turned into the Literary-Memorial Museum dedicated to his life and literary achievements. Before moving along the street much further, he pivoted and returned to the front of the building, admiring its neoclassicism. Will's enduring interest in architectural styles and forms of construction led him to explore the interior. The pretensions in the exterior design would surely be reflected on the interior. They weren't. The interior was remarkably simple and the layout simply an enfilade of rooms. He had hoped he would find personal collections of art or historical artifacts that could inform him of the possible source of some of the material in Isaac's collection that dated from the mid-nineteenth century. There weren't any.

On the opposite side of Pushkinska Street, he observed the bank 'Port-Franko', a building that of itself offered no attractions; but as a bank building whose origins as a bank dated to the mid-nineteenth century, perhaps it would offer some insight into either Günzburg or Menshikovsky bank operations. The interior had been gutted and offered no insights and no one could be found who could speak English.

He crossed back to the Bristol Hotel's side of Pushkins'ka Street where he located the Arcadia palace, constructed between 1855 and 1858, which housed the Museum of Western and Oriental Art. The collection on display presented some artifacts similar to material now in Isaac's collection. Will was able to find a curator. His objective was to identify dealers in Odessa in the nineteenth century who sold materials of this kind. Records of transactions might be in the museum archives or the curator might know where the records were if still extant.

Will was referred to the city archives for those documents. He was confident the archives would have a list of all major businesses operating in Odessa after its founding as an operational city in the early nineteenth century. It took no more, he was informed, than six or seven years after the creation of the city in 1798 for it to become a thriving commercial centre and economic boom-town.

Will continued his brief exploration of the city, passing the splendid opera house designed in 1887 by the same Viennese architects who created the opera houses in Vienna and Budapest, among others. His immediate impression was that the drum-like structure with porticos on four sides was somewhat similar to the Royal Albert Hall in London.

His goal was to go back to the Primorsky Boulevard along which he had walked the night before, but his destination was the famous Londonskaya Hotel, built as a mansion in 1827 in a neoclassical style that enhanced the overall appearance of Odessa as similar in architectural character to its northern prototype St Petersburg. The hotel had been established in the mansion since the mid-nineteenth century. Would the hotel, wondered Will, have guest registers from the start of its use as a hotel? He walked into the hotel, finding an English-speaking front desk clerk who proudly informed Will that all hotel registers were preserved and, with the permission of the hotel manager, they could be available to Will to examine. The clerk made an appointment with the manager for the next day. Will decided he would bring one of the researchers with him.

His morning had been full and involved a lot of walking. He returned to the restaurant 'Boulevard' to which he had taken his security detail the day before. He broke one of his cardinal rules not to have any alcohol before sundown; sitting on the terrace he ordered a small carafe of local white wine which he enjoyed with his lightly fried fish. Will's relaxation and comfort were enhanced by observing Frank and another of the security guards nearby professionally ignoring him.

30

IF THE MENSHIKOVSKYS had business interests in Odessa as the archival material found in the St Petersburg safe room indicated, there must be a record of their visits to the city or their residence there. One of the researchers was tasked with checking for business records and places of business connected to the family. While Penelope was reviewing the records of the largest and oldest established law offices in Odessa and the Jewish archives located in the oldest synagogue, Will set himself the task of looking at the early mid-nineteenth-century hotel registers at the Londonskaya for entries that might establish visits by the family to the city.

Will had called the London Medical Clinic the day before and had attempted to talk to Isaac to engage him in a conversation about what he discovered about Menshikovsky family businesses in Odessa, but even about something as innocuous as the weather Isaac was still uncommunicative. Isaac remained in a world of his own and was unable or unwilling to communicate. Even asking him about Sophie's health failed to elicit a comment that Isaac knew whom Will was talking about. When he explained to Isaac where he was and the purpose of his visit, Isaac remained silent, making no sound that indicated a recognition of either Will or of Odessa.

* * *

The Londonskaya hotel manager, Oleg Oransky, was a man in his sixties who had taken fastidious care of his appearance. He was of above-average height, grey-haired but with a distinguished two-tone effect, perhaps enhanced with pomade or hair colouring. His manner was almost too courteous and formal to be a statement of his real self. He approached Will at the front desk, right hand extended with only the slightest pressure in his grip, releasing quickly. Will realized that the manager was totally disengaged and he would not take a step beyond what was essential to maintain civility.

When Will explained his reasons for wishing to see the nineteenth-century and early twentieth-century registers, Oransky confirmed that he had been informed earlier that day of Will's request and that Will would be given access to the records. Will explained that he would be accompanied by two assistants. The manager looked at them and replied knowingly, "I am accustomed to gentlemen such as you having assistants in attendance on them." One of the assistants was one of Frank's security guards who looked much more athletic than studious. The other was part of Penelope's team, bilingual in Ukrainian and English.

Oransky accepted the assistants but he stated that there would be a hotel clerk with Will and his assistants who would supervise their research to protect the hotel's property.

Will was taken with his entourage to a windowless room in the basement that had a large table with several chairs around it. On the table were several hotel registers. In preparation for his research on the registers, Will had outlined the surnames he was looking for to the assistants with Ukrainian and Russian language skills, putting them to work as clerks. Any individual with the names Menshikovsky/Menshikoffsky, Mendelssohn, Günzburg, and Trotsky was to be recorded by full name, address as recorded, date and duration of stay. "And I want to know if the names were as individuals or as accompanied, and if the latter, I want the names of the companions, if given." His directions were also given to the hotel security officer who was to supervise him. "He might as well be put to work since he is here and we are paying him". The hotel clerk spoke some English and read more than he spoke so he could be helpful in reading the entries.

"It appears the entries are all made in Russian, not Ukrainian. I have studied Russian, gentlemen, but in print," said Will to his two companions. "I am not very good at interpreting Slavic languages in the cursive. My own handwriting in Russian was consistently criticized as illegible by my professor at university." That at least generated a mild smile from the hotel clerk. Will's security guard simply looked worried.

* * *

Three hours later those registers covering the years after the mansion had been reinvented as the Londonskaya Hotel had been read and documented up to the year 1905, at which point Will told the guard that they would stop and reconvene the next day.

* * *

Will and Penelope met with Frank and Will's security guard in Will's suite at the Bristol where a conference table had been set up by Frank with the guard's help. Before discussing the results of their research, Will turned to Frank: "This information I will be discussing may contain sensitive records I will wish to keep confidential. Is there any possibility that this room could be bugged with recording or live audio devices?"

Frank replied that he had checked the room before they assembled and that he could find nothing, but he agreed to check again when Will insisted on it, hoping that the hotel was neutral territory.

Frank and his assistant who had accompanied Will at the Londonskaya began a careful examination of the room: everything from light fixtures to electrical outlets and computer outlets. Half an hour later, Frank asked Will to meet with him outside on the street.

Penelope joined them as they crossed the street to the Primorsky Boulevard Gardens where they found a park bench. When Frank insisted on examining the park bench for hidden devices, it was clear to Will that devices had been found in Will's suite.

Frank reported that the room had been successfully bugged by experts. He admitted that it was his assistant Andy who identified and explained the technology.

"Whose technology, Andy?"

"As far as I can tell, I would say it is Russian-made. Very sophisticated. Not equipment I have come across before. Well disguised, but not well enough. It was buried in a thin coat of plaster. I have observed that method of disguising the technology before. Fresh plaster still slightly wet."

"Can we successfully remove the bugs?" asked Will.

"Yes, but it would be obvious that we are onto them and I cannot guarantee that I will find all the installations."

"Alright, Mr MacIntosh, I recommend we find a safe and neutral location using your living room for disinformation purposes only."

"Am I to understand, Frank, that my stay in the suite will be recorded – every cough, burp and step? Is there video recording equipment, too?"

"Yes, everything you do, every sound made in your suite and your use of the bathroom will be recorded. It appears it is a live feed as well as recording devices. Don't worry, I think these were installed while you were out during the afternoon."

"Good. I don't want to find myself on a porn site stripping or showering or God knows what."

Penelope managed a smile and suggested an alternate venue as a good idea.

Will asked Penelope to arrange for the renting of an apartment, if possible in one of the three apartment buildings on Isaac's inventory. She had visited the law office engaged to manage the Odessa properties that afternoon and had contact information that enabled her to get through to the lawyer in Moscow who had arranged matters. The lawyer informed her that a secure apartment was available in one of Isaac's buildings further along the same street on which the Bristol Hotel was located.

The suite at the Bristol would be retained in its renovated form in an effort to disguise the fact that the devices had been found.

Frank offered to pack and remove Will's clothing and move it to the apartment after dark that evening. Penelope was offered a relocation to the apartment as well, to which she quickly assented.

They agreed that they should leave the Bristol immediately and go to the apartment to see what was necessary to accommodate them. Frank's assistant Andy, it was agreed, would remain in his hotel room. Will made a helpful suggestion that Andy should smile sweetly as he entered and emerged from the shower and during dressing. Andy was acutely embarrassed and said simply, "That won't be necessary. I will manage my privacy, okay?"

It turned out that the apartment was three blocks from the Bristol; far enough away, Frank assured Will and Penelope, that the devices embedded in the Bristol Suite would not pick up their conversations at the apartment. Strategies for access to and exit from the apartment were worked out with Andy's help. He admitted there were other jobs he had successfully managed when he had been hired by celebrities who were often forced to take diversionary steps to protect themselves from the media.

"In my opinion, Mr MacIntosh," Andy said, "the Western media, particularly the British media, are a hell of a lot more skillful in setting up recording and audio devices than the Russian mafia. And, oh yes, from what I could see of the devices, the locations and methods of installation, the Bristol Hotel installations are the work of the Russian mafia."

* * *

After a quick, light supper in a restaurant in a side street close to the apartment, the group assembled in the new apartment. All present were pleasantly surprised to find it beautifully appointed, with comfortable furniture and a fully stocked kitchen which included an over-stocked bar.

"Penelope, how could this place be so well provisioned – and on such short notice?" asked Will.

She replied, "It is on permanent lease to the judiciary in Kiev. An itinerant judge from Kiev comes to Odessa a couple of times a month. I have been assured that alternate arrangements will be made for the judges – you can have the apartment as long as you require it."

"Should we relocate the liquor to the judges' apartment?" said Will. "There is enough here to keep the palates of the Ukrainian army wet."

"No," responded Andy, "the other apartment will be as fully equipped as this one. There should be as little moving of anything in or out of this apartment as possible. You will notice that there are three bedrooms: the judges travel with a clerk or two. There will be room, I think, for Mr MacIntosh, Penelope and Frank."

The large living room had a dining room table with seating for eight. The group took their places around the table.

Will spoke first. "I will need a report from each of you. Please go slowly enough to enable Penelope to take notes. While I was visiting the bathroom I discovered a large safe with the door open which we can use to store Penelope's notes and anything else we require. Frank, you are in charge of the combination and opening and closing of the safe. The judges are certainly well taken care of while in Odessa, I must say. Just as well; it makes a convenient new residence for us."

Will reported that he and Andy, during their examination of the Londonskaya registers, had found numerous entries for several Menshikovskys, Mendelssohns and Günzburgs. "Their stays spanned a period from the opening of the hotel to their end date of 1900. The length of stays were most extensive by the Menshikovskys, averaging two weeks every six weeks, the Mendelssohns only a few days every four or five months, and the Günzburgs about the same. Each visit was made by a male who was unaccompanied, at least as far as occupancy of the room was recorded in the register. The stays were consistent as to duration and frequency right up to 1900. We will check for the period 1900 to 1905 tomorrow. The individuals who visited represented, I think, generational shifts. The first Menshikovsky in the register was an Isaac. He was the sole member of that family in the register until 1875 when the name changes to Maxim Menshikovsky who lasted only five years. Then it becomes Isaac again who, judging by his signature, was quite young. His signature is frequently entered until 1900.

"As to the Mendelssohns, three names again for the same time period, the changes of individuals being about the same time. This applies as well to the Günzburgs, but there was a ten-year lapse in their visits between 1880 and 1890. This we have to explore.

"The visits from members of the three families did not overlap, which I found strange, but I guess I was expecting some joint ventures by two or more of the families."

Penelope and Frank were still to report, but as it was getting late, it was agreed that the meeting would adjourn until the next morning for breakfast. Penelope said she had arranged with the law office to have a cleaner and cook take care of the group during their stays. "I was assured both women were absolutely reliable and trustworthy. In fact, the cook was the wife of a junior partner who welcomed the opportunity to make a little extra money."

31

WILL'S ROUTINE WAS similar no matter where on the planet he was. Early rise at 5:50 a.m., breakfast by 6:30 and underway before 7:00, with a clear focus on his agenda for the day. While the agenda differed from day to day, the routine seldom differed. On his third day in Odessa, with an increasingly complex set of issues and questions, he was in overdrive.

A meeting was arranged with Penelope and the security detail for 9 a.m. at the apartment. This gave Will an hour and a half to stretch his legs and to give further thought to the growing information and complexities of Isaac's family in the southern Ukraine region – in Novorossiya, as the area was known in the years after the region was taken from the Turks at the end of the eighteenth century.

He walked from the apartment building further along Pushkinska Street, passing an amazing mixture of neoclassical architecture; each building had a unique fusion of various pure styles, giving the streetscape a visual coherent interest, and for Will, an architectural entertainment.

The fresh sea air gently flowing into the city from the Black Sea only a few city blocks from the apartment led him towards a civic park he had visited on his last and only other visit. It led him happily to Shevchenko Park where he decided to revisit the Glory Avenue obelisk which formed a memorial to the Unknown Soldier. This early in the morning the only pedestrians he met were sleepy and bored policemen on horseback, none of whom acknowledged his existence. The long, broad downward sloping sidewalk was designed to be a processional route for military remembrance ceremonies. He stood at the top of the ceremonial route admiring the simple but elegant landscaping framing the obelisk further down the hill in the distance.

Virtually the whole of the seafront of Odessa was a

park-like reserve of pathways and children's play yards. One could walk for miles through manicured parkland and see little evidence of human occupation or endeavour.

When he reached the obelisk standing at the edge of the north bank of the Black Sea, he was able to roughly translate the Russian inscription, which was to remind residents and visitors of the horrific seizure of Odessa by the Nazis during the Second World War, which lasted over fifty days. His reverie was broken by a parade of diminutive soldiers marching down the promenade towards the obelisk. Will moved to one side of the obelisk to take a seat on a park bench to watch the ceremony that was sure to follow.

As the small army arrived he observed it was comprised of young adolescent boys and girls in uniforms he recognized as those worn by the Russian equivalents of the Boy and Girl Scouts. Over their uniforms, each had a sash that extended from one shoulder to the opposite hip. The three colours in which the sashes were decorated seemed to speak to a status the wearer had in the youth organization. The two leaders in full military uniform, both male, gave an order that resulted in the children forming two lines facing the memorial, and on another order, each line saluted, then stood in silence with heads down for a few minutes. Then, with considerable dignity, most of the parade marched back up the promenade to the street far above. They left two of their companions to continue guard duty, one youth on one side of the memorial and the other on the far side. In perfect balance and turning, they periodically marched around the memorial, faced it directly at each 90° compass point and saluted, then returned back to their respective primary stations.

Will was aware of the extensive loss of life and property the citizens of Odessa had faced during the war. To see the continuing observance of remembrance was impressive and moving, particularly seeing it conducted by the youth. Clearly, they would have the duty of remembrance impressed on their minds as a responsibility for the rest of their lives.

As Will watched the ceremony, he was reminded of the numerous sieges and invasions of this region since its

Russification and after the First World War its identity as a Ukrainian city. There were few periods of lasting peace and stability. His reading of the histories of other war zones in Europe during both global twentieth-century conflicts taught him that fortunes were made, many assets destroyed or confiscated and social standings lost with the disappearance of land and businesses.

How did those periodic uprisings and wars affect the Menshikovskys, Mendelssohns and Günzburgs in this area? It was apparent that there would have been a major impact on any business ventures or assets held by the families.

His long-standing question of how the families came to be connected was underlying his speculations. He knew that the Mendelssohns came from a German Jewish family whose paterfamilias was Moses Mendelssohn, an intellectual, theologian and banker. For a Jew in Germany, he held the highest status a member of his race could attain. The Günzburgs were Russian Jews whose origins on their path to fortune and status were centred in St Petersburg. The Menshikovskys were a modest Russian Jewish family probably viewed by the Mendelssohns and the Günzburgs as nothing more than upstarts, with their center of activity in the small regional capital of Smolensk.

What brought these families together? Intermarriage among the families with the Menshikovskys was the connecting link, the Günzburg's title of baron even passing on to the Menshikovskys.

Will ruminated on these thoughts, becoming increasingly convinced that it was not St Petersburg, Berlin or Warsaw that had forged their common bond as equals.

The rise of the Menshikovskys in the highly competitive and conservative society of a Jewish family in central and Eastern Europe was equivalent to the majordomo of Isaac's dacha becoming the inheritor, son-in-law and cultured successor to the Baron Menshikovsky; so improbable as to be unthinkable.

The hour and a quarter Will took that morning during his pleasant and undisturbed walk gave him a focus and renewed energy to pursue Isaac's investigations. He reminded himself repeatedly, though, that the assumptions he reached that morning were only that – assumptions. There would have to be evidence to support them.

* * *

The meeting convened on time at the apartment. Will started the session with the caution that since evidence of intrusive listening and recording devices had been found, they must now assume there were adversaries in Odessa aware of who they were and what they were investigating. Will asked each around the table for an opinion as to who these adversaries might be. Everyone passed without comment until it was security guard Andy's turn.

"Mr MacIntosh, the nature of the installations in your suite at the Bristol have the hallmarks, as I have said earlier, of the Russian Mafia, or Bratva. In Russia, as in Ukraine, the Bratva usually is the active arm of the plans and objectives of the oligarchs. It is my opinion, therefore, that what I have discovered represents the invasive techniques employed for one of the oligarchs. Which of the oligarchs, in particular, and what his actual interest might be here, I don't know, but I think it is important to find out."

"Agreed," was Will's reply. "Please follow up that line of investigation, but not to the detriment of your duties as personal security for Penelope and me. I remind you that Penelope is your particular responsibility, as Frank is for me."

Will and the group theorized about who the oligarch might be. They had suspicions arising from the events in Smolensk. Will gave his opinion that it was unlikely that the Smolensk gangster Polansky was behind them here in Odessa. "There is nothing here that would interest Polansky – nothing we know about, anyway. But we will have to be careful not to rule him out until that is proven."

Penelope, who had been virtually mute since her arrival in Odessa, limited her contribution to being on time for meetings and helpfully accepting instructions from Will and then carrying them out in a highly competent fashion. Now she asked, "Would it be helpful, Mr MacIntosh, to ask the manager at the Bristol or the head of in-house security there, whether they know anything about the bugs?"

Silence ensued. Penelope blushed, obviously thinking she had misspoken.

"What harm could that do, do you think, Frank?" said Will. "Sounds like a practical idea to me. If the hotel is aware of the bugs, they may know who installed them, which could, in turn, decide whether they are hostile or neutral – for some other purpose. I worry, however, that merely asking the question will reveal that the nature of our visit to the city is such that a search for invasive recording devices would be necessary. Frank, your opinion."

"The inquiry, if made, should not be made by you, Mr MacIntosh. I am known as chief of your security detail. The fact that you have one will tell them you're up to something – I will say you believe you require protection both personal and for the confidentiality of what you are about which is legal in nature – something about an inheritance. So, no, I don't think the hotel will be surprised or alarmed at the question. Whether they will answer it is another matter. Remember the oligarchs and their minions, the Bratva, are a continuous threat to many people and institutions in this city. I don't think we would be giving anything away by asking. It should be Andy to conduct that investigation since he is known to them as a junior member of our team, and therefore it would appear less threatening coming from him and that his inquiries are being made at a low level of importance where you are concerned, Mr MacIntosh."

"Right, Andy, you will see Penelope to her destinations this morning – one is the law offices or the Jewish archive, I think – then back to the hotel. Do you need a translator?" The answer was no. The manager and security chief at the hotel both had a basic vocabulary in English.

They then moved on to the results of the investigations conducted the day before by Will and his team, Will taking the lead: "We learned yesterday that representatives of all three of our families of interest visited Odessa with some regularity – the Menshikovskys more than the others and none at the same time as the others. We learned, too, that there was a protracted gap of a few years in the third quarter of the nineteenth century when no one from the Günzburg family visited. We are justified in continuing our investigation here. I am convinced that Odessa holds vital clues as to the origins of the connections among the families and the serious money the Menshikovskys came into. Later this morning I will continue my research at the Londonskaya Hotel then I will go to the Bristol to continue my review of its guest registers. Penelope, I haven't had an opportunity to discuss your findings at the law office yesterday."

"Well," Penelope replied, "I think my research may help somewhat but I suspect there is much more to be found. I visited the two oldest firms in Odessa, both of which date back to the Imperial period as far back as the 1840s. First, there were no members of any of the three families who were themselves lawyers. Each of the two firms had Jewish senior partners. Each firm was strategically mixed in terms of representation of the various Ukrainian or Russian regions in Novorossiya, ethnic origins and class. Each was designed to appeal to every layer of society and it seems the various sources of business required legal services. The records of each also disclose that members of all three families had utilized the services of both firms."

"Penelope, were you able to identify the precise services provided to each family?"

"No, Mr MacIntosh. We did not have time to get into specific files, but I agree that will be necessary."

"What specializations, if any, did the two firms have? For example, was one firm more focused on banking than another? Was one firm more involved with railways and transportation than another? Odessa was founded and continued until the 1917 Revolution as a 'free port'. This meant that maritime law would have been an important specialization in the city. Which firm specialized in company law and mergers?"

"I have nothing to offer you on any of those themes, sir.

As you spoke, I and my research assistant have noted each of your queries. We will follow up with those today and tomorrow. It will take at least two days to go through the files as carefully as is required."

Will then turned to the researcher brought from London who specialized in archival research and the antiquated storage systems used for preservation of records. Her report was brief: "I was able to pull numerous files, identify several annual registers of businesses and telephone books starting about 1900 for telephones and businesses in the city. My source material has been assembled but not yet reviewed. That is my target for today. I expect I will need at least two separate days for the research."

"One last category – for each of you to consider in detail," said Will. "Court cases by and against each of the families. Remember, when I say each family, I include every corporate identity in which they functioned. Watch in particular the creation of trusts, or references to trusts created elsewhere. When you get to the bank records, I want to know business and personal transfers, to and from banks, trust companies and other legal entities located in the West.

"You will find the linkages I suggest to be thorough and we must follow all leads to find them," was Will's final instruction.

Will, Frank and the researcher brought from London returned to the Londonskaya Hotel as had been pre-arranged at the end of the session the day before. Will returned to the reception desk where an unfamiliar face presented herself. Will explained that he had a meeting arranged with the manager and the hotel's head of security. The clerk knew nothing of the meeting and displayed a complete indifference to Will's request for help. When asked whether the manager could be brought to the registration desk Will was told, "Busy," and he faced the woman's back as she buried herself in filing or something that involved sorting a large pile of papers.

Not to be deterred, Will searched in his briefcase for the telephone numbers for the manager and the chief of security. He went to the in-house telephone located close to the elevators and dialled the manager's number. It was picked up on the third ring. A tired female voice answered and after Will introduced himself, she said simply that the manager was not available but she would give the manager Will's request for an appointment.

He then called the security manager who was much more forthcoming: "Yes, I do remember Mr Oransky agreeing to your continuing your research today. He has informed me he is not going to be available to meet with you. However, it was left to me to decide whether it was safe for the hotel to continue to permit you to have access. Before I make this decision I want to meet with you to find out much more about why you want this information, whom it affects, and what you will do with it. We get a lot of inquiries. Some of them are for illegal or problematic reasons. I will meet you in a secure room next to my office. You may bring your security person – the one you had with you yesterday."

The meeting convened a quarter of an hour later. At that point, it was about 10 in the morning. The security chief's questions lasted about an hour. When Will asked whether the interrogation was being recorded he was not given a clear answer. Will realized either he could continue with the interrogation or he would not receive permission, and if the latter probably important information would be lost – information that could be important in linking all the details gathered by each of the researchers. If lost, it could result in false conclusions being reached.

"I will proceed with this interrogation," he said to himself, "even if it is recorded. I will try to keep my answers as vague and non-specific as to the families as I can."

An hour later, the hotel's chief of security looked bored, frustrated and tired and he announced that Mr MacIntosh, as the proposed author of a book on the Deutsche Bank and its earlier incarnation under the name of the Mendelssohn Bank, posed a risk neither to the hotel nor to the management of the hotel.

As the security chief walked Will, Frank and the researcher back to the room they had visited the day before, now laid out with the remaining hotel registers, Will leaned over to Frank and whispered, "Not once did he ask about the families involved or their names, although a reference to the Mendelssohn Bank implied that family's involvement."

Four hours later Will suggested that Frank and the researcher call it a day. The hotel security guard who supervised their work spent most of the time with his head cradled in folded arms resting on the far end of the table. Frank had to wake him to gain his attention to secure an exit from the room and the hotel.

Not only did the hotel not inquire for whom and about whom the research was being conducted, the security chief did not require proof of the names of his researchers and did not write down his name or any of the names given.

* * *

Will, Frank and the researcher met back at the apartment. After Frank thoroughly checked for bugging devices and found none, the meeting got underway with Will taking the lead. In Penelope's absence, the researcher took detailed notes.

The research conducted that afternoon was somewhat similar to that of yesterday. It differed in that the Günzburg visits stopped in the 1880s and the Mendelssohns before 1917 when they, too, ended.

"From the information gained today, we know that at least in this city and probably in this Novorossiya region the Menshikovskys became the prominent entrepreneurs by the 1870s or 1880s, at least among the three families. As to why that became the case, it remains to be determined, perhaps from the research being conducted by the others."

Will closed the meeting asking those attending to assemble the next morning at eight. Frank remained with Will after the others had left. The researcher was directed to prepare a computer-generated report which would be circulated as a hard copy in the morning.

Penelope reported back to Will and Frank about 6 p.m. with information she believed would help in the investigation.

She determined that the Günzburgs were the first of the three families to set up business in Odessa and by 1840 the Mendelssohns had a presence in the city. The Menshikovskys first established a business office in the city in the 1850s. Each family, she said, appeared to have their own areas of interest: the Günzburgs in banking and later railways, the Mendelssohns also in banking, but, it appeared, banking specifically related to import and export of goods and later in oil and gas explorations. The Menshikovskys, on the other hand, simply operated a branch of their Smolensk bank in the city to accommodate small-scale businesses and the agricultural sector, much as they had managed in Moscow.

The three banking families were not the only banking enterprises in Odessa. There were several others, one or two primarily Jewish in ownership, which were involved in servicing co-religionists' business requirements. Up to about 1850 nothing in the research suggested why such prominent banks as those of the Günzburgs and the Mendelssohns would have joined forces in any manner with the minor banking enterprise operated by the Menshikovskys.

Just as they were about to leave for the evening, the researchers assigned to the public archives arrived, somewhat flushed and excited.

"I have news that will interest you," said Penelope's principal researcher. "I have found several very old files containing public records of law cases dating back to the 1850s. In particular, there were three cases that linked the three families. In 1850 the Günzburg family was sued by a shipping company with an international scale of business, and then a year later a similar case was filed against the Mendelssohn Bank. Each case alleged not only misappropriation of investment money, it alleged that members of both families were personally complicit in the thefts and irregular transactions. The two cases were exceptionally important as the plaintiffs were the same – the Imperial government – and because the amount of money alleged to have been misappropriated, I mean alleged to be stolen, was in the hundreds of millions of roubles. The decisions rendered by the Russian courts – remember, Odessa was part of Russia in the nineteenth century – were against the two banks and against the named individual members of the two families.

"I read the defence documents and I must say they offer a set of facts very different from those in the claim. The defendants were being tried in courts by judges beholden to and subject to direction by the Imperial government. Bottom line: neither the Günzburgs nor the Mendelssohns stood a chance of success in the cases against them.

"Enter the Menshikovskys. At this time in the history of their bank, they had had no business dealings with the Imperial government. They were too small to attract the interest of the Russian authorities. So what appears to have happened is that as soon as the Günzburg family got wind of a possible case against them in Odessa with major implications for their bank and businesses elsewhere in Russia, they sought and found in the tiny inconsequential Menshikovsky Bank the ally they needed. They divested over 95% of the capital assets held by their bank, transferring the assets to the Menshikovsky Bank through skillful devices we would now consider money-laundering. By the time the decision came down by the court, the Günzburg Bank was virtually a shell, which promptly went into bankruptcy and disappeared... at least in the form and with the structure it had at the time it was sued. Exactly the same thing happened with the Mendelssohn Bank. Its holdings were not as extensive in Russia as those of the Günzburgs, but the judgment entered against the Mendelssohn Bank in Russia bankrupted it, too. That bankruptcy, too, resulted in virtually no loss to the Mendelssohn family as it had followed the exact path that the Günzburg Bank had carried out months earlier. Through devious means, quite legal at that time in Russia, both banks transferred their assets to the Menshikovsky Bank. Because the head office and accounting and transit office of the Menshikovsky Bank was located in the small city of Smolensk in western Russia, the vast wealth transferred to it by the two banks was effectively lost to the Imperial government.

"The Menshikovsky Bank in Smolensk went from a very

inconsequential regional bank to one of the wealthiest and most important in Russia. Remember, there was no centralized auditing of banks. No one in St Petersburg knew of the incredible wealth suddenly vested in the Menshikovsky Bank.

"This is where the Menshikovskys displayed their genius. They could have splashed it around prompting suspicions. No, they remained apparently small and discreet."

There was awed silence. Will finally said, "I suspected something but I had no idea of anything this clever and devious. But there is one flaw in this scenario: why didn't the Günzburg and Mendelssohn Banks come after their money?"

"Again, this is where the Menshikovskys proved equal to their competitors. The Menshikovskys knew that the Imperial government would watch for any sign of the money surfacing which would enable them to get at it. After all, the lawsuits were nothing more than an extortion racket by the Imperial government against two very wealthy Jewish banks. The Imperial government needed money for wars, railways and palaces. What the Menshikovskys skillfully manoeuvered was an agreement with the Günzburg and Mendelssohn families (not their corporate entities) for interest-free loans to them – for one half only of the vast wealth transferred to the Menshikovsky Bank in Smolensk. The two families were so grateful for the scheme devised by the Menshikovskys for a relatively safe return of even one half of the money that they readily accepted the scheme.

"The next step was equally clever. The little Menshikovsky Bank in Smolensk set up a branch in St Petersburg and Warsaw. That created four branches of the bank. The total assets received from the Günzburgs and Mendelssohns were divided equally among the four branches. Remember, the capital was in the form of gold bullion. It was carefully assembled near Smolensk where Dr Menshive's dacha is now and from there the bullion was shipped to the four branches. From the four branches the Menshikovskys, late at night, simply had cartloads of bullion transferred to a Günzburg or Mendelssohn address in the city where the transfer took place. For the purposes of appearances, the Menshikovsky

Bank recorded the transfers as loans to the heads of the two families, as personal loans on a demand basis repayable at a greatly reduced interest rate. It was always the intent that the demand loans would not be called. In fact, none ever were.

"While the transfers were being handled for the Günzburg and Mendelssohn families, transfers of substantial bullion accompanied their share which left Russia and was deposited to the credit of a new Menshikovsky bank in Warsaw and in Berlin. The largest deposits were made in Berlin."

"Do you mean to tell us that all this information is contained in the public archives in Odessa?" asked Frank.

"Yes. In a well-secured, anonymous file – no markings except the name Menshikovsky. Hidden in plain sight. Very few if any interested parties would look under the Menshikovsky name. They certainly would not bother with the Menshikovsky name. I then checked to see if there were any searches under the Günzburg or Mendelssohn Bank names, and there were numerous inquiries, primarily in the mid and late nineteenth century."

Penelope interjected: "Positively brilliant on the part of all three families. Does anyone know the amount of money involved?"

The researcher replied: "One can only estimate that from the amount of the judgment and the assets left in the two banks to honour the judgment. The judgment was for £350,000,000 pounds sterling in all for both banks: for some reason, the Imperial government collected only £1,000 pounds sterling from each bank. My guess as to the amount transferred to the Menshikovsky Bank was in the vicinity of £50,000,000 pounds sterling, which in terms of the value of the pound today in 2008 is worth over twenty times that amount."

"Why pounds sterling?" someone asked.

"The international currency in the nineteenth century was the British pound, much as the American dollar has been in the post-World War II period," explained Will.

Will announced that it was time for a drink to celebrate. Food and several bottles of celebrated Moldovan wine were ordered in and were enjoyed by the whole team... perhaps a little more vigorously than was in the best interests of their health and of their performances the next day.

32

HEADS WERE HEAVY, with slower synapses than usual among the parties who had celebrated the evening before. Conversation was sporadic and dull during breakfast at the apartment. Will was almost on time and Frank a little later.

As Will and Frank studied their granola with little interest and sipped their black coffee, Penelope joined them. She had prudently held back on her liquor intake and was in better shape than her male companions. Her enthusiasm for further exploring the banking schemes identified by the researcher the day before persuaded, if not forced Will to concentrate and focus on the investigation.

As a way of controlling the pace of the research for the rest of the day, Will suggested that he and Penelope take the day to visit local museums and galleries to get a sense of what was assembled by the museums in the nineteenth and early twentieth centuries. He was particularly interested in donations made by residents of the city. Who were the notable collectors and what were they collecting?

Fortunately for Will, Penelope thought Will's suggestion an appropriate step in their research, and it would give them an opportunity to ruminate on the research findings to date. A late morning start was agreed to, justified by Will's insistence that he would need to have a list of the museums and galleries and their areas of specialized collecting. Could any of the considerable cultural assets now owned by Isaac acquired by or for the trust have been obtained in Odessa?

The Odessa Fine Arts Museum was housed in a fine nineteenth-century neoclassical building with a two-and-a-half-storey portico supported by six massive Corinthian columns. The collection contained, as tourist promotional brochures proclaimed, the most complete collection of paintings, drawings and works of art by local artists who had achieved national recognition in Russia.

As Will and Penelope walked through the galleries, Will identified a number of artists whose work was sold at Isaac's New York auction sale held at Christie's a few years earlier. He had wondered where those obscure paintings had come from – at least obscure to him and to the specialists at Christie's. They were not obscure to the predominantly Russian buyers at the sale who had forced prices well above the reserve bids.

The museum contained numerous artifacts from musicians whose origins were in Odessa and who had achieved international acclaim, such as Emil Gilels, a favourite pianist of Will's during his student days, the violinist David Oistrakh and the celebrated pianist Sviatoslav Richter. As Will thought of the eminence of each, he was reminded of their worldwide reputations and numerous accomplishments – and that they were all Jewish. It also reminded him that the opera house in Odessa he had passed so often in the past few days and had visited during his last trip to the city required another visit to attend a performance there.

The Archaeological Museum was the next stop. Will had read that the most important artifacts in the collection had been assembled by a private citizen and with a transfer from his ownership the museum had been established. The particular items in the collection that Will looked for were examples of the craftsmanship of the Scythians who were native to this region and had developed many of their metal working and crafting skills from the Greek colonies that dotted the north and western shores of the Black Sea.

The museum had a few examples of Scythian art, but fewer, much fewer, than Will expected to see. Had the most important pieces been transferred to national museums in Moscow or St Petersburg? Or, as he suspected, acquired by private collectors and had found their way into locations both public and private in other areas of Russia or the world? He knew Scythian gold was currently a particularly hot topic for exhibitions mounted by Western museums.

Will was lucky to find the principal curator of the Scythian collection in her office. She was willing to talk to him. Penelope quietly followed Will without comment or argument, taking notes as they progressed through the museum.

The curator confirmed that the earliest collection was assembled by a private individual as early as the 1820s. She also confirmed that the collector divided his paintings and artifacts roughly in half: one half went into founding the museum and the other half he sold to investors. "Very clever," thought Will, "In effect, he created an interest in and demand for and valuation of Scythian gold."

Will asked whether it was known whether any of the three banking families had acquired Scythian gold. The curator replied that the Günzburgs had an interest in the artifacts but did not know whether the other two families had acquired any. She added, however, that it was known that in the mid-nineteenth century, perhaps in the 1850s, a small local bank acted as an agent for collectors and conducted several archaeological expeditions searching for the artifacts and had also bought some for its own use. How much they had excavated for their client or clients was unknown. When asked which bank was involved, the curator replied that it was small and as the Scythian gold was little regarded at the time, scant attention was paid to the bank or its clients who wished to assemble a collection. And no one particularly cared if the artifacts left Novorossiya.

Penelope asked quietly, "Was it was legal at the time for private individuals to dig for or purchase historical cultural works like Scythian gold?" and she was informed, "There was no law to prevent it."

"Therefore," Penelope said, "those who have the artifacts now, acquired in the nineteenth century, appear to have clear title from their original acquisition."

Will was equally grateful for the questions and for the answers.

There were several galleries in the museum with fine examples of antique Greek statuary, many of them of exceptional quality. They reminded Will that Isaac's father had a collection of such statuary. "Could it be," he thought, "that some of his collection could have been assembled by his ancestors through the bank in Odessa?"

The Literary Museum, the next to be visited, was housed in a former Gagarin Palace. As Will and Penelope walked through the museum they were both astonished at the literary greats with origins or strong connections to the Odessa region who were recognized as giants as much in the West as in Russia. In particular, they were interested in the city's associations with Pushkin and Gogol, among others. He knew Tolstoy had fought in the 1850s Crimean War for Russia and that his family had at some point in the latter part of the century acquired a palace in Odessa, still referred to as the Tolstoy Palace in current tourist literature.

Two other museums were of interest to Will, but a combination of exhaustion and fallen arches required him to call it a day. He invited Penelope to join him for an early dinner in the courtyard restaurant, the Summer Garden, at the Londonskaya Hotel. They shared a bottle of Moldovan wine, Penelope deferring to Will, recognizing his greater need for alcohol. It was the first opportunity they had to be off-duty with each other and to relax.

Will was pleasantly surprised that Penelope, who had said little during their forced march touring the museums, had enjoyed herself; she spoke with enthusiasm and knowledge of what they had seen. In addition to compatible interests, Will was awakened to her beauty and considerable charm. She may have been only twenty-two or twenty-three, but her natural grace and apparent innocence suggested someone much younger. And she did not respond to him as a decrepit older man, which was highly flattering.

33

A CONFERENCE WITH the two researchers and security guards was convened early the next morning.

The first to report was the researcher who had discovered the legal proceedings against the Günzburgs and Mendelssohns by the Imperial government. She expanded on her report given a couple of days before: "I have gone through the archives carefully as I have the court records, taking an interest in the name 'Menshikovsky', either as individuals or as a bank or business name. The bank, as I said, had been opened by 1850. There is nothing in the public record to distinguish it. It always simply appeared to be a small bank with a limited clientele. It never advertised or promoted itself.

"The original location of the bank remained at its original address until the 1917 Revolution. I checked property registration and mortgage registers. I found the bank acquired three properties near the bank offices. However, I suspect it acquired several others under other names, often with the names Smolensk or Smolinsky. I wonder about a Menshikovsky connection, as I do for four major waterfront warehouses and office buildings bought in the 1890s in the name of the 'Dnieper Holdings Ltd.'. As both Smolensk and Dr Menshive's dacha are on that river, I thought there might be a connection. I then contacted the oldest law offices in town and one confirmed they had a record of the purchases but not the incorporations. Each company was fronted by a non-Jew, but the signatures of the signing officers appeared to be – indeed I think they were Menshikovskys, but the writing was so poor, or had been obscured, who could tell? This was consistent in each transaction I encountered. I will offer the opinion that the Menshikovsky investments, except for the bank itself, operated continually through frontmen. It appears to be all legal, according to the law offices I consulted. There was nothing, however, to publicly represent the Menshikovskys as the owners. From the other documents, including newspapers, I could not find any reference to the family. They were private and isolated to the point of being hermits – at least here in Odessa. Very clever, though. Their properties were never damaged in pogroms or confiscated by the Imperial or municipal governments."

The *modus operandi*, as Penelope said, was now clear and clever.

The second researcher reported for the first time: "The municipal records show that there were one or two Menshikovskys, always single men, living here from and after the bank was established here. They paid their taxes on the due date, never before or late. I reviewed the records of the three synagogues here in Odessa. The principal synagogue has a record of one male at a time, one succeeding another, throughout the time span of 1845 to 1917, the first name changing about every ten years. No women or children. I suspect the membership in that congregation was for the record, for show, to establish a presence. None of them held any office or position in the synagogue, the city or business associations. They were here but not really here. I wonder if the Menshikovskys who were resident here were junior members of the family in training for higher positions in the bank operations located elsewhere. At that time it was customary for men not to marry until they had a stable income and could afford to support a family."

Andy, the auxiliary security guard who had been relegated to stay at The Bristol in the room reserved for Frank, reported next.

"I have checked the security devices today in your suite, Mr MacIntosh, as I did yesterday and the day before. They remain installed, but I have discovered that they are not operational. There, but not working for some reason. I wanted to know why not, because it could be that those who installed them had discovered that Mr MacIntosh had moved out. I carefully cultivated a friendship with the hotel's head of security. Last night and the night before he joined me for dinner.

He is a compulsive drinker, as I have found many people, I mean men, are around here. During our time together before, during and after dinner he had a bottle of vodka at his elbow at all times. I can't stand the stuff, so I had a little wine. He was happy to have the bottle to himself and consumed a whole bottle at each of our two dinners together. The strange thing is that he never seemed to get drunk. But as he drank he talked more and more, which was really helpful. I learned a lot. I will tell you.

"It didn't take long for him to inquire who Mr MacIntosh is. I told him he is a very rich collector of art and antiques who is exploring Odessa as a possible source of stuff he could use in his collections. I said he had to be secretive because if those who competed with him for the potential collectables found out where he was and what he was looking for it would drive up prices and perhaps cut off supplies. He said he knew of your visits, Mr MacIntosh, to the museums today which worked really well to support my story.

"That gave me an opening to ask why there were bugging devices in the suite. He didn't act surprised. Perhaps he was too far gone to be cagey, but he answered that he knew they were there, but he claimed none were working. I asked why they were there. He said to record some of the guests – particularly, he said, when the judges come to visit the city, some insisted on being in the hotel where they could get all the luxuries only a hotel could provide here. I was shocked – you couldn't do that in the States or Canada. 'I know,' he said. 'The judges' bosses in Kiev want to keep them safe, so they want to know who they have as visitors – he said, so that they couldn't be blackmailed. You know,' he continued, 'we have a huge problem with Ukrainian girls being bought and sold and pimped. Men from Russia, America and Western Europe come to Ukraine to buy a wife. Some judges have been involved in that trade. Attempts to stop it meant the judges would have to be monitored so they could be punished if they misbehave here, as many do.' Amazing. So, Mr Macintosh, the hotel was not interested in your sex life because you brought your own woman," he said.

Penelope blushed a vivid purple that must have been visible back on the street. Her only answer to the comment was, "Ridiculous. I don't believe that goes on here in a modern country like Ukraine."

Will quietly replied, "The security chief's story has all the elements of truth. I've read about and witnessed it firsthand on my earlier visit here. I'll tell you more about that later if you are interested."

Everyone felt sympathy for Penelope's discomfort and they agreed to break for the day to reconvene early the next day; possibly, Will said, their last day in Odessa.

34

WILL AWOKE THE next day with a feeling he had accomplished all that he could in Odessa and that it was time to get back to Isaac and Isaac's family. As he mentally tabulated the significant information gleaned while in Odessa he took satisfaction in the achievements of each member of the team. They had all pulled together well and operated as a cohesive unit. He was to be shocked and unprepared for the information the team would find during this last full day in the city.

Frank joined Will for breakfast, always the first on duty after Will's punctual early morning appearance, at the table spread by the chef hired for their stay at the apartment. Will took advantage of the calm in the day's activities to call London. He contacted the clinic where both Isaac and Sophie remained receiving treatment. He was informed that Isaac was gradually emerging from his profound withdrawal from life around him and was engaging with the clinicians and support staff at the clinic. He was also beginning to visit with Sophie and was spending at least an hour a day with Little Isaac and Anna. Sophie was also improving, at least to the degree that she would respond to simple questions. It was Little Isaac who generated the greatest response; Little Isaac rushed to Sophie and happily grabbed onto her, keeping her entertained and requiring little effort on her part to respond.

Satisfied that the London situation was under control and beginning to show progress, Will took out his ever-ready notebook and started making an agenda for each member of the team for that day. He was interrupted by Frank who was energy personified.

"Mr MacIntosh... fascinating news from St Petersburg. Further investigation of the safe rooms at the Alexander Palace has uncovered more information on the oblique reference to Odessa. In fact, the team headed by Count Dolgoruky has discovered three handwritten journals. He interprets them as written by a senior member of the Menshikovsky family. The entries describe goods traded and assets purchased by the family in St Petersburg.

"Just as we guessed yesterday, none of the extensive assets were acquired in the name of the bank, in the family name or any of the names we connect with the family. They were purchased or traded in the name of a company the ownership of which was registered in the name of Christian Russians, but attached to the journals was a trust declaration signed by those men acknowledging that the goods were acquired in trust for the bank, the senior businessman in the family or in one of the several companies already formed by the family. The goods included an impressive array of types and values. The entries cover the period from about 1840 to 1917 when they suddenly stop.

"Now, the connection to Odessa: you recall that we found a reference to this city clearly connecting the family's business interests to Novorossiya. The journals establish that junior members of the family in each generation, actually named, were sent to Odessa to learn the business. Records of numerous transactions are listed, mostly of a banking nature, but there are copies of letters sent to the representatives in Odessa and those received from Odessa. What they disclose is interesting.

"Each member of the family sent to Odessa was given very strict rules as to the conduct of the banking and real estate businesses – and several properties are referred to as having been purchased. I will tell you about those in a minute. It is the direction given in relation to non-banking and real estate acquisitions that you need to hear about. Each junior partner sent to Odessa was instructed to develop and cultivate an interest in some type of cultural property. Scythian gold was mentioned, as were ancient Greek statuary and historic items, paintings, prints and other forms of the decorative arts. The objects acquired would form part of the collective holdings of the family, not of the junior partner who acquired them. It was clear that family money would be spent and the item retained as a family asset. Again, the acquisitions were to be in the name of an arm's-length holding company. Each junior was directed to form a collection of some specialized type; the president and vice-president were to be Russian Christians. The secretary-treasurer would always be the junior partner who was bringing the material into the collection. The trust declaration was also required from the Russian Christians who held corporate offices in those companies, one form of which was that they would act solely in the best interests of the Menshikovsky family. Each corporate officer was paid enough to keep them in line.

"Another thing, the real estate: about fifteen properties were purchased in Odessa and the location of the bank and separate business offices were identified. Reference in the journals suggests that separate business records were maintained in both the bank and in the business office. We have to try to find those buildings; if they are still owned by or for the family, we must investigate them. I think one or both would have a strong room like the ones at the Alexander Palace."

Frank concluded with: "I think we have found a gold mine of our own, Mr MacIntosh."

Will listened to Frank's information, taking notes and changing the entries he had made on his agenda for the day. Every member of the team would be instructed to explore and investigate land holdings that could still be held by the family. The Swiss bank inventory would help but it was proven to be incomplete.

"What about the bodies in the strong room, Frank? I hope they have been removed and given a decent burial?"

"Yes. Sorry, I forgot that part of the information I received. Count Dolgoruky and Prince Vorontsov have had experts from the National Museum examine them. They were killed by a poisonous gas of some kind after being tied together in the strong room. Their clothing and documents found in their clothing establish that they died in 1917. It is Vorontsov's opinion that they were Mensheviks."

"Oh, yes, Mensheviks. The dominant political party or movement during the Russian Revolution. It was the

Mensheviks who were supposed to form the post-revolutionary government. However, brilliantly led primarily by Leon Trotsky, the Bolsheviks, despite being the minority political party, defeated the Mensheviks through skill and duplicity, forming the government. Vorontsov believes that the men in the strong room were found hiding in the Alexander Palace during the Bolshevik takeover of power and were killed by one or more Bolsheviks. He says that it stands to reason as none of the valuable goods were moved or removed. Probably the Bolshevik involved in the killings intended to come back later to take the treasures and sell them all on the black market but he was killed during the military and social upheaval in Russia in 1917 and 1918, so it appears the death of these men has nothing to do with the Menshikovskys."

"Yes. That is also Count Vorontsov's opinion. That is also the opinion of the Putin government. They won't do anything about bodies except keep the information as hidden from the public as possible. Public knowledge of the deaths could reactivate the political divide between the Mensheviks and the Bolsheviks."

"What?" said Will. "After all this time?"

"Those loyalties apparently remain deeply embedded in the people," replied Frank, "particularly among government circles in Western Russia. Best left dead and buried, I was told."

* * *

By ten o'clock that morning the team departed on their specific investigations as directed by Will who declared that they would reassemble at 5 p.m. at the apartment.

Penelope was sent back to the law office with new names of holding companies, company directors and addresses for the properties known to have belong to the Menshikovskys in 1917. Her knowledge of Russian and the history of the region were invaluable in enabling her to efficiently and effectively investigate the records of the law offices. Privacy concerns were not relevant in the Russia of 2008, so no approval was required by the law offices to give access to their archives, but Will provided her with a notarized request and authorization as the qualified agent of the family to provide the information. Will's document was effective as a direction to the law offices to cooperate, which they did. He emphasized to Penelope that if she encountered any resistance at the law offices, she was to call him on his cell phone and he would come and sort out the problem; this proved to be unnecessary.

Frank and Andy were sent to check police and court records, as the thinking was that many of their records – at least those still kept – would not be in the public archives.

The two researchers were sent back to the public archives and as one was herself from a Russian Jewish family, she was sent to the three synagogues to continue to explore their records given the new names Frank had been given.

"This name, here on this document, baffles me," he said. "Menshikovsky is also the name of a noble Russian family – Orthodox, of course, not Jewish. In fact, they had a palace in St Petersburg across the Fontanka River from the Alexander Palace. Is there a connection between the families? Or did Isaac's family assume that surname as part of its strategy to hide in plain sight? It was common for serfs on the estates of nobles, when serfdom was abolished in the late nineteenth century, to take the surnames of their former owners or some variant of that name. Let's watch for any indication of the source of the surname. We do know that the family surname has been in continuous use for over two hundred years. Has it always been used by Isaac's family? Did they adopt it as former serfs of the noble family? Is the connection coincidence or significant? Certainly, the name has been used by Isaac's family throughout the nineteenth century."

* * *

When the group met later that afternoon a record of their discussion was made by Penelope and both of the researchers. Will insisted on it. He wanted no fact or evidence to be unrecorded or written down inaccurately. He emphasized that the quality of evidence gained in Odessa was highly superior to what had been obtained in Smolensk or St Petersburg. It appeared to him as he expressed it to the group that as a preamble to their reports that the primary Menshikovsky family and businesses were operated out of St Petersburg and Moscow, with Odessa as a clearing house for most of their commercial activities. The Smolensk location was the origin of the family, but by the late 1860s, with the huge infusion of Günzburg and Mendelssohn capital, its centre of activity moved east, north and south.

Penelope was the first to report. "I have found records of purchases in the secondary names we discussed yesterday. The Menshikovsky name appears only in relation to the bank. The records of the bank in the law offices indicate a relatively small-scale operation as a public bank, but massive transfers of capital through its accounts at certain times. For example, during the Crimean War in the 1850s huge capital deposits and withdrawals were made. Most – I find this amazing – were made by British banks. The transactions are not identified. Why would a law office have such records? Perhaps as a secure archive in case of a pogrom or interference by the Imperial government. That was always a major worry for Jewish businesses, no matter how cooperative government pretended to be. It always knew it could squeeze Jews for cash in exchange for being left in peace – or at least a form of peace.

"Now, as to the properties: I have found that of the large number held by Menshikovsky family interests in 1917, several were confiscated by the Leninist and Stalinist governments in the 1920s and later during the Cold War. However, there were five properties whose ownership was effectively concealed and whose location was of no importance to the authorities which remain. I have visited each. Two, you will hear more about this because I called Will" – the first time she had referred to him in the group by his first name, a fact not missed by the others – "who joined me to explore them. Luckily, he brought Andy with him. I will leave the rest of my report to Andy. He was with me during the most interesting part of my day."

Andy gave his report: "Security for Mr MacIntosh and each member of our team has been paramount for Frank and me. Frank was responsible for Mr MacIntosh. I was delegated to handle all other security issues on a day-to-day basis. For the first few days, no one cared who we were and took no interest. Today I have observed two men watching both Mr MacIntosh and Penelope everywhere they went. I have engaged a reliable security guard I discovered a couple of days ago here on holiday visiting his wife's family. He is German and has excellent credentials. He followed the two who were watching Mr MacIntosh. He has reported to me on an hourly basis by cell phone during the day. They are Russian, armed and very dangerous. He watched them at one point in a nearby park taking out what looked like a medical kit and one man was showing the other how to use a syringe. On one or two occasions, they came close enough to Mr MacIntosh to have physical contact. My assistant and I successfully distracted them. I have to tell you we are leaving this city at a good time, but we will have to be vigilant. We are all at risk. The nature of the risk is only suggested by the syringe. They mean business. I suggest that my German friend and I stay a few days after you leave to investigate who these guys are and to whom they report."

Will thanked Andy for all members of the team and asked him to keep the German security guard on payroll for as long as he was in Odessa, and for Andy to remain in Odessa until they discover who hired the two followers and discover what they were interested in. "You have my authority to get the information we require by whatever means are effective. I was going to report, as Penelope said, but at this point, our presence here has attracted interest which can only mean that someone has informed them of our purpose for being here. It would not be safe or secure for me to give any further information while we are in Odessa. We will reconvene in London the day after tomorrow."

PART 5

London – Gozo – Transnistria – Moscow

35

WITH A VIGOUR and enthusiasm he always felt on first arriving in London, after his return from Odessa Will set out from the flat in Fitzrovia, not entirely alone.

Andy's comments in Odessa on Will being followed raised the security level to high. He was well aware that anyone in Odessa looking for him could and probably would discover he was leaving Odessa, and then his airline flight number and destination. Frank had informed him after they cleared customs and passport control at Heathrow that personal security would be intensified for Isaac, Sophie, Little Isaac, Anna and Will, each to have a security detail of their own. Will, as a frugal Scot abhorring waste, particularly unnecessary monetary waste, shuddered to think of the cost, but he knew it was necessary and that it wouldn't make a noticeable dent in Isaac's bank account.

Will appeared to be on his own striding towards Portland Place and the clinic nearby, but he was being followed by Frank and two other security guards as he would be for the foreseeable future. While outside the apartment Will was instructed not to notice or communicate with Frank or the other two, the latter having been introduced to Will only that morning. There was little chance he would remember them, particularly as they would be camouflaged and occasionally changing their appearance. For Will's peace of mind Frank remained identifiable so that if Will needed him he would be able to contact him. Cell phone usage was prevalent in 2008, enabling an extra degree of contact. The threat of hacking and interception of calls was largely unknown among the general public at that time, so no restrictions were imposed in either Frank's or Will's use of their cell phone, although Frank informed Will every few days he would remove Will's phone and replace it with a short-term rental. This gave Will a certain level of anxiety as he was left to create a new password each time the phone was replaced, imposing on him the task of memorizing and keeping the passwords straight.

As is often the case in early September in London, the sun was in full intensity; a heat wave was annoying the radio and television weather reporters and causing traffic congestion and sidewalk overload in central London, slowing everything down.

* * *

At the clinic, Will went to Isaac's room first after checking with the duty nurse on Isaac's floor to receive clearance that Isaac was up, alert and willing to see him. He was greeted by a person as unlike the person he had left a week before as was possible. Isaac welcomed Will warmly, announcing he would be moved to a nursing home for a short stay before being released. Will knew that the nature of Isaac's mental state was such that he could regress if anything disturbed him. Will kept the conversation as light as he could, simply giving a positive account of his visit to Odessa and some of the conclusions the team had reached. Isaac was insistent on details, but Will managed to divert the conversation onto safe subjects to avoid anything that would induce anxiety.

An hour with Isaac was followed by a walk down the clinic corridor to Sophie's room. She, too, was better, but not as improved as Isaac apparently was. She recognized Will, however, and asked in a polite conversational fashion what he had been up to lately. The vague question informed him that Sophie did not have any awareness of recent developments in the investigations and his travels. He kept the conversation cheerful and light concentrating on Little Isaac's genius, good looks and charm – topics Sophie enjoyed and opinions she shared.

Half an hour with Sophie was sufficient for both patient and visitor. As Will was about to leave Sophie's room she asked whether he had found any improvement in Isaac's health. This gave Will encouragement that Sophie was beginning to connect with the outside world with some interest. Little Isaac was one thing, her husband another.

Both Isaac and Sophie were to be moved together to an ultra-luxurious nursing home in Chelsea in west London overlooking the Thames River in the next few days. Will was greatly encouraged by the move. He knew the nursing home was a short distance from the Royal Hospital, a building designed by Sir Christopher Wren as a home for unmarried war veterans requiring some degree of continuing care and medical assistance. Built in the decade of 1681-1691, it was one of Wren's most accomplished designs and included the development of an extensive park separating the building from the Thames River, a park open to the public. Will planned to get Isaac out daily for walks in the park. The setting and the extensive grounds would provide exercise and distance from things that would stress Isaac.

* * *

On schedule, Will arrived at Smythe's law offices in Lincoln's Inn Fields near the Strand at 11 a.m. It never ceased to amaze Will that most professional offices and appointments in London were not scheduled until 10:30 or 11 a.m. Back in Charlottetown, he was already at his law office by 7 a.m., on duty and fully operational.

Smythe greeted him warmly, saying he was interested in hearing what had been discovered as a result of the trip to Odessa, and that Penelope would be joining them momentarily. During this exchange, Frank remained outside Smythe's private office, listening to the conversation and watching activity in the office generally. Smythe did not appear concerned by Frank's presence or his supervisory role.

Penelope joined them shortly after Will arrived. They sat at an elegant Regency library table positioned in one corner of Smythe's office in a location where Frank could both see and hear them.

Will reported on the visit, keeping the information even more general if not vaguer than he had given Isaac. He and

Penelope had agreed during the flight from Odessa that secrecy was essential; while Smythe and his staff were trustworthy, no risk, however remote, should be taken in releasing information.

The purpose of the meeting was identified by Will within half an hour of arrival: "Smythe, we have discovered that Isaac's family gained the initial bulk of its wealth from transactions with two other Jewish families in Odessa. Their methodology is now clear to us. This we have discovered through the considerable investigative skills of Penelope and the researchers we took with us – but I credit Penelope with the pivotal research that led to our discoveries." He then briefly described some of the third-party corporate devices used in the development of their wealth.

"What I need from your firm is detailed information on the trust created by your firm in my home province of Prince Edward Island. At what point was it created and where does it fit in the business plan created by or for the Menshikovsky family?"

"I can tell you it was created by my predecessors in this office in the 1880s. We searched for legal systems in place in various of our British colonies, looking for a legal regime that recognized English common law, including the law of trusts, but had little or no public registry of trusts. We were looking for a jurisdiction where we could domicile our Menshikovsky Trust but where there would be no public record of its being domiciled there or a requirement for an annual financial filing. Prince Edward Island had the perfect legal structure relating to trusts for our purposes. We could legally domicile the trust there and no one would discover its existence. Now, I have to tell you that in the twentieth century certain requirements were imposed that created the need for court approval for the winding up of a trust and other matters not relevant to our trust. The trust is still in existence and domiciled there. There is now an annual report of income and disbursements filed with the court, but only as directly received or directly expended. The *cestui que trust* – that is, the person who benefits from the trust – is a company incorporated in the Channel

Island of Jersey, which is almost as secretive as Prince Edward Island where trusts are concerned.

"As to the question of where it fits in the asset-holding structure of the Menshikovsky Empire: it is the ultimate owner. It is, however, carefully controlled by a series of companies and trusts created here in London and in Switzerland. There are a few companies, as you noted, in Russia, Germany, Poland and Belarus."

Will was intrigued by the notion that such vested wealth could be controlled and owned by a trust in his hometown. "How," he asked, "did you discover that the law of trusts on Prince Edward Island was so amenable?"

"As I said, Mr MacIntosh, after considerable research according to meticulous notes kept by former partners of this firm, we knew of the place and its almost non-existent trust laws requiring disclosure of the ownership and assets held by the trust. I know that this firm and two or three of our neighbours here in Lincoln's Inn also domiciled trusts there. All of us who used Prince Edward Island have been satisfied with the arrangement. The few court filings that are now required are handled by a law firm in Charlottetown – one I am sure you are familiar with. The lawyer who handled the domiciling of the trust and maintained head office records, as limited as they are, is Mr Charles Longworth's successor in his practice. He was the lawyer engaged."

"Oh!," exclaimed Will, "there were two members of that family who in the late nineteenth century were lawyers. They were both close relatives of my great-grandparents."

"Yes, we know of your family connection to the Longworths. Perhaps you don't know that your combined connections to Prince Edward Island, the Longworths and Dr Menshive were what led to your being asked by Dr Menshive to join him four years ago on his initial travel to Europe to investigate the Swiss trust, which, incidentally, is secondary to the one domiciled on Prince Edward Island. When Dr Menshive's lawyer in New York discovered our connection with the creation of the Menshikovsky Trust, he asked me if I knew a lawyer on Prince Edward Island other than one in the firm currently representing the trust. I checked our records and had a family history search conducted. Your name came up. Mr Cohen, Dr Menshive's father's lawyer in New York, suggested your name to Dr Menshive. Dr Menshive was very surprised to have your name mentioned, but since he knew and trusted you already he happily asked you to join him."

"Good God, this is almost Dickensian in its coincidences! However, we are where we are. I am glad to discover the various connections. They bring me into an even greater comfort level with my role and responsibilities with Isaac and the assets," said Will.

"Yes. You are now considered here and at the Swiss bank the senior manager and director of all operations, and likely to remain so. We here at this firm," said Smythe almost obsequiously, "would be pleased to continue as your London solicitors."

Will's distracted response was a simple nod of the head.

Afternoon time for tea, even in a London law office, is diligently followed. While Will and his companions silently sat, giving everyone a chance to absorb the information imparted by Mr Smythe, the tea trolley with an array of biscuits, jam and butter and Earl Grey tea arrived. The receptionist was also, it appeared, the tea lady. "That," thought Will, "would not be politically correct back at the place of domicile of the trust."

As the three lawyers sat enjoying the tea and biscuits, Penelope opened her briefcase and set out papers clearly preparing for her contribution to the meeting.

After the tea things were removed and Frank served as Will's assistant in handling documents and making notes, Smythe asked Penelope to give her presentation.

It took an hour for Penelope to complete her presentation, which was in effect a revised management plan for administration of the assets. It would centralize the administration in London and secondarily in Zurich. Prince Edward Island would remain as the place of domicile of the trust but very little activity would take place there, although Penelope proposed that Will's law firm be designated as counsel of record for the trust. To which Will promptly, and perhaps too forcefully, replied that that would create an untenable conflict of interest. It would remain where it was. He would be able to supervise and critique its performance at arm's length, but as the firm's office was next door to his it was easily accessed.

At the conclusion of the discussion on Penelope's proposal, Will concluded the consultation, arranging for its resumption in a week. He then suggested that if Penelope would join him for dinner at Rules restaurant in Covent Garden, he could explore some further particulars which would enable him to consider the proposal in greater detail.

Smythe looked at Penelope with shock, as if he suddenly saw her as female for the first time. Penelope's blush announced her acceptance of the invitation.

36

AUBURN-HAIRED PENELOPE WAS certainly a blusher, a trait she had demonstrated on one or two earlier occasions. But never more so than the next morning when Frank arrived for his accustomed early morning breakfast with Will. Seeing Penelope with Will and her more than mild absorption in him, Frank understood what it meant and smiled knowingly.

Will greeted him, asking for an update on the current level of security risks to the Menshives and to those in the apartment. He replied that there were no developments in London that should trouble anyone there, but in Odessa Andy was observing increasing scrutiny, suggesting persons with adverse interests were looking for Will and his team.

"That may be the case, Frank, but we must investigate the five currently held properties located in Odessa to find out if any of them have hidden treasures or records. Odessa is remote from our principal areas of interest, so we must get at these investigations without delay. I am needed here in London and cannot go; anyway, I am now too identifiable to be anything other than a risk to myself and anyone with me. I need someone who both reads Russian and understands enough nineteenth-century Russian law to interpret any documentation that may be found."

Penelope came out of her reverie and turned to Frank and she said, "Will and I have talked about who would be best suited for this task. I have volunteered to go and to take our researchers with me. Mr Smythe has agreed to give me leave from my duties there in the law practice. Our researchers together with one more, a Dr Jellicoe, who is a specialist in Ukrainian history and speaks both Russian and Ukrainian fluently, has agreed to join me. He will be invaluable in assessing the significance of anything we find."

Frank assured Penelope and Will that Andy and his security team in Odessa would stay and join Penelope and the group leaving from London. In the meantime, he said, Andy and his team were investigating the chain of title of each of the five properties in Odessa and examining each from the street to determine which was the most likely to have been the location of the Menshikovsky junior partner's private office. Will and Frank had earlier agreed that the private office would be the place to investigate.

"I suspect, Penelope, that the private office will be located in the building occupied by the junior partners as a residence. Given the highly secretive way in which the Menshikovskys operated in Odessa, I suspect the residence will be relatively modest and unobtrusive. I bet there will be nothing notable about its external appearance but it should be in a highly secure location. This should enable Penelope and her team to check off the unlikely properties and to get at the most suitable for our purposes.

"The Menshikovskys had a property manager for the Russian properties, Mr Molotovsky, with whom we have dealt in the past. He informed me last night that he hired a Christian Ukrainian several years ago to serve as the property manager in Odessa. He thinks he knows which property is most likely the one we are looking for. He will have the local manager join Penelope's team when they visit the properties and he will make arrangements with the current tenants for access to the properties." Will added, perhaps more forcefully than was necessary: "Loose lips sink ships." The meaning was clear: absolute discretion in what was said and where was imperative.

Penelope left the breakfast table by 8:30 that morning and having already packed, she left for Heathrow where she would connect with Dr Jellicoe and the two research assistants.

* * *

Will resumed his consultation with Mr Smythe at his law office. The balance of the day was spent meticulously listing the assets by type, location, estimated value, importance to Isaac's future plans and any known competing interests, specifying the merits and risk posed by each adversary.

At the end of a day of intense concentration and debate, the list was completed. The resulting spreadsheet would be left, it was agreed, at the law office in a safe located in Smythe's private office. No copies would be taken in the short term. A more accurate assessment of risk from outside interests was necessary. While hacking into computers by devious technicians, usually employed by an adverse party, was still in its infancy in 2008, it was known to occur. At the end of the day, a hard copy of the spreadsheet was run off and the digital computer record was deleted.

Before Will turned in for the night, he received a telephone call from Andy and, at the same time, a knock on the door announced Frank who was invited into Will's room for the conversation. Speaking into the phone, Frank cautioned Andy to avoid specific names and locations in his briefing.

Andy reported: "Your lady lawyer was unrecognizable when she got off the plane here in Odessa. She had to introduce herself to myself and my team, as she did Dr Jellicoe who was new to us. She came prepared with several disguises. I commended her for those precautions. She met with the property manager and after examining each property with a drive-by and explanation from the manager she decided which one to visit first. The one she chose was a row house on a secondary street off Pushkinskaya Street. It looked like every other one but was an end unit with a back garden fenced and gated. The manager informed us there was only one resident tenant at any given time. The ground floor flat had a small plaque simply announcing that the Smolensk/Odessa Bank office was located there. The unit was unoccupied, as I suspect it usually was. The tenant on the two floors above was a Ukrainian Christian who taught literature and Ukrainian culture at the local university. A very low-level academic. No one who would attract attention. We went into the ground floor flat and found it modestly fitted as an office. There was nothing of interest on that level, but we found a concealed, well-secured door that led into the basement area. I guess the manager knew about it, but he didn't mention it even though he had a key.

"The basement was what we were looking for. It, too, was fitted as an office but with the most modern technology, filing cabinets and several conference room-type tables for laying out documents. We examined all the filing cabinets and we found leases going back to the 1850s. There was nothing in those records that appeared relevant or helpful in any way. The manager suggested we leave and seemed eager for us to do so.

"I remembered Mr MacIntosh talking about a secure room or two in a palace in St Petersburg. I thought the same strategy may have been used here, too. I insisted we examine the space more carefully. The manager was clearly annoyed. 'I know this place well, there is nothing more down here,' he announced.

"Within fifteen minutes I found a hidden door plastered over, which was designed to make it difficult to find. The manager stared at me and stood back surprised as I cut the enclosure away from the door. After removing the debris the door was revealed. It was secured with a combination lock similar to the one described as being at the palace in St Petersburg. I contacted Frank, who remembered the combination for the other lock. The room contained no treasures we could see, but it was full of detailed business journals, invoices and corporate registers. They started in the early 1850s and continued to 1917. More about 1917 in a minute.

"The records listed every transaction made at the bank, every acquisition made by the bank, or made for a third party by the bank. I'll concentrate for a moment on those.

"Extensive entries were made for purchases or trades for Scythian gold, antiquities and cultural works such as first edition books, paintings, engravings and antiques. A lot of antique Greek statuary was listed. I say 'trades' because a lot of the material acquired was from individuals who had, I would say, no need for money but wanted food or some other benefit the Menshikovskys could provide.

"In summary, I think we have the motherlode of records. You will need to see them all."

Will interrupted the long narrative saying simply, "Yes, we need everything that is in that room. Photographs are to be taken immediately of all sides of the safe room before anything is disturbed more than it has been. Penelope is to supervise an identification of every journal, document or clustered group of documents. This must be undertaken tomorrow. Photographs of as many of the documents as possible are to be taken, carefully recording each photograph by date, number and subject.

"We have no interest in retaining any of the Odessa properties, so I want the contents removed tomorrow night – in the middle of the night. You must tell the tenant that some junk which was found in the basement is being removed then as that is the only time workmen could be found. If you can arrange a dumpster to come, all of the contents should be carefully and methodically arranged in it. The dumpster is to be taken to an abandoned airfield we identified by satellite photography of the Odessa area. I will have a helicopter hired to come to that field by 6 a.m. the day after tomorrow. This will be highly illegal as we will not be informing aviation authorities or customs. If we disclose the existence of this material and our plans to remove it there will be fierce opposition from several quarters. I want Penelope and her group to head north to Moldova and from there to cross into Romania. She and her group can fly out of Bucharest on a commercial flight back to London.

"Andy, remember: oligarchs are not just located in Russia. There are numerous Ukrainian oligarchs and both a Ukrainian and an Albanian Mafia working in your area. Those following you may be any of those – it could even be worse. You may have both the Russians and Ukrainians after you – and the Russians and Ukrainians could be pursuing rival ends. They will all be heavily armed, unscrupulous and very determined. That is why my intentions must be carried out to the letter. Timing and process are vital for success. We must have all of those records back here in London the day after tomorrow. Keep Penelope and her team safe, too."

Will's normal 10 o'clock bedtime was abandoned. Arrangements were required for each step of the process Will had described. Tasks were divided between Frank and Will. All the arrangements had to be made for the support transport and logistics in London. No one in Central or Eastern Europe could be trusted. There was a history of several deaths and vicious attacks on Isaac and his family – this series of events could not expose them to further violence. It was unlikely they would survive it.

It could have been helpful to have the help of the American government or the Jewish leaders in Ukraine, but no one could be trusted with the information that would have to be imparted to them as background for a request. Will and Frank agreed they were on their own.

"Frank, how can we hire a helicopter of a troop-carrying size? We need to fly into Odessa across several national boundaries. Where would we find a 'copter and crew on such short notice who would be trustworthy?"

Frank remained silent for a few minutes and he then said: "I was in the American Air Force for several years. I know there is an underground that provides aircraft and crews. As it happens I have a contact: a great friend who owes me. In Afghanistan I saved his life from a terrorist bombing. He will jump at the chance to help. Will, is there money to pay him? It could be quite a bit."

"Find out how much – all verbal communications. We have no choice but to pay what is asked. I hope the cost is not exorbitant," complained Will.

37

AT 1 A.M. the next day Frank reported back to Will that the air transport had been arranged. "It was," Frank said, "unnecessarily complicated." Will thought it was highly risky and could result in being shot out of the sky without warning or create an international diplomatic incident between the USA and Russia. Complicated it was, and necessarily complicated, thought Will. The stakes were so high the risks had to be accepted and the plans carried out precisely and carefully.

Shortly after Frank closed the door to Will's bedroom, Will dashed out calling him back. "Frank, where will the 'copter land after it leaves Eastern Europe? Getting out of Ukraine is one thing, but landing without papers in any foreign country would be foolhardy. We need papers. The terrorist alert is so high right now the 'copter would be shot down or confiscated with its cargo intact."

"I have thought of that," replied Frank with his accustomed confidence. "The return to London will not be direct. The flight from Odessa will be south across the Black Sea which after leaving the Ukrainian zone is in international waters. The helicopter will fly south down the Sea of Marmara in Turkey and then down the Dardanelles into the Mediterranean. Once into the Mediterranean and in international territory, it will land either in Cyprus or Malta, two well-known air traffic control centres known for their lax air controls. I suspect we will try to get into Malta. As you know, Malta is actually a tiny archipelago with three inhabited islands: Malta, Gozo and Comino. We will aim for Gozo, which is north of the main island of Malta. I know there is a little-used World War II airfield on Gozo. Once there, we can bribe our way out on a private cargo aircraft licenced to transport goods from Malta to an airfield north of London used for cargo arriving by air."

"How do you get the goods from Gozo to the island of Malta?" asked Will, who was skeptical and worried.

"We don't: the cargo plane will pick them up at the airfield on Gozo."

"Frank, I have been to both islands and can tell you they are minute. What we are describing will be picked up by air traffic control at the International Airport in Malta. I have flown in a helicopter from Malta to Gozo. It only takes half an hour in a small 'copter."

"Leave it to my people, please."

Will, with resignation, agreed.

38

THE HELICOPTER ARRIVED at the small private airstrip located close to the Ukrainian border with Moldova on time and well-equipped to take delivery of the numerous large, well-wrapped packages containing the records and files extracted from the Menshikovsky business office and storeroom in Odessa. The removal was conducted at two on a Monday morning when there was virtually no traffic on the streets and no pedestrians evident anywhere.

The tenants of the apartment in Odessa had been ordered to leave the premises for three days, ostensibly to allow the installation of a new furnace in the basement. Andy and his allies in the security detail had arranged for four large trucks to arrive with forklifts to remove the packages from the front lawn; the lawn being hidden by a wooden fence separating the house from the street.

The labourers were informed that the packages contained tax records stored in the bank which were being requisitioned by the Ukrainian tax authorities. To ensure secrecy and silence they were told that a number of working-class residents of the city would be in trouble and made to pay substantial fines and penalties to Kiev if the tax authorities gained control of the records. Each of the workmen knew of relatives or neighbours who would be affected. As a matter of civic pride, they assured Andy that they would be silent. This premise was sealed with an hourly payment twice the going rate for cartage.

The trucks arrived unnoticed at the landing strip and the troop carrier-size helicopter was quickly loaded, with the forklifts being able to drive up a ramp at the back of the helicopter into the cavernous storage bay inside. The crew of the helicopter had a carefully mapped route for its departure from Ukraine and into the Mediterranean Sea through Turkish territory.

When the helicopter reached international waters in the Mediterranean Sea, the pilot sent a coded message to Andy who forwarded it to Frank in London.

Two hours later, the helicopter approached Gozo from the northeast, passing as far from Maltese air traffic control as possible. Arrangements similar to those made in Turkey eased the way for landing the helicopter in a private airstrip near Victoria, a town on Gozo, but far enough away to avoid noise that would attract attention.

The helicopter landed as scheduled without incident and taxied up to the aviation fuel pumps to fill the nearly empty tanks. It was after daybreak that the tanks were being filled; a process that would take over an hour which would bring the time to the hour of departure by working people to their places of business. The military-type helicopter flying overhead at that time of the day would have alerted the local police to its unusual presence on the island, no doubt resulting in officialdom being alerted and involved.

The crew secured the helicopter and covered the vast aircraft with a camouflage netting which they hoped would disguise it from curious eyes.

The crew, as scheduled, walked for an hour to the outskirts of Victoria, where they checked into the five-star Kempinski Hotel in the small community of San Lawrenz. It was perfect for a restful day out of sight. The hotel was within walking distance to San Lawrenz and promoted itself as a refuge for those seeking privacy in peaceful surroundings. The five-man crew arrived in military fatigues that could have been American issue. No questions were asked at registration as Will had prepaid their one-day stay, meals and spa treatments that would occupy the time and physical requirements of the crew. It was a scheme Will knew would keep the crew from getting into trouble.

The helicopter was scheduled to leave the island at three the next morning, a time when no self-respecting Maltese would be up and about. An uneventful departure was guaranteed by a branch of the Sicilian Mafia. It had effective access to forged papers ranging from flight manifests, crew identities, air corridor passage permits, and every requirement needed to enable the helicopter to proceed through Italian, French and British airspace.

* * *

While the helicopter and its cargo were on schedule, Penelope, Dr Jellicoe and her team were having less success. The plan was for her and Andy accompanied by two of his auxiliary guards and the two research assistants to enter Romania through Moldova. There was insufficient room for them on the helicopter. Reservations with Austrian Airlines had been made for a flight leaving Bucharest for Vienna in two days, a timeframe that should have been ample.

Neither Penelope nor Andy were aware of the geopolitically fractured nature of Moldova: its eastern section, while ostensibly operating as an independent breakaway state called Transnistria, was in effect under the control and governance by the Russians. It was also, of course, claimed as a constituent part of Moldova.

Andy selected a little-used area of the Ukrainian border with Moldova that he knew would require few answers on travel documents as long as sufficient cash passed hands. He was not aware that the border he crossed, while technically Moldova, was part of Transnistria.

He and his flock discovered the error in geography when they left the border station. They were met by Transnistria police speaking Russian and carrying Russian firearms. Penelope had some basic Russian language skills and she tried to explain the error in their selection of the border crossing, apologized and asked for the courtesy of being allowed to travel to Chisinau, the capital of Moldova. She took some limited comfort in knowing that Dr Jellicoe remained in Odessa to further his assigned research.

"*Nyet*," was the sole reply to Penelope's request.

They were herded into a military troop carrier and taken to what appeared to them to be a military base. While they were in transit, Andy was able to text a message by way of the helicopter back to London with the simple message: "Order being filled, may be delayed in delivery." This was compatible with the story they were to give the authorities that they were on a legal mission to Odessa to obtain information relating to an estate being handled by Penelope through the law office in London. At Will's insistence, Smythe had given her sufficient bogus estate papers in case there was a problem in Ukraine. Again, the authorities showed no interest in her story and simply took her and each of the team by the arm to cells where they were individually incarcerated.

39

TWENTY-FOUR HOURS LATER, back in London, when no further word was heard from any of Penelope's team, Will and Frank realized they had a problem that could have international implications if the Russians chose to make an example of them with trumped-up charges of some kind.

Will arranged a meeting with a consular official in the American Embassy in London, together with a senior official from the Home Office in London. Will provided only what information he thought necessary to gain some sympathy and traction in getting the team released. Both officials met a couple of hours later with a senior consular officer in the Russian Embassy. Stasis. Nothing. The Russian official didn't try to hide his boredom or yawns. His only promise was "To do what I can," which Will understood would be nothing. The excuse, predictably, was that Moldova was a sovereign country and the official knew nothing of alleged Russian influence in Transnistria.

40

IT WAS NOW day two of the incarceration of Penelope and her group. There was no record of Penelope's involuntary stay in Transnistria. And there was no consular contact or other civil niceties customary to a foreign national being held in another country.

Will realized that each of the group was without representation or a voice in Transnistria. They could be held indefinitely. No demands had been made yet. Will did not find that surprising. The local hoodlums were answerable to no one. They could keep the group locked up indefinitely, or at least until they received what they considered to be their due to release them. Will knew they would wait until inquiries and requests for release were made. It would be at that point he speculated, that their demands would be made known. How could Will set up a line of communication with the jailers?

After considering the options and discussing them with Frank, he decided to call his friend in the Canadian Embassy in Moscow and ask him for advice; fortunately, Peter MacNeill was available to take his call. Peter was now the senior consular official in the embassy and knew about developments in Isaac's situation over the past three years. Peter's knowledge of Will and Isaac's activities amazed Will.

Peter's advice was direct: "There is nothing the Canadian or American diplomatic people can do for you. Transnistria is lawless, with officials accountable to no one. The only external influence in the country is from Putin's government. If you have any access to Putin's office, use it. That is your best bet. The alternative is highly risky and I don't recommend it. That would be to hire mercenaries to enter the country and attempt to seize the facility where they are being kept. Apart from obvious logistical problems related to an invading force, you don't know where they are. I could request my counterpart in the American Embassy to join me in an approach to our counterpart in the Russian Embassy. It would be no more useful than was your talking to an official in the Russian Embassy in London. No, the only way of getting the ear of a Russian who could exercise influence is through someone who has reliable access to Putin or at least to his office."

Will hung up, deeply disturbed even though the aircraft from Malta had arrived safely in England and its cargo was being held in a secure storage unit which was guarded with four reliable security guards. He knew, however, that the fate of Penelope, Andy and the others rested with him.

"Make a list," Will instructed himself. Whenever he was perplexed by what course of action to follow, he would bring out a yellow legal length pad of lined paper and randomly jot down ideas as they came to him. He knew that the process would eventually lead to a pattern – a direction and plan.

Over a period of five hours, he wrote down his thoughts. By the time he finished his notes he glanced at the clock nearby and noticed it was an hour past his accustomed bedtime. He would resume the process in the morning when he was fresh and he would be better able to identify whatever pattern may have emerged.

41

AFTER A BREAKFAST fortified with three cups of strong coffee, Will walked back to the office he had established for himself in the Fitzrovia apartment and as he seated himself staring at his jumbled thoughts on paper, a pattern did emerge. Several familiar names appeared. Each Russian. Each in Moscow or St Petersburg and each with a professed connection to Putin or his office.

He decided he would start with Prince Vorontsov. What he would have to disclose to Vorontsov could be used by Vorontsov either to assist Will in gaining the release of Penelope and her team or against Isaac and the distribution of the assets held in Russia, perhaps even those held in Ukraine. Vorontsov appeared to be trustworthy and on Isaac's side, but he was in an official role in Russia, one he would want to keep, so he might be easily subject to adverse influence in this matter by Putin.

Did he have a choice? Will pondered the question several times before he realized that he had no choice. There were no other options. He would have to trust Vorontsov.

Allowing for the time difference, Will waited until it was four in the afternoon in St Petersburg before calling; this was when Vorontsov usually returned to his office after a liquefied lunch and an ensuing nap.

Will explained the situation his team was in, leaving out nothing. He knew Vorontsov would be evaluating the truth of the facts Will was expressing and that Vorontsov was exceptionally astute and accustomed to sifting fact from fiction.

At the conclusion of Will's explaining the circumstances and requesting Vorontsov to intercede on behalf of Isaac's group in Transnistria, there was a long pause at the other end of the line. Will was patient, but just as he was about to ask whether Vorontsov was still on the line, Vorontsov said,

"And why do you think Putin would take an interest in your dilemma? What is your offer to him that would engage him to help you?"

"I have given that a lot of thought. I believe it is in the president's best interest, because if we can get them out before the Moldovans and the Ukrainians discover the exceptional treasure owned by Isaac, that the government of Russia would like to have, an international situation would certainly develop that would prevent the kind of distribution that would largely benefit Russia and that we are now working on, as you know. I think we need to keep the lid on this process and to continue the level of secrecy that we have consistently maintained."

"You should know, Mr MacIntosh, that the president will probably have some favour from you in exchange for his cooperation."

"I have suspected as much. But I don't think I have any choice," was Will's reply.

"I have the contacts and can speak to the appropriate officials later today. I suspect they will want this wrapped up sooner than you planned," said Vorontsov almost in a threatening tone.

* * *

Two highly experienced secretaries hired through an agency joined Will at the new business office where the records retrieved from Odessa were stored. More executive assistants than mid-level secretaries, both came highly recommended not only in terms of their experience but also for their reliability and competence. As persons who understood confidentiality, they would comply with the high standards required by Will.

When they arrived Will was surprised that one of the two was a male. They were both about sixty-five years of age, recently retired from responsible positions with the Bank of England at its Threadneedle Street headquarters. Will had requested banking experience but had not expected the exceptional level of their pre-retirement areas of responsibility.

When Will expressed with some surprise and pleasure about their work experience, Gretchen Braun took what was clearly her accustomed lead in answering: "I worked with the Governor of the bank for forty years, sir. I was responsible for all secretarial and clerical recruitment and job performance in those areas in the Governor's office for the last fifteen years. After my retirement, to which I had looked forward for some time, I was lost. I had dedicated my life to my work and when it came to an end I thought my life had. So, I decided part-time work might fill the void, so I left my name with the agency. I hope I have the level of experience needed for this position."

And Harry Moore, the male member of the team, expressed similar reasons for applying. His work experience was with the bank's internal auditor and was similarly the senior clerk and executive assistant to the auditor.

Will explained the history of the Menshikovsky Trust, its transfer to Isaac and the investigation and research he and Isaac had conducted to date. He explained that what he needed was a reconstituting of the business records of the bank in each of its branches and an analysis of the assets acquired. He also explained the exceptional sensitivity of the project and that there was a potential for surveillance by hostile interests. "One of the side issues," Will explained, "to the primary tasks is to follow the Menshikovsky family, keeping a record of the names and spelling of the various forms of their names – by date, time and place, and," he said, "I think there is a possibility the surname was assumed in the early nineteenth century and that their name started in some other form, spelling or perhaps even another name entirely."

Ms Braun spoke first again: "This represents a major challenge that would fit my skills and interests. I will happily accept the challenges, confidentiality and risks you describe." She paused to permit Harry to speak.

"I agree. I look forward to working with Ms Braun and your team, Mr MacIntosh. Like Ms Braun, I have skills well suited to building the business profile of the Menshikovsky Bank. I should add that the agency said this project might be for a few weeks only. Could you perhaps give me a clearer idea of what timeline is involved? While I am financially independent I want to work, so if this is for a short term I will start looking for new employment."

"I suspect," said Will, "that the time required will be between eighteen and twenty-four months and could be much longer. After gaining insights from our work, I will need a team to administer assets located throughout Central and Eastern Europe as well as in London worth, we think, over thirty-five billion pounds sterling. I hope you will be able to help quantify the value of the assets and assist in the divestment of some."

Both Braun and Moore beamed with enthusiasm at the opportunity the project offered. Will's response was confidence that the agency had selected the correct personnel for him.

After giving instructions to the two, not designating either as chief but addressing both as equals on the team, Will instructed them to hire what assistants, office supplies and furniture as they needed.

* * *

The bank's records and numerous personal journals and diaries of the Menshikovsky managers located in the Alexander Palace were removed from Russia by truck – in fact, three eighteen-wheeler trucks, through Finland and from Tromso by ship to the small innocuous seaport of Grimsby on the east coast of England. From there they were transported by truck to the new business offices located in Canary Wharf, downriver on the Thames opposite Greenwich.

The records arrived the day after Braun and Moore had reported for work. They were amazed at the huge volume of printed and written material that they would have to organize, analyze and index for retrieval and analysis. Fortunately, recent computer programs gave them and their growing team invaluable assistance in those tasks.

42

WHILE ACTIVITIES WERE underway at Canary Wharf, Will met at least once a day with both Isaac and Sophie giving them news that was more encouraging than was perhaps warranted.

On the third day, during a visit to the clinic, Dr MacKenzie took Will aside and told him that both Isaac and Sophie would be transferred to the nursing facility in Chelsea. This was good news. It meant both Isaac and Sophie were recovering and they should soon be sufficiently strong and healthy to take part in decision-making.

When he was not with Isaac and Sophie at the business office, Will was focused on his most pressing problem which was securing the release and return of Penelope and her team.

Will's scheme to engage Putin or his office in negotiating with those exercising control in Transnistria was moving slowly and offered no immediate solution. After two days of frustrating conversation with his contacts in Russia, including Vorontsov and Dolgoruky, he reached out to the lawyer who had represented the Menshikovskys' interests for years. He made inquiries and requests but he was ignored. Both the British and American embassies admitted they tried to reach Putin but without success. "If neither the Brits nor the Americans can gain the cooperation of Putin or his officials where else do I go?" asked Will to himself repeatedly.

When Will announced to the British consular service in London that he wanted a visa to enter Ukraine and ultimately Transnistria through Russia, he was turned down. The senior official who made the final decision told him bluntly: "You not go. You not be allowed to leave if you got there. Money and staff they would take from you but do nothing."

With that advice, Will accepted that if he were to travel

into Transnistria he would be a greater hazard to his goal than a help.

Over a lengthy lunch well-fortified with first-rate English wines, Will discussed his dilemma with Smythe who was as anxious as Will to get Penelope back. The Travellers Club at 106 Pall Mall was a fortress-like, ashlar-faced structure designed by Sir Charles Barry, later to be chief architect of the new parliament buildings. The neoclassical building was one of the first gentlemen's clubs in London. It was a favourite refuge for the restless and adventurous, one of whom was Roger Smythe, QC, who as a student at Cambridge had taken a year off to explore classical ruins in Italy, Yugoslavia (as it then was) and Greece. From there he took side trips to former Greek colonies in Turkey and southern Russia. Will hoped he might have suggestions that could help in freeing Penelope and her companions.

The lunch was more of a banquet than any lunch Will had had in the past and it had a substantial volume of red and white wine, with a brandy post-dessert stomach-settler. He felt thoroughly liquored and rather muddled by the time the brandy appeared. The setting and intake had one very positive result, however. Normally removed and non-communicative, Roger Smythe became loquacious and even voluble in his comments on the situation in Transnistria. He suggested contacting one of the better-known Russian oligarchs and asking him to assist. This, Will recognized even in his elevated state, would be dangerous in every way. Smythe had nothing to add to the many possibilities Will had already considered. However, Will left the Travellers at about 3:30 p.m. treading very carefully, trying to focus through his glazed eyes which were trying desperately to close for a nap. As he walked through Trafalgar Square up St Martin's Lane into Charing Cross, he realized finally that the only way to reach Putin and company was through the contacts already made. Will realized that either he had not spoken to the right one, or those he had contacted had neglected or failed to pursue Putin with Putin-like vigour.

A name came to mind. Someone first met four years ago

when Will and Isaac had made their way into Moscow from Smolensk after burning down a campground as they destroyed their tracks escaping from attackers determined to kill them. His thought was of Dr Boris Zhukov, the Executive Director of the Pushkin Museum in Moscow. He held a position that was a personal grace-and-favour grant by Putin and he was kept at the president's sufferance. Will did not know the basis for Zhukov's elevated status in Russia. It was sufficient for his purposes that he had the position. He would pursue personal healing and restoration overnight and would fly to Moscow as soon as Zhukov could see him.

43

A MUCH LATER breakfast than usual was the start of the day following Will's visit to the Travellers. After a full English breakfast that provided him with enough calories for a week followed by three cups of full-strength coffee, he felt sufficiently in control of his faculties to call Zhukov.

The call went through remarkably quickly after he identified himself to the receptionist. Zhukov greeted Will with a robust: "Good to hear from you, my Canadian friend. How is our companion Dr Menshive? I hope he is feeling better." Will replied with the usual pleasantries and then directed the conversation to its intended purpose.

"Dr Zhukov, you will recall Isaac and me discussing the large treasure trove of antiquities and historical objects he has in his possession that might be of interest to the Pushkin. We have a real problem. You are the only one who can help fix the problem. I led a team recently into southern Ukraine to investigate some of the sources of the Scythian gold and ancient Greek and Roman statuary we would like to give to the Pushkin. I left a team of researchers behind after I departed Odessa where our searches were located. The group I left behind departed the next day. They had a flight for London through Bucharest, but on the way to Bucharest, they decided to take a road trip through Moldova. Well, that wasn't very bright, but curiosity can lead to stupid decisions. They passed through a border crossing on what their map said was the Moldovan border. It wasn't. They found themselves in Transnistria where they are now incarcerated. I haven't heard anything from or about them for several days. I call on your help because until they are returned to London they may be the object of blackmail and bribery which could affect what we want to donate to the Pushkin. Now what I ask you to do is to work through President Putin's office to have the necessary pressure imposed on the authorities in Transnistria to release our group of researchers. If we can't get them out, our discussions with you, Dolgoruky and Vorontsov will end, and plans to distribute the treasures will probably fall to the oligarchs. Time is of the essence. If the people holding my team discover the huge holdings Isaac has in Russia and Ukraine, we may all lose out. Could you contact President Putin?"

"Yes. I remember, of course, the plans for the transfer of valued treasures to the Pushkin and other museums. Your timing is good. I am asking to be named director of all national museums. If I can appear to bring such assets to the museums I would be considered. I know it would help."

"Doctor, I knew I could rely on you. I plan to fly to Moscow later today to be with you in case I can help in any way. I should say that I have full authority to commit to the transfer of certain assets that could be completed while I am in Moscow after the group is safely back in London. You know I mean those assets Isaac and I discussed with you. Only those."

"Yes, yes. Of course. I remember there were many others."

A meeting was arranged for Will to meet with Zhukov at the Pushkin the next day at 2 p.m.

* * *

The prospect of a meeting with Zhukov and through him officials who could gain access to the President of Russia energized Will with considerable force yet not a little trepidation. He had never dealt with a person in whom absolute power was vested and who exercised it in a cunning and capricious manner. How was he to interact with the president? As a person with very little to use as tools of trade in negotiating with the autocrat, he felt virtually powerless.

Will reminded himself that he had the authority to divest any of Isaac's assets located in Russia as part of a negotiation for the release of Penelope and her group. He was, however, well aware that if Putin chose to simply take possession of what he wanted, he could do so with impunity. The courts of Russia were nothing more than an arm of the president's administration and policy. He could expect nothing in terms of fairness or objectivity from a Russian court. All of his legal training in the Canadian legal system was irrelevant – worse than that, any interaction he would have with Putin would be based on false assumptions. In planning his strategy, and he knew he needed one, it must be based on a balance of power. He laughed to himself at the thought of negotiating with the president grounded on any appearance of give and take in the power available to the president and to himself.

However, Will realized that his discussions, if there were to be any, must have an underlying position of strength or at least what Putin might perceive as strength, thereby conferring on Will some degree of power of his own.

44

WILL'S FLIGHT TO Moscow was scheduled to leave early in the afternoon, which gave him time to meet with Isaac at his new quarters in the nursing home in Chelsea and with Anna when he returned to the flat to pick up his bags on the way to the airport.

The nursing home was located in a former mansion designed in the ultra-stylish Arts and Crafts Style by the architect Philip Webb, heavily influenced by William Morris. The use of natural wood exposed with stone and hand-cast bricks created an inviting and relaxed atmosphere as Will entered the building, particularly as he walked through a small pocket garden that comprised the front lawn. The planting created the illusion, as was intended, that the house was simply an original element of the landscape and setting. Will took comfort in viewing the property, knowing that both Isaac and Sophie would find the clinic welcoming and fashionable and which they both would enjoy.

At reception, the young lady at the desk was dressed in a casual but elegant dress. There was no sign of hospital or clinical attire which would act as a barrier to the feeling of this place as a temporary home. The receptionist spoke with an Oxbridge accent but without disdain or force as it so often is expressed. Will knew that both Isaac and Sophie would react negatively to any pretence or condescension. So far so good, he thought.

An assistant, also dressed in casual but fashionable clothing, took Will directly to Isaac. He was shown into what was a suite comprised of two bedrooms, two bathrooms, a kitchenette and a large lounge.

Isaac was ensconced in one of the bedrooms and Sophie in the other. The two rooms were separated by a bathroom and closets but were close enough so that the occupants could see each other or could be screened from each other. Will knew that the healing process of both patients required gradual increases in their exposure to each other, permitting each to emerge from the cocoon of withdrawal into which they had retreated as a result of their post-traumatic stress disorder.

Isaac was awake and sitting up in a wingchair with a wrap over his waist and legs which were propped up on an ottoman. At hand on a side table he had a pot of tea and some biscuits – and a book. Will was curious about the book. He knew its subject matter would tell him more than Isaac could vocalize about his condition. If it was on the latest hip replacement surgery, it would be a positive sign of his coming back into the world in which Isaac had confidence and control. If it was a book on money management which seemed to be an aggressive theme in London book stores, Will would surmise that Isaac was resuming his interest and planning for the assets and their future. On the other hand, if it was a colouring book or a book written for children, Will would know that Isaac remained in a state of regression.

Given Will's schedule for the next day or two in Russia, he was eager to discuss the meetings planned for Moscow.

Isaac was reading a book on wills and trusts. English wills and trusts that Will had given him several months ago. This Will took to be an exceptionally good sign of Isaac's health returning.

They greeted each other warmly and happily. For the first time in weeks, Isaac appeared more like his old self – happy and conversational. Isaac was the first to address their common burden: the assets and the investigation. Will was careful to keep his report as succinct and uncomplicated as he could, emphasizing the several positive aspects of the recent investigations. Isaac was fascinated by the findings in Odessa.

"I had no idea the family had any connection to Odessa, Will. How did you discover there was one?"

"Isaac, you will recall that while we were investigating the strong room in the basement area of the Alexander Palace in St Petersburg we came across business journals that referred to businesses located in Odessa. At that time we did not know whether there was anything of interest remaining there, but as there were four or five properties on the inventory listed for Odessa, I decided it would be a site to be examined. I considered it to be important particularly in light of the considerable collection of Scythian gold and ancient Greek and Roman artifacts. They had to have been acquired somewhere – I assumed most likely close to the excavation sites where the archaeologists unearthed them. So I took a team to Odessa and spent over a week there. It was highly informative and, in fact, answered many questions about the early days of your family's businesses and acquisitions. Our findings are complex and it will require a lot of time to review them with you – so for now just know that, happily, we have more extensive insights into the businesses and acquisitions than we had up until then."

Isaac's concentration had begun to slip away towards the end of Will's monologue. It usually did, so Will did not attribute the mental shutdown to be anything more than Isaac's presently limited attention span.

Will then explained that in recent talks with Dr Zhukov there was a plan to meet with an executive assistant in President Putin's office. Isaac was interested in that development. Will explained only what his objective was: a possible settlement on the division of the assets in Russia. He did not explain to Isaac that the immediate requirement for the meeting involved trying to rescue a team taken to Odessa as part of the investigation. Will knew he had to keep the conversation as upbeat as possible, giving Isaac little cause to be anxious or angry.

"Isaac, when I meet with Zhukov and the representative of Putin's government, do I have your permission to negotiate and to reach a deal that could settle the Russian problems? May I have your permission to settle on terms that seem plausible during the discussions?"

"Absolutely. We have discussed the general terms of a settlement on several occasions, Will. You know those terms better than I do now – and you remember them better than I do. Yes, go ahead. I leave it entirely up to you. What you agree to will be acceptable to me no matter what the terms. I just want the Russian connection settled. It would give me great comfort and relief if you can reach a settlement. Remember, though, that I would like some of the art and antiquities and some of the real estate. But there is nothing that I can't live without. I mean that if you have to give it all away to get us out of Russia permanently, you do it. Both Sophie and I hope we can keep the dacha, though."

It was at this point in the conversation that Isaac started to drift away into a nap.

Will knew he had Isaac's directions as to the range of settlements he could make if he had the opportunity to make one. He also knew that the journal Anna was diligently keeping of the various stages and developments would have to contain a record of his conversation with Isaac. He recognized there was a risk to his personal safety in returning to Moscow. He was cautiously optimistic that it offered a possibility that there could be some movement to a settlement if he did return.

Before leaving the clinic, Will called on Sophie. She was awake and alert when he came into her room. In the past, there had been very little response from Sophie to his meetings with her. It was not like that on this occasion. Sophie enthusiastically welcomed Will and asked him numerous questions about Little Isaac and Anna. She was now able to see her boy daily, but only for a couple of hours. She needed to know what the other twenty-two hours contained in Little Isaac's life. Will had a full briefing the night before from Anna on Little Isaac's activities and his progress in printing and vocabulary. Sophie was overjoyed to hear the child was the *Wunderkind* she had always claimed him to be. They discussed her health and Will was surprised and relieved that she had recall of the painful events that led to the loss of the baby and her own sub-coma to a state of mental paralysis as a result of post-traumatic stress disorder. "Yes, Will, I understand why I am here, and also the reason poor Isaac is here. I can tell you that my health is improving every day. I see light at the end of the tunnel, and I don't mean the tunnel of death!"

Sophie assured Will that she and Isaac were able to meet

daily for several hours and they were working towards the happy state of affection they had previously enjoyed before the Smolensk and Moscow events.

Not once did Sophie ask about the investigation, the assets, the oligarchs or others that were central to Will's life. He was greatly relieved that she took no interest in his work or the continuing problems her family faced in dealing with those issues.

They parted on the most congenial and affectionate terms, reminding Will of their relationship at the dacha in Smolensk before the horrors of the abduction in that city.

* * *

Will returned to the flat in Fitzrovia, enjoying as he always did walking into the elegance of the Robert Adam-designed square lined with mansions still expressing his original designs. Will never ceased to feel the sense of elegance and grace that prevailed in this area after Adam completed the ensemble of buildings. Someone in the Menshikovsky family, he thought, showed exceptional taste and financial acumen in acquiring the building in which the apartment was located.

He was greeted at the front door by Little Isaac, who bounded into his arms squealing with delight and then asking about 'Momma and Poppa'. Will gave him an enthusiastic report on both parents and he assured him that they were looking forward to his visit with them later that afternoon.

Anna was patiently waiting for him to finish his time with Little Isaac. "You are like a parent to Little Isaac. You know, Will, you have a natural way with children. They feel comfortable, happy and secure with you. I wish I could be like that."

Will replied that as a parent he had had exposure to children both his own and nephews and nieces and as a result, he was comfortable with children and loved to interact with them at their level. Anna again deprecated her skills, saying, "That's all very well, but I don't know those levels and if I did I wouldn't know how to act with the children like you."

Anna received the reassurances she was seeking relating

to her role with the child from Will, who commended her on the success she was having in a parental capacity in Little Isaac's life. "Anna, he would not be as happy, active and inquiring (and challenging at times) as he is, if he were not thriving with you. You are doing very well. I know both Isaac and Sophie are deeply appreciative of your time and efforts with Little Isaac."

Will briefed Anna on the discussion he had had with Isaac that morning. She recorded it so that she could transcribe it into her journal. She was eager to hear more about Odessa, but Will had only time enough to pack and get himself to Heathrow for the British Airways flight to Moscow.

* * *

On the way to the airport, Will reflected on his final moments with Anna. There was a nagging sense that Anna was trying to say something. That could only account for an inordinate pause at the conclusion of her comments to him, a pause that involved her looking at Will as if she were expecting him to say something or she herself wished to say something. He knew that their roles in relation to Isaac and Little Isaac created a more distant, perhaps formal relationship than they had formerly enjoyed. He also reminded himself that he was becoming interested in someone whose attractions were drawing him away into another compelling pursuit. His solution to what could have been an emotional contest was to persuade himself, easily done, that he was too busy to dwell on emotional attachments. Too messy, uncontrollable and unpredictable. Best left to hibernate.

Arrival at Heathrow brought him to Terminal 5 where his early check-in and printout of his first-class boarding pass would facilitate an orderly boarding of the aircraft. As he was being assisted with obtaining the baggage tags by a smart airline assistant, he looked with sympathy at the people who were confused, angry and anxious lining up at the machines non-first class passengers were subjected to. One of the few perks he experienced as Isaac's chief man of business was flying first class on a credit card with unlimited credit that granted exceptional travel amenities and clerical assistance. His memories of the tortures of being in the other line almost gave him the rush of frustration and anger he usually experienced at Heathrow.

His first-class ticket with benefits gave him access to the British Airlines lounge. He found a massage chair, pushed it back, turned it on low and opened his briefcase. Before he could gather the papers he required to continue his planning for the meeting tomorrow with Zhukov, a sharply dressed female server arrived at his side and quietly asked whether he would like a drink and something from the buffet. His rule not to take alcohol while travelling was swiftly broken, thinking this attractive young woman would be heartbroken if he failed to take what she offered. He should have declined. It seemed she was delegated to serve him alone. Numerous offers were made during the two-hour wait, including a head massage which he knew he could not refuse even though it left his hair in a mess, something that was anathema to him. Like all the attention given, the massage, liquids and food were appreciated.

When the flight was called he floated aboard and was barely into his bed when another strikingly beautiful stewardess (or whatever they are called now, he thought) arrived with a glass of champagne and some hors d'oeuvres. He resigned himself to flying higher than the aircraft on the way to Moscow.

His carefully plotted strategy for the meeting with Zhukov in preparation for a possible meeting with officials in Putin's office was rapidly swirling into chaos, so he accepted that rest might be the safest and happiest way to spend his time on the four and a half hour flight.

* * *

Peter MacNeill, his friend and consular officer at the Canadian Embassy who had been exceptionally helpful to Isaac and Will during their visit to Moscow four years before, met Will at the Moscow International Airport.

Peter took one look at Will and politely said, "First class, eh! It's impossible to resist the amenities. I can see you will need some assistance in getting settled in the guest suite you had four years ago. We had a budgetary surplus last year so it was applied to upgrading the suite. It has gone from five-star to ten-star, if that is possible. You will, at least, enjoy yourself."

Will managed to adequately express his greetings and expressions of thanks in spite of his diminished mental state. He also managed to bring Peter up to date somewhat on recent developments in their mutual place of origin, Prince Edward Island. Will wanted to share how much more important Prince Edward Island had become in Isaac's story, but he realized that he was not in any condition to exercise the discretion and judgment he should apply in any such revelation. He promised himself to do so when he was feeling less muddled.

Peter safely delivered Will to the suite contained in the hotel-like guesthouse operated by Canadian External Affairs for dignitaries from Canada who required security and absolute privacy, as most Foreign Service and senior government people thought they needed. He gave Will a new mobile phone specially encrypted for security which he said should prevent hacking or records of calls made. It would give him unlimited telephone calls to anywhere in Europe (including Great Britain, which never accepted that it was part of Europe) and North America. Will's offer of a dinner from a nearby restaurant was declined, but more in the nature of a rain check. Sleep, Peter wisely concluded, was what Will required, not more companionship or food and liquids.

Before falling into a profound sleep, Will called Zhukov's cell phone, leaving a message that he had arrived and would call before 9:30 a.m. the next morning and expressing the request that they meet at 11 a.m. He suggested the Pushkin Museum as it would be the most neutral and least obvious place to meet. Will would be observed going into the museum as just another North American culture-vulture.

45

SLEEP WAS INSTANT, deep, refreshing and restorative. Will awoke with his usual vigorous approach to a new day and its challenges. His spirits were even more elevated by the excellent Russian tea he served himself from a huge samovar. As he sat contentedly going over his notes prepared to give himself a strategy in his meeting with Zhukov, he recalled from their previous meetings that Zhukov was a descendant of the great General Zhukov who had achieved popular acclaim as a hero of Russia for appearing to defeat Napoleon in the latter's advance on Moscow in 1817. In fact, Napoleon was not defeated by any general, but by early winter weather and the Russians' strategic abandonment of Moscow. Napoleon was blindsided by the very rapid arrival of winter which, with its profoundly cold temperatures, wind and snow, effectively captured Napoleon and his forces, decimating them. However, General Zhukov was identified as the celebrated hero of the day by Czar Alexander I himself.

Genetics can pass on personality traits; so claim specialists in that field. Will mused that his acquaintance must have inherited his ancestor's acceptance and celebration of his elevated status in Russian history. Dr Boris Zhukov wore his contemporary celebrity with the same pride and confidence as his ancestor must have.

Will realized that Zhukov's pride, if properly massaged, could lead to enhanced support for Isaac and Will's mission on this visit to Russia. He refreshed his plans for advancing the arguments in support both of liberating Penelope and her team and of arranging a permanent settlement with Putin's government in relation to Isaac's assets located in Russia.

* * *

Zhukov did not play the irritating game many officials in high offices do by keeping their guest waiting a lengthy interval before the start of a meeting. Will's arrival ten minutes before the scheduled time was met with a polite offer of tea and biscuits which he happily accepted. On the dot, Will was invited to join Zhukov in his office. 'Office' it did not appear to be. To Will, it was more in the nature of a hybrid between a museum of exceptional artifacts and an elegant hotel suite.

Will sank into a well-padded sofa opposite one on which Dr Zhukov himself was seated with Russia's Minister of Cultural Affairs, Alexi Alexandrov. The table positioned between them contained several documents that Will could not identify but looked forward to reading. At a table perched at right angles to the coffee table sat a clerk who not only took notes but served as translator when either Will or Zhukov ran into linguistic difficulties. Will tried his best to exercise the little conversational Russian he had learned at university many years before.

After the traditional Russian formal greetings were delivered and returned, Zhukov asked Will what he thought he could do to assist him and Isaac.

"Get to it straightaway," Will reminded himself. He did.

Will explained in detail what had been discovered in St Petersburg and in Odessa and he said that with part of his investigative team now incarcerated in Transnistria there was a very high probability that the team would be used as pawns for some of the assets or some benefits not yet known that could compromise Will in his negotiations with the Russian government.

"Isaac and I have discussed the type of settlement he wishes to make here in Russia. In fact, I confirmed it with him a couple of days ago. He was unable to join me this time because of a health issue he must take care of. Not serious, but one that requires attention.

"Dr Zhukov, the risk to Russia, as I see it, is that many of the Menshive treasures were acquired elsewhere than in Russia. The Scythian gold and the classical Greek and Roman archaeological artifacts were taken from Novorossiya – which as we all know is now southern Ukraine. If the extent of the treasures becomes known publicly, you will have competing claims from Ukraine, Greece, Turkey, Moldova and Bulgaria and probably Romania. Some of those governments can be readily managed by President Putin; others cannot. In the resulting chaos, enter the oligarchs and the Russian Mafia – yes, sir, there is a Russian Mafia, the so-called Bratva. Please do not demur. Our discussions will be useless if for our private conversations that is not accepted as the fact that it is."

Zhukov sank back into the sofa, stifling the objection it was clear he would express. "What do you want me to do, Mr MacIntosh?"

"I request you to engage President Putin in solving the problem of releasing my team from Transnistria and in exchange I will enter into binding voluntary agreements transferring title – or if you prefer – releasing all of Dr Menshive's rights and interests to the Russian people to an agreed list of treasures held here in Russia. You, sir, would benefit immensely. The bulk of the cultural materials would be passed on to institutions for which you have or aspire to have administrative responsibility. Yes, virtually all of the assets are held in Russian institutions now, but the records of all of those institutions classify them as on loan subject to recall on demand owned by a trust administered by a Swiss bank. Our government engages in underwriting loans of cultural artifacts which benefit the international reputation of Russia. You know that the history of the collection is now known to the United National Cultural Organization, BBC Radio and Television and CNN. Each has agreed to hold off on any press coverage to enable me to negotiate. If your government refuses to cooperate in an open and business-like manner, the restraining agreement with the media will end and the full story will come out. With it, every country and thug in Russia and in the West will fight to the death to pilfer what they can get authority to obtain from the collection held by Dr Menshive."

"We have considered his request respecting having the group released from prisons in Transnistria and Dr Menshive's offer to settle a distribution of the Russian-located assets. As you know, sir, I accept for my institutions but the final decision rests with the president," explained Dr Zhukov.

"When can we have President Putin's answer?"

Dr Zhukov turned to Minister Alexandrov who had been silent up to that point in the conversation. "Minister Alexandrov, do you have an answer to give Mr MacIntosh?"

"Yes. President Putin has followed your investigations with interest as they have progressed, has been impressed with your goodwill towards Russia and Russia's interest in the collections. Has heard your request and proposal. I am pleased to inform you that as we speak your team is being flown out of Moldova by private aircraft and will be taken to a private airstrip north of London designated by the UK government for this purpose. You will now stay with my colleagues until the final agreements have been reached and signed." Minister Alexandrov bowed slightly to Will and then to his colleagues. Without a further word he rose, turned and left the room.

It was quickly agreed that there had been enough discussion for one day. It was with relief that the meeting was postponed to the next day to convene at the Armories located in the Kremlin – a location which housed several highly significant treasures of Isaac's on loan. Will was pleased with it. The discussion would be kept in absolute privacy with little opportunity for leaks. His immediate task was to verify that Penelope's group had been released and were safely on their way to London. He returned to his suite at the guest house.

There were messages from Penelope and Andy that the group was on its way back to England. There was also a message from Isaac, which expressed confusion about what the group was and where they were to be released – but Will guessed Isaac had been told and had forgotten.

46

BEFORE WILL LEFT the guest house the next morning, he received a message from Dr Zhukov informing him that the governments of Ukraine, Bulgaria and Turkey had discovered the Menshive collection, some of which had been found within the borders of their modern states.

"Looting. Theft. Rapacious pillaging," were terms applied through diplomatic channels to Minister Alexandrov. The Minister instructed Zhukov to terminate the meeting scheduled for that day, saying a delay, possibly lengthy, would be required to enable President Putin to deal with his counterparts in those countries claiming an interest in the treasures.

Will was acutely disappointed the meeting would not be held. It appeared he was close to a settlement. He thanked Dr Zhukov and promised to be available at any time or place to continue the discussions. Zhukov sounded as disappointed as Will and he promised to press forward with resumption of the negotiations for a settlement.

After sending an e-mail to London announcing his imminent return, Will caught the first flight back to London.

* * *

The process of the investigation in Odessa and the retreat from there was long, tortuous and fraught with personal risks to Will and, particularly, to Penelope and her team. With her arrival and that of her team back from Transnistria, it may have appeared to be the end of the investigation, but it proved not to be. Certainly much had been accomplished. However, the loose ends were many and the need to resolve and conclude an agreement with Russian authorities with finality had proved to be far off.

Will went to the designated airstrip to meet the returning

team. He had with him three first-aid specialists and three of his London-based security team arranged and led by the redoubtable Frank who could always be counted on.

As Penelope entered the private arrivals lounge, Will approached her with the degree of familiarity they had shared when they were last together. Will was shocked and troubled by her appearance. No longer a young woman demonstrating good cheer, confidence and blossoming good health, she was now withdrawn, agitated and appeared not to have eaten or bathed in many days – which turned out to be the case.

Will's affectionate approach, with arms up for a hug, was firmly rebuffed as she walked back towards the entrance. She did nothing. She said little. Her behaviour was statement enough. He knew he must find out what had happened to her to have put her in this hostile attitude.

Andy and his team followed with the few suitcases and boxes that had been taken by Penelope and her team from Transnistria. Andy looked almost as distressed and defeated as Penelope, as did the rest of the team. He did not withdraw from Will as he advanced to shake his hand. As Will did so, he quietly said to Andy that they must meet to discuss the experience the team had endured in Transnistria and the reason for Penelope's appearance and lack of engagement with Will.

It was decided that Frank would deliver Penelope and her few belongings to her flat in Bayswater. Frank's assistants agreed to take Andy and the guards in Penelope's team and the researchers wherever they wished to be taken.

Each member of Penelope's team, when asked whether they would be ready for a debriefing session with Will and Frank the next day, excused him or herself and said they needed one full day to recuperate as much as they could. Will instructed the paramedics to accompany those members of Penelope's team who most appeared to need physical or psychological assistance. When the services were offered, Penelope and those needing the assistance accepted them without argument.

The boxes returned on the aircraft were taken by Frank

directly to the office and conference room rented in Canada Tower in Canary Wharf.

* * *

Will met with Frank late that afternoon to hear what reports came back with the security team when they were delivering Penelope and others to their destinations.

"Mr MacIntosh, the unanimous opinion of Penelope's group was that they were subject to horrific conditions and personal abuse; none of them would give details, at least not yet. I watched Penelope carefully as she was given a preliminary examination by a paramedic. You couldn't imagine the bruises and cuts to the few exposed areas the paramedic was able to see. You will have to be very careful, sir, as you question her. She may have suffered psychological trauma that will take time to heal. From my military training, I have observed soldiers who with less cause developed post-traumatic stress disorder."

Will told Frank that he was to retain the services of a general practitioner and a psychologist and take them without advance warning to Penelope and the others for a professional diagnosis.

"They will be entitled to have whatever medical care, specialized or generalized as may be needed to assist in their recovery. Some of it will be covered by the UK National Health Service, but what isn't will be paid by Isaac. The National Health Service can take a long time to provide the necessary preliminary medical examinations. If you find any delay in obtaining appropriate care, hire qualified professionals to act immediately. Psychological trauma, I am told, is best treated as quickly as possible after its onset. We must do everything we can for each of Penelope's team."

* * *

Later that afternoon Will received a telephone call from Frank informing him that he had gone through the few documents

Penelope had taken with her from Odessa. The boxes, three in number, held items she decided were too important to have transported by air freight.

When the three boxes were opened it was clear that they had been opened and thoroughly examined at some point after Penelope left Odessa – almost certainly after they entered Transnistria. None of the boxes contained monetarily valuable items that could be converted into cash on the black market; there being no other market that would have an interest to buyers of items such as journals and legal documents. Will concluded that it was from examination of the boxes that authorities in Moldova, Bulgaria and Romania discovered the existence of the treasures.

Each document removed from the boxes was examined by Will and was identified, dated, described and a journal entry made for it. There were over two hundred documents. Many short, many longer, but very formal and legalistic in nature with impressed metal seals of a notarial type impressed on wafer seals – some actually embedded in early nineteenth-century sealing wax. The language of the legal documents was either German or Russian. Since neither Will nor Frank had sufficient fluency in early nineteenth-century Russian or German, particularly in their highly stylized cursive forms, they were carefully put aside for Frank to deliver to the Canada Tower rooms where all the materials removed from Odessa would be examined in detail.

The third box contained what Will would have called a cookie tin; no doubt a nineteenth-century container for storing and preserving important documents. It was a large container about eighteen inches on the long side, twelve on the narrow and ten inches deep.

Frank put on gloves a gardener would use – the only ones he could purchase on short notice – and he carefully opened the box. It contained important-looking documents – boring and of no interest or value to anyone other than historians or those investigating the owner of the box.

The owner of the box was identified on the inside hinge cover. Will's knowledge of the Russian alphabet and vocabulary, while limited, enabled him to read the name of who must have been the owner, actually owners. The first name was a Menshikovsky: an early Isaac.

"It is curious," announced Will, "the Menshikovsky name has two other names below it: 'Bronshtein', and faintly below that, 'Cann'." None of the documents could be deciphered; they were about to be put back into the can when Frank put his hand out, forcefully preventing the box lid to be closed.

"The bottom of this box is shallower than the depth of the can. There is a secret storage space at the bottom. There are two other cans, smaller, but similar in appearance to this one. We must check them as well in case they also have a hidden compartment. Now, while it is tempting to hack into this box to expose the hidden compartment, we will have to do so with great care. It might be booby-trapped with an explosive or a deadly liquid or gas. I will arrange to have a friend in the Metropolitan Bomb Squad assist us in opening each of the three hidden compartments."

"Great. Good idea, but you will have to be very careful not to allow your police officer friend to examine the contents. It could result in inquiries about how it came into your possession, particularly if the contents turn out to be Turkish drugs. Turkey was a supplier of opium and marijuana to Britain in the nineteenth century. I agree we need assistance in opening the cans, but much care must be taken in keeping the contents a secret. I suggest a ruse such as, 'This is potential evidence in a civil legal proceeding involving conflicting bequests in an old will'. Would that work?"

"Yes. Well enough," said Frank. "It sounds fishy but it at least offers an explanation. I will tell my friend that I am dealing with a New York lawyer who is difficult and will tell them the lawyer will bring in embassies and the Met if anything happens to the stuff at the bottom of the boxes."

"Worth a try," was Will's resigned response.

* * *

Frank's contact with the bomb squad stayed beyond his usual

hours at Scotland Yard examining the contents. Will waited for Frank to emerge from the front entrance on Victoria Street a short distance from Westminster Cathedral. Will sat drinking coffee at a Costa Coffee shop and ate a light sandwich trying to dilute its fortified caffeine. He was thankful to have a few minutes of peace to read the *Evening Standard* newspaper which he picked up at the Victoria underground station. His enjoyment of the newspaper every day was enhanced by the fact that it was free.

No one Will could possibly know would walk by, so he turned his attention to the newspaper. He was in London with its more than eight million residents and many visitors. As he was turning to the editorial page which was often critical of all politicians and pretentious celebrities, his eye was caught by someone standing outside the entrance to Scotland Yard. What caught his eye was the amateurish disguise the person was wearing and his awkward stance off to the side of the entrance, obviously waiting for someone or something.

Frank had provided Will with a secure cellphone after they returned to the city. Will stared at the strange-looking individual for several minutes and was just about ready to turn back to his newspaper when the mysterious man was joined by another man; this time quite prosaic in appearance but no less intent on watching the front door.

"They can't be up to any good. It may be helpful that there are CCT scanners all over that building. Every movement on this street will be recorded."

The second man walked to the sidewalk and back. It was his gait that told Will he had seen this man somewhere before. Will stared at him intently for several minutes watching the man's movements more than his face. Suddenly it came to him that he had seen this man recently in Odessa on or near the Menshikovsky bank office and apartment. The man had made himself obvious to Frank by continually watching the building from the opposite side of the street. Will told himself that he would never have noticed him without training; it was Frank's experience that enabled him to pick him out. As Will stared at him further, the Slavic heavy brow and narrow forehead confirmed his suspicion.

Will had watched the drama unfolding across the street for no more than ten minutes before he made the connection. Whether the pair outside Scotland Yard were waiting for Frank or someone else didn't matter. He knew he couldn't risk not alerting Frank. He dialled Frank's cell number, expecting immediate pick-up. No answer. The call could not be completed. Will knew that if the pair were waiting for Frank they obviously knew him by sight; so too, they would know him. He couldn't leave his vantage point in the coffee shop and walk into Scotland Yard. They would recognize him immediately. He didn't worry that he would be at any physical risk in that location, but he would give himself away as being in London. He hoped they didn't know he was in the city.

Will tried several more times to reach Frank. No success. Will was new to the wonders of cellphone technology so he assumed he was doing something wrong in making the call.

On his fifth call, he could see Frank approaching the entrance. Both of the men he had observed stood back watching Frank intently. Frank picked up Will's call just before he was about to push open one of the revolving entrance doors. He stepped aside inside the reception hall and spoke.

Will cut him off before he could complete a sentence. "You are being observed; I think stalked by one or two you identified in Odessa opposite the bank office and apartment. Pretend you have forgotten something and head back to the elevators mouthing the words, 'Thanks. I will be back for it'."

Frank managed a derisive laugh after following Will's instructions. Just who was the expert security guard? It did strike him, though, that Will had appeared to have learned something from their covert activities together during the investigations.

Will waited for a call from Frank as he knew he would call with instructions. A few minutes later Will received the call. "This is a secure landline. The cell signal will not penetrate the security systems in this building. The Met is already printing the CCT scanner coverage of the two idiots. Obviously as amateurish as you can get them. But with the images on the scanners, they will be able to identify them and bring them in for questioning."

"Just as you said, Frank. Two sturdy cops are now apprehending the two. They appear surprised and are looking around for the source of their trouble. When and where will it be safe for us to get together?"

"Leave by the side entrance of Costa and walk over to Westminster Cathedral and from there walk up to Victoria Station. There is a W. H. Smith bookshop on the main level. I will see you there in a few minutes."

As planned and on schedule they met and took the Circle Line and then the Northern Line to a tube stop close to Fitzroy Square, travelling several seats apart and not acknowledging each other.

Both Will and Frank agreed it was too late that day to have their debriefing.

47

FOR THE FIRST time in weeks, Will enjoyed a deep, full and refreshing night's sleep. This reflected his profound exhaustion pervading his faculties after the stress of the visit to Odessa. Preparing to meet with Anna and Little Isaac for breakfast and Legos, Will recalled the bizarre episode at Scotland Yard the day before. He knew that there were several factors involved in the incident that required immediate investigation and resolution. His comfort and relaxation arose from his confidence in Frank to get to the bottom of the quandary of how the Odessa agents could have followed Frank so quickly to London and could have turned up at Scotland Yard at exactly the same time that Frank arrived there.

So it was that when Anna and Little Isaac arrived for their breakfast, Will was in a happy and welcoming mood, looking forward to a couple of hours with them.

The past couple of months had distracted him from his intention to get to know Anna better and to act as a surrogate father to Little Isaac. Will's companions arrived as eager to see him as he was to see them.

Little Isaac devoured his porridge, juice and toast, drank his two glasses of milk and delivered his accustomed burp – a requirement for many two-year-olds experimenting with bodily sounds, no matter how disgusting they may be to others.

While Little Isaac was underway with his enjoyable tasks, Anna inquired about the visit to Odessa. Her question was framed in a way that indicated that Anna had little knowledge of her family's connection with the city. Will replied, giving her a brief history of her family's connections to Smolensk, Moscow, St Petersburg and Odessa. As her eyes glazed over with indifference, he simply explained that his team had been successful in finding documents that would assist them in getting the property matters settled sooner than he thought. That was sufficient to satisfy her interest.

The conversation reminded Will that the ancient family trust and the assets held by the trust transferred by her father to Isaac and to her was of no interest to Anna. She had been consistent in that attitude since her renunciation and the assignment to Isaac of her one-half interest in the trust assets. It also gave him a message he needed at this time in managing Isaac's assets, a task that he alone was now handling. Anna, he knew, could not be encouraged or engaged as part of Isaac's family in the ongoing management of the assets, including the important task immediately before him to arrange a distribution of the assets in Eastern and Central Europe in a definitive solution which would leave Isaac holding assets secure from competing claims. Anna could not be counted on to represent her family in any business planning or management. Will knew that this would have long-term consequences at various levels.

Strangely to Will, Anna's interest was focused on Penelope. What was she like? Did Will like her? How did they get along? Would he be having her involved in the investigation on a continuing basis?

Will replied, bored with the triviality of the questions, that she was a great help and proved to be smart and interested in what the investigation was trying to accomplish. He then changed the subject to Little Isaac.

Anna assured him that Little Isaac was seeing his parents every day for between two and three hours at the Chelsea Clinic. Will was delighted to hear that both Sophie and Isaac were responding with great affection to Little Isaac. The little fellow appeared, Anna said, not to be worried about why his parents didn't live with him and why they were surrounded by people who looked and worked like doctors and nurses he had seen in his few visits to clinics for his shots and check-ups. Anna assured Little Issac that when his parents got better from their sicknesses they would return home to him at the flat and that his parents would play with him a lot.

Little Isaac asked Will where he had been while he was

away. Will explained that he had been in a faraway country called Ukraine where Little Isaac's family had businesses long ago. The business topic interested him not a bit, but he wanted to know whether Will could build a Lego castle with him like the castles in that place. "Are they like the big castle next to Tower Bridge?" To which Will said they were a bit like that in Ukraine, but different, and he agreed to join Little Isaac in building what Little Isaac knew castles to look like.

The two hours had stretched to almost three hours, but happily for Will. Playing with Little Isaac gave him a deep sense of connection to Isaac's family and normalcy. Normalcy: he had wondered if he would ever have that sense again as he encountered the numerous challenges and threats during the investigation. There was little in his background or life experiences at home on Prince Edward Island that had prepared him for the encounters he had experienced since travelling to Europe with Isaac over four years before. A warm family life both immediate and extended was what he was used to, longed for, and required to ground him in a life of reality. His time with Anna and Little Isaac did just that for him.

Will arrived at the Chelsea Clinic by 11:30 that morning, in time to meet with Sophie before her accustomed early lunch. As usual, she demonstrated no interest in anything east of the east coast of England. Amazingly, she seemed to have no interest in anything to the west of England either. Will realized that her contentment was the result of the exceptional medical care she was receiving at the clinic and her re-engaging with Isaac.

Sophie spent most of her time with Will discussing the brightest, most advanced and perfect child ever born. Little Isaac was her preoccupation. Will took that as an indication of her healing and a return to her life before Russia and its terrors and disappointments. At no point in their time together did she mention the baby lost just a few weeks before. She was returning to the world she knew and had loved before Russia, which Will recognized as a very good sign. In relation to Isaac, to whom she had demonstrated detachment and occasionally hostility in the last few weeks, she now spoke warmly, saying he spent several hours with her every day and that she looked forward to it. Out of the clear blue, she announced that she liked London and wanted to stay there. "People are so courteous and helpful here. I am going to ask Isaac whether we can stay here for a while, perhaps always."

When Will asked whether she would like to hear about his investigations in Odessa, her reply was crisp and decisive. "No, dear Will. I don't know where that place is and it is probably dangerous. I don't know why you men go to such places. As to the business, I leave that to you and Isaac. I know we have enough money to live on, Isaac tells me that a lot, so I don't worry about businesses."

* * *

Will's meeting with Isaac was surprising to him; it was similar to Sophie's. Isaac had limited curiosity about the current investigations or Will's progress in working on a settlement, less than he exhibited the day before. Will understood that this was a characteristic of PTSD. "I don't care anymore, Will. You are my attorney and CEO of all of my business interests. Just do what you will to sort it all out."

This left Will somewhat rudderless and anxious about the position he was left in. He knew he would have to make critical decisions but he hoped that he could have continuing discussions with Isaac. He knew that in time Isaac was bound to return permanently to his accustomed interests, determined once more to have his business arrangements meet his exacting standards. Will knew there would be an accounting of the decisions he had made and any agreements he had reached as part of a settlement. "Too much authority is vested in me. I don't like it, but I have to continue as the sole decision-maker no matter where it takes me." Will asked Isaac whether he was well enough to give Will a statement in writing confirming what he had said. Isaac agreed immediately. As a competent lawyer and one who knew his vulnerability, Will put Isaac's statement in the form of an affidavit, and when Isaac's attending in-house physician arrived on his rounds to see Isaac, Isaac signed the affidavit which was witnessed by the doctor and then notarized by the clinic manager.

"That's as much as I can do." Will reasoned – finding his worried reasoning with himself increasingly frequent.

"Isaac, before I leave to meet with Frank, I want to talk to you about bringing someone from your family into the management of your assets. Neither Anna nor Sophie are remotely interested, and you have just attested to your renunciation of any role in those tasks. I would like to bring in a member of your family who could be an administrator with me, in the event of your death. I remember your will. You have left a substantial but minor share in the overall portfolio to your three daughters. Are any of them interested or capable of taking an interest?"

Isaac paused, taking his time to answer. "Will, you know my fractured relationship with the mothers of my three girls. We have communicated only by e-mail when there was a crisis in my life that could put them or the girls at risk. Neither of the women has any legal interest in my business or assets. That was all settled by my lawyers, you may remember. The only one of my girls who has tried to connect with me is the eldest, Ruth. Before I came over here, after I married Sophie, I met with her in New York and introduced them. They got along very well. After Little Isaac was born she showed interest in knowing him as her brother. I think she might be worth connecting with. The other two have been thoroughly poisoned against me by their mother. I have left them something, but in the scale of things, not much. Why do you want to complicate your work and my life by bringing one of the girls into this mess?"

Will's reply was as forceful as he dared make it in light of Isaac's condition: "Because I am in an untenable conflict of interest, Isaac. You have vested in me 100 percent of the responsibility and power to investigate and settle the conflicting claims on your vast fortune. I want a member of your family to oversee my management and to sign off, at least on their own behalf, as I make decisions. I am not recommending that we add her to the authorities you have given me, but I think it is important to have a family member overseeing my administration, particularly for Little Isaac's future interests. I am certainly not suggesting any of your wives, legal or common law, be brought in. That would be a recipe for disaster. Do you object to me contacting Ruth? You gave me her contact information when we were working on your will before Little Isaac was born."

"Go ahead. I wouldn't mind getting to know Ruth. She, among the three girls, is more like my family than the other two. She is the most likely to help you and perhaps be willing to become part of my immediate family. I will discuss this with Sophie. Don't worry about Sophie. She has been encouraging me to bring the three of them into our immediate family. Ruth is the one I want you to contact," was Isaac's comforting reply.

"Good, I will do that straightaway. How old is Ruth and what is her marital status? Does she have children? What are her education and employment? All of that information will be important in my approach to her and in deciding whether she could be helpful," said Will.

"You certainly ask a lot of questions, friend. Will, as I remember and I hope I am not confusing her with the other two, she is thirty-four, unmarried, a lawyer and in a corporate practice of some kind. What you will find interesting is that she is a collector – at an amateurish and modest level, so far. But it was her collecting and her interest in Dad's collection that brought her into contact with me. I enjoyed meeting her and was really encouraged by her business-like approach to collecting and managing her own affairs. Incidentally, before I came over with Sophie, I gave her two million dollars as an inducement for her collecting. She was really surprised and grateful. Yes. The more I talk about Ruth, the more I would like to see her and if she will agree, have her involved. Go to it, Will. Great idea. Thanks."

48

HEIGHTENED ANXIETY ABOUT the extraordinary responsibility imposed on him extinguished the feeling of calm security with which Will had awoken that morning. In the past, for most of the four and a half years of investigations he had had Isaac at his side sharing the decision-making and the consequences of those decisions. Even his solitary visits to St Petersburg and Odessa were relatively straightforward; it was simply a continuation of the investigation. No decisions were required that would have a long-term or permanent impact on Isaac or his family. As Will thought further about the incident yesterday at Scotland Yard, he realized that he, and probably all of Isaac's family, were back at risk and perhaps literally in the firing line. What courses of action he would take now and in the weeks ahead would affect all of Isaac's family and Frank and his team, as well as Penelope and her team of researchers.

Into this maelstrom, Will was about to invite Ruth to join Isaac's support group under his guidance. Was it reasonable to expose Ruth to the risks inherent in her becoming involved in the process? Well, he had discussed her participation with Isaac. At least Isaac gave his opinion that it was a good idea and had even encouraged him to do so. Would he remember what he said to Will if anything happened to Ruth that harmed her in any way? It was some comfort that he had the affidavit. He knew the doctor and the nurse who were present when it was signed and affirmed would confirm Isaac's authorization to contact her.

His meeting with Frank to discuss the Scotland Yard situation was scheduled for two o'clock that afternoon. It would be five hours earlier in New York. It was a Friday, so Ruth should be at her workplace by now with her cell phone at hand. He called, receiving a recorded message that she was late that morning and that the caller should leave a message.

Within ten minutes, Will received the return call from Ruth. She started the conversation with confidence and assurance stating she knew who Will was and his role with her father.

Taking comfort from her straightforward manner and knowledge of at least some of his role and responsibilities with her father, Will informed her of the several developments in her father's life since he had arrived in Europe a few weeks ago. He explained that investigations on the assets were continuing and that negotiations with Eastern European governments would continue to be required and were difficult and probably risky to Isaac's team. At that point, without a comment or question from Ruth, he stated that it was important for Isaac's family that there be a member of the family, particularly of her generation, to be involved to protect the family's interests.

He got to the point with little delay: "Ruth, you impressed your dad at your last meeting as someone with a strong sense of family and a mindset similar to his own. He wonders if you would consider taking a leave of absence from your firm to join me as a strategic member of my management team. I have to be clear with a warning that there have been several deaths directly consequential on our investigations and of course, your dad himself has received serious gunshot wounds and now suffers post-traumatic stress disorder, as does his wife Sophie. So, I invite you to join me, but I do so worried I may be putting you into physical harm. I have two daughters, one about your age. I'm not sure I would risk her doing this, Ruth – but I leave it to you to decide whether you would be prepared to take on this risky assignment."

Ruth replied, "Mr MacIntosh –"

Will immediately interrupted: "Please, it will be 'Will', no matter what you decide."

"Alright, Will, I hear you. I understand the risks and the reasons why Dad and you have asked me to join you. Have you asked my half-sisters? A question I must have answered before I go further with this conversation."

"No. I discussed this with your father. He said, frankly, that he felt their mother had poisoned him in their eyes and as a result, there has been no contact for over fifteen years. He has made it clear to me that if his ex knew the value of the assets and his overall scheme for settling the issues involved, he would end up in court facing an injunction freezing his access to the assets and his ability to wrap this up."

"I think Dad is correct. I have had no contact with either of them for even longer and I do not wish to do so. Another question: to what extent will they have any long-term role in the administration of the assets?"

"No involvement in any part of the investigation or the administration of the businesses. A bequest of a modest amount has been specified for both, and having drafted the will, I can say it contains a precise explanation as to why it is modest – at least modest in comparison with the overall value of the assets. I think the will has been drafted in a way to prevent an attack on it after Isaac's death. While your father is recovering from post-traumatic stress disorder and was for a few weeks legally incompetent, he has healed to the point of being occasionally competent in a legal sense. I don't think the will can be overturned, but you as a lawyer will know that courts can't always be predicted."

"I am honestly flattered by my father's request. Dad is correct that we had a wonderful meeting earlier in the summer. I agree that he and I share a similar personality and manner of doing business. That is why no man would put up with me, I think! I'm very determined and outspoken, very much like Dad. I have to tell you that my mother and I communicate only when it is needed and then it is like walking on thin ice. You would not have to worry about Mother interfering and trying to become a third-party administrator."

"Spoken, Ruth, like the competent lawyer I know you to be. Now, as to compensation – I mean I am asking you to take a leave of absence from your work. I have no doubt you are well paid and, like most of us weak souls, you have financial commitments that must be met. You will be paid what you request – no negotiation required. You will also have an unlimited credit facility with a British bank to enable you to pay whatever residential and household expenses you may incur. There will be a general accounting for tax purposes, but that will be light."

"Well, I was wondering. I am no less weak in spending than you suggest. I will do some calculations and let you know what I will need. I will not be greedy or exorbitant in my request. I am thankful my living expenses will be paid: I gather these can be crippling in London."

"Yes, your father has several properties in the London area. In fact, I have a beautiful apartment in a building Isaac owns in Fitzroy Square which I share with your aunt Anna and your young brother, who we all call 'Little Isaac'."

"I'm becoming really interested in doing this, Will. I don't know my little brother but I would love to get to know him. Aunt Anna has done her best to keep in contact with me. I have really appreciated it. It has kept me emotionally feeling part of the Menshive family, but she knew little of the family's history and never showed much curiosity. I am curious. I want to know much more of who I am and what I have received genetically, as it were."

Will concluded the one-hour conversation, welcoming her to the 'team' as he repeatedly referred to Isaac's support system. Ruth said she would be able to join Will after giving her firm a month's notice – but said they might be prepared to reduce the notice period. Will concluded the conversation by cautioning her to give absolutely no details of her father's wealth, the nature and location of the assets, or of the investigations conducted to date to anyone other than those on the team. Ruth responded that she had heard about the auction sale at Christie's some years earlier and the problems that arose during the sale. Will was greatly relieved to have Ruth aboard to help him.

* * *

Will's meeting with Frank was scheduled later in the morning in the recently rented space in Canada Tower at Canary Wharf. They agreed that they would take separate routes and would arrive half an hour apart. Frank was to arrive early and was to bring his Bible for the 'prayer meeting'. That brought a faint mumble, almost a suppressed laugh, from Frank who was the antithesis of a religious person.

The space actually occupied at Canada Tower was underground, what Londoners occupying residential accommodations in similar spaces referred to as 'lower ground floor': a euphemistic way to disguise the degradation of not living in a detached villa in Kensington. The access was the most secure Frank could arrange. One of Andy's team met him in Greenwich across the Thames from Canary Wharf and walked him through the underground tunnel to Canary Wharf to assist him in finding the place; the reason for taking that route was that the tunnel was seldom used and little known, particularly to visitors to London, as the would-be attackers at Scotland Yard appeared to be.

Will enjoyed the walk, marvelling at the fact that just a few feet above him the Thames River flowed freely in its passage eastward to the river mouth, interrupted only by the tides which twice daily reversed its flow.

As they emerged from the Thames tunnel they were in a small building on the edge of the river; they passed a park adjacent to some of the original pre-development residences. They then entered the complex of business towers and condominiums and hotels in Docklands of which Canary Wharf is a part. Canada Tower soared over other high rise structures and it contained sheltered lower ground floor shops configured as a mall. The crush of workers was such that Will and his guide were safe from being observed by anyone who might try to identify and interrupt them.

After being admitted to the vast area that served as the storage and office space, Will was taken to an office having dimensions of no more than fourteen by twenty-five feet in size and containing IKEA furniture of the cheapest and most functional type. He sat at a conference-type table and was quickly served tea from a thermos; his reputation for taking tea by the gallon having preceded him. He pulled a notepad forward and took a pen to start an agenda, a process as predictable as his penchant for tea by the gallon.

Before he could get a line or two down, Frank walked in followed by a trolley similar to one used to transport meals in a hospital. On it were three metal boxes, the tops slightly ajar, promising easy access.

"Thanks, Frank, for all your arrangements for this place. It appears to be as secure as we require. Who could find us down here? More secure it seems than the American Fort Knox."

"Yes, and those boxes contain artifacts worth almost as much as the money stored in Fort Knox."

"Alright, please give me an explanation of what you discovered in the top compartments and in the bottom compartments of these boxes."

"In the top, Scythian gold: numerous artifacts, made of more than twenty-four-carat gold. They contain so much gold that they are almost pliable by the naked hand. The pieces are early and identifiably created by Greek craftsmen, perhaps from the classical period of Pericles. I know this because Andy and I went online last night and we studied the Scythian gold research found there. Not only are the pieces valuable for their gold, they are even more valuable for their rarity, the quality of their making and for the period of their creation. I would venture a very amateurish guess that they are incapable of a valuation. They would be so sought after by museums, collectors and governments that only a bidding war could establish their value.

"Apart from these stunning pieces – and I am not one who is into antiques, as you know – they are incredible even to a layman. What we found below in the bottom compartments was just as interesting. In the largest and what appeared to be the oldest box, the bottom compartment contained a signed statement by a David Bronshtein dated May 1895. It states that he and his son Lev found this cache of gold objects in a field on their farm near Odessa and that they sold it to their friend Isaac Menshikovsky. Who are these Bronshtein people? Are the farmer and his son important?"

"Hugely important, Frank. Christ, I can't believe this. Lev Bronshtein was to later reinvent himself as Leon Trotsky, one of the leaders of the October Revolution in Russia in 1917 that overthrew the government. The fact that there is a Trotsky connection will make this collection invaluable to Putin and his government. They are continually trying to create an image of legitimacy and continuity in spite of the fact that the Soviet system failed. If I am correct from my memory of Russian history, Trotsky was initially one of the leaders of the Bolsheviks and after meeting and helping Lenin to organize the Bolsheviks, he joined Lenin ultimately as his second in command, a position he continued to hold until Lenin's death. The connection with Trotsky will have other connections, I am sure, in the assembling of the Menshikovsky assets. Amazing! Truly amazing. That connection is even more significant because David and his son Lev Bronshtein were Jews. David would have chosen to trust only a fellow Jew with this treasure. He would have known that if the Imperial government in St Petersburg had found out about the discovery it would have confiscated it.

"Frank, we must move the three boxes with all of their contents to an absolutely secure location. That, more than anything else, must be our immediate priority."

49

PENELOPE AND SMYTHE welcomed Will and Frank at the law office the next day, early – ten o'clock being early by London law office standards.

Will greeted Penelope with warmth but he received none in return. She was meticulously polite. As polite as she would be to an elderly maiden aunt suffering from dementia.

The detailed record of proceedings in Odessa and particulars of their captivity and escape that Will had requested be created was brought out by Penelope and presented, somewhat formally, to Will who read it aloud and approved it. Will reminded Penelope that Anna Menshive also maintained a record of those activities in which she was involved. Penelope's journal was to be appended to the one prepared by Anna.

Smythe appeared to be pleased with the record as he heard it: "It is essential that we have iron-clad proof of possession of the assets to which Dr Menshive lays claim and the method and legitimacy of their acquisition."

After Will gave an accounting of the three boxes and their contents the room fell silent. Smythe spoke first, ending the pause: "It was illegal to bring those artifacts into this country without declaring them at UK customs. In fact, they should have been declared entering and leaving Ukraine. While the value of the objects is unimaginable, they are explosive in the wrong hands. Both the Russians and the Ukrainians might even start a war with each other to secure them for their national museums. Tourism alone would be a huge consideration to both, Scythian gold being much in the news. If you involve UK customs at this point after they were illegally brought into this country they would be confiscated and held, and released only after protracted legal proceedings that would become a public spectacle."

"Alright. They must either be surreptitiously hidden in

the UK or removed elsewhere," said Will. "Any suggestions, Roger?"

Smythe replied, "I am not ethically permitted to counsel you on the illegal use of these artifacts. Any comment of that kind would make me an accessory after the fact, if I am not already. I do not want to know where these artifacts are located or where they go until they have left the UK."

"Roger, I remind you of solicitor-client privilege. Our discussions cannot be revealed by you to investigating authorities or in a court of law." Was Will's surprised reply.

"In this country, sir, any advice I give you relating to the transporting, secreting or removal of these artifacts in or out of this country would be in itself an illegal act which would not be protected by privilege. At this point, I am safe from challenge or charge but I can go no further."

Penelope remained silent throughout this exchange, looking decidedly uncomfortable and worried.

A discussion then ensued as to the creation of a foundation for holding the assets. "Where would be the most satisfactory domicile for the foundation?" asked Will.

"I suggest that Switzerland remain the domicile for your new foundation," offered Smythe, "but it should ultimately be owned and controlled by the Prince Edward Island Trust. The Swiss bank would be the safest location for storage of the artifacts. We could draft the documentation here if you wish."

"That had been my intent," said Will. Seeing Smythe's face fall and realising the other man's apprehension that he would lose a valuable client and the substantial fees that client would bring to his firm, he added: "However, as we have compromised you with the information on the Scythian gold, it will have to be drafted elsewhere. I will make that decision later. I will, however, invite your firm to review and comment on the documents." Smythe was visibly relieved.

"As to the large number of documents brought back from Odessa, they must be analyzed one by one and information gleaned from them to establish a narrative and proof of how the Odessa assets, assets of every kind, were acquired and kept establishing legitimate ownership and possession. You need that, Mr MacIntosh, before you start detailed negotiations with the Russian, Bulgarian, Polish and Ukrainian governments. If they identify any defect in the title to any of the assets, they will simply declare them forfeit to their government based on indeterminate ownership. I understand a number of documents found in a palace in St Petersburg were transported from there to Odessa and have likely been transported here. The Russian authorities, if they find out, will be very angry that they were removed without authorization – they will assert they are national treasures and should have remained where they were."

"Yes. But they have no record of what those documents were. They have no way of determining what was in the palace or what we removed. Nothing on any of the documents says they were stored and removed from St Petersburg. Russian Museum officials were present when the strong room was breached. Their attention was taken by the shelves full of artifacts – a most impressive array of jewellery from the Czarist period, perhaps the best outside the Armory in the Kremlin in Moscow. Remember, this may be a mess for me to sort out, but it is also a mess for the governments of those four countries to sort out, not only with me on behalf of Dr Menshive, but in relation to the competing governments. This is going to be a rocky road to settlement, I think," said Will.

"I hope you survive it, sir," was Smythe's ominous reply.

After the meeting adjourned Will asked Frank to invite Penelope to join them for a debriefing on her experiences in Transnistria.

Will stood aside while Frank approached her. She was noticeably less cool with Frank than she had been with Will. With quiet grace, she agreed to meet with Frank and Will in a conference room on the ground floor of the law office which was removed at some distance from where they could be overheard by Smythe, who by now was beginning to worry Will.

Penelope, without prompting, gave her story. It was essentially one of mistakes. They thought they could get to Bucharest airport more quickly by taking a flight from Chisinau, the capital of Moldova. Penelope and Andy examined a map of the region but it was in Ukrainian. They noticed unusual markings along the eastern border of Moldova, but as they did not understand their meaning they simply drove to the nearest border between Ukraine and what they thought was Moldova after leaving Odessa and without difficulty crossed the border.

"Were there no border crossing points requiring customs or passport checks?" asked Will.

"Yes, of course," replied Penelope. "We passed those easily. We were no more than half a mile into what we thought was Moldova when there was a fleet of police cars and a couple of army vehicles approaching us – herding us like sheep. The horror started immediately. The females in our group were put on the back of an open-back army truck. The men were taken by police cars. The females in my team were poked and prodded from the moment we got into the truck. I did my very best to protect them. A couple of the young women in my team were well dressed and were very pretty. They were selected for what became sexual slavery. I was spared that indignity, but I am traumatized just the same. I am overwhelmed with guilt that I did not do more to protect them. During the four days or more we were with these thugs, the girls were subjected to the vilest treatment imaginable. They are, the two of them, still in a state of profound shock. They have been examined medically and steps have been taken to prevent pregnancies."

"Was there any indication, Penelope, that they knew what your mission was in the Ukraine?" asked Frank.

"No. We discovered we were in Transnistria, eastern Moldova. They had stumbled on us as fresh stock to exploit and they were going to harvest us. They did not appear to have a political or financial objective. It became clear after a couple of days that the prison authorities where we were incarcerated had notified the Transnistrian authorities. We received a visit from officials who would not identify themselves who were interested only in whether we had a political purpose for being in the country. Our ignorance of the political and military situation in Moldova and in Transnistria convinced them that our story about being in Odessa on a private estate matter was true. They continued to hold us, though, hoping to gain something from our captivity. I assume they planned on holding us for ransom. While we were held in that prison we were given mouldy bread twice a day and something they described as drinking water but looked more like toilet water. I have never known such fear and revulsion. It was truly terrible," sobbed Penelope.

Will tried to comfort her at first with words and then by holding out his arms to envelope her with his arms and body as they had so often done in Odessa. As Will got nearer she put up her hands and screamed. It was not clear who was more terrified by this reaction, Penelope or Will.

Will asked Frank whether any of the documents and objects that had been taken with the team from Odessa were seized in Transnistria by her attackers.

"No," answered Penelope. "I had everything assembled and wrapped in sealed packages. None of the wrappings were removed. Everything taken from Odessa has arrived intact in London. Incidentally, Andy has safely taken our documents and other materials to your storage facility here in London. I want to say that Andy is not in any way responsible for our bad luck in entering Transnistria by mistake; he was wonderful. He was allowed to see me daily for a short time," said Penelope. "He got me and the two young women through the ordeal. Don't put any blame on him. Don't you dare!" Penelope explosively announced; perhaps 'warned' would be a better description, since there were actions accompanying the words – her arms raised in an aggressive stance that shocked Will and Frank equally.

"Before we leave you this morning, Penelope, did you examine any of the journals and documents you brought with you?" asked Frank.

"Yes, of course, as I said to you, I assembled the journals and documents in packages. I didn't just pick them up at random and stuff them together. Of course, they were sorted by subject matter and chronology. Carefully. As I would do in assembling evidence for the first day of a trial."

Will spoke: "Thank you, Penelope. I'm sure they are exceptionally well prepared and will greatly assist us in reviewing them. We would like to have you with us to do that if you would agree. I know that is not possible today or tomorrow, but I hope you will be well enough to join us soon," said Will with genuine sadness. He knew his special connection with Penelope had come to an end. The most he could hope for was that they could resume their arm's-length professional relationship.

* * *

For the first time in several weeks, Will had a well-lubricated lunch in Canary Wharf with Frank before moving on to the store room and office nearby. As they sat at a café table overlooking the canals and the Thames River inlets that permeate Canary Wharf, Frank was in an agitated state, tapping his right foot. Will was about to tell him to stop. It was a mannerism he disliked in others although he frequently engaged in it himself. Will then noticed something unusual about Frank's right shoe. Something about the heel was different.

Will casually commented, "Frank, I like frugality. I see you have kept your shoes for more use by having the heel of your right shoe replaced. I hate waste, as you know. It is often difficult to find a 'shoe doctor' as they grandly call themselves nowadays. I guess cobbler sounds too common!"

Frank removed the shoe, turned it over and said, "I did not have the heel replaced. I haven't noticed this new heel until you pointed it out, sir." He then picked away at the margins of the new heel and commented, "This is professionally installed. It was installed to look as much like the other heel as possible." With that, Frank took his Swiss army knife and quickly lifted each layer of the heel. Will was about to remonstrate when it became clear that there had been a hole bored through the middle of the interior layers. Inserted in that hole was a tracking device. It had been adapted for listening as well.

"That, Frank, is how we were tracked so quickly and accurately after arriving in London."

The device was removed. Will insisted on having the honours, and with his size elevens he stamped repeatedly on the device, crushing it to smithereens; then, having picked up all the pieces, he walked over to the canal in front of the café and threw the remains into the water, watching with satisfaction as they sank.

An explanation had been found for the efficiency of the surveillance placed on Frank and by extension on Will and all of his team since they arrived back in London. However, just how much had been heard or recorded since the device had been inserted in his shoe and how it got there were questions to be answered.

Frank submitted to Will's questions willingly but with humility, knowing in retrospect just when and how it might have happened.

It was well known that there were websites advertising beautiful Ukrainian girls for sale as wives. Men from all over Europe and the United States who could not hope to attract a blonde, shapely young woman on the basis of their own physical gifts, flew into Odessa on every flight on their way to meeting in person a young woman found online who agreed to return with them to the United States; married or unmarried mattered little as long as the girls had a passport holder from the States with a visitor's permit for her. Will had overheard numerous gross and crude men in the airport as he left Odessa after his first visit bragging about their conquests. The only real conquest was made by the girl in gaining entry into Western Europe or America.

Frank admitted he had met such a girl while walking in the park near the apartment in Odessa. She was exceptionally confident and aggressive in approaching him. She had him in a cheap hotel room nearby within an hour of their meeting. She made it a condition of his receiving her services that he take a shower, but he must do a strip for her in the bedroom. She claimed it was a necessary prelude to her being ready for him. She told Frank that it was necessary... it turned out it was not for that purpose but for him to leave his clothing in the bedroom while he was in the shower. After his shower, he noticed that his clothing had been moved but before he could inquire she offered an explanation: "To make room for us I moved your things and mine to the chair by the door. It is easier for us now." No further prelude was required. It was over in very few minutes. She looked bored during the exercise given exclusively by Frank. She was out of the room less than half an hour after they entered it.

Will's reply was, "As a trained professional I don't understand why you didn't read the situation from the moment she approached you."

To which Frank replied: "Stupid. Yes, I was stupid. It had been a long time since I had been with a woman. It was not my head taking the lead, sir. I'm sure you understand how it is."

"I understand all too well, Frank, but when you are hired to undertake highly sensitive security surveillance to protect me and my team you are expected to be on duty at all times. I need you on my team for the next two or three days, then you will leave my employment. Your appearance is now well known to the person who is after my team and me. Your continuation as part of the team will compromise us all. The time left before you leave us will be limited to debriefing. I need to know what else you may have been up to that could have compromised Dr Menshive and me. You have served us well on several occasions, and that guarantees a severance payment that will be more generous than it should be. You know, however, that you will now be a personal target by our opponents. They will believe you have continued to work with me. It would be best if you hop on a flight to the States in three days. I will give you sufficient money for steerage on a charter flight from London to Toronto. You can take a train from Toronto to wherever you will be going. In the meantime, you will remain here in this space. There is a small sofa bed against the wall that you can use. All of the material in this space will be removed while you are here. You will not ask where it is going. To ensure your compliance with my directions, I will have Andy and one of his assistants with you at all times – and I mean at all times. I would never have believed you could have failed me and Dr Menshive so totally. Just so you understand, it was probably the listening device in your shoe that enabled the goon squad to discover where Penelope and her group were going. I wondered why they had such little trouble getting into Transnistria. Why did you include those shoes with Andy's baggage? That in itself was irresponsible. They were happily waiting for Penelope."

"These shoes are the same size as Andy wears and were more suitable for him to wear as he went through customs in England than the heavy-duty boots we were wearing loading the plane," replied Frank.

"I think I now understand why Penelope was so cold and hostile to me. She probably suspected there was a security breach that exposed them to the terrible violence they were subjected to after getting into that damned place. She will never forgive me and I don't blame her. I was responsible for her security and that of her group. I failed every one of them.

"One other thing. You have an in-depth knowledge of the investigations that Dr Menshive and I have been undertaking for over four years. You know the assets almost as well as Dr Menshive and I do. If you disclose one word of any of this to anyone, I will find out. You will not last long enough to talk to anyone else. Yes, that is a threat. It is one I will carry out personally if necessary.

"Yes, and one more matter. Have you had any contact with Anthony Cann directly or indirectly at any time in the last five years in the States or anywhere for that matter?"

"I admit that I had a couple of telephone conversations while we were in New York and perhaps one here in London. And one brief meeting in Central Park. He was trying to deliver a message to you and Dr Menshive but he meant Dr Menshive's family no harm."

"How much did he or someone on his behalf pay you, Frank?"

"Not much, sir. Really, just out-of-pocket expenses."

"All of your expenses had been generously paid."

"Did he give you a tracking device of any kind or a recording device which would enable him or those for whom he may have been acting to follow us and to hear our plans?"

"No."

"Did you check your clothing, your hotel room and anywhere else a device like those could have been planted?"

"No, I didn't think it was necessary," said Frank.

Will pointed to the IKEA sofa bed and said, "Stay there and don't move. Make no effort to record or document anything you see here. Any attempt to benefit from your knowledge of the Scythian gold or any of the other artifacts will be discovered and you will pay the price."

"I won't. I promise. I really wanted to be part of your team with Dr Menshive even after all the settlement arrangements were made. I think you believe I have exposed your information more than I have. I will try to prove my value to you and my sincere wish to continue to provide protection to you."

"Not until I know the full depth of your betrayal, Frank. In the meantime, consider yourself charged, tried and convicted of breaching our trust in you. You are now dead to us," was Will's final reply. It was, he hoped, the final communication of any kind he would have with Frank.

* * *

Will was shattered. Frank had been his primary security detail since Isaac's shooting and his incapacity by post-traumatic stress disorder. Will had no one to help him. He knew from Anna that any relationship with her would be limited and she would lack any interest in the decisions and solutions that lay ahead. He had been hopeful that something might come out of his relationship with Penelope. That was now dead as well. He was well and truly alone.

Fortunately, Frank had three security guards who had been part of his team since Will and Isaac had arrived in Europe four months ago. Andy was one – a relatively recent recruit but one who had performed very well. Will knew he would have to interview them all and try to discern whether they were trustworthy and could be relied on as permanent replacements. He had found a replacement in Frank for poor Ben who was killed in Isaac's service in Moscow four years ago. For the most part, Will was sure, Frank had served Isaac and him well.

Will took Abraham and Mendel, the two other guards into a secure room in the storage facility, explained the situation and put it bluntly: "Did either of you know Frank was putting us at risk?"

"No. At no time did we sense he was anything but professional and dedicated to your service and that of Dr Menshive. I knew he had a hyperactive libido but I assumed he could manage that without putting you at risk. It can be done, but it is really difficult to pull it off while on duty as we are 24-7. Please remember, we were not conducting surveillance on Frank, only those we thought were or could be a risk to you."

"And Mendel, how about you?"

"Same as Abraham. I can't believe what has just happened. I have to say, sir, that you had no choice but to fire Frank. He has compromised you and Dr Menshive and it is too soon to tell how deeply."

Will explored in depth, exercising his considerable skills in cross-examination, whether each man, including Andy, was suitable for the security role for which they were being considered. They were each interviewed separately. Mendel was the second to be interviewed. He stated that he had absolute confidence in Andy's judgement and skills and recommended him as the lead on the security team. "And one more thing, Mr MacIntosh, both Abraham and I are Ashkenazi Jews whose family, like Dr Menshive's, came from Europe about the same time. There is a tie and bond among many of us with that family history. You have that as an added protection. We will not, neither of us, betray Dr Menshive and his remarkable family. Sir, his family is part of the American Jewish success story. We couldn't countenance any risk or failure to protect that story and Dr Menshive's family itself."

Will was grateful that Frank had left such a strong team, including Andy, to take over from him. Perhaps that was part of Frank's overall security plan. Andy was accepted and confirmed as a permanent replacement for Frank and given a probationary period as a lead, with Abraham, on the team as a 2-I-C.

Before leaving the remaining team, Will instructed Andy to hire three more security guards. He emphasized that they must be British citizens with strong military backgrounds. If possible, he said, they should be Jews. He had heard Mendel's words and was impressed by the loyalty issue he had described as a motivating factor for him.

As he was leaving, Will told them that if they proved themselves to be trustworthy and effective they would have permanent jobs with Dr Menshive and whatever organization was created to manage his assets. He knew that promise would be a motivation for diligent and reliable service.

When Will instructed Andy to hire three new security guards, they were assigned to Isaac, Sophie and himself. Andy would remain responsible for Anna and Little Isaac – and for Ruth when she arrived.

* * *

From Canary Wharf Will returned to Smythe's law office; he explained what had happened with Frank and that it could have been Frank's indiscretions that had led to Penelope and her group being so disastrously compromised. He requested Smythe to contact an executive employment agency to enable him to add to the management team to assist him and Ruth. In the short term, he needed new space for all of the documents and artifacts located at Canary Wharf.

Will asked Smythe whether Penelope would consider continuing as part of Isaac's team or whether she would discontinue her connection with Isaac, knowing her connection with himself was gone, at least on the personal level.

Before he left Smythe's office Penelope came in on another matter not expecting to find Will. She looked at him with blatant hostility, staring for a few minutes, and seeing how devastated and remorseful Will appeared she said: "As I came in, Mr MacIntosh, I heard you ask whether I would consider continuing to assist Dr Menshive. The answer is that I have great admiration for what his family has achieved and for what he is trying to do with this immense wealth. You may recall that my mother's Ukrainian family are Jewish. While I am a member of the Church of England as were my parents, I feel a loyalty to my Jewish cousins such as I consider Dr Menshive and his family to be. I will continue to serve them. I take this role, taking comfort in knowing that I will have Andy's support and intelligence to help me."

Will had the good sense to blush as a red-haired Celt is wont to do when humiliated.

* * *

An alternate location was required for storage and office space, given the breach in security established by the incident at Scotland Yard. Several alternate locations for the documents and artifacts brought to London from St Petersburg and Odessa were considered. Several properties near the former Battersea Power Station could be acquired at a reasonable price (several projects planned for the area having failed): a site near the Oval in south London and a site near the planned redevelopment of King's Cross in north London were all considered. Each was ruled out as either too remote to be readily accessible or too obvious to the curious or those pursuing the documents for the treasures brought from Russia.

Canary Wharf continued to be the perfect location, Will reminded himself. It was accessible and escape was possible by road, rail, air (London City Airport nearby) and most importantly by the river.

It was necessary to relocate from the current site at Canada Tower, however. Frank remained a potential problem and his knowledge of the location of the workshop and storage facility was an immediate concern. Any relocation would have to be carried out quickly and without attracting notice.

The solution lay before him. Move, but only a short distance. Space was available in the semi-basement area of the

Docklands Light Railway terminal at Canary Wharf. It was much larger in area than the space currently occupied in the basement of Canada Tower and had well-secured windows admitting natural light in two of the rooms which would be suitable for the visual and manual inspection and analysis of both documents and artifacts. The windows, Diocletian in form, had heavy steel bars on the inside, and an added element of security was that they looked into a large airshaft that had no access or other onlooking windows.

The main feature of the new space was that it was fifteen minutes from the existing storage facility. Everything was on the same level. Three electric goods transfer vehicles could and did move all of the contents from the first site to the new one within a couple of hours. This was carried out between two and four o'clock in the morning when only the premises' security were on duty. They had been forewarned and were requested to be well away from the move. The pretext was that highly sensitive court documents requiring a high degree of security were being moved and could not be observed to protect national security. The ruse worked well.

50

THE DAY AFTER the move, Will arranged a meeting onsite with those who would be located and working there.

The research group was led by Penelope, who by now had either forgiven Will or was so obsessed by his successor Andy that Will was a matter of indifference to her, at least emotionally. She led her team which included all but one of the personnel she had taken to Odessa. They had assembled the Odessa documents relevant to their investigation. The team was clever in leaving in Odessa masses of old receipts, sales slips and meaningless (to them) bank records to hide the fact that many documents had been removed. It was known that the bank premises would be searched, probably already had been searched, by those who had engineered their captivity in Transnistria.

The objective of the research team was to examine the records to establish the legality of the acquisition of many of the assets held now by Isaac, and to develop a precise understanding of the motives of the collectors of the assets, their methodology of collecting and how the assets were retained safely in spite of numerous wars, pogroms against Jews, and confiscations of Jewish property by several governments in the geographical area that now bears the name 'Ukraine'.

Will explained to Penelope: "As we move into detailed negotiations with the governments of Russia, Ukraine, Belarus, Bulgaria and Poland we know that each will claim an interest in assets acquired in southern Ukraine, because each of those current geopolitical entities had a direct or indirect historical interest in that area. For example, Belarus will have an interest in any assets found within its current borders, but as a part of the Russian Empire it will claim an interest as part of its share of the treasures formerly held by the Imperial government when the empire broke up into individual countries. We need to be better prepared for arguments they and others will make. We also have to be prepared for claims by individuals – family and co-religionists who may claim the treasures were simply stored and kept for the true beneficiaries of the material stored there."

"Yes, Mr MacIntosh," interjected Penelope with the new tone of formality which emphasized, as much to herself as to others, that the relationship was now business only. "And the other possibility, and the one you want to establish as fact, is that the treasures were acquired by members of the Menshikovsky family for their personal use and investment. From a legal point of view that is your strongest position in negotiating with others."

Having earlier made that point clear to Penelope on several occasions, he did not correct or remind her that her statement, while correct, was not in truth hers. He realized that there would be a certain degree of roleplay and competition in their ongoing relationship, albeit reduced to the business at hand.

* * *

After the meeting with the research team, Will met with the security group. Andy, Abraham and Mendel, hired in Odessa, were new to this group but, having been thoroughly briefed by Will and others including Penelope on the requirements for security in each aspect of their investigation, they were prepared to meet the challenges that lay ahead. Protecting the storage and research site was one priority, as well as protecting the Fitzrovia site and its residents. Will had a separate round-the-clock team engaged to protect Isaac and Sophie. Their mandate was separate. Will decided to keep the two security groups separate to limit the amount of collective knowledge each of the security guards had. Will recognized that the risk Frank had posed to Isaac and his family and to the investigation was greater because of his comprehensive knowledge up to the point of his termination.

Communications with the outside world would be handled

by a professional public relations person recently hired by Will who would be located in a separate and isolated location. The PR person would receive inquiries and if directed by Will she would answer them as: "Ms Baker, executive assistant to William MacIntosh, CEO of the Menshikovsky Trust."

Jointly with Smythe and Penelope, Will had discussed the 'front' or 'cover' they would use as the operation under which the investigations and negotiations would operate. Will's identity was too well-known to hide it. The 'Menshikovsky Trust' had been restructured four years ago by the Swiss bank, but it was that identity by which governments knew of the owner of the various treasures found within their jurisdictions and for which loan agreements had been written.

* * *

Will and Andy as his principal security officer, met with Smythe to develop a strategy for security for each aspect of the investigation and the assets themselves. This had become a priority in light of the incidents in Odessa, Frank's betrayal and their encounter with hostile interests earlier at Scotland Yard.

"How can we flush out those pursuing us or the assets? The last time, four years ago, we were fairly successful in doing that by holding a public auction at Christie's New York. Again, we don't know whether those pursuing us are interested in Isaac and his family personally or whether they are after specific treasures."

Smythe, as usual, rubbed his nose with long sensuous strokes, then his chin and earlobes, before answering: "What would you sell? You have an extensive variety of assets. You wouldn't sell the whole. You would force national governments to protect their interests by confiscating them."

Will replied: "I agree. Nothing that is of particular interest to governments, such as archaeological artifacts and art created within their current borders and that could be viewed as their national treasures, would be sold. After the numerous discussions I have had on each of these countries, Russia in particular, I know what cannot be sold. I think we could sell objects that are of limited interest in a final assembling of the assets free of competing interests, but the sale might bring out those who would identify themselves by attending the sale as having an adverse interest. I think we could assemble a significant collection of artifacts and art of marginal interest to the trust and see where that takes us. Incidentally, I would disclose our motives and the actual list to the government authorities we have dealt with. An advantage we have now is that we do know who to talk to and who can give us reliable undertakings."

Smythe: "Alright, a rhetorical question: what do you have to lose if you do this?"

Will: "We would be selling assets and thereby depleting the extent of the holdings. However, we will have to dispose of a substantial number of the assets anyway to create a manageable portfolio. I look now at the huge list of assets as more of a burden and potential liability than I do valuable goods and investments that must be kept. There is simply too much and spread over too much geography to enable us to manage on an ongoing basis. No, to answer your question, I don't see a downside.

"I do see an advantage, however. You know that the Jewish factor is prominent there. It works two ways. The governments of Central and Eastern Europe (and often in the West, notably in Germany) have in living memory had a resurgence of anti-Semitism. We have to work against that atrocity. The other is the counter-balance, namely that international Jewish organizations are much better prepared to defend hostility against their community than in the past; indeed, any attacks that could be linked to discrimination against Jews would attract the United Nations which would bring condemnation and public attention to the attempts. Now that we are in the twenty-first century, governments, even Putin's, are sensitive to allegations of racism – particularly against one of the most prominent, wealthy and influential groups in the world.

"I think a sale that is well-publicized and offers a few treasures would build public interest. Support for the objective of the ultimate solution Isaac has in mind would be enhanced by advertising the sale as part of a plan to raise money for international charitable work in the arts, education and spiritual awareness as expressed in the major monotheistic religions of the world. Yes, if we promote the sale around that theme, I think it would inhibit some aggressive positions or interference; it would be seen as an attack on the charitable objectives more than an attack on the trust.

"I think there is merit in having the sale," concluded Will.

To which Smythe replied: "Well thought out, sir. I agree. Where do we go from here?"

"To Isaac and his wife. His daughter Ruth arrives tomorrow. She will form part of our team. I will involve her fully in the plan. And I will start talking to various national interests who need to know.

"Another advantage, I think, is that this may interest Isaac and help in his healing and re-engagement with the world."

* * *

Isaac and Sophie joined Will in an elegant Edwardian parlour at the clinic for tea that afternoon.

Will was considerably encouraged to observe both Isaac and Sophie looking much better and interacting as in the days before Smolensk.

The Smolensk visit and the Moldovan problems were briefly described, to which neither Isaac nor Sophie expressed any interest, simply accepting the information as facts. The nature of the records found in Odessa and what they might reveal to assist in a total solution enthused both Isaac and Sophie. This was the first expression of enthusiasm from them for anything other than each other and Little Isaac. When Will explained his plan for another auction and the benefits the auction might bring, both Isaac and Sophie gave their opinion that it should go ahead. Sophie showed relief that the path ahead could lead to finishing the nightmare they had been experiencing.

Isaac's response was what Will hoped it would be: "I want

to be part of this sale, Will. Between us we will identify the stuff that will go into the sale and Sophie and I will discuss the 'charitable' connection – that is brilliant, Will. It's where I want to go. I think now is the time to go public."

"Before I leave you two, please remember that Ruth arrives tomorrow. I will bring her over for tea after she has a chance to settle in."

That news brought tears to Isaac's eyes for the first time in several weeks, not of sadness or despair but of happiness, an opportunity to reconnect with Ruth and to bring her into his family as a full partner. Isaac's happiness was shared by Sophie who reached over and took Isaac's hand. It was time for Will to leave.

51

"MR MACINTOSH, WE NEED you to come in as soon as possible. Our research has unearthed some remarkable evidence…," blurted out an over-excited Penelope, who could be heard in spite of the raucous cheering in the background.

Before she could finish her sentence, let alone her message, Will interrupted. "Stop. That's great, Penelope! Please keep it canned until I get there from Fitzroy Square. I will take the Central Line on the Underground until I get to Bank and then I will jump onto the Docklands Light Railway. I should be with you and your team within the hour. Thank you for starting your day so early. I guess your dedication has been rewarded! May I gently remind you we have to be very discreet in our messages by telephone or on the computer? We know that all these technological advances have not been perfected – they can be hacked into, so there is no security on any of them. We know we are being followed and there is at least one source of information on many of our activities and location."

* * *

When Will arrived at the research centre located in Docklands Railway Station's basement at Canary Wharf, he could see, sense and hear the excitement. He held up his hand with a finger raised to his mouth demanding silence until they were safely gathered in what had become known among the team as the 'Diocletian Room'.

"Thank you," said Will, sharing the enthusiasm electrifying the room. "We are now in a secure zone. Abraham and Mendel have had specialists in overnight to scan for bugs and to install devices that will block any attempts to infiltrate our space here. Okay, I am ready. Notepad and pen poised for action. As agreed, Jeanna" – this was one of the researchers on the team taken to Odessa and later confined in Transnistria – "will take handwritten notes of our discussions which will be stored in the ultra-secure place that I identified late yesterday."

Penelope had set up a flip chart in true lawyer fashion, as if she were giving evidence at a trial or at a utilities hearing, the latter being her specialty. She began:

"You will recall that in Odessa we found a reference to Scythian gold being acquired either by the bank, stored by others at the bank, or by one or more of the Menshikovskys. As you already know, the vendor or person recorded as discovered it in was a David Bronshtein. The reference we found in the false bottom on one of the cans stated that he brought it in with his son Lev who found most of it. We wondered whether they sold it to a Menshikovsky, or the bank, or delivered it to be kept in safe-keeping for them. As you suggested, sir, the Bronshtein in question is the father, and Lev the son, the man who would become known to the world as Leon Trotsky. That much we guessed. We now have proof.

"We have a statement from Bronshtein that all of the Scythian gold brought to the bank was found on his farm. Like most Jews in Novorossiya, David Bronshtein was dirt poor. The statement discloses that he wanted money to send his son to a school in Odessa – a place of higher education. At the bottom of the statement, there is a declaratory statement intended to establish his entitlement to possession of the gold and his assertion of a right to sell it."

Penelope paused to pass the document to Will to read, "... You will see it is dated 1885 and signed by David and amazingly by his son Lev who declares himself to have the legal right to sign off his interest in the gold. The purchaser is identified as Isaac Menshikovsky (one of the several in the records). The Bronshteins were paid a substantial sum for the gold. Clearly, Menshikovsky wanted the document to establish that it was in itself an open and fair transaction that could not be impugned by either the sellers or the buyer."

Will gave a brief history of Trotsky in Odessa including the fact that he attended the equivalent of high school in Odessa at a school celebrated as one which provided a high standard in its educational achievements.

Jeanna spoke up, confirming Will's observation and she added, "And it is significant that Lev was known at the school as Leon Trotsky. We have found proof of that. It appears Leon, while attending the school, worked part-time at the bank and assisted the resident Menshikovsky.

"Trotsky, we now can prove, maintained a close contact with his friends the Menshikovskys and their bank – in fact, we have proof that the Menshikovsky Bank as a front for the Mendelssohn and Günzburg Banks lent millions of roubles to the Bolsheviks in the early days of the Revolution. The signing officer for the St Petersburg headquarters of the Menshikovsky Bank was a Vorontsov, a junior member of that noble family, who was the public face of the Menshikovsky Bank. Remember, 'Menshikovsky' is almost exactly the same as the name of an important noble family, the Menshikoffskis."

Will was beaming as he heard this account. He had suspected something like this: hiding in plain sight with the connivance of one of the most important revolutionary leaders. "Are there any agreements between Lenin and Trotsky with the Menshikovskys or their bank related to repayment of the loans?" asked Will.

"Yes. Loan agreements were signed and are in the records. However, there is a side agreement that lists the several promissory notes and which states that in lieu of payment, the Bolshevik government should give the Menshikovsky Bank absolute freedom to acquire land, buildings and assets of all kinds on condition that fair market value was paid to the Bolshevik government for them... and with the unbelievable proviso that the bank would be immune from 'seizure, confiscation or nationalization'. All three words are used in the agreements.

"The Communist government of Stalin and his successors continued to borrow from the Menshikovsky Bank until 1939, the start of the Second World War and the date when the bank was closed."

"I believe the accuracy of what you have reported. But

why would Stalin, who had no connection to the Menshikovskys, have honoured those agreements?" asked Will, in his usual Socratic fashion, before going onto answer the question himself. "I guess for two main reasons. First, Stalin must have discovered that it was a Jewish bank and, given the policies of the Nazis in Germany relating to their hostilities against the Jews, Stalin's Jewish policies were as adversarial as the Nazis. And, I think even more important, the bank had documentation in its possession that if it became public would demonstrate how vulnerable and beholden the Bolsheviks were to the Jews for the survival of their regime, and of course, the special treatment accorded to the Jewish bank for those loans.

"It all falls into place. The Mendelssohn and Günzburg Banks, we know from other sources, had transferred and released their interest in the loans made by them through the Menshikovskys. This, I think, was during the threatening years for the Jewish population of Central and Eastern Europe during the 1930s. I think we can assume that both the Mendelssohn and Günzburg Banks received some major benefits from Russia in exchange – probably protection for other assets or the right to remove substantial assets from Russia before the onset of the Second World War. We know it little benefited the Mendelssohn Bank, as the Hitler government in Berlin confiscated the Mendelssohn Bank and renamed it the Deutsche Bank, now one of the largest and most powerful banks in the world.

"Meanwhile, with the liberties conferred by the agreements on the Menshikovskys, the bank and the family acquired a wide range of assets in Central and Eastern Europe of such variety and sensitivity, secretly acquired, that when it came time to collapse the trust, the trust would have powerful information potentially devastating to the Soviet government that they would not want released. Even Putin today would prefer to have the records expunged and destroyed in exchange for a few concessions to Isaac.

"The Menshikovskys were incredibly astute in the selection of the assets they acquired. The assets had to be not only of considerable value, but they had to be vital to the national identity of the Russian, Polish, Ukrainian and Belarusian governments, so significant that those governments could not appear to lose them or to have allowed them to be acquired by other governments."

Silence prevailed for several minutes while each person in the room thought about what Will had said and they came to realize the significance of the findings of the research disclosed by Jeanna on the part of Penelope and their team.

"I must emphasize something of paramount importance to each of you," said Will, dropping his voice into its most emphatic and dictatorial. "You are at personal risk now to those who would want even part of this information becoming known in the Western media. There must be no discussion outside these walls as to what we have heard. None. You will put yourself at risk and everyone else connected to the Menshikovsky story – and of course, I include Dr and Ms Menshive and their son and Dr Menshive's daughter from his first marriage, who arrives in a couple of hours.

Then Will's demeanour changed: "Congratulations! I mean it! Your work is exceptionally important. It is more important, frankly, for the documents you have found than for the assets Dr Menshive and I have found. Your documents are our bargaining chips. The originals of those documents, Penelope, must be copied and delivered as soon as possible. The originals will be taken to a location I will identify only to the person or persons who will be engaged to deliver them. The copies will be kept here in London at a location I will also arrange; don't speculate where. It will not be Mr Smythe's law office. That would be too obvious. Penelope, if you could wait for a few minutes we will discuss where."

* * *

The meeting with Penelope followed. All tensions and hostilities demonstrated by Penelope towards Will had evaporated. They were now co-conspirators. When Will announced where the documents would be stored, however, she looked at him as if he were out of his rational mind.

As Penelope left the room Abraham and Mendel entered it. Will gave them a summary of the findings of the research group – but only enough to establish what was valuable, where the originals would go, where the copies would go, when, and by what means. They, too, reacted as Penelope had.

"Just have the originals at the London City Airport by two o'clock tomorrow morning. Make sure, Penelope, that your group has copied them. Both on memory discs or sticks – whatever it is that is used to digitally record them these days. The crew on the chartered aircraft will not know what is in the containers. Their destination will be revealed to them only when the aircraft is loaded and ready to leave. You, Mendel, will accompany them. I will meet with you separately and will reveal what you need to know at this stage. Yes, ladies and gentlemen, the contents of the boxes are of great significance and value for our purposes. Don't worry, if customs chooses to examine any of the boxes they will only find very old documents – nothing to be declared or illegal."

* * *

Will took the Docklands Light Railway and then the Underground back into central London. As he was seated, overheated and restless as the underground train moved towards his destination, he was planning the next phase of the operation: to transport the originals and to secure them. One of his most immediately pressing issues was where he would find a safe location to make the several telephone calls to put his plans in place.

As he was walking along Portland Place he entered Oxford Circus and he turned as a truck driver went into hyper-aggressive honking. His turn was instinctive as it was for the crowd encircling the junctions of Oxford Street, Portland Place and Regent Street. Will's eye was caught by a church located at the juncture of Portland Place and Regent Street, a church he knew well as having been one of Hawksmoor's most inventive. The bowed front steps led him into a narthex or entrance hall and from there into what had been the sanctuary but was now part of the BBC presence in London. He entered the building and found it empty, although there were numerous seats and a few tables in the middle of the former sanctuary. A perfect place. "If anyone comes in, I am just a tired and lost tourist trying to find my way back to Covent Garden." He took out his cell phone and got to work.

Several calls later Will smiled, took several deep breaths and he then left the building. He looked at his watch. It was now almost 5 o'clock. Ruth Menshive would be arriving at the apartment in Fitzroy Square in the next half-hour or so. His walk to the apartment was no more than twenty minutes from Oxford Circle which enabled him to get back, freshen up, meet with Anna, ensure that a welcoming tea would be ready, and to relax… as much as he ever could relax.

* * *

Ruth was not known personally to Will, and she had not been seen by her father for over ten years. Their wish to welcome her on her arrival at Heathrow Airport would have been futile since they would not have been able to recognize her, even if Isaac's health would have enabled him to be there. Will arranged to have Mendel, the junior security guard, there with a sign outside the exit from customs along with many others similarly meeting strangers.

When Will met with Isaac and Sophie the day before, he proposed that Ruth be introduced to the family in London in stages. First, she would go to the apartment on Fitzroy Square to meet Anna and Little Isaac in preparation for her stay at the apartment for as long as she chose to reside there. After she was refreshed and ready to come to Chelsea, Will would bring her over to see Isaac and Sophie, probably in time for tea at five that afternoon.

Sophie listened to the plans carefully and expressed her feelings clearly: "Will, I agree. We do not want to overwhelm either Ruth or Isaac. I look forward to meeting her. Isaac has known so little of her that I don't have any idea of what she looks like, how she behaves or how she will react to us. I am very pleased, though, that she is coming. I want her to be a vital part of this family. I know Isaac would like me to take an active interest in the investigations and planning for the new foundation, but my recent experiences have left me with nothing but hostility and fear as far as they are concerned. I want nothing to do with either. It is my hope that Ruth will fill the role I suppose I should be taking. Little Isaac and care for my husband are all I am going to give my attention to… as the wedding ceremony says, 'for better or for worse'. Even if all of Isaac's money dries up or is lost, I don't care. Dad has told me he will take care of the three of us. My comfort and financial security rest on Daddy and Mommy."

Isaac waited for her to finish before gently and softly replying: "It would be impossible for me to lose the financial security I can provide to you and Little Isaac from the Menshikovsky Trust. But I know your Dad and Mom would also step in to help if it is needed. It won't be needed, but if you find solace in their offer I am glad they have given it. I take joy in it for another reason: I am fond of them both and want them to be active as inner circle members of our family, Sophie. As to your role in the investigation and planning for the foundation – forget it. Will, with highly competent help, will do all that is necessary. When I am able to concentrate better and think more clearly, I want to be more involved, too. For now, our reliable friend Will is carrying the burden."

"Will, I hope your reward is not only in Heaven!," said Sophie. "Isaac has taken over your life for years. I want you to know how deeply grateful we both are. I hope I have been expressing that often before and since Moscow."

"Sophie, it is out of friendship and affection for the three of you that I am involved as much as I am, but I must admit everything I have been engaged with assisting Isaac for almost five years now has been a great adventure. It has been a fantastic antidote to the career blahs I was going through at home. Don't worry about me. I am with you and the family – even Isaac! – as long as I am needed."

"You may be needed even longer than Isaac… you are more so at the moment, certainly. Perhaps he will return to the overbearing brute I married," sighed Sophie with a twinkle in her eye.

* * *

Will's cell phone chirped repeatedly while he was waiting for Ruth's arrival; fortunately, the volume was so low only he could hear it. He went into a secure room in the Fitzrovia apartment, closed the door and answered the calls; all were from one source. It was one of the security guards sent with the boxes of documents on the private chartered aircraft. His message was that they had arrived at the designated destination, were met as planned and that the boxes were safely deposited where directed. The security guard was certain that no one observed their departure from Canary Wharf or from the London City Airport. At their place of arrival, there was mild curiosity expressed by the two or three airport and customs officials while they were being processed, but there was no problem. The strategies and explanations planned in advance had all worked. Will cautioned the caller that the researchers at Canary Wharf might find additional material that would have to follow the same path to security storage.

The next call Will received was less benign. A frantic Penelope was screaming into the phone, "There has been an explosion – a huge explosion here at Canary Wharf – huge structural damage to the building! I don't know what to do."

"Are the documents and assets all lost? Is anyone on your team injured or worse?"

"Oh! I wasn't clear. I am sorry. I am so frazzled. The explosions occurred at or in the storage space we had before our move to where we are now. Our new space, as you know, is no longer in Canada Tower; we are almost a quarter of a mile away from there. No, no one was injured here. No damage to anything here. My anxiety and worry is because we were the target of this bombing or whatever it was. Those responsible will soon find out that the space was empty and that they missed us. I'm sure they will try again to locate and attack us. What are we to do?" asked Penelope.

"Nothing. Absolutely nothing. I think you are right that the perpetrators will try again. But they have to find you first. If you try to move any of the contents from our new facility they will be watching for activity of that kind. It would lead them to you. Stay in the space until after hours this evening. Leave after dark – try to disguise yourselves. As cleaners would be a good bet. There are numerous fast food outlets in the subterranean tunnels there. You won't be short of food and water. Keep in touch with me during the day. I know several of your team have cell phones. Don't use the same one twice. Change from phone to phone and do not discuss anything specific about the investigations that could identify you or your location. I'm sure you and your team are safe if care and precautions are taken; you will all come through this harrowing experience safely. Just think how much interesting work you can all carry on with during what will be a quiet day. I will contact our security detail engaged at your location. I will remind them of the need for enhanced vigilance. Call me if you need me."

Penelope and her team were safe and likely to remain so. Will was relieved that he had acted so quickly in removing the primary documents and some of the lesser artifacts brought from Russia and Ukraine out of Canary Wharf.

* * *

Will, with Andy and Abraham, now the principal security guards, decided on what enhanced security was required – not just at Canary Wharf but at Fitzroy Square and in Chelsea. Abraham was, in military-trained fashion, decisive and in command, giving Will considerable relief. Will asked him to make discreet inquiries about the bombing from emergency and on-site security officials. What was it the bombers thought they were destroying?

"Never a dull moment," Will kept saying to himself. "Even a day or two of peace would be very nice." He knew in the immediate future there was little likelihood of that.

* * *

Before he could get his head into gear to prepare for meeting Ruth and Anna, while in the Jaguar touring car purchased to transport Will around London, a call came in from the security guard assigned to Penelope and her team. Will preferred to sit in the front passenger seat to give him better visibility and legroom, but given the heightened risk levels to all of the team, today he sat in the back; the blackened side windows provided some security against being observed by anyone along the way. He took the call and quickly cautioned the caller to be as non-specific as possible.

"Sir, I have been in contact with my counterpart over at the site of the activities this morning. It is believed by officials that it is a terrorist matter. A thorough examination of the site to identify the persons responsible and the type and place of manufacture of the device will be carried out. My contact knows the reason for my interest and will keep me fully informed. And they will beef up security throughout the whole area. There was no inquiry from them about the use of the space that was destroyed and I did not reveal where we are now. I say that knowing even if this call is overheard those responsible will have discovered their activity ineffective. I hope it has exposed them. The investigation will be thorough. Some of the most important international banking and insurance transactions in the world are carried out from this site, my contact tells me."

"Thanks. Very helpful. Call me immediately with any new developments. Incidentally, food will be needed for your people. Discreet pick-up and delivery would be appreciated. Be sure to assist them in their comings and goings. I know it sounds theatrical, but disguises such as wigs, hats and changes of clothing are useful. I know you have a couple of females on your team; they will be helpful to your team for planning in that area."

* * *

Anna and Little Isaac greeted Will warmly and without Little Isaac catching a second breath Anna was abandoned and Will and Little Isaac were on the floor building Lego castles... of the type he imagined were found on Prince Edward Island. Will's attempt to explain that there weren't any castles on Prince Edward Island was met with disbelief. "Castles everywhere I see," was Little Isaac's confident opinion. It didn't matter, Will was flat out on the floor with at least 6,000 Lego pieces — to him it seemed that many. He wondered if Little Isaac required them all to be used. In spite of the challenges Little Isaac set for him, it was relaxing and a welcome period of normalcy, which was in itself refreshing.

Anna tried not to interfere in the construction project underway at her feet, but she quietly assured Will that there were no issues of any kind at the flat. She said Sophie's parents came in for an hour every morning with bagels for everyone. Little Isaac and his grandparents had become great friends and both grandparents melted as they watched and played with Little Isaac. The grandparents did not have a son of their own, so Little Isaac was a novelty as well as a grandchild. Anna emphasized that they were not in the way or disrupting Little Isaac's schedule or Anna's privacy. They knew Ruth was expected soon and while they were eager to meet her, they wanted reassurances that their usual visits with Little Isaac would not be a problem in the new routine that would be required to accommodate Ruth. Anna assured them there would not be a problem with their visits or with the occasional excursions to the London Zoo, a favourite destination for Little Isaac with his grandparents.

Will called the new place of storage to make sure the material was safely stored, sealed and guarded. The reassurances he sought were received.

As he was waiting for Ruth to arrive at the apartment he had a call from the new facility in Canary Wharf. "Right, what do you have for me?" asked Will without identifying the caller.

"Sir, it is amazing. You will recall that our earlier location was made up of several rooms. The most valuable stuff was stored in three fireproof safes hidden in a cabinet and the paper archives in another room on open shelving. As you know, all the significant stuff that could not be lost has left this country. Almost all of the rest came with us to our new facility, but there were duplicates and stuff left behind that Penelope and her team planned to go through again and then destroy what was to be discarded. The very few valuable things in the safes were left there to be picked up later today. No attempt was made by the bombers to open the safes. Actually, the safes were well-hidden in a sealed room. The rest of the space was empty. With the explosive devices the bombers had, they could have blown the safes easily. Some of the duplicates on the shelves in the sealed room were collateral damage. I am told nothing of value – but, and I think this is significant, the safes were not found. Their interest in bombing the place is unknown. I thought you should know this. I think the fact it was bombed may tell us something. You may know what."

* * *

Anticipating Ruth Menshive's arrival, Will assumed he would be meeting a short, dark-haired, round-faced, somewhat sneering female version of Isaac. When the knock came on the door at the apartment in Fitzrovia he was faced with the exact opposite. His first reaction was that this person was lost or looking for information about someone else on this side of the square. His quizzical look was greeted by a gentle giggle and a confidently thrust right hand, "Mr MacIntosh, I presume!"

Will regained his composure while still displaying the red face that surprise and embarrassment usually brought on, "Ruth, I presume!"

Both had a chuckle as Will examined this ravishing creature more carefully while she walked as directed to the sitting room. Where Isaac was short, she was tall; where he was somewhat fair-haired in a balding sort of way, she had a luxuriant head of golden blonde hair stylishly arranged to accentuate her Viking-like facial features. Unlike her father, Ruth was dressed in a style that accentuated her many assets, giving her an air of elegance and grace.

Little Isaac was introduced and Ruth responded warmly and she instantly attracted the attention of Little Isaac who was, even at his age, displaying his father's weakness for blondes. Affectionate greetings were exchanged by Anna and Ruth.

The next hour passed among them with candour and good cheer, building by the minute the grounds for a happy family reunion and bond that had every chance of continued success.

The conversation was personal: Ruth talking about her life until then, Anna about hers, and Little Isaac at more length than was necessary or informative about his. Anna had offered to take Ruth to the guest bedroom she would have, but Ruth declined wisely, stating she wanted time to get to know her brother. This endeared Little Isaac to her, knowing that he was being given a priority in her choices. As Ruth spoke and engaged with each person in the room she captivated each in equal measure.

When Anna commented that she must have received her height and colouring from her mother, whom Anna had never met, she replied, "Yes, I do take after my mother in appearance, and I am very much like my father in personality and interests. I look forward to getting to know him – yes, I have met him on several occasions but there was so much aggression and hostility between my parents that I knew him very little. Over the past three or four years I have taken an interest in the Menshikovsky family – my family – although my mother did her best to alienate me from them. I suppose my interest started when I read and watched on the news about Dad's famous auction sale in New York. It appeared to me that he was a much more interesting person and one from whom I could learn a lot more than I had realized. Mom and I disagreed on what he was like: she obviously had first-hand knowledge but all that I discovered about him made him increasingly interesting to me. A hugely complex person he must be, with a character not unlike my own, I have come to realize."

Anna wisely refused to give her assessment of her brother except to say, "Ruth, from my teen years even into my early thirties I couldn't talk to Isaac with a civil tongue. I now regret those wasted years. I have come to respect, admire and love him dearly. You will reach your own conclusions as you come into frequent contact with him, which I believe is Will's plan for the two of you – a plan I heartily agree with. It's nice to have a niece to get to know and to share the abominations of men with. We will have lots of private talks that the men will not want to hear."

"*I* will, Aunt Anna," said Little Isaac, believing all conversations he heard were directed toward him. "I want to hear your stories. I could tell you lots," was Little Isaac's amusing contribution to which the women enthusiastically agreed. Little Isaac would be part of their 'secret club', said Ruth. The idea of a club, particularly a secret one, pleased Little Isaac enormously.

* * *

Ruth and Will left for the Chelsea Clinic at 4:30 that afternoon. During the ride, Will gave her a brief summary of the last four-plus years of the health issues facing her father and more recently her stepmother. Will described the role he hoped that Ruth would play in the future with both the investigation and the new foundation. The violence surrounding many of the stages of the investigation was left for later. Deliberately, Will wanted to bring her into her father's family as a committed participant. The threats and potential terrors that might bring could be left for a time when there would be enough time to discuss them fully without unduly scaring her.

Surprisingly to Will, Ruth did not ask about money or the kind or value of the assets. Perhaps she already had information that had given her some indication of what the issues were. He knew that one of his first tasks would be to measure her honesty and motivation for agreeing to be involved, and what terms and conditions she might have for it. That was his plan until they were walking to the elegant hooded entrance to the Edwardian neoclassical building that housed the clinic. As they stood briefly on the front step, Ruth turned to Will and said, "I am very wealthy in my own right, Mr MacIntosh. I don't need or want Dad's money. Don't worry about my reasons for being here. They are exactly what I told you over the telephone."

* * *

Sophie was dressed to impress and she had her hair done in a style that brought out her best features and which declared her fashionable taste. Isaac, on the other hand, was dressed in casual clothing, although recognizing that a jacket and matching trousers were necessary. The open-necked shirt was his declaration of independence.

The next two and a half hours flew by. Will's several attempts to leave were rebuffed by both Isaac and Sophie. It seemed to Will that he was there to silently provide support and help in the conversation if necessary. After the five-star formal tea staged for them by the clinic was finished and its remains were removed, both Isaac and Sophie began to show signs of fatigue. Will took the initiative to suggest that it was time for him and Ruth to leave for the flat.

On the way back to the flat Ruth expressed pleasure in meeting Sophie and in getting to know her father a little better. Will said that Isaac had thoroughly enjoyed the occasion and that he looked at her frequently with the same pride he demonstrated when he was with Little Isaac. Ruth was pleased with the introductory visit and happy that she and Will would meet at the office and storage facility the next day.

52

THE NEXT DAY, before leaving Fitzroy Square, Will conferred with Andy and discussed security plans for Ruth, and he was assured there would be two dedicated guards assigned to her round the clock, both women, one of whom was trained in anti-terrorist techniques.

On the way to the Canary Wharf location, Will explained that there was a current risk of attack by persons unknown and for reasons yet to be understood. He was pleased when he explained to Ruth that subtle disguises would be necessary from time to time.

"That's fine with me, Will" – the 'Mr' had disappeared – "I acted in several plays at Columbia University in my undergraduate days. Actually, I had one brief gig in one of the best plays of the season in Manhattan a couple of years ago. It's not my type of living. I played out my contract but that was it. However, I did learn the art of disguise which included change in body movement. It was fun for a while, but acting became mindless and tedious."

Will's assessment of his new collaborator grew with each conversation he had with her.

They arrived at the working research and storage facility at Canary Wharf, Docklands Rail Terminal. Will introduced her to Penelope and he asked Penelope to brief Ruth on the contents of the space, the material transported out of London, and the role Penelope and the research team wished to share with Ruth.

That gave time for Will to sit down in a separate soundproof room for a meeting with the security guard on duty who was to brief Will on the security issues that arose from the bombing.

The guard reported that the investigation on the bombing now included MI5 and MI6. "Both terrorism and criminal activities of a more conventional type are being investigated," he announced. He assured Will that he was continuing his private investigation with the help of Abraham and Mendel. One factor in the bombing that continued to intrigue the guard was why it appeared that the attackers demonstrated little interest in trying to find or take the few documents on the shelves.

Will brought Penelope and her team into the conference room and he asked Ruth and the senior security guards to join them.

"Alright, let's have your theories as to what the attackers were looking for. What was their objective before they tried to blow the place up?"

Penelope stated the response: "Your attackers could have several motives; the most obvious being to steal anything of monetary value – of value to them – that could be converted into money. As I consider the numerous attacks on Dr Menshive over the past four and a half years, it doesn't appear to be saleable stuff they want. Next, they could be angry with Dr Menshive for any number of reasons – perhaps because they think they have a superior claim to the trust assets or some of them. If that were the case I assume they would have attempted a kidnapping of Dr Menshive himself. The Smolensk situation, I think, was a local matter. Yes, attempts have been made on Dr Menshive's life, but they didn't succeed. Perhaps they were meant to scare rather than kill him. Among the many other motives, there is one that has occurred to me after examining the St Petersburg and Odessa documents. They contain highly sensitive and potentially damaging information that if it became known to the public would be embarrassing to Putin and his government, and I mean the agreements between Trotsky on behalf of Lenin and the new Soviet government and the Menshikovsky Bank and two other prominent Jewish-owned banks operating in Eastern Europe.

"This may have occurred to you, Mr MacIntosh: could there be two separate groups attacking Dr Menshive and his assets – one after the assets themselves and the other those after those agreements?"

There was a long pause while Jeanna took down detailed notes of Penelope's suggestions.

Will replied: "An extremely fine analysis, Penelope. Thank you. The first group you identify could be made up of persons who think they are more entitled than Isaac to have received the trust assets – that could be distant cousins or people like Anthony Cann who claim a family relationship. It could be a group made up of people who believe the assets were assembled during the Holocaust and so should be distributed among survivors or their families. And in relation to the second group you suggested, could it be Russian government agents who are after the documents with the objective of destroying them to reduce the bargaining advantage they give me?"

Abraham offered the comment: "It appears, sir, you have half of Europe after Dr Menshive or his assets. Can you really narrow this down to those actually challenging Dr Menshive?"

"The answer, Abraham, is obvious," said Will. "We have no choice but to find out and to identify and neutralize those who are pursuing Dr Menshive. Over the past month, we have moved forward in our understanding of the motives of our attackers much more than we had before."

Penelope asked, "Would it be a good idea to look for help from Putin's government in solving this problem?"

"The answer is no. I have worked cooperatively with very highly placed government officials in Russia and I have been given valuable assistance. The documents found in Odessa, particularly, added a new dimension that we have not recognized before: namely, the highly sensitive agreements from the early years of the Bolshevik Revolution in Russia. I am certain, Penelope, you will find similar documents from the Stalin years and perhaps into the Cold War years.

"The Russians will not want any of those documents made public – nor will they want them in their historical archives. The current government of Russia, if it is aware of these documents, and I bet they are, will want them destroyed as quickly as possible."

Ruth accompanied Will on the way back to Fitzroy Square, this time travelling by high-speed jet-boat with official-looking markings painted on the side. Those seated in the boat were shielded by opaque glass that was bulletproof. Will was impressed that Ruth was neither intimidated by what she had heard nor expressed a wish to exit the team immediately. Either reaction, he knew, would be reasonable.

When they arrived back at the apartment Will excused himself to go to his suite to check messages that came in during the day and to have some quiet time to reflect on what had occurred at Canary Wharf.

53

EARLY FALL IN London is usually the most inviting time of the year for visiting the numerous districts of the city – most of which are relatively self-contained villages. One of those districts that has a particularly well-defined and enduring identity is Chelsea.

The elegant housing reflects its earliest role as a suburban enclave of wealthy professionals, merchants and scions of the aristocracy – independently wealthy and able to lead a life of leisure. It served as a refuge from the frenetic clamour and noxious odours of the horse-dominated Victorian transportation system. Houses were designed and built around various squares as speculative projects which provided a consistency in style and scale that did much to establish character and refinement to the housing, but also a degree of anonymity, given the lack of individuality in most of the terraced facades. Closer to the river where land was more expensive, lots were subdivided for wealthy aristocrats and artists among others who built villas expressing an individualism that provided a varied interest in buildings. Those who were fortunate to have the means to build along the river had the sense and taste to ensure that the scale of their villas, while pointedly larger than the development houses, were complementary to the urban design of the district.

It was the special calm and quiet of Chelsea with its attractive streetscapes that led to the adaptation and interior reconstruction of three of the villas in the 1990s into the nursing home that housed Isaac and Sophie. The views of the river and the subtle scent of flowing fresh water from the Thames River enhanced the virtues of the Chelsea Clinic. The clinic provided an atmosphere most conducive to healing for those suffering from severe physical or mental problems.

The Chelsea Clinic proved to be the ideal choice given all its amenities.

For Will, visiting Chelsea was as much motivated by visiting Isaac and Sophie as it was in the pleasure he took from viewing the elegant architecture and the apparent sophistication of the ambiance of the streets and sidewalks which offered a place of solace from the busy pace of central London.

His visit at the clinic that afternoon was to brief Isaac on recent events at Canary Wharf and to prepare him for his departure from the clinic. Both Isaac and Sophie had progressed so well in their recovery that Dr MacKenzie and other specialists had informed them that they should prepare to move out into the real world and to accept the challenges of day-to-day life.

Subsequent to Ruth's arrival and her introduction to her father and stepmother, and after the adjustments to a renewal of family connections had successfully transpired, Will developed a strategy that would bring Isaac and Sophie closer to living on their own, outside the clinic.

Where would Isaac and Sophie move to as a residence after leaving the clinic? Will had recommended London, and in earlier conversations with the clinic, both Isaac and Sophie thought Chelsea would be where they would like to live permanently.

Over the past four years, Will had extolled the many features and virtues of London, eventually persuading Isaac that London should be the headquarters for the new foundation he planned to establish and for his permanent residence. These plans had been frequently discussed with Sophie before the terrors of Smolensk, St Petersburg and Moscow. She had been sent as a teenager to a music school located in Highgate, north London, for a couple of semesters. During her time in London, she fell in love with the exceptional cultural amenities and quality of life available to those whose bank accounts did not require annual, let alone daily, attention.

As Will and Isaac sat in a conference room at the clinic with the maps and guides spread out on the table, Will asked

Isaac whether he had any preferences for a district of London that would appeal to him.

"Yes, we would like a residential area that is more likely to be quiet and to have shops nearby where we can pick up daily supplies, perhaps here in Chelsea. Well, we won't be picking them up, but we will have people who will do that for us, I guess. Leafy districts with clear air and a reliable freshening breeze would be best. The property will be detached, as they say over here – a standalone house of a rather large size. It will need to be large because Sophie will want a boudoir on the floor near the master bedroom and on the ground floor a music room large enough for a grand piano. She is determined to continue piano lessons. I want my own den – I guess they call it a study over here – and a large library so the rest of the house would be of a scale that would accommodate rooms of that kind."

To which Will replied: "There are numerous districts like that, from Richmond upriver from Chelsea to Greenwich downriver opposite Canary Wharf. I think that you both would like to be close to private schools and easy access to the theatre district in central London."

Isaac's nod told Will he was on the right track. Will then identified several districts that would be considered to be part of central London, but he narrowed them down to three. All three districts Will and Isaac had discussed months before, but the experiences Sophie and he had had in the last six months gave an overriding requirement: "Security will be foremost in any district we choose," said Isaac.

"The security can be provided anywhere with enough guards. I suggest that security will be most reliable in a district where there will be many people with similar requirements to yours – where there will be lots of CCTV cameras and instant access to and service from the local constabulary. In my opinion, the three choices that fall into that category are Highgate or Hampstead, both in north London next door to each other, Dulwich or Wimbledon in south London, or Chelsea or Belgravia in central London, close to Westminster. Isaac. Of those districts I suggest you consider north London

– incidentally, that could include a district called Little Venice north of Regent's Park: this is interlaced with numerous canals formerly used for transport of goods from the north and west of England into the shipping districts along the Thames such as Canary Wharf. I would rule out Little Venice even though it is popular with aristocrats, movie stars and ultra-rich people, like you. The reason is that the properties are quite close to each other, 'cheek by jowl' as it were. Of all the locations, I think you should start looking in the Highgate/Hampstead areas."

"Why rule out Chelsea, Belgravia or Knightsbridge?" asked Isaac.

"None are family-oriented communities. You will want to be close to families with young children, excellent schools, health facilities and fresh air. Both Highgate and Hampstead are located at the top of a former Thames River escarpment, now an elevated setting with parks and villas of the separateness and size you would like, and which attempt to spread that park-like atmosphere to their individual landscapes. I repeat, the air is noticeably better up there. It is also easy from there to access anywhere in central London by road, tube or bus."

Further discussion led Isaac to accept Will's recommendation. Will added that a move to Hampstead or Highgate would likely be acceptable to Sophie given her happy semesters at the music school in that area.

Will left Isaac happily mulling over the maps and tourist information guides. He also had available to him an excellent computer with digital real estate listings that included the districts Will had recommended. Early that afternoon Isaac brought Sophie to the conference room to look at the maps and computer images of potential properties. He was reminded of her continuing mental disorientation and confusion when she admitted that she couldn't understand either the maps or the computer – and this, he thought, was a woman who was proficient in the use of computers and had loved to navigate with maps as they had taken excursions through New England many months before.

54

THE NEXT DAY, Will returned to the clinic and met with Dr MacKenzie who expressed amazement at how much better Isaac appeared to be. "All he can talk about is the house search. He is demonstrating great enthusiasm for the project and actually has Sophie interested, although somewhat confused. I think that will pass when she is taken to see the final selection," he offered. Then, as an afterthought: "I think you should take Little Isaac with you. His boundless joy in every novelty will capture Sophie's attention and help her make up her mind in any final decisions. This is a remarkable healing experience for them both. It helps, Will, that middle-class worries about the source and quantity of money and how it dictates the choice of location and style of house are not an issue. These two have sufficient money to buy whatever appeals to them. That removes the stress and anxiety most people feel while house-hunting."

"Yes. Shopping for a house in London is a daunting task. Isaac has no budgetary restrictions, but there are requirements that must be met – the two most obvious are privacy and security."

Having received Dr MacKenzie's blessing for the project, Will joined Isaac and Sophie in the conference room. Both were intently staring at the computer images. They pointed out the properties that appealed to each of them. It was curious that those they selected were characterized by being cozy, intimate and spatially impractical in terms of their collective requirements.

Will suggested that they look at a wider range of properties. When he showed images of the villas that he knew would meet their needs, Sophie angrily announced that she could read the prices and knew what they would cost in US dollars. "We can't afford these, Will! Don't tempt Isaac to spend more than we can afford. They may be what you would like in your fantasies, but we have to be realistic."

Before Will could turn to Isaac for help, Isaac had put his hand on Sophie's, gave it a gentle squeeze and quietly told her reassuringly that both he and Will knew what the financial limits were and that she was to leave that to them.

Somewhat mollified, Sophie said, "Alright. If you get carried away, Isaac, I know Daddy will help me with the money we will require. I will never understand, Isaac, why you have to pretend you are as rich as Daddy. Don't compete with him. It will upset him, Isaac."

Will suggested a solution. Three possibilities should be selected and each visited. To make sure they were located where they needed to be and whether they were in their price range, he thought he and Isaac should visit them first and if found to be acceptable, then Sophie and Little Isaac would come along for the next tour of inspection.

Sophie thought that was a good idea, but added: "Yes, and Daddy will see them before a final decision is made. I know he will have to finance it, so Isaac, you must be sensible. Small and on a quiet street will do."

* * *

A tour of Dulwich, which housed the first English purpose-built public art gallery and had exceptional schools set among landscaped properties, was attractive, but on reflection, Isaac decided he did not want to be on the south side of the river where he knew he would feel isolated and cut off from the vibrancy of the city.

Will moved on to the villa-clustered, very high-end district of Belgravia. They walked the area for an hour. It was apparent to Isaac that it had become more of an apartment and embassy area than a living community with family-oriented amenities, as Will had suggested earlier. A drive through Knightsbridge and Kensington left Isaac equally cold.

As they drove up Parliament Hill into the Hampstead area

the sun came out, the drizzle had stopped and a gentle breeze gave a freshened air to the district at the crest of the hill.

"Alright, Will, I see a large pub here at the top of the hill. The parkland below us is open so we can see St Paul's Cathedral and as far as Canary Wharf. So far, so good. The atmosphere here is good."

They parked the car opposite the pub and walked the myriad of twisting streets undulating with the hilly terrain. Will pointed out several substantial villas that were obscured by landscaping, mature trees and fencing. Many had gates operated by electronic remote control. "This is where I think you should concentrate your search, Isaac. Privacy and security are as important as the style and layout of the house. You will have it all here. It has the added benefits of some of London's best private schools, an efficient fire and police department and an active community of engaged residents determined to preserve the special qualities of this area. There is a community here. Some of the most famous and rich inhabitants of planet earth live here. Whether you ever meet any of them is unimportant. You will know, however, that they will be as protective of their neighbours' properties as their own; that is an effective way of protecting themselves."

"Will, how much do these properties cost?" asked Isaac, reverting to a pre-trust mindset.

"Get a grip, Isaac. You know damn well you could buy half of Hampstead in cash without batting an eye. Money is not the determinant here. Safety and security are... where Sophie and Little Isaac will be safest and have a garden with privacy – perhaps even a swimming pool to enjoy."

"I guess you are right. As Sophie says, if we go over my budget, her father will chip in."

Isaac's persistence on that topic proved to Will that Isaac was not fully back into the real world he had inhabited before Smolensk and Moscow. It reminded him that Isaac was vulnerable to reversion to his PTSD.

"Right, Mr and Mrs Posen will help in a pinch, I'm sure. They, too, will consider Sophie and Little Isaac's safety as paramount to any other consideration," was Will's resigned answer.

Real estate properties in this district, with prices high enough to pay off the debt of small countries, were not posted at street level as they would be in middle class neighbourhoods.

Before they joined Abraham at the pub, they did their duty to the pub by visiting it, sitting on its outside terrace overlooking the view over Parliament Hill down to the city and beyond. As Isaac mellowed with his first beers in several months, he announced rather more forcefully than necessary that this would be his 'local' and he would live nearby. Will was amazed at how quickly Isaac had picked up some of the London expressions, a clear indication he was literally buying into the project.

After Abraham picked them up in the Jaguar he dropped them off at the clinic. On the way into the clinic, Isaac announced that his days in captivity would end as soon as he could acquire a house in Hampstead… "No, Will, I know, not a house, a villa. I've got to get it all straight. I am going to call my father-in-law right away and find out whether he can help with the purchase."

* * *

When Will got back to Fitzrovia, he called Mr Posen and explained that Isaac would be approaching him for a loan to purchase a house in Hampstead. "Mr Posen, I don't know whether you understand the scale and nature of Isaac's wealth, but let me tell you, absolutely no contribution from you or anyone else will be necessary. However, if he or Sophie asks whether you can help, I suggest you agree. I assure you, you will not have to part with an American dollar or English pound." Will was comforted by Mr Posen's laughter at the other end of the line. It told him Mr Posen had a realistic idea of his son-in-law's fortunate circumstances.

55

DR CHARTERHOUSE, THE RECENTLY hired psychologist, a specialist in post-traumatic stress disorder treatment, and Dr Walter MacKenzie, the Menshives' loyal and patient physician, were astonished at how quickly both Sophie and Isaac appeared to re-enter the world after Will's suggestion of purchasing a house had been made to them. The doctors cautioned Will and Ruth that Isaac and Sophie might be re-engaging in the present, but they suspected that there were substantial periods in their lives for which there would be amnesia – periods that would re-emerge from their traumas that could cause regression of their symptoms. "Certainly take them on this exciting path of acquiring a new home. See how far that will take them. But do not assume they are consciously back in full command of their whole lives, background and history. There are and likely always will be trouble spots," was Dr MacKenzie's admonition to Will, as he waited for Sophie and Isaac to join them. Dr Charterhouse nodded his agreement.

Sophie arrived in the clinic's reception room preparing for the excursion to Hampstead to house-hunt. She was glowing with happiness, not less so for having Little Isaac in hand. "Will, you said the viewing this morning should just be Isaac and you. When I told Little Isaac about your sightseeing adventure today, he was insistent on us coming. Yes, I want us to come, too. He will add a lot of joy and spontaneity to the outing." Will did not confess to his having orchestrated Little Isaac's addition to the party.

Isaac arrived equally relaxed and if men can be referred to as radiant, he was.

Will commented quietly to Isaac while Sophie was fussing over Little Isaac, "I think I know the source of your good cheer this morning, old chum. According to Mendel, who sits in the corridor outside your rooms, you and Sophie had the bedstead in her room rocking last night. I hope you will have the strength to last the day viewing the properties."

"Yes, Will, you're right as usual. Several times. Made up for lost time. Several cutaneous layers of my dick have been worn off – can hardly pee this morning. Watch Sophie, she may be unsteady on the pins. How could I have been away from what I do best for so long?"

"Great. You are getting back to the Isaac I have come to know well over the last five years. Enjoy. Be yourself, but not with the variety of partners you were accustomed to. You don't need that stress in your marriage or turmoil in what remains of your emotions. I hope, though, that you can get through the day before bedding her again."

"*Oy*, you pious Presbyterian – I have watched you and that lawyer girl you had with you in Odessa. You would be telling me a lie if you said you didn't sleep with her. I see it on her face as much as yours. The truth…!"

"OK, perhaps, but we have other fish to fry today. Let's go!"

"Will, I'm glad there is a man under that dour and rigid manner. I will get you into the groove yet."

With a grunt from Will, Abraham led them out to the vehicle he was going to use for the day. Isaac took one look at it and exclaimed in shock, "What the hell, Abraham! What's this? Where is my Jaguar with all its fittings and polish? What I see is a bloody Hyundai Santa Fe SUV. Good vehicle for you, Abraham, in your spare time, but not for me. What's up?"

Before Abraham could reply, Sophie commented, "Looks good to me. Big enough for all of us and high up enough for us to see over fences and hedges."

Will added: "My instructions exactly, Isaac. Today you are travelling as incognito as possible. You know you have been pursued by hostile people in the past. We know there are similar people even here in London. For your safety and that of your family, we will travel as anonymously as possible. In fact, you will notice that Sophie is in a raven-black wig hiding her natural colour and wearing clothing that is both elegant and obscuring her appearance. Before we get to the first house you, too, will be camouflaged. You will wear a wig – yes, you will or we don't leave here – and an oversized padded Burberry all-weather coat and silk scarf.

"Another thing. The houses we will view, as far as the realtor is concerned, are not being bought by you or Sophie; they are being viewed as a residence for me as a CEO of a Canadian IT company establishing a headquarters in London," announced Will as part of the security strategy for the day. "Sophie is my half-sister and you are her peculiar husband. Leave the questions and any negotiations to me. Yes, enjoy yourselves but save your comments until we are safely out of each house. My story is that my sister and her husband insisted on coming when they heard about my interest in a London base. Sophie in this theatrical outfit is a New England decorator who wants to visit upscale London homes. We don't have time for further explanations now," said Will.

"You are always scheming and strategizing, William. You will tell me what this subterfuge is all about when we get back to the apartment later this afternoon – incidentally, this will be my first visit to the Fitzrovia apartment. I look forward to it."

The first appointment was at 2:30 that afternoon in Highgate. The Santa Fe left the clinic as Will intended at 10:30 in the morning. This gave them time to drive through some of the neighbourhoods Will suggested as possibilities. They drove along the Grosvenor Road bordering the Thames until they got to Pimlico, a highly popular, expensive, upper middle class neighbourhood. Abraham turned into St George's Square and as he did so, Will had him pull over into a parking spot so he could show Sophie and Isaac a Regency row house of seven stories, identical to each of the other houses in the row. Will explained that the price was exceptionally high as it was one of the few Cubit-designed houses in the row that had not been subdivided and was on offer as a single-family residence. Before Will could add any further information, Sophie quickly said, "Not interested. There is nothing particular or stylish about the place. And no yard for Little Isaac. Let's move on."

Without directions being given verbally by Will to Abraham, the route had been preplanned and required nothing more than directions as to how long each stop would be. Will knew none of the properties viewed from the street would interest either Isaac or Sophie, so the planning worked well.

From Pimlico, they drove north into Belgravia, visiting Eaton Square and its precincts. "This is just like St George's Square, but grander. There is nothing homey about these places. They may be palaces inside, but I want something that says me and my family on the outside," said Sophie. South Kensington didn't appeal to either Sophie or Isaac, for the same reasons. Will sat back, satisfied that his plan continued to work well.

They then moved further north to Primrose Hill where separate villas from the 1840s stood on dignified but minute lots cheek-by-jowl with their neighbours, many of which had been converted into boutique hotels or fashionable flats. This district, as fashionable as it was for Londoners, missed the mark by a mile with these property seekers.

Further north and within the time allotted, Abraham and his Santa Fe entered the Highgate and Hampstead area. Abraham drove slowly past the pub Isaac had decided was to be his 'local' and as soon as Isaac noticed it he shouted, "We're in the right district up here. Drive over to the top of Parliament Hill. Sophie, take Little Isaac – we are going to take a walk along the top of the park here. Look at St Paul's Cathedral way down there. You can even see downriver to a bit of Canary Wharf. Feel and taste the air up here. It's much better than down at the clinic or in central London… and it's better for Little Isaac up here."

"Oh, yes," said Sophie, "I see that. How about schools and shopping?" Will was prepared for these questions and brought out local promotional brochures listing all the amenities of the district. "I agree with Isaac. This is the district of London

I must be in. Can we find a house up here? I guess they would be cheaper because they are so far from central London."

Will replied with: "Let's not worry about money yet. I think it is much more important that you find a house you really like. Then when we identify what it is about that house you like, we will try to find something in a price range you can afford."

Sophie agreed. It was the rule of thumb her father expressed for shoes, art, Florida seasonal properties and exotic travel destinations. She sat back with a beatific expression, satisfied she was following her adored father's precepts. Isaac just smirked and kept his mouth shut, pleased that Will had planned this excursion so well.

Two properties in Hampstead were viewed. Both were mid-nineteenth century and to Sophie's taste very old fashioned, dark and, as she put it, not 'homey'.

They drove back to the pub for tea, sitting out on the terrace as Isaac and Will had done a couple of days before. They got there in time to get a nice table overlooking the park and the expansive view beyond. The tables around them filled quickly. Sophie expressed surprise at how late people seemed to have their lunch in London, not understanding yet the English tradition of tea in the late afternoon, often with little for lunch. Even more surprising were the substantial quantities of wine both the male and the female guests consumed. "Can they all be on holiday or retired, Will?"

"No, Sophie. The workday for many people starts later in the morning, often at ten because of the distances people must travel, and they work until seven-thirty or eight in the evening. So meals are later and I guess they need fortification to get them through the rest of the day. Something else: in London, very few people entertain in their homes. They meet in restaurants or gastro pubs like this one to meet friends and business associates."

Sophie's work ethic-centred upbringing induced the obvious comment: "Well, I don't see how fit they would be for work in the afternoon when they consume a bottle or two of wine for lunch. I noticed the two tables next to us, each with beautifully dressed, elegant, middle-aged men and women who consumed two bottles at their tables. Isaac, you must not adopt these habits. I won't have it. Daddy would be horrified. I think he would speak to you about it."

Isaac remained mute, much to Will's liking. The day was unfolding even better than he thought.

"Alright, we have viewed several properties in central London, none of which suited you. We have visited two large properties in the historic area of Hampstead but they didn't meet your requirements. I have only one left for today. It may not be suitable, but I want you to see it. It is quite new and located in a nearby subdivision called 'Hampstead Garden Suburb'. It overlooks a golf course and is very close to Parliament Hill and this pub – walking distance, at least. So let's have a look at something newer."

Abraham drove them through some of the main thoroughfares of Hampstead and Highgate, showing them the least attractive areas of the district. On time, the clock on the dashboard of the SUV showing 5:30 p.m., Abraham stopped in front of the house to be visited.

Isaac took Sophie in one hand and Little Isaac in the other and walked to the entrance of the driveway to the house. They faced a new, exceptionally large, ultra-stylish neoclassical mansion, referred to as a 'villa' in London. The four-story building was dominated by an open porch sheltering the front door supported by Tuscan Doric columns. Like the rest of the design, there was nothing small or cramped. The several stairs that led up to the front door were as wide as the porch, which took up half the width of the house. The two windows on the main level on each side of the porch were a modern interpretation of the Regency style and were exceptionally tall, which anticipated the lofty ceilings that would be found within. The second level, which the English strangely call the first floor, had four windows: two on each side above the windows below, contained in projecting pavilions on each side of the porch, and three beautifully scaled windows, called Palladian windows, above the porch. Dormer windows in the roof indicated extensive living space at that level as well. The house was on an elevated foundation into which small windows were inset below the principal windows above. Will pointed out this part of the house to Sophie and explained that this basement area in London was called the lower ground floor and that it was also fully developed.

"Look, besides the steps up to the porch, slightly sunk below the level of the driveway, there is a garage door that must lead into internal parking."

"Good. I wondered what I would do with my car."

Sophie's immediate reaction was, "Gorgeous! Will, you should not have taken us here. You know we couldn't afford this even with Daddy's help. You are cruel. I love it, but we shouldn't go in."

She started weeping, trying to hide her disappointment from Little Isaac who was bouncing up and down and pointing to the wide lawns inviting him to play and the pebbledash concrete driveway also inviting him in to ride his new bike with safety.

Isaac took Sophie by the hand and walked her closer to the front entrance. Will held Little Isaac and Abraham back, while Isaac and Sophie had their discussion.

"Sophie, Will has told me how much this house costs. You have probably guessed this is the one he thought we would like. OK, money. Listen, love, money is not a problem. I have some money from all that Russian art I sold in New York a few years ago. We don't need your father's help. I can pay for it in cash. No debt. Now, I want you to come through the house with me and tell me if you like it. Remember, you do not think of money. Will and I have carefully looked at my financial records. We can afford it."

"Oh, Isaac! How much is it?"

"Remember it is being sold in English pounds sterling. I would have to convert it into American money and I don't know what the exchange rate is. Remember, we have been out of contact with the business and banking world for months. Will has made the calculations and assures me it's alright. Actually, I discussed this with your father yesterday and told him the price. He and your mother drove by and they love it and see nothing wrong with the price."

The tour of inspection took place. Each of those viewing the property remembered the planned ruse – that it was Will who was the purchaser in the discussions with the realtor. Sophie, in particular, showed considerable business-like restraint in her response to the house as she pointed out its features to Will.

* * *

The apartment – or maisonette, as London realtors would refer to it – located on Fitzroy Square was as elegant as it was when originally constructed. It was designed by Robert Adam who applied his neoclassical architectural suburban design concepts and interior decorative elements to the property. To Sophie and Isaac, it was small, cramped and hopelessly old-fashioned. After the visit to Hampstead, they toured the apartment with Anna and Little Isaac, both of whom had come to love the place and because of their expressed affection for it, they were reserved in their negative comments. But, it confirmed Isaac's and Sophie's decision for the Hampstead villa, having the maisonette as a comparison.

Dinner was arranged to be brought in and served by a professional catering firm Anna had used on several occasions, to celebrate Ruth's arrival. During their pre-dinner rendezvous in the sitting room, each enjoying a gin and tonic, Anna gave Sophie and Ruth a more detailed description of Little Isaac's amazing accomplishments over the period Sophie was in the clinic; more than Sophie was able to absorb in the past. Many questions were asked and answered; all of which confirmed Anna's opinion. Mrs Ellis the nanny was brought in and joined them for coffee and dessert, a time for further interrogation from both Sophie and Isaac.

When the topic of Little Isaac had expired and he was showing a need for sleep, Mrs Ellis took him off to his room.

It was about this time that Ruth joined them. She had been sharing dinner with a school friend from the States who had been on the same flight from New York at The Ivy in Charing Cross, one of the more fashionable restaurants in London. While she had visited Sophie and Isaac in the clinic since her arrival, this was the first meeting she had with them in their reinvigorated and somewhat restored state.

Ruth was eager to hear how the house search had gone. Isaac led the reply by describing its size and rooms, as he gave his assessment of the house: "It has a movie theatre room and a swimming pool. Huge. It overlooks Highgate Golf Course so it is quiet with lots of greenery around it. A huge backyard with amazing landscaping lit at night to dramatically highlight the features. It has 17,000 square feet and is spread out over four floors. Inside underground parking for two or three vehicles. Eight bedrooms, most if not all with private bathrooms. It has staff living quarters for a cook and a maid who could double as a server at meals. There is also a detached security office which we need, as you know. The house was built within the last two years and it has been beautifully maintained. I think the current owners are Russians who occupied it only sporadically. I don't know why they are selling but I will have a thorough security inspection. It will be cleared of any recording or listening devices and of hidden cameras. Now, Sophie, would you like to answer Ruth's question?"

"Everything Isaac has said is correct. I don't like the colours or furnishings, though. Ruth, your father has assured me there will be enough money to pay for it in cash and to refurbish and to change a few decorative features. Yes, Ruth dear, I love it. Little Isaac loved it as soon as he saw the lawns and when we showed him the pool and theatre room we had trouble getting him to leave. I'm worried about the money, but Isaac tells me that is OK. If it is, I want it… I will check with Daddy first. He will tell me if we can afford it. He may have to give us some money, though."

Isaac's impatient response was, "I have told you I can pay for it in cash and even for the new things you want for the redecoration including new furniture. The interior was glitzy and vulgar, but that is easily changed. Everything else about

LONDON

the place is perfect, including the security arrangements we must have."

The discussion moved on at the suggestion of Sophie as to who would live there. She turned to Anna and asked her to move into the new house, "After all, Anna, you and Little Isaac have bonded well. He relies on you. I know Isaac and I will travel some so it is important that Little Isaac have continuity and stability. There will be room at the top of the house for Mrs Ellis if she agrees to continue with us. Part of the attic area will have to be walled off for our security guard. We will have twenty-four-seven security. The detached security office will be perfect, but we should have sleeping arrangements for the security man if it is needed."

Anna's blush seemed to confirm the necessity of that arrangement. Ruth looked at her with interest, telling herself that she would have to find out just who was of particular interest to Aunt Anna.

Isaac looked at Ruth with affection, thanking her again for joining the family and he asked her whether she would like to live with them. He confirmed that she would be an integral part of the family unit, and as part of Will's team on the investigation and management of the assets. Ruth's reply was simply to agree that was her plan and that Will had spent a lot of time briefing her on everything that had transpired so far and what his plans were for the future. Ruth thanked Sophie for the offer but she said she would find a place of her own. She was accustomed to living alone and wanted to continue to do so.

Sophie said she would consider Ruth more as a younger sister and friend than as a stepdaughter. "Ugh, what an awful connection that would be," she said. "Cinderella!"

Ruth observed to Sophie: "I want a place right in the heart of the London scene. Perhaps the apartment will do. The flat is decorated in a historicist style with period furniture. This is me. I love it here. So, if it is okay with you and Isaac, I think I would like to stay here."

"Of course you may, Ruthie," was her father's reply. "You can make whatever changes you would like to suit yourself.

You should know that the building is one of my holdings. You will have a demanding landlord, though, as Will handles the real estate for me and I don't interfere. Oh! Remember, Will is living there, too."

"Oh, if Will is my landlord I will have no trouble with him. I'll try not to be too demanding – I commit to trying to get along."

Will, who was present but had not contributed to the conversation up until then, simply said that if there should be a battle of wills, he expected to lose.

"That is all well and good, Will, but will you stay here, too? Ruth says she doesn't mind sharing the apartment in Fitzrovia with you. There are over 3,500 square feet of living space. I assume there is enough room for you and Ruth to share but that is up to the two of you," said Isaac, genuinely concerned for the welfare of his friend.

"I would like to stay here for the time being, if that's alright with Ruth," said Will. To which Ruth replied, "Oh, yes. No doubt I, too, will need his guardianship."

* * *

Isaac needed a private meeting with Will before he and Sophie returned to the clinic. They rose, leaving the others in the sitting room chatting merrily, but before they were out of the room Isaac asked Ruth to join them. "You are now part of Will's team. He says he wants an immediate member of our family to be part of the investigation and decisions he will be required to make," said Isaac, to which Will responded, "Yes, Ruthie, I would like you to join us." While this was simply confirmation of why she was in London, the request was a courtesy. She confirmed her acceptance of his request, clearly happy to do so.

They went back into the dining room which by now had been thoroughly cleared and polished and was ready for the next round of use by the occupants.

"Okay. Now, Will, I want to know what all those disguises and camouflaging was about that we had to endure during our house-hunt. I don't doubt they were necessary but I need to know."

"During my tours of Russia and Ukraine," Will said, "our teams learned much about the methods and people who had acquired the assets. The disguises today were to continue your protection and since I think you may need it as much in London as you did in Russia, I am going to give you the 'Shorter Catechism' version reply of what we have learned so far during our investigation."

"Ever the Presbyterian, Ruth. Get used to it," was Isaac's resigned response.

"No problem. That was my church in Washington. I was happy to be associated with it and I plan a similar affiliation here. Go with your Catechism, Will."

"First. Many of the assets were acquired between 1812 and 1912 primarily during periods of military, political or social turmoil.

"Second. The assets, both the real estate and the artifacts like the art and Scythian gold, were acquired primarily as a hedge against confiscation of your family's money.

"Third. The money and other assets were held by a bank in trust for your family. If the assets had been held publicly in your family's name, they would have been subject to confiscation by anti-Semitic pogroms in Russia, of which there were many, or by the Imperial government in St Petersburg and later the Communist era governments in the Soviet Union.

"Fourth. This is the very clever part – the assets were all acquired in the names of companies or trusts, the owners of which were Russian non-Jews, all of whom acted as agents for the Menshikovsky family.

"Fifth. All frontmen negotiating acquisitions held out that they were representing what appeared to be non-Jewish interests.

"Sixth. The Günzburg and Mendelssohn connections arose in the third quarter of the nineteenth century. Money was given in good faith and for what we as lawyers call 'valuable consideration' by the Günzburg and Mendelssohn banks to your family's bank, transferred for reasons we have yet to discover. It resulted in a vast fortune being assembled and held legitimately by your bank.

"Seventh. And this leads to my strategy today – the assets were assembled discreetly and held in plain sight by a complex structure of companies and trusts, the parent of which is domiciled in Canada."

"You mentioned Trotsky earlier as somehow being connected with the acquisition of the assets. Trotsky! How on earth could Trotsky have been involved?" sputtered Ruth in amazement.

"Later, not now," said Will firmly, before continuing with his list.

"Eighth. The network of holdings companies and trusts defeated the curious; you will recall that the fundamental owner is a trust established in my home province of Prince Edward Island. It in turn has trusts established in Switzerland which has subsets in London, Berlin, Warsaw and Russia. Newer trusts, established for tax-saving purposes, in turn own companies incorporated in the Channel Islands to hold assets located in the British Isles where public disclosure of the identity of the shareholders is limited and easily obscured.

"Ninth. And for our purposes at the moment, the last of the various devices for owning the assets were strategically placed for political and economic stability – and the Swiss trust, which was at first assumed incorrectly to be the master trust (that's the Prince Edward Island trust), secured the assets with the expectation that they would be paid out and distributed to a family member only at a time and to a person who could securely receive them without jeopardizing the assets. For example, Ruth, if you look at what your father owns in his name, it is very, very, little – a nice holiday in Spain would spend the cash."

"What! After all this time and trouble and killings, Dad really doesn't own the assets worth billions?" asked an ashen-faced Ruth.

"He has the sole beneficial interest in everything. So, his ownership is somewhat indirect to protect the assets, but ultimately the only person who can access them and can convert them into cash, as it were, is your father. Yes, he can easily liquidate some or all of the assets and convert them into billions in assets – but he won't do it. He could destabilize the economy of several Central and Eastern European countries if he were to do so. He therefore has substantial clout for what he may choose to do with the assets. For example, the mixed assets result in the Scythian gold being an effective trade-off for real estate, art or some other asset. It is a brilliant scheme," said Will, gradually running out of steam.

Isaac, who was a party to this monologue, responded with, "*Oy*, you have been a busy Canadian beaver while I was whiling away my time in a coma."

"Back to how this affects your interests here and now, Isaac. This explanation, as detailed as it is," said Will, "is necessary to brief Ruth adequately. You remain as vulnerable to attackers as you have been in the past, especially if your personal ownership were to be discovered. We will discuss those another time. However, I recommend we apply the brilliant strategy employed by your ancestors as we move forward. You and Sophie want that house. It will not be bought in your name. It will be bought by a trust also established in Prince Edward Island which names you and Sophie as the *cestui que* trusts… kind of like the sole beneficiaries entitled to possession. I will be the trustee, with Ruthie as a successor trustee to act if I die or go gaga, which you are likely to drive me to. So, in the meantime, I will hold myself out as the interested party in the purchase of the house… ostensibly for the IT company which I will create here. The IT company will be owned 100% by your Prince Edward Island trust."

"Will, you lawyers are as devious as those Russian oligarchs we have been fighting."

"Perhaps, in some sense, but we do so within the strictness and strictures of the law. Will we carry on with my strategy, or do you wish to come up with one of your own? A gentle reminder that anti-Semitism is resurfacing throughout the world. My scheme should limit risk to you and your family if it is discovered that you and Sophie are Jewish – the truth is that you will simply be tenants answerable to me."

"God help us, Ruth," replied Isaac. "Do you see how this Canadian lawyer has taken control of my family? You will have to protect us, Ruth!"

To which Ruth quickly replied: "You have very little risk, Dad."

56

WILL RECOMMENDED THAT Isaac and Sophie give some further thought to the house in Hampstead Garden Suburb which they had viewed and fallen in love with. As a lawyer with an extensive practice in real estate back on Prince Edward Island, Will knew impetuosity in purchasing property invariably ended in disaster.

Sufficient time had passed for a renewed visit to the house. They met the realtor there who was representing their interests. He confirmed that he had followed Will's instructions to play around the edges with the listing agent asking for inconsequential information but by doing so keeping Isaac and Sophie's interest active as far as the vendor was concerned.

As they approached the front door Will quietly reminded Isaac and Sophie that they were only along for the ride, the purchaser being a company represented by Will. They understood and agreed, particularly when Will reassured them that if they had any questions or wished to view any specific part of the property in detail that Will was not paying attention to, the notes both Isaac and Sophie were taking as they were touring the house would remind Will to deal later with the matters raised in the notes.

The viewing party was joined by a professional quantity surveyor and an interior decorator of considerable fame from Pimlico Street in west London. When Will informed Isaac that he had brought along a quantity surveyor, Isaac looked baffled and asked whether the boundaries of the property were uncertain or in dispute. Will informed him the surveyor he brought was not one who prepared survey plans: he was an experienced and highly qualified 'quantity' surveyor. "That is," Will said, "a chartered surveyor who examines the structural integrity, materials quality and potential weaknesses in the structure of the buildings."

Isaac expressed his satisfaction that the property was receiving professional scrutiny. Sophie was thrilled to have with her a woman she introduced as her decorator, Ms Campbell, with her to answer questions on everything from the flooring, fabrics in the curtains and paint colours. Notes were taken by Sophie and Ms Campbell; Sophie said that they would share these later when deciding what renovations and redecorations would be made to the house.

Three hours after they had started the inspection, Sophie and Isaac announced that they had an important matter to discuss and that they would go out into the backyard to do so, apologizing for disrupting the tour of the house. Will replied by turning to the two realtors and saying that he would continue his inquiries and examination of the property, which he did, ending a short time later with a suggestion that the realtors join him in the dining room

"It's time for a chat about money and terms," Will said.

"Don't you want your friends with you, Mr MacIntosh?" said the owner's listing agent, clearly suspicious that the real purchasers were Isaac and Sophie.

"No, of course not. They have an issue with one of their children in a school-related matter. No, they would not be part of this discussion in any event. They have been somewhat helpful to me for their opinions but they are not necessary at this point."

Will went on to state more as a confirmation than as a disclosure that if the house were purchased it would be for his occupation as CEO of a Canadian IT company setting up an office in London.

Money was the primary topic. The listing price was repeated by the owner's listing agent, and the secondary conditions the owners required were also raised and discussed.

Will listened to the two realtors bargain and argue for half an hour. This was the strategy agreed to before the house inspection began. Will required the information that would be gleaned from the babble between the realtors to discover the core elements required to enable him to put the deal together.

"It is clear that the owners require a quick turnaround," said Will, preparing for a counteroffer on the list price. "It is also clear that there are several others viewing the property. My company is interested in making an offer but will not have me wasting my time on negotiations or lengthened by a process that would expose an offer I might make to gazumping – this bizarre procedure over here in England that can enable a valid offer and acceptance to be superseded by a later higher offer.

"I understand your list price. It is simply an asking price. In my opinion, it is ten percent above fair market value given the values of other houses in this area of equal quality and size that have sold here. However, to get this house search over, I am authorized to offer the list price plus a premium of five percent on condition that no counter offers will be entertained or accepted. In addition – and this is highly important in terms of the instructions from my board – in order to ensure that I am back to work immediately, the sale must take place within seven days. To lock in our offer and your client's acceptance we will make a deposit of 25 percent of the purchase price which will be held in trust by my company's solicitors here in London. This will be a cash deal. No financing is required. Our inspection is complete. While there are issues my quantity surveyor has identified, we accept the property as is, where is."

The listing agent was surprised at the generous level of the increase in the list price and stated that he would consult the owners.

"Make it clear to your clients that this is our one and only offer. This is not the start of the process. This is the end, or I walk. I have anticipated that the owners may try to improve my offer through continued negotiation. That will not happen. There is another house in this area privately listed that could be satisfactory. If my offer is not accepted, I will meet as scheduled with the listing agent there at 3 o'clock tomorrow afternoon. I require the owner's answer this evening – by 7 p.m."

It was agreed that if the owners could be reached for a decision the listing agent would have their decision by that time.

"When I made arrangements for this tour of inspection I instructed my realtor to inform you that if we made an offer, the owners would have to be available to make a decision on the offer. If they are not available to give me a decision by the time specified, my interest is over and I will move on up the street where I know the owners are eagerly waiting for my arrival. In fact, I might go along to that property while we are in the neighbourhood and kill time until the decision comes in."

"Sir, I don't think that will be necessary," said the listing agent.

Will overheard a brief conversation between the realtors on his way out in which the listing agent said to Will's agent, "Christ, is that the way things are done in America? He is a pushy bastard." And his realtor's reply: "I don't know anything about real estate practices in America, but I will say that this gentleman means what he says. You've got a fabulous deal here; I hope the owners are wise enough to accept the price and the terms."

* * *

Will, with his party including Isaac and Sophie, stood at the elegant double-doored front entrance under the neo-Baroque swan-necked pediment at the specified time.

The door was opened by the listing agent who showed Will and his realtor into the dining room, trying to cut off Isaac and Sophie. Will put a quick stop to that. "This couple," he said, "has an interest in what I purchase because they will be short-term tenants of the house. I can't take personal possession until I conclude my lease on a flat in Fitzrovia. Alright, what is your client's answer to my offer?"

"Is there any possibility of an improvement? There are other potential offers expected this afternoon."

"My offer and my conditions were clear. I will not waste my time further," said Will, as he stood, directing his realtor to also stand in preparation for leaving.

"Stop. Please. Alright, I do have instructions from the

owners. I am instructed to accept your offer as long as the deposit is paid before 5 p.m. tomorrow with proof of payment from your lawyer that it is in his firm's trust account. But they have a request. This is a very large house with six occupants: the owners and their two children, a cook and chauffeur who doubles as a gardener. They need some time to move out. Could they remain in the house as tenants for three weeks after the closing? Could you check with your board? They need an answer immediately before they will sign."

"My decision is final. I will grant them the three weeks as over-holding tenants, but they will be required to sign a fixed-term tenancy agreement that will specify that I or agents or representatives of mine can view the house on one hour's notice between 9 a.m. and 6 p.m. at any time between the signing of the sale/purchase agreement and the date fixed for vacant possession. That condition must be accepted by the owners as part of the agreement."

"Thank you. Yes, I had hoped you would agree on terms like that. I have the owner's instructions to accept your terms," replied a relieved listing agent, now the selling agent. "I will have the agreement drafted by our lawyers and will have it ready for you to sign at 9 p.m. this evening."

"Not until my lawyers have had time to review and comment on it," announced Will. "Your offer to draft the agreement is not necessary. You have noticed that I have an extra person with me this afternoon. She and the lady who has been viewing the property with me have apparently been inspecting the decorative elements. She is actually a lawyer in my company's London firm of solicitors. The notes she was taking were related to the offer and the final terms of agreement. She will prepare the sale/purchase agreement. It will be available for execution by the owners at 9 p.m. as I said. It can be signed either here or at our lawyer's office; your choice," said Will somewhat firmly.

"Oh. That is highly unusual here."

"Perhaps. Consider the terms of the deal and the exceptional expense my company is accepting; there will be no room left for exit or uncertainty. Either you accept my lawyer's agreement or I walk. So, where will we sign? Here or at a lawyer's office?"

"Could we have a draft of the agreement to review before 7:30 p.m.?"

"Of course. I am informed by my legal counsel that it can be ready before seven this evening. Give me the information on the contract for your lawyers. We will have our lawyers get it electronically to your lawyers by 5:45 this afternoon."

Before the listing agent could get the words out, Will added, "Proof of the deposit having been made to your firm's trust account will be included with the sales/purchase contract. A word of caution: unless there is a material error in the draft agreement it is not, and I repeat, not open for negotiation."

With that Will rose and he announced that his group would leave the selling agent to get on with their day. As they left, the selling agent stood, shaking his head saying quietly but not too quietly, "Remarkable. I would not want to meet that fellow in any other negotiations." Little did he know what lay before him.

* * *

The group at this point led by Isaac and Sophie left for what had become a preferred destination: the pub at the top of Parliament Hill, where seating had already suffered considerable wear and tear from its frequent use by the Menshives and their guests.

When the drinks arrived, a Pimms for each around the table, Isaac looked at Will and said, "*Oy*, friend, you can be an over-bearing brute! I have observed it in the past but never more than today. I don't want you negotiating against me ever, Will," said Isaac.

Before Will could reply, Sophie said: "Oh, Will, it was like in a movie. It was quite a scene, except it was real. You should have a TV sitcom... perhaps no one would believe it, though."

"It was the only way to get this arranged so that it would

not be stressful for you. Yes, I was somewhat theatrical, but that was deliberate for making a firm offer to the owners. It was also a way of keeping your attention and distracting you from anxieties you would otherwise have had with the negotiations. I hope you are satisfied with the results."

Isaac replied, "I am terrified to suggest otherwise!" which brought a ripple of laughter around the table. "Actually, I couldn't be more pleased. The more Sophie and I saw of that house, the more we realized that it was perfect. It needs redecorating, but that is all."

"Easily done, with the real Ms Campbell's assistance. Since we arrived here, Penelope Wright, representing our lawyers, has confirmed that the agreement will be prepared on time and that the money I had transferred last night to her firm's trust account in anticipation of this result has been received."

The agreement was signed, witnessed and sealed with proof of the deposit being given to the owners' lawyers on schedule.

* * *

What had been a pleasant diversion for Will, purchasing the house in Hampstead Garden suburb, ended abruptly with a call from Reuben Molotovsky. He was calling from St Petersburg where Will had sent him a month earlier to complete the inventory of assets located in that city.

"Mr MacIntosh, good news and bad news. Which first?"

"Always the bad news."

"The inventory has identified and has listed the valuable artifacts found at the Alexander Palace, but we have also found a large quantity of gold in a hidden compartment in the storeroom at the palace; that is probably bad because it appears it was stored there during the 1917 Revolution. The gold bars are stacked in multiple rows. There must be at least two hundred of them. I think the gold is somehow linked to the bodies we found in the middle of the principal strong room. If I am correct, whoever stored the gold was either for or against the Revolution. It looks like it was by either the Mensheviks or the Bolsheviks. If it was revolutionary forces, it means historically that whichever political party it was, that much gold was intended to be used for party political purposes and not for feeding the starving masses that both the Mensheviks and Bolsheviks were supposed to be supporting. Also, from whom did they acquire it, compromising their revolutionary principles in getting and secretly hiding the gold? My worry is that if this becomes known to Putin and his administration, they will do all in their power to suppress the information. I think that would put every one of us who knows about this secret trove at personal risk. The good news is that the only knowledge the president has relates to the dead bodies... easily dismissed as casualties of war. The gold and the former aristocracy-owned artifacts found in the same place as the bodies could suggest that it was fleeing aristocrats who had assembled the treasure and not either Bolshevik or Menshevik forces."

Will listened intently, understanding the significance of the discovery. He already had representatives of Putin's administration involved in documenting the assets found in St Petersburg. If, however, the gold was linked to early revolutionary figures like Lenin, the discovery would contaminate the reputation of the early founders of the Communist state.

Will considered at length whether he should disclose the gold to Dolgoruky, Vorontsov or Kutuzov, each of whom had one foot historically in the former aristocracy and another in modern times, and all of whom were in the employ of the Putin government. Would they support Putin in disclosing the treasure trove, or would they attempt to smuggle it out of Russia for distribution to descendants of the aristocracy, many of whom were their relatives and who had become impoverished by the Revolution?

And the big concern for the Menshikovsky interests was how the family was connected to the gold.

Will's imperative direction to Molotovsky was right to the point: "I understand the gold was found by your team which of course is loyal to the Menshikovsky family. If I am correct, you must keep this information to yourself. Do you know how much gold there is and what its current value could be?"

A question he needed an answer to before he completed his direction.

"Yes, sir. I and two of my assistants, both distant cousins of Dr Menshive, have weighed, counted and evaluated all the gold. Its street value, calculated by current world market values, is in excess of three billion – that is with a 'b', sir."

"Seal that chamber, disguising it as much as you can. Swear them on whatever your assistants consider spiritually, morally or ethically compelling not to disclose any information on what was found. If they comply with my directive, Dr Menshive will make it monetarily worth their while. You know, Reuben, that we cannot remove it from Russia. It would be illegal and easily traced, given the quantity involved. I have a further direction for you: I want you and your assistants to go through all of the gold and identify, if you can, its assay date of making. Any gold coins are relatively easy to date – any created in the nineteenth century would have impressed on them data that would identify the year of making. Gold bars were usually so impressed as well. This information may, I say *may*, tell us who assembled the gold. Was there anything found in the secret chamber that could give us any explanation of whose gold it was and why so much was assembled?"

"No, sir, but we will get at that immediately. We will conduct this research at night and will go into the palace under cover of darkness."

"You will *not*, Reuben," instructed Will. "You will enter the palace where and when you always have and you will leave at the same time and in the same way. Now, I want you to call Vorontsov and Dolgoruky, telling them the call is at my request and asking them to continue their work identifying what they think the Putin government would demand as its conditions for a settlement of the division of the assets. Tell them I will be with them by the beginning of next week. I will bring the security detail you are familiar with and someone new you haven't met. She is an American wealth planning specialist who can assist us in clustering the assets into categories for the purposes of negotiating a settlement. Keep as much of our past activities and problems away from her as possible."

* * *

Will understood the ramifications of this information relating to the trove of gold bullion. He worried that the gold and the dead bodies, if connected to Trotsky and his revolutionary compatriots, would exponentially increase his problems well beyond what he had already encountered.

His immediate reaction to the call from Molotovsky was to meet with Smythe and his ever-attentive assistant Penelope Wright. They listened speechless to Will's latest news.

Without waiting for either Smythe or Penelope to respond, Will said he required Smythe to examine Russian and international laws that could provide them with directions on how to get the gold out of Russia. Also, he directed Penelope, who was still traumatized by her experience in Moldova /Transnistria, to double or triple her team's analysis of the books, journals, ledgers and other documentation brought to London from Russia and Ukraine to ascertain any reference to the acquisition of the gold.

"Penelope, we need to know when, why and by whom the gold was assembled. It may have nothing to do with the Menshikovsky family. It may have been stored there by the previous owners. It may have been assembled and stored by revolutionary forces; if so, we must know which and when. Could it have been assembled by Czar Nicholas, his family or other aristocrats? To enable me to develop a strategy to deal with the damn stuff, we have to be fully informed or we will have no bargaining room."

After receiving Will's instructions, Smythe turned to Penelope and asked her whether she was prepared to accompany Will to Russia to assist with translations from Russian or French, the latter being the *lingua franca* of the eighteenth and nineteenth centuries used by Russian aristocracy and royalty.

Before Penelope could reply, Will interjected: "No, I will

not have Penelope subjected to the very real physical risks to our safety this trip will bring. She will be most helpful here in London reviewing and decoding the documentation we send from Russia. I will assemble a team that will be adequate for my purposes, but I really need the legal research I have asked for, Penelope, as soon as possible – if possible before I leave for St Petersburg next Monday."

He received the assurance he required.

57

FIRST THING THE next morning, over breakfast with Ruth and Penelope, Will briefed them on the problems that had arisen from finding the gold and trying to discover who had assembled this trove. At the conclusion of his lengthy dissertation, Penelope paused from taking notes (in a special form of shorthand) to say: "Mr MacIntosh, you couldn't keep me away from this adventure. Yes, I will go under the guise of a wealth management specialist. What the hell, I have been sort of absorbed into this case... it has become part of my purpose in life. I believe in what you are doing with Dr Menshive and the cultural and ethnic issues involved. Dr Menshive's mission has become mine."

"If you are coming, you will have to disguise your appearance. Gone will be the long blonde hair. You will have it cut into some other style and have it coloured, something dark. And I want you to use a makeup that darkens the tone of your skin... something Mediterranean, perhaps. Your overall appearance will be a dull researcher type, assuming there is a predictable look for such people. I don't know. What I want is for you to be unrecognizable when you leave this house at one o'clock next Monday morning. I will have a private jet on standby at London City Airport which will whisk us off to St Petersburg directly."

"Are the disguises really necessary?" asked a shocked Ruth.

A brief history of the last four years given by Will with emphasis on the violence he and Isaac had encountered persuaded Ruth that a bullet-proof vest should form part of her disguise.

"We have to keep you alive and well, Ruthie! Your dad cannot withstand another loss of a family member because of the trust. You will remember that I told you not to discuss any aspect of your role or experiences as part of my team for the same reason. When he is stronger, we will brief him fully on this development."

As he was quaffing his second decaffeinated coffee, Will received a call on his cell from Piotr Dolgoruky.

"Mr MacIntosh, I received a call this morning from Reuben Molotovsky. Vorontsov and Kutuzov are available to meet with you Monday afternoon. I suggest we meet at the Museum of Decorative and Applied Arts in St Petersburg. We have an invitation from Director Vorontsov. Incidentally, while I was talking to him a few minutes ago he was enthusiastic about the meeting, telling me he thinks he has a formula for a settlement of many of the claims that might lead to a wrap-up."

Will thanked him, expressing his hope that the situation with the many competing interests could be resolved soon.

58

TWO DAYS LATER, just before noon, Will received a call from Penelope excitedly inviting Will to join her and her team at the research and storage headquarters at Canary Wharf that afternoon at 2 p.m. "I think you will be shocked at what we have discovered. Shocked certainly, but it may be a key to understanding many of the unanswered questions we have been struggling with."

* * *

Arrival at the Canary Wharf site was not as simple as it had been. His identity and appearance were well-known by then, as were the two routes he customarily followed to get there. He decided that the circuitous route of a river taxi to Greenwich, walking the Thames tunnel and then walking the path to Canary Wharf following the DLR track, should provide some cover. In any event, he got to his destination safely and he was greeted by Penelope and her team with a degree of calm and purpose he had not witnessed since they had returned from Odessa.

"Great to see you all so cheerful and full of happy news! Now, Penelope, what do you have for me?"

"We have a direct connection between revolutionary Russia in 1917 with the Alexander Palace, Trotsky and the artifacts and bodies found there," Penelope announced excitedly. "We have Imperial Russian documents, some of the very last made before the abdication of Czar Nicholas II that prove the Imperial government had assembled the artifacts as a repository for the nobility and the fleeing aristocracy with the intent that they would be stored in a safe location and distributed to those fleeing the Revolution or to those who remained in Russia. If the Imperial government survived the

Revolution, any of the artifacts that were not used as intended would be removed from St Petersburg through diplomatic pouches to either Geneva or Berlin. This document is not found in the minutes of the Czar's Council or any other official group. It appears that Czar Nicholas' brother was assumed to be the heir to the throne. It was the brother and his private secretary, with the help of security agents of his own, who put the treasure trove together.

"Why the Alexander Palace? At last an answer. The Menshikovsky Bank was the survivor of Günzburg and Mendelssohn interests in Russia. The Menshikovsky Bank was requested – I think, rather, it was ordered – to lend the failing Imperial government gold to help run the closing days of World War I. So the bank made it a condition of the loan, knowing it was a gift to the Imperial government, that it receive something of substantial value in exchange. The Czar owned several properties in St Petersburg which were used, as the British would say, as 'grace and favour' accommodations for Romanov relatives. The Alexander Palace was one such asset. The Imperial government had little else to give the bank – the palace was one of the most valuable properties in Russia in 1915 when title was transferred to the bank. At the close of the war when the gold had not been expended, the short-lived Imperial government intended the gold to be used to assist fleeing aristocrats, as I said earlier."

"And the Trotsky connection?" asked Will.

"Title was transferred to a holding company incorporated in Switzerland as the sole shareholder which is a trust of some kind. Apparently, before the gold could be safely transferred to the Imperial government for its intended uses, Revolutionary agents exterminated many of the ruling Romanovs, including the Czar and his immediate family. They, of course, were followed by the Bolsheviks after a battle between the Mensheviks and the Bolsheviks. We have documentation from the Lenin archives that the Lenin collaborators, which included Trotsky, discovered the plans to transfer gold to the nobility and aristocrats. Trotsky was assigned to deal with the Menshikovsky Bank to take the artifacts and gold it promised to the new government. Why it remained at the Alexander Palace isn't known, but I suspect it has to do with Trotsky's fate – assassination by Stalin in 1940, which obviously prevented Trotsky arranging his safe return to Russia and transfer of the assets.

"We are just getting into the rest of the documentation on this stage of the story. Incredible! It all begins to make sense. There is more to come."

59

FOR SECURITY REASONS, the documents available to Penelope and her team at any given time were deliberately limited. Will carefully arranged for the bulk of the Russian and Ukrainian records retrieved from Odessa to be stored in a secret but safe place. It had been assembled in groups based on similar subject matter, but as the divisions between the groupings blurred with overlapping information, Penelope found that any given group of documents was deficient until all the remaining documents in similar but separate groups were explored. However, the apparent threats to Isaac or to the ongoing investigations required the utmost control of the material both in its storage and its use as part of the investigation.

Will and Penelope agreed on the repository of the documents and the organizational logic of the groupings. When she abruptly announced, late in the afternoon of the day before, that she was just getting into the information on the revolutionary period, Will knew it was necessary for two new groups of documents to be taken from the secure storage unit and delivered to Penelope. However, fear of the originals being misplaced, stolen or destroyed meant that the documents available to the research team had to be carefully photocopied and then scanned and e-mailed to the research unit at Canary Wharf.

The caution being exercised by everyone on the team was made necessary on a daily basis with the reports Abraham and Mendel brought to the operational centre in Docklands. They had observed intense interest by unidentified individuals in following members of the research team coming and going in Canary Wharf. They expressed fear of an inside source of information, someone close to the investigation or the family.

If any of the team was required to carry handbags or large

totes that could be used to transport documents, they would be followed by one or two of the security team in case those carrying them were intercepted. Abraham sent out two or three of the research team with bags filled with meaningless paper and objects, hoping the bags would be seized.

When documents in a particular grouping were read and analyzed, a summary was encrypted by a specialist on Penelope's team in compliance with her directions, and in the process, each new detail, fact, or assumption was added to the growing narrative and history of the Menshikovsky family. At the end of each day those working documents, always in copy form, were shredded and incinerated.

By noon of the day after Penelope's excited report on the latest Trotsky connection, Will arrived eager to discover more. His upcoming visit to St Petersburg would be with government officials, some of whom, he suspected, had mixed loyalties. He knew he required much more information on the connections to the Menshikovsky Bank by those hostile to the Menshive investigation; these would probably include connections to Trotsky or the remnants of the Bolsheviks still active. Certainly, Penelope's preliminary conclusions, now generally accepted by Will and others on the team, were that the connections existed. This was no surprise to Will, as he was fully briefed on the Bronshtein/Scythian gold acquisitions in Odessa. That Lev Bronshtein, who grew up in Novorossiya, became Leon Trotsky, one of the key leaders with Lenin in the early years during the creation of the post-revolutionary Communist government, was an established historical fact. But what, if any, connection was there between Trotsky and the Mendelssohn Bank? Was he in some way involved in the Mendelssohn Bank, providing the new government with funding – and, if so, on what, if any, terms were the funds advanced?

"Proof, Will. We have proof that it was Trotsky personally," said Penelope, "who negotiated with the Menshikovsky family to provide loans in substantial amounts in the early years of the new government after the Revolution. We have discovered an actual memorandum found in a sealed plain envelope written by a Menshikovsky – it appears to be Isaac's grandfather's writing or that of his great-grandfather. The author details the number of meetings he had with Trotsky, the amount of gold demanded, its source and method of delivery. Needless to say, the memo makes it clear that the transactions were to be secret and absolutely confidential. Mr Menshikovsky added at the bottom of his memorandum that there were several threats of violence and possible death to members of the Menshikovsky family if there were any breaches in confidentiality.

"Menshikovsky identified the terms on which he agreed to provide the gold: that there would be no records kept by the new government of the Menshikovsky Bank or family in the loans, and that in exchange the new government would accept all land and buildings held by the family and bank prior to the Revolution as effectively owned by the family and bank and that they would be free to deal with the properties as if they owned them outright. Now, the remarkable thing is that we actually have a handwritten document, signed by Trotsky *and* Lenin, giving that undertaking. Next, Menshikovsky informed Trotsky that the bank had no real estate in St Petersburg large enough to store the amount of gold the new government required, hence the transfer of ownership of the Alexander Palace, with its vast basement and cavernous subbasements being given to the bank – well, not to the bank, but to an agent of the bank who was recognized by Lenin and Trotsky as holding it for the bank.

"The ledgers dutifully made and maintained by the bank record each acquisition of gold, from whom it was acquired, how much was paid and how much was to be transferred to the new government.

"The story gets deeper. The bank legitimately acquired the gold, almost all of it, for a fraction of its international value from nobility and aristocrats seeking papers enabling them to flee the country.

"The trove of diamonds and other precious gems, including the fabulous jewellery found in the storerooms in the palace, were used as barter, given in exchange for those documents required by those fleeing aristocrats. It appears that, during the intensely destabilized post-revolutionary period, the new government was frantically trying to get out of the war and establish some fiscal stability. The one bank that was reliable but not 'on the high street', as it were, was the Menshikovsky Bank.

"Trotsky's familiarity with the Menshikovsky family was key to the relationship. Trotsky knew his father trusted the Menshikovskys in Odessa and was never betrayed by them. The Bronshtein family, as Jews, were subject to having their assets seized at any time; however, the Menshikovsky Bank kept secret accounts and records for the Jews in Novorossiya: records that were never disclosed or found by the authorities in St Petersburg or later in Moscow when the capital was moved to Moscow. Trotsky knew he could trust the Menshikovskys. On the other hand, what he knew of the secret banking system operated by the Menshikovskys for the Jewish population in Novorossiya – and probably in Smolensk and Moscow, too – would give the Lenin government the ammunition to destroy the bank. However, the Lenin government had more to gain from using the bank and the Menshikovsky family than destroying them.

"On another note, Dr Menshive's grandfather or great-grandfather, we are still not sure which, had a personal journal like his predecessors as head of the family. He recorded in one of his journals that in 1921 and 1922 the political situation and the threats of pogroms had become so intense that he decided to leave Russia. He did so very quickly; the journal stated that his decision to leave was made after he discovered the pile of dead bodies in the basement of his Alexander Palace. He took it as a message to him and to his family to leave immediately.

"Why leave the gold and priceless artifacts? Well, Mr MacIntosh, I think you can tell us why," said Penelope.

"Incredible. The reason he left it all behind was that he had created the archive documenting everything the bank owned and where it was. It was not safe to remove it from Russia, but it was there should he or a later member of the family need it as a bargaining chip in retrieving some or all of the assets. So Mr Menshikovsky simply left it to his successors to deal with the mess. He knew eventually there would be a beneficiary who would have to straighten it all out. Enter Dr Isaac Menshive."

"Perhaps, Mr MacIntosh, but actually this mess has devolved onto you to sort out."

"Yes. But there is a symmetry to that. One of the strategies employed by the Menshikovskys was to front their business operations by a non-Jew to divert attention from the assets being owned and controlled by a Jewish family. Actually, as you know, I have used that same strategy in purchasing a house in Hampstead for Isaac and Sophie.

"What is your opinion, Penelope, as to the ownership of the gold? Does Isaac own that gold?"

"Based on international law he does. Based on current Russian law he has a claim on it; however, Putin is desperate for capital to shore up his declining economy. He can certainly prevent it from leaving Russia – that would put it in limbo. Eventually, they could fabricate a tax bill claiming every ounce of it. I recommend that you treat the gold as one of the offsets or one of the trade-offs for other benefits such as the art and real estate," Penelope advised.

"The Putin government is aware by now, from several sources, of the value and location of most of the Menshive assets. I don't see any way out except to negotiate a settlement with the government. The gold may be the clincher for us. There is no public record of it. It could be transferred to the State Treasury very easily and show up in the public accounts (to the extent they disclose anything) as a finding from a Second World War source not earlier known, for example. They have the creative energy to come up with an explanation, if they want one, that best serves their purposes."

Will had, he thought, as much background as he needed to arm himself for negotiations with Dolgoruky, Vorontsov and Kutuzov. Before leaving the research centre he asked Penelope and her team to carry on with their research. "If anything significant surfaces, Penelope, that you think might assist me while I am in Russia, please contact me on this new telephone. It is supposed to be secure."

* * *

Will returned to the Fitzrovia apartment, where he met with Andy, the security guard who had been with the team in Odessa and who was now engaged in providing security to Penelope and her team during the day (and bits and pieces to Penelope after hours, evidently to their mutual satisfaction). Will gave him directions for continuing security for his charges, which included Anna and Little Isaac until they relocated to the new house. Will and Andy were joined later by Abraham and Mendel.

The need to provide security for Isaac and Sophie continued to be a high priority, he explained. While the historical records were being reviewed and explanations developed for most of the mysteries surrounding the Menshikovsky Bank and family, Will emphasized, everyone involved in the process at that time continued to be under hostile surveillance and likely under threat to physical harm. An immediate priority was to identify who were the hostile elements and what their motives were.

"We will have no peace or safety until we track down our opponents and in some manner neutralize them. However, I have enough information from the Russian documents to establish that Putin's government would lose face and have major international issues to resolve if the Menshikovsky archives become known. I suspect that at least one of our hostile pursuers is representing Putin who wants to destroy the archive before it becomes public knowledge and contaminates the integrity of the Communist system in Russia – at least what is left of it. We know Putin deeply regrets the loss of the Soviet system. I am certain he would stop at nothing to destroy anything that could discredit the early Communist leaders still considered heroes in Russia. That is one likely threat. If you require more security forces you have my authorization to hire them – but make sure they are trained, sufficiently informed of the background, and are on our side only.

"There is a third, possibly a fourth, source of attack on the Menshive interests," cautioned Will. "The most likely would be existent relatives of Isaac's who believe they had an interest or claim to the assets. Think of Anthony Cann, who murdered Isaac's family lawyer four years ago. He has to be watched carefully. There may be others in league with him. The possible fourth is a group of Holocaust survivors or their descendants who mistakenly believe they have a claim against some or all of the assets. While we have moved forward incredibly well in understanding the Menshikovsky family and the assets, there is much more to do to settle all of the claims and establish peace and security for Isaac and his family. Just because there has been a lull in the violence, don't assume it will continue."

* * *

While Will was briefing Ruth in preparation for their visit in three days to St Petersburg, Will's encoded cell phone blipped, demanding his attention. Ruth watched him carefully, concerned, as his face turned first red and then progressed to purple as his blood pressure rose to strategic heights.

"Keep me informed. Don't worry about what time of day. I want a report from Andy on what happened and the level of destruction. Keep Penelope and her team away from there – permanently. If they were carrying out their duties as I instructed there will have been nothing in the research centre that would matter in the least."

Ruth asked quietly, "Has anyone been hurt? It's the research centre at Docklands?"

"No one hurt on our team. Nothing should have been lost. Yes, the research centre was destroyed by a bomb an hour ago. The authorities ascribe it to a terrorist attack. It wasn't. It was an attack on us. There was an injury – not one of our people – a young woman who is a financial trader at Citi Bank who was passing by on her way to the DLR railway platform. I will have our security detail make inquiries – but we cannot reveal that we had an interest in the space destroyed. We will have to relocate: I have an idea which I will discuss with you. In the meantime, I need to be briefed by Penelope on what, if anything, was left at the research centre last night when everyone left and what was removed – if that can be determined from the mess left after the bombing. This is the second time our research facility has been attacked. Someone knows too much," said Will quietly, greatly concerned.

60

THE CONTRACT FOR sale and purchase of the Hampstead house prepared in Smythe's office had been delivered as promised to the owner's solicitors on time, so when Will received an urgent call from Mr Smythe he suspected something had gone awry. His call confirmed it.

"Will, the deposit is in my account and the purchase documents delivered, but this morning I received a call from the owners' lawyer informing me that a judgment and attaching order have been filed against the owners. This has the effect of freezing the transfer of title until the judgment has been lifted. I am trying to find out what the judgment and attaching order relate to. The judgment is an additional problem because the total liability to the owners arising from these legal proceedings is not fully specified – costs, interest and other unknowns. Do you have a suggestion?"

"Yes, our contract is valid and I expect was registered as I required in the contract. The transaction is for more than fair market value so it cannot be attacked on that ground. The assurance of registration has been received. That being the case, the sale goes through according to the terms of our contract unless there is a title problem or fraud of some kind. Please follow up with appropriate inquiries immediately. What is clear, Roger, is that the owners are in a desperate financial situation. Our money is safe, given that it is in the other lawyer's trust account. Let's see if we can clear matters with the creditors – but only within the limits of our liability under the contract – and proceed with the purchase immediately. I can arrange to have the remaining cash sent to you by the end of the day. As to vacant possession being delayed, the property is at risk as long as the owners are in it. If necessary we will assist them in their move, but they must find a place into which to move."

Abraham arrived during Will's conversation with Smythe. He had additional information. "The owners are Russian, as you know, Mr MacIntosh. We checked them out. London isn't known as 'Moscow on the Thames' for nothing. Our sources checked out the owners to be okay. It turns out that the owner goes by other names and identities, one of which is as one of the more notorious Russian oligarchs who got himself into financial and legal difficulties with one or two of his companions in crime.

"You will be surprised to learn who our source of inside information has been. Frank. He has been diligently keeping an eye on your activities. I have seen him around in areas where we were active. I was getting worried. I needn't have been. He called me with this information about the owners. The claimant has helped considerably in informing me on who is after the owners, what it is they want from the owners, and what it will take to clear the judgment and attaching order. He is legitimate. I tested Frank on the basis that his information came through some role he has with the creditor oligarch. He convinced me he had no conflict of interest and he was only interested in protecting you and Dr Menshive. I am persuaded that he can be trusted. He says he also has information related to Anthony Cann which you need to know."

"Good God! This is surprising. It could be very helpful. I think we have to act on the assumption that he is acting in our best interests. Abraham, direct him to get to Smythe's office immediately. Smythe's staff will debrief him and if his information checks out we might be able to get this cleared before other creditors can surface. I will call Smythe's office immediately. Tell Frank I want to meet him at the Fitzrovia apartment at 5:30 p.m."

* * *

Ruth was waiting patiently in the dining room at the apartment to discuss their planned visit to St Petersburg. Very little of the details of what had been discovered in Russia had been disclosed to Ruth. Basically, Will thought, to protect her. It was now clear that if she was to be of any help she would have to be fully informed.

Ruth sat watching Will multitask, dealing with several major threats to their plans for resolution of the many conflicts facing Isaac and the family; she listened with interest as he explained how with compassion, gentle encouragement, and desperation he secured Penelope's agreement to join the team going to St Petersburg. Since her earlier decision not to join the team, she had changed her mind; not unexpected, as it was part of her post-traumatic stress disorder that her decision-making and emotions would take wild swings. Her skills as a Russian language translator made her participation in the trip essential.

* * *

"We will meet with Penelope, Roger Smythe and an expert in appraising art and historical artifacts from Eastern Europe whom I have hired to assist us," said Will later, when briefing the team assembled to travel to St Petersburg. "My plan is to use the next three days to develop a comprehensive proposal for settlement with the governments of Eastern and Central Europe. After we have developed the proposal I will have to have it vetted as well by a representative of UNESCO and the governments of the United States, Germany and the United Kingdom. The government of the United States has assured us of its protection – which it has consistently failed to provide, notwithstanding its assurances of protection. However, we need them onside for legal and tax reasons. And for similar reasons we need the United Kingdom and Germany."

"There is nothing straightforward in any aspect of this, Will," offered Ruth.

"None, and every party involved puts us at risk because we don't know who we can trust. Take, for example, the former American Ambassadress to Poland. We had repeated guarantees that her embassy would provide an effective security for us there. Your father and I were almost killed; others were, under her watchful eye. She and your father developed a relationship of a more personal and physical kind, which just complicated matters further. She is well out of the picture, but who knows what will surface as we move forward? I desperately need your help, Ruth, in watching for problems and to assist in formulated solutions."

"I will, and not just because it is for my father and little brother, but because I like overwhelming odds when I am trying to solve legal problems."

"Yes, I am aware of the excellent reputation you have developed in that regard. You will be in your element here, Ruth!"

Confessions ensued from Will as to his personal relationship with Penelope in the past. Two minutes after doing so, for some reason he could not fathom, he needed to assure Ruth that the affair, while intense, had been brief and was now over. Frank's role and the reasons for his dismissal were also part of the background Will knew Ruth required. As he progressed through the rather sordid aspects of the multiple relationships, Ruth's amusement increased, resulting in, "William MacIntosh! This tale is one of libidos gone wild. All of you, including Dad particularly, seem to have let loose years of frustration in a middle-aged spending spree!"

"An appropriate *double entendre*, Ruth. Yes, it was, even at times of high risk and danger, a lot of adrenalin-pumping fun. I hope this trip to St Petersburg will be more sedate and full of successful resolutions to our problems."

"A little pompous, Will. I understand that the glamour of the earlier adventures may have rubbed off, leaving you with the one less objective of getting this all settled."

Abashed in the presence of this savvy and highly intelligent young woman, Will managed 'stage purple' on the facial scale of emotional revelation. Ruth observed the intensifying colour with curiosity and humour. Her reaction was somehow reassuring and comforting to Will.

* * *

The call from Smythe at 2:30 p.m. that afternoon was welcomed. It took Will away from the embarrassment of his discussion with Ruth which had left him perplexed and agitated.

"Mr MacIntosh," said Smythe – Will never invited Smythe to use a more personal first name basis; he knew how to maintain top-dog standing in the relationship – "good news. Your man Frank has given us very explicit details of the demands being made by the creditor oligarch who filed the judgment against the Hampstead house. Through a reliable source I will not identify, I was able to reach the oligarch earlier this afternoon and have reached a settlement that will be satisfactory to our client the purchaser, and it is one the seller cannot refuse. I have discussed this with the seller's lawyer. We have a deal. I propose it works like this: we close tomorrow. From the deposit, we will pay out an amount required by the judgment creditor to lift his judgment and settle in full the claim against the seller. In return, we will have a memorandum of settlement signed by the creditor, the seller and the buyers. The deal will go ahead as scheduled tomorrow. Seller agrees. I think they know there are other potential claims.

"As to vacant possession, I told the seller's lawyer we must have vacant possession tomorrow. We can't risk more legal claims against the seller that could result in encumbrances or restrictions of any kind on access to or possession of the house. The seller has agreed on condition that you will purchase the bulk of the furnishings. The value ascribed to the furnishings is modest – who knows what they owe on them? There are no registered charges against the chattels we could find. So, if you agree, they will move out before 5 p.m. I believe you agreed to assist in the costs of their moving. It turns out they are insolvent, so to get them out, you pay."

"Agreed. An excellent solution, Roger. I will have the balance of the purchase price and the money for the furnishings and moving costs by noon tomorrow. Remember, please, the IT company you incorporated, which is owned by the Swiss trust we set up for Isaac (in turn, ultimately owned by the Prince Edward Island Trust), is the owner. Therefore we do not need to seek instructions from Isaac or Sophie. I will inform them when the deal has closed safely and finally. Thanks again.

"Incidentally, if I didn't do so already, thank you as well for lending Penelope to me again for a Russia trip. This one may see finality to our problems. Oh, yes, another thing: thanks are also due to you for accepting Ruth as a member of your staff. I know she can't be a practising full-time accredited lawyer, but she can have occasional appearances here through your office. She will be a long-term member of my team. I think she wants to sit the bar exams and become a full-time member of your Inns of Court. Not so, me. I will only remain qualified back in Canada. My role over here will be one hundred percent management and investment. Thanks again. I will check with you tomorrow."

* * *

The meeting at 5:30 p.m. with Frank was with Will alone. If the meeting passed in a way acceptable to Will, he might invite Frank to rejoin the team.

Frank came to the Fitzrovia apartment he knew so well, on time, and brushed, polished and pressed to military standards, his shoes glistening with an almost vulgar gleam. His embarrassment and deferential demeanour gave Will hope that he could regain trust in Frank, someone who had been the saviour of Isaac and himself on numerous occasions.

"So, Frank, what have you been up to that has brought you back into our lives? I refer to Dr and Mrs Menshive and myself."

"You can't know how deeply I regret failing you as I did. It was a lapse of judgment that put you and the Menshives at risk. I won't ask or expect forgiveness, but you may have some sympathy for me when I tell you my story. I was lucky to have saved most of the money Dr Menshive generously paid me as a security guard, so I didn't need immediate employment elsewhere to keep body and soul together. I had been checking several leads that I knew could be important to the settlement of at least one of your adverse claims. It takes us back to Anthony Cann. I knew he had a tail on us twenty-four-seven since your arrival here six or seven months ago. When Ms Wright took her team back from Odessa, Cann was having them followed – I think it was Cann who tipped off the Transnistria authorities to Ms Wright's entry into the country and the potential documents she would have with her. I have found out that, in exchange for Cann's turning Ms Wright and her group over to the authorities in Transnistria, Cann was to receive whatever documents they had with them, while the authorities there would keep what valuables the team had taken out of Odessa.

"The 'tails' engaged by Cann following the team in Odessa were experts at subterfuge and disguise. Your security people had no knowledge they were being followed. But followed they were. Cann's crew discovered just about everything your team did while in Odessa. They certainly learned about the early acquisitions of assets in that region and the inconceivable value of the assets, including the Scythian gold.

"It turns out, or at least so Cann claims, that he is a direct relative of both of Dr Menshive's parents through a daughter of the second Menshikovsky who was stationed in Odessa. That daughter and her husband, obviously a Cann, were hired as staff at the Odessa bank and the husband served as manager while the senior Menshikovsky was away. Cann claims that a lot of the wealth acquired by the Menshikovskys in the mid-nineteenth century was acquired by his own ancestors. He said he used to discuss this with Isaac's father. So what Cann hopes to do is to force Dr Menshive into sharing the bulk of the assets with him. I know he will be in St Petersburg early next week having something to do with the trust and the assets. I think it is important that I continue following Cann and his security team even when he goes to St Petersburg. Yes, I am asking to be rehired as part of your team."

"Hired! Carry on as you suggest. You will meet me in St Petersburg on Sunday evening at a location I will give you later. I don't need to tell you that your undivided loyalty is to the Menshives and that you are to follow to the letter the instructions I give you."

"Yes, sir. You can count on that. I won't fail you again," replied Frank, an abashed and genuinely apologetic friend of Will's and the Menshives'.

61

BEFORE LEAVING LONDON, Will met with Andy, Abraham and Mendel at the Fitzrovia Square apartment and he informed them that Frank had applied to him for reinstatement to the security group. He observed the hostile reaction, particularly from Abraham, who knew personally the risk Frank had created for the team and for the family. Will interrupted Abraham before he could say something he would regret, informing him that he was persuaded of Frank's sincerity. He reminded Abraham of the valuable services Frank had provided since he had been terminated.

"Frank will be on your team, Abraham, but not as team leader. Abraham, you will continue as operations director and Mendel 2-I-C. Andy is assigned to Penelope –" (there was laughter at this point) "– and her group. Frank will be encouraged to show the same diligence and resourcefulness as he exhibited in his active role before he was terminated, but in my absence, he takes his instructions from you, Abraham; in your absence, Mendel will be his guide. That's it. There will be no debate on this matter. If, however, you observe behaviour on Frank's part that is suspicious or disruptive to the work of your team you will inform me so I can take appropriate action, but again, if I am not available and decisions must be made you have my authority to do so. Given Frank's extensive knowledge of both Moscow and St Petersburg, he will accompany us to St Petersburg and he should be helpful to us all. You will all get along and work effectively as a team. Those are my instructions.

"The flight on our private jet leaves London Stansted Airport at six o'clock this evening. There will be food and soft beverages. The seats will recline and enable you to get some sleep. We arrive in St Petersburg early tomorrow morning and will be immediately into our investigation and meetings of the highest level.

"Incidentally, in addition to Penelope, who will be identified as our Russian translator, there will be another passenger who has recently joined me as an administrative assistant. She will be my 2-I-C, but as she is new to this, she will have only as much authority as I give her, and I tell you she has been given appropriate instructions. Her name is Ruth. For the moment that is all you need to know. Mendel, get that simpering grin off your face. We are going into a highly dangerous phase of our investigation; there will be no time for any diversions."

Mendel, the more outspoken of the Abraham and Mendel team, interrupted to say, "I see our translator from Odessa, Penelope coming on board. She has Andy, one of our Odessa team of security guards, with her. Is she carrying secret treasures?"

"No doubt Andy will think so," was Abraham's caustic reply.

"Yes, Andy will be with us," Will replied. "He will be an auxiliary to your team, but as I said, he is assigned specifically to Penelope and a small group of specialists who will be joining her later tomorrow.

"It may be difficult for you, but over the length of our stay in St Petersburg you are all to be celibate monks. Rein in your libidos. Forget the fleshly temptations to which you have each proven to be susceptible. You will be given ample time to release your nether-region energies when we get back to London. Mendel may need help in that department. We may be able to find an agency who can provide him with the necessaries back here in London."

Will left the security team who would travel with him, and he then met with the team who would remain in London to provide protection for the Menshives and the research facility. The continuing investigation of the bombing of the facility, along with a relocation to a new site already selected by Will, would occupy their time.

* * *

Will and Ruth met in the spacious dining room at the apartment with doors closed, the room having already been searched for listening and video devices. He spent an hour and a half explaining in detail the history of the investigations he and Isaac had undertaken over the past five years and he set out the objectives of the meetings in St Petersburg.

"You will recall, Ruth, that I explained the other day the possible sources of the opposition or hostilities we are currently facing. While we are in Russia I emphasize that each of those potential sources will be there and active. We do not have a definite face or motive for any of those operatives who are acting for those groups in opposition to us and to our activities, but my assumption is that they are separate from each other and are as much in opposition to each other as they are to us. Our primary suspicions at this time relate to Anthony Cann. Our security team will be thorough in protecting us to the extent possible, and to tracing down our enemies. Please remember that our discussions must be secure and we must always be suspicious that we are being heard or recorded.

"Our objective on this trip is to make a deal with the Putin government for distribution of the assets held in Russia, including a substantial part to be released to Isaac's new holding company of which you and I are the only directors."

"Will, your briefings have been thorough. I have reviewed the original inventory and the incredible supplementary lists. I see plainly why there could be several groups trying to get a part or all of the assets. Let me assure you, I am fully with you in trying to preserve as many of these assets as possible and the release and transfer of as many assets as possible to the new holding company as we can."

"Ruth, I am going to see Isaac and Sophie now to brief them on the purchase of the house which should go through today, and on our mission to St Petersburg. Thank you for agreeing to come. It is important that Isaac fully realizes the degree of your integration into my team and the personal risks to which you are being exposed as part of my team."

"You know I am on side. Apart from family obligations

that bring me into this situation, Will, as I told you earlier, I am enjoying the 'cloak and dagger' fun of it – yes, it is dangerous. There was no danger, challenge, or excitement in my legal work in the States. I look forward to working with you and the others in the negotiations – and in creating a management structure to administer the retained assets. I honestly feel this is my destiny – as if my ancestors are encouraging me to be part of this. I know you were instrumental in bringing me in and I will always be grateful."

* * *

The meeting with Isaac and Sophie was the most joyful experience Will had had with Isaac in over four years. Both Isaac and Sophie had fully reconnected and were once again acting as a bonded team of their own. Doctors MacKenzie and Charterhouse had warned Will that their current mental state was a veneer that could be quickly ruptured, sending one or both into regression of their PTSD to a degree of seriousness equal to or worse than that from which they had come.

Plans for moving from the Chelsea Clinic to the new house were to be delayed for a month while essential renovations were made. These involved the removal of extensive ceiling-to-floor mirrors, crystal chandeliers hanging from the many wall brackets and vulgar rosettes on the ceiling. It took great imagination to see the potential through the narcissistic exuberance of the Russians who were moving out. Ms Campbell, Sophie's interior decorator, had persuaded Sophie that she could reinvent the interior spaces with a more reserved and classical sense of modernity. Ms Campbell's sketches were nearly worn through by Sophie repeatedly reviewing and noting changes to them. Isaac announced that he would make all decisions related to historical carpets, art and artifacts. Sophie would have a room of her own adjacent to the master bedroom, equivalent in size and purpose to Isaac's huge library/study on the ground floor. She was assured that her space was hers to decorate as she chose. "No statues or portrait busts in my sitting room, Isaac. I know what I would like. The room has a double aspect with lots of light. French or English Impressionist works of art would work well. That's what I want."

"Would you like my help...?" started Isaac.

"Absolutely not. Right or wrong, garish or sophisticated, vulgar or refined, the choices will be mine. It will be my refuge."

"Agreed," was Isaac's only answer. The only answer he was safe to give.

They were so preoccupied with the house that they had little attention or interest available for the St Petersburg briefing Will gave them. Isaac refused to take the time to listen to a more detailed background for the St Petersburg trip, saying only, "I'm glad I'm not going, Will. Thanks. I owe you a lot for all of what you are doing. I hope Ruth enjoys herself. I am content to stay here and be domestic."

This remark proved to Will just how detached and disinterested Isaac had become in the process he and Isaac had been engaged in since they first came to Europe over four and a half years ago. He was very pleased to have Ruth as a substitute for Isaac on this next phase of the work. He knew as he left for St Petersburg that he had no preconditions from Isaac for a settlement. With Ruth he would have *carte blanche* to enter whatever arrangements they decided were best at the time. There was comfort in that; a feeling he shared with Ruth, who gave her opinion that: "Dad and Sophie have been through enough. I don't blame them. We will do our best, Will, and that's all we can do."

* * *

On the way to Stansted Airport, while comfortably seated in the back of the late-model Jaguar XS outfitted with every conceivable security, luxury and entertainment device, Will tried to get some rest with a brief nap. Of course, it was not to be. His cell phone contained every anti-tracking, anti-hacking and other security system available in 2008. It rang abruptly and stridently demanding attention (as he had programmed it to be heard in a howling gale).

The call was from the security guard on duty at the Canary Wharf research facility. "Mr MacIntosh, the police have contacted me. The bomb was not that of a terrorist. It was made to look like it, but it was a specialized device that the police with MI6 have traced to a Russian oligarch. He is one of the oligarchs suspected in the situation in Odessa and even back to the problems you and the doctor had while you were travelling between Smolensk and Moscow a few years ago."

"I suspected a Russian," replied Will. "They believe they have a license to kill anywhere on our planet – and because they are seldom pursued or caught by Western security they essentially *do* have a license to kill. Does that individual know we have his identity?"

"No. We don't think so. We know he remains in London."

"No, he won't remain in London. You and two of your auxiliaries will follow him. He will take a private jet today or tomorrow to St Petersburg. We have our sources at Stansted who will inform us who is leaving the airport over the next twenty-four hours. Follow his flight path and once the plane has landed don't lose sight of him. He will have others in his group. You will need to have each followed. Logistically this will be hard to do – just do it.

"Do you have any idea who this creep represents? Himself, the Putin government, private interests or a foreign government?"

"I did ask my source. It's weird, sir. My sources tell me he appears to be interested only in the documents. What was stored at the research centre has been carefully buried by our team and cannot be found."

"Do you know which documents?"

"No. Nor do our sources, but I have to tell you they know that the documents contain top secret information that could be used to manipulate Putin and anyone succeeding him. Jeez, I don't know what that is all about, but I hope you do. These guys are professionals and desperate."

"I will have further instructions for you relating to the

documents," instructed Will. "In the meantime, don't lose sight of those who are attacking our interests, and report to me frequently on this phone."

The full conversation was on speakerphone to enable Ruth to hear. When the conversation ended she turned somewhat pale. Visibly perspiring, she said, "What does that mean, Will?"

Before answering, he checked that the dividing glass between the front seat and the back was securely fitted and closed. He replied to her with a hand on her left arm, "I will not talk now about what the documents are. I will tell you when I know we are in a totally secure place. You need to know. They are of immense security concerns to not only Putin and his administration but to the integrity of past and future Russian governments. Now, you will excuse me while I make a number of calls."

Over the next hour, Will made contact with the research group, giving them instructions to accept directions from Roger Smythe. That call was followed by a call to Smythe who required few words to inform him of what was required and who was to do it. Smythe was instructed to call back within the hour confirming that his instructions were being followed exactly. The calls did not end there. Will then called the security detail in New York enquiring what information they had from or about Anthony Cann. Cann, of course, had been convicted of the murder of his employer, the senior partner at the New York law firm which handled Isaac's mother's and father's estates, which resulted in the gift of the assets and mess to Isaac. He was informed that Anthony was on day parole but he was being followed twenty-four-seven with a tracking device on his phone and a government wiretap, the results of which were communicable to the security guard.

"Nothing much came from Cann through these channels, Mr MacIntosh, until two weeks ago. Numerous calls were made on a telephone line he would have thought was secure. While the conversations were coded, just this morning we have had them decoded. He was calling a woman called 'Anna' and asking for information on Dr Menshive, his family and yours. There was other stuff that didn't make sense to me".

"Forward it immediately," directed Will, greatly alarmed by the mention of the name 'Anna'.

The next call was to the head office of Christie's Auction House on King Street in the St James area of London. Three weeks ago Will had set up a listing of art and artifacts similar (in theory) to those in Isaac's collection. There was a sale of some of Isaac's lesser Russian art and a few archaeological artifacts scheduled, but the sale would not be held until a date in a few months' time. This unusual arrangement was agreed to by the auction house only because Isaac had been a volunteer on the board of Christie's in New York. Will asked whether there was any particular interest in the goods listed on the schedule of items to be sold.

"Yes," the representative from Christie's replied. "Over the past two weeks there has been a very active series of computer searches related to the Russian art and artifacts – almost all that had originated in Novorossiya – around Odessa. We have tried to trace the sources of the e-mails but haven't succeeded."

To which Will replied, "I have an IT specialist, Mr Weatherbie, who will likely be able to trace the sources. As earlier agreed by your director, I will have Mr Weatherbie come to Christie's at three o'clock this afternoon. This is highly sensitive. You must disclose none of this except to your director."

PART 6

St Petersburg – London

62

THE PRIVATE JET was loaded with boxes, cases and luggage when Will and his group arrived at Stansted Airport. Plans to fly out of London City Airport had been scrapped for security reasons. He examined the schedule of flights and their destinations compiled by Frank who had been sent ahead that morning from central London. As Will and Frank with the others on the security team examined the schedule, Abraham pointed out that at least two of the private jets leaving that evening were taking similar paths to St Petersburg. The names of the lessors and lessees of the jets had been surreptitiously obtained by Frank. The names were checked against known oligarchs, Russian mafiosi and notorious Russian gangsters, though they did not fall into any of those categories. However, one jet in particular was identified as being suspicious.

Frank gave his analysis, concluding with: "It's my recommendation that we switch aircraft. We have a private jet hired with a reliable crew landing here from Gatwick Airport in half an hour, Mr MacIntosh." (Formalities had been resumed as he tried to rebuild his status on Will's team.)

"It is what I had expected, Frank," replied Will. "The materials loaded on the jet in front of us are all fakes. The material aboard is worthless and is intended to distract our enemies from the aircraft containing our actual cargo. There is no need to offload anything from this aircraft. We will board it as planned; however, in fifteen or twenty minutes the pilot will advise the control tower that the jet has mechanical problems which will need examination and possibly repair before we can leave. We will go into the terminal, but not to the public lobby. We will be taken to a secure boardroom from which we will be taken immediately by runway bus to the incoming aircraft which contains the cargo we require. It will land and leave from a remote part of the airport."

"Why all this subterfuge, Will?" asked Penelope, who was still somewhat unhappy with Will and as a form of revenge was prepared to challenge him on any issue that she thought would irritate him.

Will ignored the question and led the group onto the aircraft, taking Andy aside to tell him that he was to silence her and bring her along quietly and obediently. He also reminded the security team that 'loose lips sink ships'. It was impossible to tell where listening devices would be mounted.

The aircraft was boarded following standard practice after the flight was announced on the airport public address system. The jet started moving within minutes of the doors closing. Abraham, who was sitting next to Will, asked: "Why are we moving? Aren't we going into the terminal?" To which Will gave him a not-so-gentle elbow and a finger to his lips.

Five minutes later the jet stopped beyond the sightlines of the terminal public rooms. Immediately the exterior door was opened, and Will rose quickly and announced, "Leave, now. Nothing is to be left behind."

A bus was waiting against a hangar wall. The passengers walked sedately to the bus, herded by the security team. The bus left as soon as the last person was aboard. Frank walked along the aisle and instructed the passengers to take 'crash position, now'. He was obeyed.

A few minutes later, the bus arrived at a distant edge of the airport tarmac where another jet was standing. Its crew was crowded around the wings, apparently conducting repairs.

"Hiding, as I directed, Ruth, in plain sight."

"Great, but what is the point? This aircraft needs repairs. Are we to wait here for some time while the maintenance is completed?"

"Wait, you'll see what happens next."

As the passengers quickly climbed aboard the jet on the external stairway, the crew disappeared in a truck that had been hidden on the far side of the jet. No more than five minutes after the passengers were aboard the jet started to taxi and took off almost immediately, waiting only for ground speed to reach take-off speed.

Frank was directed to walk along the aisle reminding the passengers that absolute silence was to prevail until they were off the aircraft in St Petersburg. "A good time for a nap, ladies and gentlemen. You are going to need your rest. This may be a challenging trip."

Penelope was heard to say, "Oh God, not another one." Before Frank could get to her, Andy had directed her to feign sleep.

Two hours into the flight, the pilot asked Will, Ruth and Abraham to come to the cockpit. A murmur of discontent arose from the passengers: this brought Frank to his feet, with predictable instructions.

Shortly after take-off and attaining cruising altitude, the pilot asked the crew member who admitted Will, Ruth and Abraham into the close confines of the cockpit to close the door to ensure privacy. It was amazing that so much human flesh could be crammed into a space about the same size as a public washroom toilet stall. However, it was accomplished.

"Mr MacIntosh, I have just had a report of a major problem with the jet you were supposed to be on. An hour after leaving Stansted, as it was heading north along the North Sea, it was approached by two unmarked private jets that herded it into the Baltic Sea in international waters. The three aircraft are heading east-north-east. I suspect they will be taken to Murmansk in the far north of Russia."

"As I thought would happen. They have played into my hands. I have a security team in plain clothes made up of British, American and German specialist investigators who will have one task only, and that is to identify who has hired the two attack jets and who is ultimately behind this attack. I assume this had more official sanction than otherwise." No one asked what he meant.

As soon as the news had been relayed to Will he asked the pilot to head north over Belgium and then east over Germany and Poland, on the way to St Petersburg.

* * *

ST PETERSBURG

After arrival at Pulkovo Airport, the principal St Petersburg international airport, Will led the way as the passengers disembarked. They were quickly taken by bus to a terminal entrance for private jets which was often used by government officials and wealthy oligarchs. No attempt was made to disguise or limit their exposure to others in the airport. It would be understood by other passengers by then that Will and his group were on their way with the cargo on the jet travelling to Murmansk. Will was confident that no one would be watching for the group at this airport or suspect that the cargo had already safely arrived in Russia.

Their arrival at the Alexander Palace was timed to be after dark so that the speedboat, with capacity for all the passengers and cargo, could take them openly to the Fontanka river embankment in front of the palace which had a water-edge access to the palace.

The passengers were taken to a windowless basement chamber containing comfortable seating for everyone and several dining room-type tables, onto which the cargo was placed for opening by Penelope and her group.

"Well, Mr MacIntosh," said Penelope with asperity, "you somehow got us here in apparent safety. So what the hell was that all about?" She was ignored.

Will made a speech to the assembled group. "This building has been searched thoroughly, from roof trusses to basement foundations, for audio and video surveillance devices. Those that were found have been neutralized – but in a manner that will not tell our enemies that we have discovered them. So, if you should find any 'bugs' in your room or the areas where you will be working, leave them, don't tamper with them – that could reveal we are onto the people who placed them there. Know that you are free anywhere in this palace to speak and carry out your assigned duties.

"The cargo our aircraft carried contained copies of the documents I assume at least some of our enemies are after. You were never at any risk of being shot down or killed, I don't think. They would have taken you to a holding space while the cargo was removed. They will think they have sensitive documentation their employers need on the jet they commandeered. Whom their employers are, I am quite certain I know, but I will keep that surmise to myself. In the meantime, the boxes will be emptied and arranged as I instructed Penelope and her assistants at our research centre in London. None of these documents are originals, so if this building should come under attack the documents are to be burned immediately. You will have seen that incinerators have been installed. Now, I will give you a measure of comfort: we are here at the personal invitation of President Putin and have been assured of our personal safety. My talks over the next few days may lead to resolution of the conflicts Isaac and I have been facing for almost five years now. I know many of you would like to visit the city. It is one of the most beautiful in Europe, if not the world. However, the answer is absolutely no – not unless we have an agreement with Putin and his allies both political and non-political. If we do, I will arrange tours of the city's highlights which will be led by some of the most knowledgeable expert specialists in Russian history and culture in the country."

No further questions were raised. Will's abrupt departure pre-empted further questions. Abraham reminded the teams represented in the chamber that it was time to get to work, and that there would be surveillance by his security detail throughout the visit. It was going to be thorough. If any behaviour emerged that could threaten the visit and its objectives, it would be stopped by a member of the security team immediately.

* * *

Will met with Ruth, Penelope and Abraham in a sitting room on the Piano Nobile overlooking the Fontanka river. As they stood looking through French windows covered in sheer drapes, they could see enough of the neighbouring palaces to be awestruck by the homogeneity and elegance of the architecture in the embankment area. Will gave them a few minutes to enjoy the elegant Russian Empire décor from the 1820s with which the room was furnished.

Penelope was the first to express her amazement: "How did the Menshive family acquire such a building as this?" To which Will said simply, "Another time for an explanation; simply enjoy what you see. I bring you to this room to remind you of the quality and nature of some of the assets held by Dr Menshive. This and a great deal more like it are what we are trying to protect and preserve – not just for Isaac and his family but for the special groups here in Russia and in the West he wishes to benefit."

After a Russian tea served from a huge eighteenth-century samovar which Penelope recognized as solid silver with vermeil highlights crafted in St Petersburg. "I don't think," she said in awe and with a notable change in attitude, "I have seen anything of this calibre in any museum in Europe or the States. This is almost fairytale-like in splendour. Thank you for bringing me here. It is truly motivational. I am proud to be part of your efforts to protect these treasures."

* * *

Ruth joined Will for a lavish Russian-themed dinner in one of the formal dining rooms. Just the two of them. Will knew he had to introduce Ruth to the reality of what her father had received and was trying to protect.

"Is there much like this, Will?"

"Far more than I can tell you this evening. We start our discussions tomorrow with three of the most important museum directors in the country who have been engaged by Putin to negotiate with us. They have authorization to arrive at interim agreements, perhaps a final agreement. They are subject to approval by the closest advisers Putin has. Just a reminder: what we may agree to with Putin's administration is subject to adverse claims by Germany, Poland, Ukraine and Belarus and probably Bulgaria as well. So we are dealing with a task that is almost impossible in which to succeed. I will have some help from three external experts who may assist with negotiations. Kind of like mediators. Day after tomorrow we will have the director of the British Museum, a representative of UNESCO and the cultural attaché from Germany to Russia, all of whom have reputations of the highest stature and acceptance."

"My God, I had no idea. Your explanations, Will, were detailed, but only a visit to this place has given me a sense of what we are dealing with," exclaimed Ruth, awestruck by what she saw.

"Wait until you see the secret storeroom in the basement. It will amaze you. That is where we meet tomorrow morning with our Russian delegation.

"Now, I want to suggest that you be introduced as a lawyer from Washington who has been engaged in inter-museum loans and exchanges often on an international level. You have taken your mother's maiden name, so there is nothing about your name to connect you to Isaac. They will probably discover it while you are here. If they do, they will try to divide you from me to their advantage. However, please remember I make the final decisions. I know you will respect my position and not allow them to come between us. A gentle reminder: I have exclusive legal standing and control."

Ruth looked shocked and flustered. "I won't do anything to create difficulties. I am simply overwhelmed with the scale of things being discussed. I also know that I am not in Dad's will or if I am it is for a small fraction (I hope!) of what is going to be decided. Good luck to you, Will! I will try my best to support you as a solicitor advocating for a client would."

63

A REPORT FROM the pilot of the jet that had landed in Murmansk was available to Will at breakfast the next day. Several direct quotations from the hijackers who removed and examined the cargo added to Will's enjoyment of the report, particularly the comments about secret ink and concealed messages being embedded in the surplus industrial wrapping paper that was used to stuff the boxes. He had instructed the packers at the research centre at Canary Wharf to take ink from an old-fashioned fountain pen and sprinkle the sheets with clustered but random drops: this had led the hijackers to believe there was a code to be deciphered. The ruse worked well, because its real purpose was to make the thieves believe what the flight crew also believed: that the cargo was full of secret messages of great significance and value. The crew was released only when they were of no help in interpreting the dots. Actually, the pilot said the hijackers were helpful in arranging an approved flight plan for departure from that frozen city and an exemption from passport and customs clearance. At the time of the report from the pilot in Murmansk, the paper contained in several boxes included in the fake cargo were spread out in a large conference room at the airport, while four or five academics from the local university and National Museum tried their skills at deciphering the material.

The presence of Peter Dolgoruky, the legal authority and a representative of the board of the National Museum – which had its headquarters in St Petersburg, less than a kilometre away downstream on the Fontanka River, and whose director, Dr Vorontsov, was part of the delegation Will was meeting in a couple of hours – revealed to Will what he already suspected. Dolgoruky had proven to be trustworthy in earlier encounters as a legal adviser to Will and the trust. There had to be a leak or a source of information from a prominent official giving the active pursuers advance knowledge of the assets, their location and significance. This would give Will a decided edge in dealing with the potential threat, namely Director Vorontsov, during the meetings.

Will's mood shifted when he considered the information relayed to him from the investigators in the United States that identified whom Cann had been contacting in Russia. Someone by the name of Anna. Of course, Anna is as common a first name in Russia as it is in the United States. There was little on the face of it that could be taken as linking Cann with Isaac's sister Anna. However, Will knew that they had been friends and probably lovers at some time in the past.

Ruth joined him for breakfast and, after sharing a hearty laugh over the success of the Murmansk caper, he briefed her on Anna's former connection with Cann. Ruth was incredulous that her aunt could have been duped by Cann. Ruth had met him on two or three occasions and rapidly assessed his character as a shyster and a fraud. She agreed to use Will's e-mail address to contact Anna asking her to call her that evening at seven. The excuse was to give her an update on where they were and what she and Will were up to. Will had told Anna only that he and Ruth were visiting a museum in Berlin to discuss a possible loan of some statuary. "Ruth, you will conduct the interview – but we will discuss and formulate questions before you call. I will be with you but silently listening as you have your cell phone on 'hands-free'. We will make the call after our negotiations have started."

* * *

A detailed agenda had been prepared by Will the night before the meeting with the Russian delegates. It was laid in front of Ruth, who gasped. At Will's puzzled look, Ruth clarified: "Will, this agenda is handwritten! If you propose to put this in front of each delegate, it will not only be the fake documents in Murmansk that will require translation. Help me to decipher your cursive writing and I will type it and run it off at an IT shop I saw nearby."

Once this task had been accomplished, Ruth was as efficient as she said she would be in getting a print copy run off in numbered copies.

Half an hour before the meeting was scheduled to start, Will reviewed the agenda outlining the points for discussion with her. It read:

1. *Paintings and artworks on paper located in Russia or located elsewhere held by Dr Menshive with a substantial Russian connection;*

2. *Statuary and other decorative items including furniture located in Russia or located elsewhere held by Dr Menshive with a substantial Russian connection;*

3. *Archaeological findings including Scythian gold found in Russia or located elsewhere held by Dr Menshive with a substantial Russian connection;*

4. *Real estate located in Eastern Europe including Russia, Belarus, Ukraine and Poland;*

5. *Investments being traded on the Moscow Stock Exchange;*

6. *Bank accounts held in banks located in Russia, Ukraine and Poland;*

7. *Archival documents and historical documents relating to Russian history foundational to modern Russian identity wherever sourced and now located in Dr Menshive's collection.*

Note to Delegates: each of the above topics must be considered in light of potential or actual competing claims by other governments such as Belarus, Bulgaria, Poland and Ukraine although there may be others.

Objective: to reach an interim or if possible a final agreement that will serve as the basis for discussions with other national governments.

Ruth accepted the range of topics as the representative of her family, which is what Will expected of her. She understood the objectives of the agenda and she agreed to take detailed notes, as would Penelope who would also serve as translator when needed and as an expert in Russian cultural identities. Penelope's assistant would also be present as part of Will's team to assist with locating and displaying assets.

* * *

The conference room arranged in the basement of the Alexander Palace had ample light and air through windows facing into a courtyard in the centre of the palace. Virtually all of the artifacts, not including the gold bullion found in the safe rooms further down in the sub basement, had been brought up and were displayed to maximum effect, like a display in a jeweller's shop on New Bond Street in London. In fact, one of the team had been a window dresser in the Asprey shop on New Bond Street in London.

The delegation was preoccupied with their examination of the artifacts; as a result, they failed to notice Will and Ruth enter the room. The effect of the display was what Will had hoped to achieve. He wanted the delegates distracted and preoccupied with glittering minutiae contained in the artifacts during the negotiations.

Ruth was introduced as a distant family connection of Dr Menshive's who was a lawyer and specialist in tax and cultural property law in the United States. She was there, Will announced, to assist him and perhaps the delegates in their discussions.

The delegates eventually accepted Will's invitation to join him at the conference table. He reminded them that no audio or video recording devices were permitted. It was essential, he said, that there be an opportunity for a frank and non-binding discussion; in Western legal terminology, a '*without prejudice*' discussion. All agreed.

"If we are able to agree on some or all of the agenda items, please advise whether you have authority on behalf of

President Putin and his government to enter an interim agreement. And will there be a Memorandum of Settlement after the interim agreement is reviewed and accepted by President Putin's delegates here today? A formal resolution of claims and agreement on distribution if possible is a necessary protection for us all."

Vorontsov, Dolgoruky, Kutuzov and Zhukov agreed they had explicit authorization to engage in the negotiations and to execute a Memorandum of Settlement.

"Let's start with this intriguing collection of nineteenth-century jewellery; some of the finest created on the planet at the time, having inset on them some of the most fabulous nineteenth-century precious gems. Some of the pieces were crafted in Paris or London, but they were acquired by Russian nobility and form part of the Russian patrimony."

All agreed.

Within fifteen minutes it was recognized and accepted that many of the pieces were essential parts of Russia's cultural heritage. Will commented only that Dr Menshive had no personal interest in retaining any of it except for five rings and three brooches, each weighted heavily with diamonds and other precious gems and pearls. There was a murmur of dissent. *All* must remain in Russia. Stalemate.

Then the UNESCO delegate, Seamus Casey, rose to the occasion, as was his role as a mediator. "Three of the rings and all three of the brooches were created in either Paris or London. They should remain with the owner Dr Menshive and his family".

Will explained that Dr Menshive and his newly married wife had examined photographs of the jewellery a few days ago and that these were the only pieces she would like to have. "Dr Menshive," he said, "was adamant that his wife would have these pieces as a memorial to his family's sophisticated collection".

Grudging acceptance of that compromise resulted.

Before moving onto the next lot, Will said that he deliberately started with the jewellery because the outcome was predictable, and the process of arriving at an agreement could prevail similarly for every category with that positive start.

When Will asked what group or category of assets on the agenda the delegates would like to discuss next, he could not resist a smile when his prediction as to the response came true: "The archival material surely stays here. Dr Menshive would have no use for it."

"Not quite true," replied Ruth. "A significant component of the archival material relates to the process and proof of the acquisition of the assets. Dr Menshive requires the originals of those documents for proof of authentication of ownership and for tax purposes. We can discuss certified copies of the documents for distribution. Also, note that many of the historical documents relate to an interest in assets Russia shares with Belarus, Poland and particularly Ukraine. If it is the originals you wish to have, there will have to be a consensus among the countries having an interest."

A fevered debate ensued. "Let us examine a few of those documents now," proposed Vorontsov. Will chuckled to himself, knowing that Vorontsov had been part of the plot to hijack the jet to Murmansk. "Of course," he thought, "they haven't been able to interpret the documents, so they want to know where the originals are and in what condition."

"I have a representative sample of the documents I can show you in the form of photocopies. Some have redactions because they appear to have highly controversial statements or claims that would be divisive among Russia and her neighbours."

"No. We must see the originals. Where are they?"

Will explained that he was worried about the safety of the documents and related the Murmansk hijacking as proof. "Someone in this room, Dr Vorontsov, informed senior Russian officials – I suspect in President Putin's inner circle – that we were bringing original documents and attempted to seize them to prevent them from forming part of our negotiations."

He paused for several minutes, waiting for a reply from the Russian delegates. Mr Casey, the UNESCO official, quietly broke the silence, saying: "It is clear that Mr MacIntosh was prudent in leaving the originals wherever they are at the moment. I recommend that the documents be left until all other matters have been negotiated. In the meantime, these talks will cease – at least, I will leave if there is any other skullduggery, as we would say in my hometown of Westmeath. If we cannot trust each other in these negotiations, we are wasting time. Incidentally, I want to make it clear that I have received a legal opinion from a specialist in international law that all of the assets and items listed in the inventories presented to you this morning are the sole property of Dr Menshive and that there are no valid competing claims to any of them. I do recognize that each of the named countries have export and expropriation laws relating to the important objects we will be discussing. It is to accommodate those conflicts between private and national interests that we come together."

The Russian delegates asked to be excused so they could have a private conference. The fifteen minutes they asked for extended to ninety minutes. When they returned it was Zhukov, not Vorontsov, who spoke. "I accept the advice given by our UNESCO friend. I do so on behalf of and with the authority of President Putin who personally conferred that authority on me. He has appointed me the principal delegate and speaker for the Russian delegation. Our interpretation of the legal ownership, I have to say, differs from the opinion you received, but for the purposes of this distribution we agree to work with your premise, Mr Casey. I will reply to all inquiries and give answers when required."

A mollified but angry Vorontsov sat brooding as he listened, not chastened but isolated. Will knew he had an enemy in Vorontsov and possibly Dolgoruky, so he decided he would move forward carefully, addressing Zhukov and Mr Casey, the UNESCO delegate.

Mr Casey prefaced his comments on his role as follows: "Before we go further, I wish to assure Mr MacIntosh, whom I have known for almost five years, to be an honest and capable negotiator and protector of his client's interests.

I extend warm regards through him to Dr Menshive whom I understand is recovering from certain injuries sustained here in Russia." Dr Zhukov commented in an attempt at conciliation: "If there is anything the president and I can do to help him we have only to be asked."

Vorontsov had the good grace to acknowledge his complicity in some of the attacks on Isaac and Will by turning a vivid scarlet.

Shortly afterwards the meeting adjourned. Lunch was served in an adjacent chamber to the Russian delegates, and to Will and his group where they were.

During lunch Ruth was about to ask a question that Will sensed should not be asked or answered with appropriate confidentiality – he put his hand on her arm, with finger to lips pointing with the other hand to the briefcases and shoulder bags brought with the Russian delegates and left in the room when they went out for lunch. It reminded Ruth that the cases and bags would almost certainly have been bugged.

Four hours of negotiations took place that afternoon. The last item was the one, Will knew, that would be most contentious. The others were settled with goodwill and common sense including the real estate, most of which was to remain with Isaac. The one item on the agenda was the Scythian gold.

The Scythian gold was a very high priority, not because of its monetary value which was virtually impossible to evaluate. If it came to the marketplace the bidding would be astronomical and probably more than any Eastern European government except Russia could afford. It was of huge importance to the cultural identity of each of the countries in the region, so it was of no less significance to Ukraine and Bulgaria than it was to Russia.

"The Scythian gold is next on our agenda. We have only an hour left for our deliberations today. We should start the negotiations. Perhaps resolution will have to wait until tomorrow, but I must remind you that what we agree as a consensus today will be subject to negotiations with Ukraine, and if Turkey finds out about this it will also intervene, as may Bulgaria," cautioned Will.

The hour passed, not peacefully, but in an atmosphere of high energy and strident demands. It was Seamus Casey who closed the discussion for the day. He asked Will, as chair of the meeting, to adjourn until the next morning. In the meantime, Casey said he would meet with the members of the Russian delegation individually.

Will agreed and he repeated what he had said during the afternoon's discussions – that Isaac had decided that all of the Scythian gold, except that which he had personally acquired before receiving the trust, would remain in Eastern Europe. He restated with emphasis that "Anything acquired by Dr Menshive not forming part of the trust he acquired is his, and none of it is open to negotiation or distribution."

What he required, Will said, was "A proposal from the delegates for the distribution among the governments who could make a claim for the assets." He also reminded them that if they could not agree on a reasonable proposal that Isaac could accept, he would make a decision himself that would settle the matter. There were no indications of opposition or dissent; Will's tone and demeanour precluded adverse reaction.

* * *

After a restful nap late that afternoon, Will met with Ruth to review the plans for the interview they would have with Anna by telephone. "Interview it would be," said Will. He was suspicious that Anna was the source of the compromising information that connected her to Anthony Cann. They finalized the questions and the call was made to Anna who was waiting for it. Will, as planned, remained mute while listening carefully to Ruth who conducted the questioning. He was ready to give Ruth notes and to give her directions if needed. Pleasantries were exchanged between aunt and niece, then the questions from Ruth began:

Ruth: "We have information that Anthony Cann has been communicating with someone called Anna. We know you two were friends. Are you the Anna with whom he was communicating?"

Anna: "I was a friend of Anthony's years ago. Sure, I have communicated with him on several occasions."

Ruth: "How recently?"

(A very long pause ensued.)

Anna: "Well, from time to time I want local news of my friends in the States. Anthony and I were in many of the same circles, so he was a useful person to talk to."

Ruth: "How recently? Please answer."

Anna: "This sounds like an inquisition, Ruth. You are being very rude. I am your aunt. Show some respect. Don't talk to me like this."

Ruth: "Anna, you know many injuries have been sustained recently by your brother and his wife. They were in no small part caused as a result of information given by persons trying to attack them or their assets. We must have the answers to my questions in order to settle some pressing issues here in St Petersburg in order to provide protection for them. Now, please answer: how recently?"

Anna: "No, I won't answer. Is Will there with you? Has he put you up to this outrage?"

Ruth: "No, but he knows I am calling. Now answer. Your answers are important as we try to protect people, including your immediate family, who have been injured – many times."

Anna: "I am going to hang up if you don't stop."

(Weeping was heard at Anna's end of the line.)

Ruth: "Alright, Anna. If you won't answer my questions, I can tell you now that I think you have been complicit with Anthony Cann in revealing information to him that has enabled him to lead to the deaths of two security guards and very serious, permanent injuries to your brother and sister-in-law. If I do not have your answers now, Mr Smythe, our lawyer will inform the Metropolitan police in London, and charges will be laid against you which will result in your being interrogated by them. I believe you are at least an accessory after the fact in the murders and there is sufficient evidence to convict you which would result in prison incarceration."

Anna: "I hate this place. I am lonely. I want to go back to the States. You can't make me stay here. If I answer you, will you leave me alone? Will I be allowed to return to the States? I'm useless here. The nanny does everything with Little Isaac and anyway I don't know how to be part of his life."

Ruth: "I can't guarantee that there will not be a follow-up to our conversation this morning. You have my assurance that I will do what I can to protect you."

Anna: "What about Will?"

Ruth: "You are family. My aunt. My blood. Will has left decisions affecting you and me, including instructions for this interview and the information we require, to me. I agree he should and I accept the responsibility to conduct this call. Remember, Will is Dad's attorney under a comprehensive power of attorney. Now, your answer."

(Anna could be heard sighing heavily.)

Anna: "Alright. Yes, I spoke to Anthony on a mobile phone a friend of his gave me before I came over to Russia with Will. My most recent call was two days ago. Before that, I guess we have spoken about once a week – and sometimes when he can't speak to me, a friend of his calls me – all in all, between the two of them, about once a week.

Ruth: "Did you have that frequency of calls since you were informed you had received the gift of the trust from your father? – your half share, I mean."

Anna: "Only after I signed papers turning my share over to Isaac. Anthony was furious I did that. When he found out through his job at the law office in New York that handled

Dad's estate, he went ballistic. He said I had given away a lot of money he was entitled to. He said Dad had agreed with him that he should have some of the money. I feel so sad. I am in the middle of Isaac and Anthony. I want to keep everyone happy. Anthony thought I should accept the offer to come to London with Will. That's why I am here."

Ruth: "Did you know that anything you said to him about where you were and what you were doing here would inform Anthony and his pals where Isaac and his family were?"

Anna: "Oh, no. I never told him any secrets. Will told me not to."

Ruth: "Did you tell Anthony which city you were in over here in Europe?

Anna: "No. But he had my cell phone number which I changed to a London server, so I guess he would have known where I was."

Ruth: "Did you tell him or describe to him where you lived in London?"

Anna: "Well, I talked about the buildings I had visited like Will explained them to me. Anthony was really interested in architecture so he wanted to know what I was seeing."

Ruth: "You know that Will and a group of researchers went to southern Russia a few weeks ago to investigate certain matters they thought would be informative for their investigation. Did you tell Anthony about Will's trip to southern Russia?"

Anna: "Well, no, not exactly. Anthony was actually very jealous of Will. Anthony said he was envious of all the paid travel Will was getting and the money he must be making from his work on the trust. He asked where Will was and where he was going. He said he wanted to look up Will's agenda and follow it on Google maps and trace Will's travels to give himself something to do. You know he has been in jail and is on parole so he can't go anywhere. What harm could this information do?"

Ruth: "Who is the friend who calls you? What is his name?"

Anna: "Sid Brown. I haven't met him. He has the friendliest voice and is very entertaining on the phone. He has asked me to go out with him – well at least for a dinner date. I hope it happens."

Ruth" "Does he have an accent?"

Anna: "Oh yes. Russian. He denied he is Russian. I asked him but he said no he was from a little country called Slovakia. Perhaps he is from there, but I can tell you it sounded Russian to me. Isaac and I had old aunts who were straight out from Russia. He sounded like them."

Ruth paused, looking to Will for directions on further questions. He replied with a very sad shake of his head and he signalled Ruth to end the call.

"Excellent interview, Ruth. I am very surprised that Anna has betrayed us. When we first arrived in Smolensk to visit Isaac and Sophie shortly after Little Isaac was born, we were close – yes, we were lovers for a few weeks until her cloying demands for attention became too much for me. I told her repeatedly that she was not to talk to Cann. So she has been his inside source – look at the incredible harm that has come from that. I didn't see that side of her. I should have been more vigilant or perceptive, I guess. Perhaps I was blinded by her professed affection for me and her avowed loyalty to Isaac. She gave me her assurances she wouldn't talk to Cann.

"What we have learned from this conversation with Anna is that Cann is the source of many of the threats Isaac and I have endured over almost five years. I will inform our security details on both sides of the Atlantic. We will have to track down Cann's accomplice – I suspect he is one of the more prominent Russian oligarchs. Probably one or more Ukraine oligarchs, too. We will also report him to the New York police and ask them to revoke Anthony's parole. It was a condition of his parole that he would have no contact with Isaac or any member of his family, and that included Anna.

"We are at least finally identifying our enemies. We are successfully neutralizing most of the hostile forces working against us."

Drained, thoroughly exhausted and dispirited by Anna's betrayal, Will left Ruth and went to his room for the night.

64

THE NEXT MORNING, Will asked Ruth to brief Penelope on her conversation with Anna and to request Penelope to contact Smythe on Ruth's cell asking him to arrange with American justice officials to terminate Cann's parole.

"What do you suggest we do about Anna?" asked Will.

"There's only one thing to do. Have her escorted this morning without advance notice from the apartment. It must be without notice and as quickly as possible before Little Isaac could be upset or put in jeopardy."

"It is clear," said Ruth, "that he already has been. Don't tell Dad, Will; leave that to me. I will call him to tell him a little white lie, explaining that Anna has taken a few days to explore Paris as she has always wanted to do. Little Isaac will be safe with Nurse Ellis and with the assignment of the extra level of security you suggested, the family in London should be safe."

"Thanks, Ruth. I need this help. I think we can assume that the bombing at the research centre and the jet being hijacked are the result of Anna's indiscretions."

"No doubt about it. Mom always referred to Anna as 'Poor Anna – the flake'. I dismissed the comments as bitterness over her divorce from Dad, but I see now her assessment was right on."

* * *

Frank asked to see Will before the negotiations would resume later that morning. He said he had been in frequent contact with the security detail in London and he also reported that Anna had been escorted out of the apartment and was put on an American Airlines flight to New York where she would be met by the New York police who would interrogate her about the Cann communications. He warned Will that the New York City police might charge her as an accomplice.

Will thanked Frank, growing in confidence with him after Frank's return to service.

"Well," said Will to himself, "Frank was always dedicated and effective in the past, but more motivated from time to time by his hormones than loyalty to his functions as a security guard. It looks as if he is back on track now, but I will still have to watch him carefully."

65

THE NEGOTIATING RESUMED late the next morning. Ruth observed Will's detachment and distraction. She took the lead in conducting the meetings. She did so with considerable skill, resolving several disputes that could have derailed the negotiations. Will watched with growing respect and admiration, as did Seamus Casey, the UNESCO representative. She was firm, focused and decisive, keeping the negotiations on track.

The meeting was scheduled to end at 4 p.m. It did. Ruth turned to Will, asking him for his closing comments.

"Thank you, Ruth. I have been out of sorts because of bad news from Canada. You have managed the negotiations exceptionally well. Actually, if I am not mistaken, we have achieved agreement on everything except the Scythian gold. Gentlemen, am I correct?"

There was unanimous agreement.

"Well, that being the case, are you ready to give me a proposal for the Scythian gold? You have met with Mr Casey who was hoping to facilitate a settlement."

There was silence.

"Mr Casey, may we have a recommendation?"

"I have met with each of the three delegates representing the Russian government. I am going to make the following proposal which might bring them together and enable settlement.

"When the Scythian gold artifacts were found and bought by the Menshikovskys either personally or through their bank, it was in a newly developed part of Russia on the Black Sea, then known as Novorossiya. In my opinion, both Russia and Ukraine have an interest in these wonderful objects. Both governments would agree that they should remain in Eastern Europe, to be in Russia or Ukraine. So my proposal as to a division is that they be divided equally by categories comprised of location of acquisition, period and historical and cultural significance. An equal division seems the only fair distribution. A third-party expert should be engaged to make that division. The current collection held by the two governments should be considered, too, so there are no unnecessary duplications."

Will asked what the response was to the proposal from the Russian delegates.

The three Russians left the room. Will expected a lengthy delay before hearing from them. In fact, he was not optimistic they would agree.

Ten minutes after they left they returned and announced they agreed to the proposal. The meeting was then terminated and an announcement was made that Penelope and Ruth would draft an interim agreement.

Will gently reminded them that the next hurdle would be the negotiations with other governments. Seamus Casey agreed to help and to participate in meetings with representatives of the other governments if he were requested to do so. "Please accept my invitation, Mr Casey," said Kutuzov, on behalf of the Russian National Museum of Art and Antiquities. Zhukov, as Executive Director of the Pushkin Museum agreed: "You have been a great help to us all."

Will added, "Thank you all for your cooperation. My group and I will take a day to recuperate – probably by playing tourist to explore this exceptionally beautiful city. In a couple of days, we will leave St Petersburg for London. In the meantime, Ruth, Penelope and I will be available if any of the delegates wish to meet with us."

"Mr MacIntosh, we still have one category to attend to," said Mr Vorontsov with considerable vigour. "The historical documents."

"You, Director Vorontsov, or agents of the Government of Russia have hijacked a private jet on which the documents were being transported as cargo from London, an aircraft that was known that I, or one of my team, would be on," said Will in an accusatorial tone of voice. "So what have you learned from the documents you have seized and have been studying according to the pilot who has kept us briefed?"

Both Kutuzov and Zhukov looked at Vorontsov with amazement. Before Vorontsov could reply, Dolgoruky responded, "I knew Vorontsov was up to something. What has happened to you and your cargo was a breach of domestic and international law. I apologize on behalf of my government. The instruction for this travesty did not come from the President. I admit the involvement of my colleague, Mr Vorontsov. Will, you and I know you could turn this into an international scandal and could defeat what we have accomplished in the last three days. What do you need to prevent this travesty from going further into a public scandal?"

"I require the names of those co-conspirators outside Russia who were engaged with your colleague, Director Vorontsov – who else is involved and a disclosure of what their motives were. Yes, Mr Vorontsov, what I have put in place is the old 'switch and bait' tactic that your own government has been effective in playing for years. You can tell your scribes to call off their examination of the 'documents'. What they are examining are nothing more than carefully splotched ink marks in apparent paragraphs that have absolutely no meaning."

"I double my apologies, Mr MacIntosh," said Dolgoruky, "and congratulations on your clever device for defeating Vorontsov and his co-conspirators. You will receive what you have asked for: a truthful report with accurate details on his involvement in those incidents that resulted in harm to you and Dr and Mrs Menshive. You have earned it. I agree with you that the sooner this is wrapped up the sooner you can leave Russia and we can get back to what we are meant to be doing."

Dolgoruky now turned his attention to Vorontsov. "Director Vorontsov," he directed, "you will wait until Mr MacIntosh and his group leave this room. You will be accompanied under police escort to the appropriate authorities located in the Lubyanka Prison." He added as an aside to the general group, "Vorontsov knows that interviews and incarceration there are no less unpleasant now than in the Soviet era," before turning his attention back to Vorontsov: "I will have my executive assistant call your former executive assistant director, former director, I should say, to pack the one small bag to which you are entitled for the long stretch of incarceration you will have there."

Finishing with Vorontsov, Dolgoruky now addressed Will. "I will have all the details you require, Mr MacIntosh, by 5 a.m. tomorrow here at the Alexander Palace. I give you my word and that of President Putin that you and none of your team will be bothered after this by anyone while you are in this country. I look forward to seeing Dr Menshive, his wife and son as soon as they come back to Russia. They will continue to have his dacha in Smolensk and this incredible palace to enjoy, as they say in England, 'in quiet possession'."

Will informed Director Zhukov that the originals of the documents were safely in storage outside of Europe and had appropriate security. Undertakings were given by Dolgoruky along with the settlement agreements, as reached over the last two days.

"When I have the promised information tomorrow," answered Will, "we will arrange a date and time to meet in London to examine the certified copies of the original documents. I recommend that we arrange for their delivery to the Russian Embassy in London."

Zhukov agreed that delivery to the Russian Embassy would serve the purpose well, and he added, "We have accomplished a settlement that defied any expectations of such a generous gift from Dr Menshive. Please ask Dr Menshive and his wife whether we could hold a reception in their honour to celebrate the settlement… with appropriate media disclosure. We would request that you, Mr MacIntosh and Ms Menshive attend as well."

* * *

The enthusiastic reception Anna had been given by her brother Isaac and his wife on her arrival in London from New York was sincere and an optimistic attempt to bridge past differences between the siblings, hoping to form a united family unit. To all outward appearances, Anna had obliged and had given herself a role helping with Little Isaac to whom she became almost as vital a part of his life as his parents and Mrs Ellis. Her betrayal was a shock and profound disappointment. Her ultimate fate as a convicted accessory after the fact on several criminal charges in New York resulted in federal time in an upstate New York prison.

When Ruth and Will left for Moscow for the negotiations there, they hoped they would see terminated the claims and demands of Russia and other Eastern European countries related to the former trust assets. Ruth's arrival back in London had already seen the termination of Anna's relationship with her brother and his family. It would be as decisive and permanent as the successful distribution of the assets Ruth and Will had negotiated.

The immediate goal after their arrival in London was to announce the terms of the Memorandum of Settlement reached in Moscow in a way that would most likely satisfy Isaac. He had numerous pre-conditions and reservations that were to be embedded in the memorandum, both for the division of the assets and for his continuing role with those assets that were to be distributed under the Memorandum of Agreement.

However, the memorandum as Ruth and Will drafted it contained little continuing involvement for Isaac or anyone in his family in the use, preservation or display of the gallery and museum pieces and none in relation to the archival materials, except to acknowledge the generosity of the donor, Dr Isaac Menshive. The substantial property and income tax relief Will was effective in negotiating for Isaac, Will was sure, would placate any disappointment that Isaac would have with the agreement.

The Anna issue, Will and Ruth agreed, should be left until Isaac was satisfied with the agreement. Will insisted on a clause being included in the agreement that made the agreement subject to Isaac's ratification. There was a thirty-day period within which objections could be advanced for further negotiations, if required, by Isaac.

Isaac's health had improved considerably but he still had and probably would continue to have vestiges of post-traumatic stress disorder that could result in unpredictable mood swings and erratic behaviour. Will discussed with Ruth her father's mental health as clearly as he could. His physical health was easier to explain and deal with.

As for Sophie, she was independently wealthy in her own right. She found discussions about the trust money and assets tiresome and annoying. She preferred to leave most decisions relating to the assets to Isaac, taking only enough interest to ensure protection of her son's interests.

"Ruth, Sophie will not be a problem after we explain the agreement focused on Little Isaac's continuing role in relation to the divided assets. Simply put, he would be his father's successor as a representative of the family in any ceremonial uses or commemoration of the family's gifts of the assets when he attains the age of thirty. He would have no say in the management or display of the artifacts, but as with a prince of the Royal Family, he would be a token representative of the family, as will Isaac during his lifetime. There will be no burden on either Isaac or Little Isaac," said Will, "so Sophie should be amenable to accept the agreement, I think."

Ruth was still relatively new to her father's new family, but having observed family strife and Menshive personalities at first hand for many years, she had correctly analyzed the dynamics of her new family with insight, compassion and affection. She knew that with Anna's departure her own role in the family would almost certainly change to one of greater intimacy in the immediate family as well as in the legal and administrative affairs of the new trust. Ruth's increasing participation in family activities would expose her intimately to the personalities, behaviour and prejudices of her father and stepmother. She recognized herself in her father, which gave her a rapid and profound understanding of both her father and by immediate extension herself. The female side of her personality enabled her to anticipate friction and opposition and to avoid them. She had proven to be exceptionally adroit in doing just that since her arrival in London.

66

THE DAY AFTER Ruth and Will arrived back in London from Moscow, arrangements had been made to meet with Isaac and Sophie at their home in Hampstead, rather than in the new office in Battersea which was a replacement for the two bombed sites in Canary Wharf.

"I want your father to be relaxed and amenable for our discussion about the settlement, Ruth. I think we can best achieve that by having a visit at home. What's your reading on the upcoming meeting with your father and Sophie?"

"You will recall, Will, that I was present at each of the telephone discussions you had with Dad while we were in Russia. He has been thoroughly briefed on the negotiations and the terms of the agreement in broad outlines. He expressed satisfaction and, I should say, happiness with what you are doing and the decisions you were making on his behalf. I don't expect any problems, but we must engage him in a way that will leave him believing that the terms were what he wanted – that you were simply implementing his instructions," said Ruth, with a twinkle in her eye, knowing the colossal egos of both her father and his friendly attorney.

Will responded: "One final note before we walk up to the front door, Ruth. I want you as much a presenter of the agreement as me. I want your father to know how effective you have been in the negotiations. I suggest you express your interest in the trust and the agreement and show your satisfaction that your family's interests were preserved, if not enhanced." Will said this with the satisfaction that an enhanced role for Ruth would result in a diminished role for himself.

* * *

"I love this gorgeous room, Sophie. The view towards the

heath and Parliament Hill are outstanding. '*Rus in urbe*' – 'the countryside in the city' – is the term I have read is the appropriate description of your location. The large Regency-style windows, particularly the canted bay at the front of the room, give so much light and a feeling of openness and cheer as one looks toward Parliament Hill. I love this view. Thanks for your invitation to join you this morning. It is a treat to be here with you and Dad." Ruth knew the most effective way to the heart of most homemakers was to compliment them on their homes.

"Ruth, dear," replied a grateful Sophie, "we love the view and the house, too. Thank you. Isaac and I love having you with us. You are welcome any time. You have been here in London or based here for a few months but you have fitted in so well it seems you have been with us for years. I think we better shift our discussion to business matters or Isaac will explode."

Isaac dutifully changed the subject to business as Sophie suggested. "Alright," Isaac to Will, preparing for a tiresome lecture, "I see you have a briefcase no doubt full of documents I must read or have explained to me, so which of you will lead?"

Will replied: "Ruth has been no less engaged than me in the negotiations. She has taken an equal role in achieving an agreement in Moscow. She had a hand in drafting the Memorandum of Agreement, so I ask your permission to have Ruth give an explanation of the contents of the draft Memorandum of Agreement. She will call on me – or you may – when I am needed."

Isaac showed considerable surprise. Will had for years been his team leader and he had taken the initiative on every significant step they had taken. Surprise turned to pleasure and then pride: "Ruthie, if Will treats you as an equal in this matter, then I accept you must be. Let me hear from you first, then."

Ruth explained the process that led to the actual negotiations, the goals she and Will had set for the negotiations and the end result. "But, Dad, I want you to know that I was led every step of the way by our trusted friend and guide Will MacIntosh. He was wonderful to work with, always treating me as an equal and inviting my opinions on every decision."

"As he will continue to be, Ruth," said Isaac, beaming with pride. "I hope and expect the two of you will serve as a team – I remind you – with you as the junior partner. I don't want any friction."

"There won't be, Dad; I assure you."

Ruth then broke down the negotiations into the categories, the issues involved and the debates on each. When she completed her analysis, Isaac turned to Will and asked: "Anything to add, friend?"

"Nothing. I think Ruth has explained this well. I would be repeating if I were to add anything. Now, Isaac, if you have no questions so far, I will ask Ruth to give you the details contained in the Memorandum of Settlement."

The approach Ruth would take had been carefully orchestrated before she and Will arrived at the house. She started with the easiest categories – easiest in terms of Isaac's expectations being met. The most contentious issues were left to the end when, as expected, Isaac was growing tired and impatient to end the discussions. Again, when Ruth completed the explanation of the terms of the final category of assets, she spoke carefully, not omitting any detail, but not disclosing any of the distress and anger some of the final debates had created during the negotiations. When she finished her report, she asked her father whether he had any questions.

"No, dear, none, but I may have some after I read the memorandum carefully. Will earlier told me I have a limitation period, as he calls it, within which I have time to raise objections. I will have my final decision in a couple of days. I want both of you to be available to me then to discuss any points I want clarified. Will, you have been so quiet. I have never sat with you so long without comment, instructions or protracted explanations. Ruthie, you delivered the whole thing in a little more than an hour. I bet our friend here would have had us gripping our chairs for at least a couple of hours, eh, Will?"

"No doubt, Isaac. I commend Ruth for her succinct explanations. I don't think I could have done better."

"Well, enough of the agreement for now," said Isaac, turning to Sophie. "Have you seen Anna recently? Little Isaac told me this morning as I was having my breakfast that he hasn't seen Anna for a long time, which could mean an hour or two or a week or two. Have you any news of Anna, Sophie?"

"No, sorry, I have not called her for a couple of days. I have been tied up with the museum group I joined. They have me doing a million things. They had even asked me to chair an exhibition of new artists. Apparently, it is a new trend that artists are experimenting with, 'realism' as they call it. Much of what I have seen looks like late eighteenth-century art. I like it better than the abstract stuff that has been so popular. Anyway, that's what has been occupying me. I even took Little Isaac to the group yesterday. He played beautifully with other children who had been brought there with their mothers. I had Mrs Ellis with me to assist in the child care. The other parents were appreciative to have her help."

"Well, Sophie dear, I suppose there is an answer to my question in there somewhere."

"Yes, if you were paying attention."

Before the conversation could veer off into negative territory, Will announced that he and Ruth had a lot of work to do in the Battersea office, and he suggested that Isaac meet them there the next morning at an early hour.

67

IT WAS DURING the meeting at the office the next day that Will introduced the subject of Anna. He took the lead and left Ruth on the sidelines. He deliberately wanted to avoid any appearance of rivalry or hostility between Anna and Ruth. His approach was simply one of describing as gently as possible Anna's betrayal of all her promises made to Isaac and to Will with respect to confidentiality and in particular to avoiding Anthony Cann. Will delivered his message calmly and gently even though he was seething with rage internally.

"Will, I know you too well. Your colour has shifted from Celtic grey to red and with the heat of anger to purple, which means your blood pressure is at boiling point. You are right, of course. She has, as you say, betrayed us. There will be consequences which I will discuss with Sophie. I cannot trust Anna in the future to have anything to do with Little Isaac and the new baby. I really thought she had turned a corner... particularly, Will, when I saw you and Anna developing a relationship. I had hoped that would go somewhere. Well, that's 'dead in the water', as my sailing buddies would say. It makes me really mad, though: she has betrayed all of us, including you, Ruthie, but I can't forgive her for betraying my parents. I will never be able to understand that."

Will tried to mollify Isaac's rising anger: "Isaac, I didn't know your sister quite as well as I thought I had. Please give her some considerable latitude and try to forgive her. She was and will continue to be a vulnerable, weak, childlike person whose emotional needs will always expose her to manipulation and deceit. I feel bad for her and worry about her future. But I will never forget that she was responsible, or at least partially responsible, for your injuries and those of Sophie... and the death of some men who did their damnedest to protect us. Their loyalty and service were betrayed by a member of your family. I say 'betrayed', since there is no more accurate or descriptive word I can think of."

68

THEY ALL MET two days later over dinner in Isaac and Sophie's elegantly appointed dining room which was hung with paintings, most of which had been carefully chosen by Isaac and Sophie together. However, some were purchased by Sophie from the new 'realistic' painters she was meeting through her museum group.

Isaac successfully restrained his negative response to virtually all of them to keep the peace and to appear to support Sophie in her volunteer work. He was sure the hangings would change periodically with Sophie's changes in interest and taste.

Isaac rose in a formal and somewhat intimidating manner for a family dinner party; he said he had an announcement to make.

Both Sophie and Ruth looked frightened and apprehensive of what was to come.

Will was the only non-family member present. He exhibited none of the anxiety displayed by the women: he was aware of what the announcement would be.

"I rise in this formal way for a purpose. Over the past five or six years, I have been struggling with difficulty and have incurred devastating injuries and other personal afflictions being thrown at me by persons unknown until very recently. I have survived these struggles primarily through the loyalty, intelligent insights and affection, I must say, of my friend Will MacIntosh. The next best thing that happened to me, after having Will as my companion and adviser, was finding the love of my life, my Sophie. I never thought I would find someone like her. She is my life, my constant helpmate and loving friend. And most recently Ruthie has entered my life, just in time to see me through the betrayal of my sister Anna. I will not say more of her now or in the future. There will be no further contact with her. Forgiveness, Will tells me repeatedly in his tiresome Christian way, is a virtue. Well, I have never claimed I was virtuous, as Will in particular knows."

There was a murmur of light laughter from the company before Isaac continued.

"I have read the document, so typical of legal minds, grandly referred to as a 'Memorandum of Settlement'. To refer and respond to such a portentous document, I believe, requires me to stand giving it due deference –" Another murmur of laughter. "So now, my decision on its contents and whether I require further negotiations. My decision has been made without consulting you, Sophie…"

"Not necessary, Isaac dear. My only interest is to protect the interests of my children, and I must add, that of your eldest daughter. Ruthie, you are truly one of us after your heroic efforts to resolve this mess with Will."

"So my answer is that it contains an acceptable resolution of all of the issues… a resolution I did not think possible. I truly worried that we as a family would be fighting with governments, oligarchs, criminals and errant family members for years if not generations. I have no issues requiring further discussion.

"I raise my glass to our true best friend Will MacIntosh, without whom none of this happy resolution would have been possible.

"I will say only that Will deserves more than my thanks. He will discover in due course just what I will do to try to compensate him for giving up his law practice and being away so much from his now departed dear wife, whom I had the great pleasure to meet and his children, now adults, who were without his nurturing advice for much of those years. They may thank me for taking over the receiving of his reforming words, though. They were frequent and abundantly given but needed and effective!

"We have resolution, Will. How often we agonized over whether it would be possible. Yes, here we are. And I have my Sophie and a gorgeous child."

"You do not, Isaac," said Sophie, standing and motioning

lovingly at Ruth, saying, "you have an additional three children. I know nothing of the other two, but my family now comprises Ruth and her half-siblings back in the States, all of whom I want to know."

* * *

"Thank you, Isaac and Sophie. Only one-half of our mission is completed," said Will.

"God, man! What remains?" asked an irritated Isaac.

"The answer is one we discussed often without ever really thinking it would rest with you to arrange. What are you going to do with all the remaining assets? That still has to be worked out, Isaac."

"Thanks for the reminder, my attorney and guide. Will, let me know the answer when you and Ruth work that out. Remember, you are the chair of my board. I am a family man now. I delegate everything to you to work out with Ruthie's help."

"God in heaven, give me strength! Thanks a lot, Isaac."

69

"WILL, I HAVE a question for you that has baffled me for some time," said Isaac a few days later. "Dolgoruky and Vorontsov are both from aristocratic families from the Czarist period. Their properties were confiscated and they were driven out of Russia with only as much capital as they were able to raise through the sale of luxury goods to my family. As descendants of those families, how were they prominent in modern Russia and in our Russia experience?"

Will smiled, recognizing an issue that had intrigued him as well. "You can add Zhukov and Kutuzov to that list. I discussed this with both Dolgoruky and Zhukov and I was given the same answer: Russia's current national identity is even more deeply embedded in Russian history and traditional culture than communism and Putin could change. So it is not surprising that some of the aristocrats would want to return. Those who did came back with a mission to restore some of the cultural successes achieved during the days of Imperial Russia. That was the motive for both Dolgoruky and Zhukov in returning. I suspect it was part of Vorontsov's motivation as well.

"But remember, the Soviet system stridently brainwashed its citizens at every turn to believe the Communist system was perfection on a governmental, societal and economic level. Both Dolgoruky and Zhukov saw it for the sham it was, but not Vorontsov. He bought into it hook, line and sinker. That, I think, is why he had no compunction in betraying us.

"Another thing. Those aristocrats who returned were useful window dressing in presenting Russian history and culture to the West. They spoke with highly cultured voices and with the supreme self-confidence and sense of social superiority, as aristocrats, which they brought with them. However, it is also true that those aristocrats who returned were always suspected of being subversive and potentially traitorous, so there were people like Dolgoruky and Zhukov who had to play their roles skillfully balancing hostile forces against the constructive role they tried to play. Whereas Vorontsov, through arrogance, fear and deceit, fell into the Soviet trap and became a pawn in the Soviet system."

"Thank you. I think I now understand. What a complex world those former aristocrats lived in during the Soviet period," exclaimed Isaac dismissively. For him, the ordeal was over.

"Yes, Isaac, and remember the episode in St Petersburg when you and I were meeting with the former aristos. They reverted to their titles and styles of address, including you as a baron of the Russian Empire. That, to them, was a validation of their reason for being in Russia."

Epilogue

ONE HALF OF the mission Isaac had set for himself and Will MacIntosh had been resolved with the Memorandum of Settlement.

A thorough study of what was retained by Isaac and could be constructively and meaningfully used by him and his new trust within each category of the assets would take weeks or months, or perhaps even years.

The value of the assets and the location of some of the immovables in Eastern and Central Europe would require years of challenging work ahead.

The assets would now be held in plain sight by Menshive families but would continue to be held in a complex form of ownership. The Memorandum of Settlement, however, was a public declaration of what was held by Isaac's new trust.

Now that connection between the remaining assets and Isaac's family would be known publicly, and that the owners of those assets were seeking a solution as to what to do with them, both Isaac and Will knew that the demands on their time, patience and intelligent creativity would tie them in many knots as numerous demands would be made for donations over the next few years.

DRAMATIS PERSONAE

ISAAC'S FAMILY & FRIENDS

Menshive, Isaac: Dr Isaac Menshive (aka Baron Menshikovsky).

Posen, Sophie: Isaac's third wife.

Isaac, 'Little': Isaac and Sophie's son, aged two in the story.

Menshive, Anna: Isaac's sister.

Menshive, Ruth: Isaac's eldest daughter, a lawyer; becomes active in investigation.

MacIntosh, Will: Isaac's companion and asset manager.

SMOLENSK

Alexi: the farm operations manager at Smolensk dacha.

Anastasia: Nurse and child care nanny, with Sophie.

Bernstein, Rabbi: Resident rabbi in Smolensk.

Frank: Isaac's principal personal security guard and team leader for all security guards.

Igor: GRU officer in Smolensk, who assisted in recovering Sophie and Little Isaac.

Menshikovsky: Manager of the dacha farm and outside operations at the Smolensk Dacha and real estate in Smolensk.

Polanski: Town counsellor in Smolensk, agent for oligarch Poliakov.

Polanski, Dimitry: Son of town counsellor in Smolensk (also an agent of Oligarch).

Sergei: the majordomo at the Smolensk dacha.

ST PETERSBURG

Casey, Seamus: a UNESCO mediator involved in the final settlement talks held in St Petersburg.

Dolgoruky, Peter: Count and lawyer in Moscow and St Petersburg, expert in international law and property law in Russia.

Vorontsov, Dr Ivan: Gallery director of the Museum of Decorative and Applied Arts in St Petersburg; specialist in jewellery, decorative arts; descendant of Prince Vorontsov (see below).

MOSCOW

Alexandrov, Alexii: Minister of Cultural Affairs (Russia).

Antonov, Dr Alexi: Kutuzov's deputy at the Russian National Museum.

Golovine, Inspector Nicholai: GRU Chief Inspector, Serious Crimes and International Incidents, Moscow.

MacGregor, Dr Philip: Isaac's family doctor from New York, attended on him in Moscow.

MacNeill, Peter: Canadian Consular official in Moscow.

Molotovsky, Reuben: Moscow general manager of all Russian Menshikovsky properties.

Poliakov: One of the Oligarchs fomenting attacks on Isaac and Sophie in Smolensk.

Ushakov, Pavel: Moscow lawyer, long-term counsel to the Swiss bank and to Molotovsky.

Valentin, Dr Alexander: A post-traumatic stress specialist in Moscow.

Zhukov, Dr Boris: Executive Director of the Pushkin Museum in Moscow.

LONDON

Abraham: Andy's 2-1-C who stepped up to replace Frank after Frank was fired.

Andy: Frank's #1 Security Guard in Odessa and assistant in London.

Braun, Gretchen: former Bank of England executive assistant who worked with the Odessa records in London.

Campbell, Ms: interior decorator advising Isaac and Sophie on the selection of furniture and decoration of their new home in Hampstead.

Charterhouse, Dr Damian: an eminent clinical psychologist specialized in the treatment of post-traumatic stress disorders.

Cohen, Rabbi: Chief Rabbi in London (Isaac's branch of Judaism).

Ellis, Mrs: the London nanny.

Jellicoe, Dr: Specialist in Ukrainian history.

Jeanna: one of the research assistants who was assigned to be the recording secretary at each meeting of the researchers at Canary Wharf.

Kutuzov: Director of National Museum of Art and Antiques in Moscow.

Levin, Rabbi: Chief Rabbi in Moscow.

MacKenzie, Dr Walter: Isaac's physician in London at the clinic, a specialist in post-traumatic stress disorders.

Mendel: Abraham's 2-1-C as a security guard.

Moore, Harry: former Bank of England executive assistant who worked with the Odessa records in London.

Posen, Levi and Helen: Sophie's parents.

Smythe, Q.C., Roger: London lawyer, involved in managing trust assets for Isaac.

Thornhill, Edward: UK property manager of Isaac's real estate located in London.

Wright, Penelope: Smythe's Junior Counsel, legal expert in UK Trust Management.

ODESSA

Adamchuk, Dr: Assumed name of Penelope Wright (see above) for security purposes while in Ukraine.

Oransky, Oleg: Manager of the Londonskaya Hotel (in Odessa).

NEW YORK

Cann, Anthony: Legal Assistant, Isaac's putative distant cousin, jailed for murder of his principal in a New York law office.

Rayskill, Dr Ben: Sophie's NYC gynaecologist and obstetrician.

Trombley, Gus: Head of Isaac's security team in the US.

Weatherbie, Mr: A specialist in Russian art and antiques with the Metropolitan Museum of Art in New York.

TRUST HISTORY

Bronshtein, David: farmer in the Odessa region of Southern Russia, (Novorossiya), father of Lev Bronshtein (aka Leon Trotsky).

Günzburg: one side of Isaac's Russian ancestry. A banking and investment family.

Isle St Jean Trust: the principal owner of all trust assets.

Longworth, Charles Q.C.: Prince Edward Island lawyer who created the Isle St Jean Trust.

Menshikoffsky: Russian noble from the Russian Imperial Period.

Menshikovsky Trust: the identity used as the 'front' in public relations and negotiations.

Menshive International Holdings Inc.: Isaac's holding company.

Strogonov: Successor to Prince Vorontsov (see below).

Vorontsov, Count (later Prince): Governor-General in Odessa.

Van Stieglitz, Ludwig: nineteenth-century Jewish collector and donor in St Petersburg.

Trotsky, Leon: (Lev Bronshtein) one of the principal revolutionaries in the 1917 Russian Revolution.

ABOUT THE AUTHOR

James W. Macnutt has been a practising lawyer for longer than he cares to remember and is a Queen's Counsel. He has been an active volunteer in numerous community organizations and initiatives. He is married with two children and four grandchildren.

An inveterate traveller for more than 55 years, the author based his first work of fiction, *On Five Dollars a Day* – published by Austin Macauley in 2017 – on the diary he kept during his first trip to Europe in 1965. His extensive knowledge of the many European countries he has visited since then forms the background for this book, the second in a trilogy of conspiracy thrillers.

In addition to the other books in the trilogy – *The Mendelssohn Connection*, published in October 2021, and the forthcoming *The 9-11 Connection* – Austin Macauley published the author's ghost story *The Spectre of Stanhope Lane* in 2019.